BLACKMADDIE

'Blackmaddie can be beautiful or terrifying, my angel,' my father had said. 'She's a huge, turreted castle on the edge of a deep loch, and when the sun gleams on her spires and throws her reflections on to the shimmering water, she's very seductive and beautiful. At other times she's shrouded in a mist that swirls and creeps around her. Then the mountains are black and overcast, hiding her in shadows, and you can't help but be conscious of the power she holds.'

'Why do you call it "she"?' I'd asked curiously. 'As if it's a person, not a house.'

'You must go there to know the answer to that,' Father had said softly. 'She has an aura about her as destructive as a possessive woman, and just as captivating, and according to legend she puts a curse on all those who try to escape from her clutches. The local people call it the "curse of Blackmaddie".'

BLACKMADDIE
ROWENA SUMMERS

Pan Books

First hardback edition published in Great Britain 1990 by
Severn House Publishers Ltd of
35 Manor Road, Wallington, Surrey SM6 0BW

First hardback edition published in the U.S.A. 1990 by
Severn House Publishers Inc, New York

This edition published 1997 by Pan Books
an imprint of Macmillan Publishers Ltd
25 Eccleston Place, London SW1W 9NF
and Basingstoke

Associated companies throughout the world

ISBN 0 330 37012 X

1 3 5 7 9 10 8 6 4 2

A CIP catalogue record for this book is available from
the British Library.

Printed and bound in Great Britain by
Mackays of Chatham PLC, Chatham, Kent

1

'I won't go!' I exclaimed furiously.

My mother's normally calm face was tight with controlled anger as she looked at me. I knew she would not want to enter into a stormy argument while the thin-faced solicitor sat in our cramped living-room in embarrassed silence at this reaction to his news.

I glanced at him, mutely begging his support, but he stared stonily down at the laboriously written letter in his hand and offered nothing.

'Charlotte, you will do as your grandfather wishes,' my mother admonished. 'Is it too much for you to understand that he wants to see you – and me – before he dies? I thought someone of your perception would be able to appreciate that an old man gets these whims. It will do no harm to comply with them.'

It would do *her* no harm, but what of me? I thought waspishly. Mother would have no compunction at leaving the shabby rooms we occupied on the teeming waterfront of Bristol. Neither would she object to giving up her work as a seamstress, sewing far into the night by the flickering gaslight until her fingers were pricked and calloused from holding the needle. I could see that more clearly than anything else.

Gowns for the rich, she'd say caustically. Rich as she might have been if my father had been the older son and not the younger, and if he had not had in his veins the lust for the sea that had drowned him. And according to her romantic memories of him, which were even now the only things that ever softened her tongue, his lust had applied itself to her too. I still felt uncomfortable when she talked about him, with an old woman's memories of a young, fervent love that sounded unreal to my ears. Given time, she would always add positively, his father would have taken him and all of us back into the family home, and there would have been no more finger-pricking and hardship, only the soft life.

I conceded that she had cause for wanting to go to Blackmaddie. But I had no wish to leave Bristol.

Mr Higgins, the solicitor, cleared his throat. The letter he held in his hand was like an echo of some half-forgotten past that was best kept buried. What did Mother and I have to do with some family in the Highlands of Scotland who bore our name? They were no more than strangers to us, and I wished they had remained that way.

'What is there to hold us here, Charlotte?' Mother went on. 'You cannot give me one good reason why we should not leave!'

I had a reason, but not one that I was prepared to tell her about. His name was William Derry, and he was a tutor at the school where I taught the little girls to sew. She did not know of my attachment, nor that I was not lacking in the knowledge of how it felt to have a man's arms around me. Mother would doubtless consider a mere tutor someone of little importance. And from her uncomfortably lurid descriptions of my father's physical prowess, she would probably dismiss William's trembling hands on the fastenings of my bodice as the fumblings of an adolescent schoolboy. Even so, he had the power to stir me, and he was a friend as well as a lover.

She waited impatiently for me to provide her with the reason for staying here, and I steadfastly refused to give her an answer. I knew I should be a dutiful daughter and try to see it all through her eyes, knowing that she had had little enough of the niceties of life. She rarely left our lodgings except to attend fittings at grand houses and to bring back bolts of material and sewing threads. When she returned home she would often be discontented and irritable because of the glimpse of fine living she had seen for such a little while, and the irritation would not leave her until the material was spread out on the huge table that took up nearly all the space in our living-room.

Only then, as her eyes contemplated the shot silk that gleamed in the gas-light, or the freshness of fine voile, did her expression grow animated. As her hands got to work with scissors and pins, she treated each new piece of work with the adoration of a lover. While she worked she was transported into a fantasy world, and in her fantasies I knew that each new garment was intended for me; I would be admired and fêted at balls and receptions, and young men would jostle for my favours.

I sighed, wishing Mother were not so ambitious for me. I had a normal young girl's desire to be loved, but my destiny did not lie in any of the grand houses where she worked. There was not the remotest possibility that I would ever wear such a gown as she sewed, except when some young lady insisted Mother brought a cast-off home for me. Or when Mother tried one of her creations on me when it was half-finished to see the effect and the fit. Those occasions were almost the only times she looked fondly at me.

Then she would caress each fold in the skirt with reverence in her touch, running her hands over my figure to feel that it fitted snugly and showed the full swell of my breasts to best advantage, and when she had done all that, to my acute embarrassment, her voice would be almost accusing.

'Charlotte, you're much too beautiful to be wasted like this. It's hard to believe I looked so like you once. Somewhere in this world there must be a young man capable of giving you all the passionate love your father always gave me.'

I usually fidgeted out of the gown at this point, before I had to hear yet more revealing details of their intimate lives together. I knew it all so well already – how every homecoming from my father's ship was like a second honeymoon. I had long ago decided that she had lavished so much love on my father that there was none left for me. I was just the constant reminder of what had been, and a great disappointment to her as well. Sometimes I was restless for a love of my own that would equal hers for my father. But she wanted too much for me: a great love and a grand life. I was too realistic to share her dreams. I would settle for William.

My own memories of my father were dimmed by time, but I too could still register the excitement of being caught up in his arms and hugged half to death between the two of them after Mother and I had waited for what seemed like hours at the quayside of the winding river Avon for the tall ships to unleash their cargoes of goods and men.

Those halcyon days had been highlighted by the thrill of the excursions to the waterfront, for we did not live in such mean lodgings or in such close proximity to it then. We would watch the crates being unloaded, listening to the raucous blasphemies of sailors and the creaking of timbers and ropes, the shrill screech of seagulls diving and swooping, and then at last there would be the salt tang of my father's rough jacket as he held me tight in his arms.

The smells that pervaded my life now were the musty ones of gas-lit rooms, tailor's chalk and cotton dust and the smell of new fabric – and, in my day-time world, the smell of the classroom. I had always been sharply receptive to scents, recalling instantly any occasion by the sweetness or the sourness of a place. The sweetness of my father, and the sourness of that stuffy classroom in the early morning; such a tame, dreary existence I led now compared with the exciting world my father used to describe to my mother and me after one of his travels.

Mr Higgins' dry voice made me jump as I came back from my dream-world.

'Miss Brodie, your grandfather is offering you and your mother a home, and such a home! You would be an extremely foolish young woman to think of refusing it.' His voice told me, too, that I should think myself extremely lucky for the chance to get out of this dreary lodging-house, where he sat perched on the edge of a chair as if afraid of catching something. He leaned forward and stared at me disapprovingly. 'They tell me the Highlands of Scotland are very beautiful, with great recuperative air . . .'

'I am not sick,' I informed him spiritedly.

'Charlotte, please do not interrupt,' Mother reproached.

I listened to Mr Higgins droning on, knowing I hated the very idea of going to Blackmaddie. I should pine away in some great turreted castle of a place from sheer boredom, and I did not feel the slightest form of kinship with this family in the north. Besides, there was William, and I knew he was hovering on the brink of proposing. That was more the kind of escape I sought, if any. I was not wildly in love with him, but he satisfied a need in me, and I in him.

'As you know, your grandfather's request has been prompted by the death of his eldest granddaughter, Katrina. Your cousin, Miss Brodie. It was some months ago now, at the very start of the year. An unhappy beginning, and Mr Brodie has been ill ever since. Now a great sense of insecurity has beset him, as often happens with old people. He wants the whole of his family around him, and to make his peace with those who are estranged.'

'He waited a long time,' I said crossly. 'Why could he not have made his peace before, when Mother and I were first struggling alone to pay for renting these dreadful rooms?'

Mother's face went a furious red at this disclosure of our means, but it could hardly have been more obvious, I thought contemptuously, that we lived a hand-to-mouth existence.

'I must apologise for my daughter, Mr Higgins . . . '

'No, Mother, you must not.' My voice was clipped with anger. 'I will have my say, since you have clearly made up your mind to agree to this old man's whims. Well, I will not. I will not go to Blackmaddie. I will stay here in Bristol – '

'I fear that arrangement will not be possible, Miss Brodie,' the solicitor interrupted. 'The request is for *you* to go to Blackmaddie. It is you the laird wishes to receive, and your mother may accompany you if you wish it. I am afraid if you do not go, your mother may not go either.'

There was an oppressive silence in the room for some minutes. I was conscious of the sound of my own heartbeats, of the inevitability of the past claiming the present, of the sound of birds, free and high on the wind outside the window, and of my mother's sharp, ragged intake of breath. And then she stopped standing on her dignity and turned to me beseechingly.

'I have asked little of you before now, Charlotte. I have worked my fingers until they were raw, and it was all for you. You cannot deny the truth of that. We *must* go to Blackmaddie. It is your birthright, and who knows what doors might open there for you? It would be denying your father's name to throw away this chance.'

It was her trump card, and she knew it. I felt a slow, sick anger, and something else besides, gnawing away at my insides like a cancer. A feeling of being drawn into something against my will and my judgement. It was like an inexplicable portent of evil, as if the Brodies I had long forgotten existed were even now sucking us back within their grasp.

I shook myself out of such ridiculous, hysterical fancies and glared at Mother.

'Very well.' I gave in at last, speaking in a shrill, taut voice that must surely have told her how tightly my nerves were stretched. 'But we shall compromise on this and go to Scotland on a visit only. We cannot be expected to give up our home because of an old man's dictates.'

'Our home!' Mother dismissed the three rooms with a sweeping gesture. 'My dear girl, when you see Blackmaddie you'll wonder how we ever survived in this hovel.'

I fancied Mr Higgins did not often make such visits as this one, to a place of such meagre furnishings, nor be offered refreshment on a table loaded at one end with scissors and pins and measuring tapes, and a pile of rich fabrics that only served to show up the shabbiness of our own clothes. For a brief moment I too felt a twist of shame at the way we lived, and a fleeting affinity with Mother's ambitions for the future.

Mr Higgins acquainted us with the necessary details and said that he would contact my grandfather immediately and be in touch with us again as to travelling arrangements. He left his card in a prominent position on the mantel-shelf in case we should need to consult him again.

Mother showed him out. I heard him clattering down the

10

narrow stairs of the tall building. Our rooms were at the very top, being the cheapest. When Mother came back into the room, her look of triumph was only tempered by her usual irritation with me.

'Now, Charlotte, get that mutinous expression off your face. Your father would have wanted us to go to Blackmaddie and there's an end to it.'

'Would he?' I said hotly. 'I seem to recall he could not get away from it quickly enough! He used to say it was like being buried alive to live in that tomb of a place. You cannot have forgotten that among all your other memories, surely.'

'Your tongue will cut you one day, my girl,' she snapped. 'Sarcasm won't find you a husband, you can be sure of that.'

She went back to her work again immediately, throwing the great bale of material across the table in a ripple of blue silk. Her voice never stopped as she worked, until I thought my head would burst with her grumbling. I had hoped she would cease now she had got her way about Blackmaddie, but grumbling was a way of life to her.

'How many people are there at Blackmaddie anyway?' I said sullenly, more to stop her tirade than from a genuine desire to know.

'You weren't listening to half the things Mr Higgins said, were you, Charlotte? There's your grandfather and Uncle Andrew and his four children – no, three now, of course, since Katrina died. The three boys are his step-sons, his second wife's children. She's dead too. Then there's your father's sister, your Aunt Morag, and her daughter, Kirsty.'

'The place must be big enough to house an army,' I commented.

There was a strange gleam in Mother's eyes.

'Maybe one of your cousins will take a fancy to you, Charlotte. They're not blood relations, after all, and you'll all be much of an age ...'

'Mother, don't start matchmaking for me,' I said edgily. 'I'll choose my own husband in my own time.'

She stopped the snip-snip-snipping of the blue silk for a few seconds, and her eyes were like dark coals as they looked at me.

'I remember your father once saying that Blackmaddie always clung to its own. There's been a lot of intermarrying in the past. Morag married one of her cousins. My marriage to your father was condemned without them ever seeing me, though of course he was cut off from the family on more than one count. He ran away to sea, and he dared to marry an English girl. But he always maintained that there was a power about Blackmaddie, even if he did not believe in it strongly enough to stay there. He left when he was still young enough to scoff at such things and risk the consequences, though I often suspected that deep down he believed in it totally. I never had much time for stories of houses having influences over people's lives and early deaths. Now I'm not so sure. Your father did die at little more than thirty years of age, and we are going to Blackmaddie.'

I felt a cold, crawling sensation at her words.

Into my mind at that moment came a vivid picture of myself climbing on to my father's knee and begging him to tell me about the fairy-tale castle that seemed so unbelievable to my childish ears. He'd laughed and cuddled me into his rough seaman's jersey.

'Blackmaddie can be beautiful or terrifying, my angel,' my father had said. 'She's a huge, turreted castle on the edge of a deep loch, and when the sun gleams on her spires and throws her reflections on to the shimmering water, she's very seductive and beautiful. At other times she's shrouded in a mist that swirls and creeps around her. Then the mountains are black and overcast, hiding her in shadows, and you can't help but be conscious of the power she holds.'

My mother had always stopped him at this point, saying it would frighten me, but I had been fascinated with a dryness of throat, loving the prickling sensation his words evoked in me. Blackmaddie then was too far removed from my everyday world for me even to think of it as real.

'Why do you call it "she"?' I'd asked curiously. 'As if it's a person, not a house.'

'You must go there to know the answer to that,' Father had said softly. 'She has an aura about her as destructive as

12

a possessive woman, and just as captivating, and according to legend she puts a curse on all those who try to escape from her clutches. The local people call it the curse of Blackmaddie.'

I shivered now, recalling his words as clearly as if he had just spoken them. They had been said so long ago, and yet they were suddenly, frighteningly vivid, more vivid than anything since Mr Higgins came here with the letter from my grandfather. I felt oddly light-headed, imagining for a moment not the old laird sitting down to compose the letter, seeking out a Bristol firm of solicitors to contact us, but Blackmaddie herself, willing the old curse to come true through the sudden whim of an old man, calling back her own across the years.

I scraped back my chair as the snip-snip-snip of Mother's scissors grated unbearably on my ears.

'I'm going out for some fresh air, Mother,' I said quickly.

'You could call in at the baker's for a fresh loaf then, Charlotte,' she eyed me sharply. 'And tea will be at four-thirty. I have to deliver Mrs Henderson's gown at six o'clock tonight, so don't dawdle by the river. It's not safe there when it begins to get dark.'

I knew that without her telling me. We had not lived in the tall house near the waterfront all these years without my being well aware of the dangers to which she referred. I rarely went out after dark alone. I only had to lean my head out of our attic windows in the late evening to know what went on in some of the taverns. And to hear the high-pitched, excited giggling of the waterfront girls who hung around waiting for the ships to dock.

I hurried down the dark flight of stairs, praying Mr Ruskin would not choose that moment to come out of his own door, and this time I was lucky. The dank smell of the river rose to meet me as soon as I opened the front door of the house.

For the first time the thought ran through me that at least when we got to Blackmaddie there would be clean mountain air and space to breathe, and a dignity of living that we did not find here. We lived in the poorest part of town, among the flotsam of the waterfront where the cobbles ran with filth, and there was usually a stench of fish and rotting vegetables in the air, combined with the strong mixture of human smells. In high summer it was almost beyond belief.

But if Blackmaddie had peace and tranquillity, it did not have William Derry. I hurried up the steep hill leading across the Downs above the Avon Gorge. I had to pause for breath several times before I reached the top. Eventually I made my way to a house larger than our own, and which William Derry grandly referred to as his residence. His attic room was more spacious than ours, and this he called his studio, despite the fact that it held a settee-cum-bed as well as all his painting equipment. William taught art, among other subjects, and spent most of his spare time painting and sketching, though I knew that as soon as he saw me that would be the end of his sketching for the day.

As soon as he opened the door to my knock he pulled me into his arms. We were overtly discreet at the school where we taught, so much so that William was even more ardent on the occasions when I agreed to come to his rooms. To arrive unexpectedly was enough to make his pale skin tinge with pink, and the perspiration to stand out on his forehead.

'Charlotte, what a wonderful surprise.' His face was animated as he spoke. 'I was just thinking about you at that very moment.'

His words were always the same, I thought suddenly. As if they had been carefully rehearsed to make the recipient feel wanted and desirable. And so they did, of course. But I was being unfair, I told myself quickly, and began at once to tell William of Mr Higgins' visit and its purpose. He registered complete astonishment, for he had known nothing of my Scottish connections, and the thought flitted through my mind that if I hoped for a knight on a white charger to carry me away from my problems and the prospect of Blackmaddie, William Derry was most certainly not the one to fit that description.

He led me to sit down on the makeshift bed that still looked like a settee and vice versa. He had a pleasant, earnest face, with side-whiskers curling to his chin. They always tickled me deliciously when he became passionate. His smile, when it came, warmed his face to a degree. He was not a devastatingly masterful man, I realised clearly for the first time.

'I shall miss you, Charlotte,' he said finally, when I had poured out the whole story.

I stared blankly into a paint-stained overall hanging on a hook behind the door, for at that moment I could not quite look into his eyes. I felt a wild desire to laugh. He would miss me; was this really the man I thought might beg me to stay, to give up my chance of a fortune, if my mother were to be believed, and marry him? William mistook my sudden sharp intake of breath for emotion, and quick to seize his advantage, his hand went at once to the bodice of my dress, caressing the fullness there, while the other one fumbled beneath my petticoats.

We usually had a little tussle before the inevitable happened. It excited him and inflamed me. But not today. I was almost dispassionate, bemused by the strange working of the male mind that could think only of animal desires while my own state of mind was so confused. Some devil inside me wanted to watch and feel and absorb everything about him, and maybe prove to myself that his was too feeble a passion after all, and that there must be so much more.

William's forehead was glistening freely and his face was rose red from the heat of his desire and the excitement my body always provoked in him. I watched him pounding away above me, lips parted over his teeth in a grotesque smile, and I pretended to moan with an ecstasy I did not feel while his hands pressed into my thighs until they felt bruised and sore. He was an energetic lover if nothing else. And there was nothing else, I thought sorrowfully. He had aroused me once, but not any more. I felt saddened at the knowledge, as if it was truly the end of a part of my life.

William noticed nothing unusual. For an artist he really was the most insensitive man. He finally rolled away from me with a beatific smile of satisfaction on his face, while I straightened my clothes and gave a deep sigh.

'Well then, William, it seems we shan't be doing that again,' I said calmly.

'You aren't going to Scotland immediately, are you, Charlotte? We have a little more time, surely,' he said with surprise.

I was suddenly impatient. After just making love to me, any other man would surely have declared his love and made some kind of plea to me to stay. I had never realised before what a shallow man he really was, that in William there was no wild passion except that of momentary lust. My feelings for him had died, except for the friendship we had shared even before his desires manifested themselves.

'Will you take a walk with me, William?' I felt the same sense of claustrophobia I had felt at home, and he agreed at once. We walked across the Downs, walking companionably along the edge of the high cliffs, where far below the waterfront looked as if it were peopled by ants. Distance lent the scene a certain enchantment, bathed as it was in the dying red glow of sunset.

A sudden gush of nostalgia struck me, misting my eyes with tears. A wave of seagulls flew up from the cliff-side, screaming in protest at the noisy tug-boats far below. It would certainly not be everybody's idea of heaven, and the muddy Avon was less than palatable at close quarters, but it was home. It was dear and familiar, and I did not want to leave it.

2

We walked on across the Downs, each immersed in separate thoughts. I could not tell what William's were, but I was convinced now that his future plans did not include me. I had been a pleasant interlude in his life, that was all. When he suggested we went into the tea-rooms at the top of the steep hill, I agreed thankfully. It was odd to discover I had no more wish to be alone with him.

I looked at him across the lace-covered tablecloth of the tea-rooms, and a small sigh escaped my lips. Since the visit of Mr Higgins that afternoon, I was increasingly aware that my emotions had undergone a subtle change. I did not want to go to Blackmaddie, but now I was seeing the alternative – a life shared with William – in an entirely new perspective. Instead of grasping at the thin idea that he might have asked me to stay and marry him, I was more than relieved that he had not. I saw that life with William would have been placid and ordinary – and deadly dull.

I smiled more warmly at him, suddenly glad that he had dispelled a dream for me so painlessly, without even realising it.

'Perhaps your visit to Scotland will not be for too long, Charlotte.' He spoke with a sudden urgency, as if it occurred to him that there may have been something stronger between us and he was in danger of losing it. But it was too late. It had been as ethereal as a will-o'-the-wisp, and it was gone.

'Perhaps, but I think it may well be permanent.' A cold little thrill ran through me as I said the words, knowing the truth of them. I tried to make it all sound more interesting to William, but it was really to reassure myself too.

'It seems my grandfather wishes to gather all his family

into Blackmaddie like a spider catching flies, before it is too late.'

I tried to sound flippant, but a gust of fear caught at my throat as I realised anew the power of this old man who could dictate the lives of two women at the other end of the country by signing his name to paper.

'It sounds a marvellous place,' William said speculatively. 'I almost wish I was going instead of you, Charlotte. They say the scenery is magnificent, and can almost equal Switzerland for snow and mountains.' He was seeing it all with an artist's eye at that moment, but I shrugged indifferently. I preferred warmer climates.

'And to have a real castle for an ancestral home!' His voice suddenly changed to being almost deferential. 'The pupils will certainly look up to you when they hear about it. You'll find them all begging for invitations to come and visit you, and expecting to see you coming to school wearing a tiara.'

I started to laugh for the first time since that dreadful Higgins had come to our rooms and made me feel so inferior. It was ridiculous, of course, but I could suddenly see that living at Blackmaddie was going to give me status I had never had before. Even though I was certainly not going to be the fine duchess William pretended, I should be one of the Brodies of Blackmaddie, instead of a nondescript little sewing-mistress, and the thought gave me a surge of pleasure as real as it was unexpected.

'I shall still be the same person,' I laughed.

'Do you have cousins in this castle of yours, Charlotte?' Hardly *mine*.

'Four,' I told him. 'Three boys – well, young men, really, who are step-cousins, and a girl, Kirsty. It's strange to think I have a ready-made family I've never met. There is also Grandfather, my Aunt Morag and my Uncle Andrew. They're my father's brother and sister. Kirsty is the only one who makes the prospect of going to Blackmaddie in the least palatable. It will be pleasant to have a friend of my own age who is also my kin.'

It had occurred to me already that I had no real friends in Bristol save William, and no female acquaintances of my own age. Not even anyone close who would wish me a tearful good-bye and be sad at my leaving. The thought of Kirsty warmed me.

'And what of these three young men? I fancy the sight of you will not be disagreeable to them, and that they will soon vie for your favours.'

William's voice was suddenly sulky and charged with jealousy. It was transparent that he was thinking back to the half-hour in his arms that afternoon and realising too late what he was losing.

Suddenly I wanted to get away from him. I indicated that I had finished my tea and told him I must go, or Mother would be getting impatient.

'You sound impatient to be gone too, as if you can't wait to get to this Blackmaddie and away from here, for all that you protest about it, Charlotte. I hope you won't be disappointed, that's all.' He was almost glowering. 'Such an odd name, isn't it, as if it had once been two names. Black Maddie. Like some sort of evil woman.'

I got to my feet jerkily, almost pushing my way out of the tea-rooms with William hurrying after me. I was shaken by his words, but I did not tell him so, merely that I had found it hot and stuffy in there and had to get outside. I insisted that I was quite all right otherwise and we parted company, to my intense relief. I did not want to hear any more theories about Blackmaddie. She was *not* evil, I found myself protesting wildly inside. She could not be, if my father had loved her so much. I hardly noticed that I thought of the castle already in the same terms as he had, as if she were a living thing, with a mind and will of her own.

As I walked quickly down the cobbled hill towards the waterfront, the tantalising smell of fresh, new-baked bread came into my nostrils, and just in time I remembered Mother's request for a loaf.

Inside the shop it was warm and humid and spicy, with trays of soft fruit buns, shiny with glaze, just being put on the shelves. I bought two of them as well as the bread, to have with our tea. I felt in a sudden reckless mood and hurried on home with the bag of buns and the smell of the hot crusty loaf teasing my senses. Even Mother's grumblings that I was five minutes late could not dispel the sudden lift in my spirits that had started as I walked along the waterfront where everything was blessedly normal. I waved the buns under her nose.

'I shall save mine for when I get back from delivering Mrs Henderson's gown,' she declared. 'It will only give me the heartburn if I eat it when it's hot.'

I thought the new bread would have done exactly the same, but she seemed happy enough to smother it thickly with beef dripping and sprinkle it liberally with salt, and to sink her teeth into it with relish as the dripping oozed out at either side. It was our usual Saturday afternoon tea, and one that we enjoyed immensely.

The gown for Mrs Henderson was packed up in a cardboard box, and the blue silk was now cut into its various shapes ready for tacking together on her return. Mother was never idle, and I felt a rush of love for she had spoken only the truth when she'd said all her hard work was for my benefit. Impulsively I put my arms round her shoulders as I passed her chair to pour out the tea.

'I shall make no more trouble about going to Blackmaddie,' I told her quickly. 'You deserve to see it, and Father would have wished it.'

Her face went pink, though she shrugged away from the display of affection as usual. But I could see she was pleased at my words, though being Mother, as always she had to put her own caustic interpretation on them.

'I'm glad you've come to your senses, Charlotte. There are far more advantages for you in Scotland than working in a little school in Bristol. I knew you'd see that I was right in the end.'

I could not be bothered to argue with her. There was no point. And at least I was thinking positively about Blackmaddie, and to me that was an enormous step forward. I had the strangest feeling that the euphoria would not stay with me for ever, but for the moment it helped me to adjust my thoughts to the new life ahead, and to mull over what little I knew of my future home while Mother was out. She stuck her hat on her head with a cruel stab of her hat-pin and clattered down the long flight of stairs with the precious cardboard box in her arms.

Being alone in our lodgings was a rare luxury. I felt guilty at admitting it, even to myself, but I always felt like throwing open the windows as wide as they'd go and letting a cool breeze blow through the rooms whenever Mother went out, always with a similar cardboard box containing a new gown inside it as if it were the Crown Jewels. It was a relief not to feel her critical eyes on me, or to hear her grumbling voice. I reminded myself that she *did* work very hard.

All the same, it was pleasant to pause in the midst of clearing away the tea things as she would never have done. To lean my head out of the window and feel the night wind in my hair. To dream a little. I could ignore the stench of the river at such moments, for my head would be filled with other things. With the mysterious night-life that began excitingly with the fall of twilight, when dark, shadowy figures merged into couples and made their way, entwined like creepers along the waterfront to some secret rendezvous.

It was a world I did not know but could only guess about. I would be too sick with fear to venture out alone at night, but I knew it must be a very different situation when a lover's arms held you close, a lover who would want me more ardently than William wanted me. I drew back from the window eventually with my eyes sparkling enviously and a glow on my cheeks as I heard the waterfront girls giggling and racing along the slippery cobblestones.

I glanced at the clock on the mantel-shelf. It was already six-thirty and growing dusk. By now Mother would be flouncing out the full skirts on Mrs Henderson's gown as the lady twisted this way and that and then twirled slowly in an elegant circle in appraisement of Mother's work. In another half-hour or so, she would be back and ready to commence work on the blue silk. It was an endless treadmill.

I took the huge kettle from the fire as it began to sing, and poured some of it into a jug. I loosened my thick black hair from its pins and leaned over the tiny sink to wash it. It took such a long time to dry that it would still be damp at bedtime if I did not start early, and Mother would grumble at me for risking pneumonia if I went to bed with damp hair. When it was done, I sat by the open window a while longer, rubbing it in a coarse towel and making my scalp tingle.

If I still did not have the tea-things washed by the time Mother got back, she would not be quite so irritated if she could see I had washed my hair. She always made a great to-do about clean shining hair and the attraction it held for the male sex.

I wrapped the towel round my head for a few minutes, leaned my head against the window frame and thought about Blackmaddie. There was no way I could forget it now. It edged into the corners of my mind whatever I did, and I could not deny the curiosity stirring inside me to see a place that made such a vivid impression on all who saw it. The curiosity fought against my resentment with my imperious grandfather, who expected his wishes to be obeyed even though we were strangers.

How long I leaned there, half-dozing, half-dreaming, I did not know. But I was suddenly aware of new sounds far below on the cobbles, sounds apart from the rumbling of carts and the calling of seamen and the cries of gulls settling into their cliff-nooks for the night.

There was the sound of running feet, and voices shouting hoarsely. I leaned out to see what all the commotion was about and my heart gave a sudden great lurch, because the name they were shouting was mine.

'Miss Brodie! Miss Brodie! Can you come down quickly? It's your mother, girl!'

The stab of panic lent speed to my feet as I jumped up and clattered down the steep stairs of the house. The towel had fallen from my head but I did not heed it. I reached the front door and wrenched it open. A small crowd had gathered outside, all gabbling separate versions of what had happened, and I had to force my way through them.

Mother lay on the ground, her head supported on a woman's lap, her face a grey mask in the pool of light from the gas lamp.

'Mother!' I heard myself scream. 'What happened?' I had to clap my hands in front of my mouth to stop myself becoming hysterical.

I watched in horror as Mother's mouth opened and closed like a fish gasping for air, but no sound came out. A little bubble of froth appeared at the corner of her lips. Her eyes were popped and staring, the veins in her neck distended and blue, and drops of perspiration stood out like beads on her forehead.

'She had a bad shock, my girl,' Ruskin, the fat, sweating, paunchy oaf from the floor below us, said hoarsely. 'A dray horse broke away from its cart and swerved into the wall right in front of her. It only winded her, and she seemed all right when she picked herself up, apart from being badly shaken. She was calm enough, considering, until she reached the waterfront. Then she suddenly collapsed like you see her now.'

'It would be delayed shock,' a woman put in sagely.

'The doctor! Has anyone thought to send for the doctor?' I said wildly. Fear made my teeth chatter. Mother looked ghastly. She had given up trying to speak. Ruskin put five sausage fingers on my arm, warm and soft.

'He's already been sent for, girl. He'll be here directly.'

Someone else spoke in a pious voice. 'We can only wait and pray, Miss Brodie. Pray it's nothing too serious.'

Pray! I could not pray. My thoughts were a jumbled mass of incomprehension. I could only crouch there on the filthy cobbles holding Mother's hands in mine. They were as cold as ice. Ruskin's hand on my arm was still warm and I shook it off with a shudder as if it were some insect.

I was stiff and cramped by the time someone said the doctor was coming. The small crowd still surrounded me, silent now, as if knowing the inevitable outcome but loath to move away, from sympathy or curiosity or both. My neck was frozen and aching with the weight of my hair, still uncomfortably damp in the cool autumn night air.

The doctor took Mother's wrist from me. He pulled the clothing away from her neck and leaned closely over her. He listened and prodded and manipulated, and all the time I felt a great desire to tell him not to bother. That she was dead, dead, *dead*. And that it was all Blackmaddie's doing, and nothing at all to do with the dray horse and shock bringing on a heart attack as that stupid fat Ruskin was blethering on about.

Blackmaddie had not wanted Mother. It was as simple as that. Blackmaddie had spat her out like a maggot from a rotten apple.

'My dear Miss Brodie, please try to control yourself!'

The sound of hysterical laughter was bubbling up from my throat. I felt the doctor holding me in a grip of iron to try and stop the sudden uncontrollable shaking that went on and on and on, and then his hand sent a stinging blow across my cheek. I went as limp as a rag doll against Ruskin's waiting, enveloping arms.

'I'm sorry,' I whimpered. 'But is she . . . is she . . . ?'

'I'm afraid your mother is dead, Miss Brodie,' the doctor said gently. 'There was nothing I could have done, no matter how soon I reached her. I'm sorry.'

There were murmurs of sympathy from the crowd. Some moved away. *Don't go*, I wanted to shriek. *Don't leave me with her.*

'Can you help get her upstairs, Mr Ruskin?' I heard the doctor say in a low voice. 'And you had better inform your wife.'

Mrs Ruskin did all the laying-out in the district.

'Jim, go and fetch your mother,' Ruskin said at once to one of his sons who was hovering about with gawping eyes. The boy fled indoors and I could hear him yelling up the stairs. Ruskin released me reluctantly, taking hold of Mother's head and shoulders while the doctor took her feet, and between them they carried her awkwardly up the steep flights of stairs and into the bedroom we shared.

I watched it happen as if it were some kind of nightmare from which there was no waking. I heard the rasping breath of the two men as they lifted the cadaverous weight of her, and the scraping of her shoes against the walls as they rounded each bend of the stairs.

I wanted to scream at them not to take her into our bedroom, and not to lay her on the narrow bed that was only a hand's-breadth from mine. The thought of sharing a room with her silent corpse was horrific.

I bolted up the stairs behind them as they laid her on her bed.

'Is there nowhere else?' My lips shook and trembled as I asked the question.

'Not before Monday morning,' the doctor said. Then his face softened. 'She cannot harm you, my dear. She is still your mother. But I would suggest you sleep in the other room if you are nervous, or perhaps in a neighbour's rooms.'

'We have room for her, Doctor,' Ruskin said at once. 'She'll be more than welcome to sleep on our couch.'

His little black eyes gleamed as he spoke, and even now, with my mother lying newly dead, his eyes raked me up and down as usual. His thighs never failed to press tightly against me whenever we chanced to pass on the stairs and his sausage-like fingers always brushed my breasts as if by accident. I was in less danger from the dead than from such as he.

'I shall stay here,' I mumbled quickly.

The doctor left soon after Mrs Ruskin arrived to busy herself with Mother. Ruskin stayed in the other room with me while I tried not to imagine what was happening in the bedroom. I seemed to have lost the power of speech. Suddenly his face was close to mine and his foul breath fanned my face.

'You'd be best off downstairs tonight, my girl,' he said softly. 'On the couch. You'll come to no harm. None you can't handle.'

The fingers squeezed my breast before I realised what he was doing, and I could only swallow helplessly and twist away from him as Mrs Ruskin came out of the room and glanced keenly at us both.

'If you have a candle to leave with her, I'll light it for you,' she said in her thin voice.

I shuddered at the thought of it, but I did not want to be left alone with Ruskin again.

'I'll do it,' I stammered. 'Thank you for – for everything.'

I gave her a shilling for her trouble, having no idea what the usual fee for such a duty could be, and then I closed the door behind them.

My thoughts were still jumbling about in my head. A candle. I searched in the drawer and stuck the candle in a holder. I lit a match with shaking hands. My tongue was so dry it stuck to the roof of my mouth as I made myself carry it into the bedroom.

I didn't want to look at Mother, but the room was so small and cramped there was nowhere else to look. She had pennies weighting down her eyes and another clenched between her teeth to pay the boatman. A chin-cloth was tied in a grotesque bow on top of her head. She was the colour of putty. I placed the candle on the table between our beds, grabbed my night-clothes and fled. I slammed the door shut once I reached the living-room.

I leaned against the adjoining door and waited for my heart to stop pounding. I still could not drag my thoughts into any sort of order. Mother had been the dominant force in my life and now she was gone. But not gone. A cold shudder ran through me as I tried not to visualise her lying there, looking, despite the pennies, as if she would wrench the chin-cloth away from her and open her mouth and begin to rail at me as usual for all the things I had not done. I tried to remember that we had parted on friendly terms for once, that I had made her happy at the end by agreeing to go to Blackmaddie. I thought of her hard life and realised she had loved me, under that critical manner. And surely I must have loved her, I thought guiltily. Father's death and poverty had made our relationship difficult. And now it was too late for us both.

But I knew I would never dare to sleep at all that night; every nerve in my body would be alive and waiting for the tinkling sound of those pennies rolling to the floor. After all my shivering, I came out in a hot sweat of fear. I could feel it running down between my breasts and thighs, and I pulled off my clothes and got into the cool fabric of my nightgown, pulling a shawl round my shoulders as Mother always instructed so I would not catch cold. I was still under her influence, even though she lay dead in the next room.

My mouth was still dry, my mind numb, and I hardly realised there was a tapping at the door. The outer door, I realised with a rush of relief. I ran to it and opened it the merest fraction.

It was Ruskin.

I stood there in a bemused state, hardly registering what he was saying, anxious for him to go, yet too afraid to be alone.

'The wife's had to go out on another job, Miss Brodie. It seems it's a bad night for dying.'

Was it ever a good night then?

His eyes travelled over me lasciviously, from my wild, dishevelled black hair to the fullness of my breasts beneath the nightgown. Fuller and heavier than usual without their constricting bodices. I saw his tongue run round his lips at the knowledge of it and I inched the door towards him, but his foot was there. He held out his hand.

'A sleeping draught for you. The wife thought you should take it. You're too shook up to think straight and it's no wonder. You'd better let me come inside and mix it up for you, Miss Brodie.'

He was inside the room before I could stop him. Across to the sink in the corner, reaching for a cup and tipping the white powder into it. He was right about one thing, I couldn't think straight. I couldn't think at all. Couldn't think, couldn't speak. I seemed to be reeling somewhere in a vortex where there was no sound at all. I was mute.

I was aware of a sound coming from another throat. Ruskin's. He was suddenly right beside me, and I had to look down on him. He was a short, stout man, but very strong. Right now his face and neck were redder than usual, his breathing heavier and rasping as he caught hold of my arm. I could feel the strength in him. He was like a bull. Bull's head, bull's strength.

'You look faint, my girl. Lie down for a few minutes until it passes. You've gone the colour of chalk.' There was rough concern in his voice that momentarily allayed my fear.

I was like a puppet, obeying any command. There was nowhere to lie but the floor. I knew he was right and that I must have lost all my colour, because the room did spin in front of me. I closed my eyes for a minute, hoping it would stop, and immediately he was on me. I felt the weight of him imprisoning me, and then the hot, slobbering kisses he pressed on my mouth. I tried to twist my head away, but his tongue was parting my lips, pushing and probing and searching.

His hands were everywhere on my body, ripping away my nightgown, tearing open the fastenings and exposing my breasts. His little eyes were glistening in their excitement, his face flushed as in a fever, his lips hanging and wet.

'Lovely, lovely,' he wheezed urgently. 'My big, lovely girl.'

He was cupping the fullness of my breasts together, burying his face in their softness. Tweaking at the nipples with his mouth, pulling them outwards into hard pellets. They betrayed me. My mind screamed out in protest, but my nipples hardened in response, despite all my revulsion.

I still had no voice. I wanted to scream, but I couldn't. I would waken Mother. I could only lie there and let it happen. All the pushing and pulling and sucking.

Ruskin wheezed like a pig, grunted like a bull. The ceiling above me rotated in front of my dazed eyes as he assaulted me. I stared down at the bull-shaped head between my breasts and tugged at the straggly hair. It seemed to delight him; perhaps it was one of Mrs Ruskin's tricks. The next minute, as if at a given signal, his hands had left my breasts, though his mouth remained, slobbering all over them.

I felt my nightgown being jerked up, and a great fumbling going on. Then the hands were pressing on my thighs, and a fat finger wormed into me. I could hear little moaning noises deep in my throat, echoing his. My head jerked from side to side in silent revulsion, but still I couldn't speak. It was shock upon shock. First Mother, now this.

There was a second's respite, and then he was spreading

me wide, thrusting into me, his thighs damp and heavy. On and on and on, with those terrible grunting sounds. His hands squeezing and pummelling every part of me, bruising me and savouring every involuntary movement I made as if I had lusted after this as much as he. He kept muttering all the while he heaved into me.

'Lovely. Lovely. My big, lovely girl. Knew you wanted it. Seen that look on your face when you walked down the waterfront with your hips swaying and your tits stuck out. Made up my mind a long time ago about you, my fine one.'

He suddenly gave an almighty jerk that almost split me in two, and a great gush of semen was the final humiliation.

But instead of rolling straight off me as I'd expected, I felt him diminishing inside me as he gripped me tightly by the shoulders. It sickened me. His face was very close to mine, his breath so foul I almost retched, but there was a sudden threat in his voice now when he spoke.

'If you tell, I'll have you out of here so fast you'll wonder what hit you, my girl. Your mother can't protect you now. But I'll see you're all right, and we'll have some more of the same.'

My eyes were tightly shut as he hauled himself off me at last. I pulled my nightgown down at once with trembling hands and lay curled up in a ball on the floor until I heard him move towards the door. He opened it.

'You drink that sleeping draught right away, Miss Brodie,' his voice was odiously normal now for any listeners below. 'You'll be needing to keep up your strength.'

Not for you, my mind screamed out, and suddenly I found my voice.

'Get out!' I screamed. 'Out, out, *out!*'

The door closed quickly. I lay there bemused for some minutes, and then my hands went tenderly to every part of my body that had suffered at his touch, and drew back in revulsion as they encountered his wetness between my legs. I felt violated. I dragged myself to my feet, staggered across to the sink and filled it with cold water. I plunged my face right in, gasping with shock as I did so. Then I scrubbed away every remaining particle of him that still clung to me, wincing with pain as I did so, but I knew I could never scrub away the memory of being raped.

Raped! But I had been unresisting, my mind argued. I had not struggled or fought or scratched or screamed. Who would believe that I had been raped? I had still been in too shocked a state after Mother's death to resist. Mother. She was in there. A door's-breadth away. She might have heard. No, of course not. She was unable to hear anything any more.

I felt illogically that she should have helped me all the same. Stopped this thing happening. It would never have happened if she had not been lying in there dead. Letting Ruskin seize his chance. I was blaming her. Resenting her, hating her for dying as I'd hated her in life. No, not hated really. Despised. That was it.

My thoughts jerked on in short staccato bursts, as Ruskin had jerked and stabbed into me. I could still feel it. He was still there, enormous, sickening, violating. I tipped the sleeping-draught down the sink, filled the cup with cold water and gulped it down. In some perverse way I did not want to sleep or find oblivion, even if I could have relaxed my taut nerves to try. I wanted my senses alert to listen for Mother's pennies to roll, and to remember the fury of Ruskin's onslaught and to revile against it.

He had said threateningly that I must not tell or he'd have me out of here. And of course he wanted me here so that he could repeat his odious performance again and again and again, whenever he wanted me. He wanted me as his personal whore. Panic almost made me retch again.

A sliver of sanity broke through the muddle of my thoughts. I did not have to stay here, and I could not possibly, not now. I must get away, and as soon as possible. To Blackmaddie, of course. She had won.

The realisation was the third shock that night. The one that released the tears from my blocked mind and sent them streaking down my face. Blackmaddie wanted me and now I wanted her. But only because of what had happened here in this room tonight.

My mouth twisted bitterly. Where was Mother's romantic love, of which she had always spoken so openly? The love she and Father had shared that was supposed to be so warm and beautiful and fulfilling? All I had known so far was William's pale shadow of affection and the animal thrustings of Ruskin. That wasn't love. Mother could never have known anything like that, unless she had been pretending to me all this time.

And I would never know. I wanted her to tell me the truth, but I could not, because she could no longer answer. Now that I wished her to speak of it, she was forever silent. She lay dead beyond the bedroom door, eternally past my reach.

3

No night had ever seemed so long. I could not fill it with sleep, and for hours I sat crouched in a chair or prowled around the room aimlessly. Painfully too, for my body was bruised by Ruskin's assault, as well as my mind. And yet, illogically, I realised I was extraordinarily hungry.

My eyes caught sight of the table, still littered with the remnants of our tea. Mother's bun that she had left for later sat alone on its plate, still shiny with glaze. It seemed a hundred years ago that I had bought it at the baker's shop the previous afternoon.

For over ten minutes I must have looked at it without moving. I had moved automatically to clear away the table but I had not stirred since I caught sight of the currant bun. A strange new freedom of spirit was taking hold of me that was inexplicable after all that had happened. But I could no longer push it out of my mind. Mother had ruled. Now Mother was dead.

Yesterday I would have been relieved beyond measure to know I need not go to Blackmaddie. Yesterday there had been no animal thrusting into my body and soul. Now that I was free to choose, I chose to go to Blackmaddie. There was all the difference in the world in making a free choice. Blackmaddie dangled in front of me like a carrot in front of a donkey, and I wanted her.

She wanted me and I must go to her. I seemed to hear echoes of Mother and Father in my thoughts. Or was something more basic than any such fancies setting me on the road for Scotland, away from poverty and distasteful surroundings? Was there, after all, more greed in me than I had ever realised?

Almost without thinking what I did, I picked up the currant bun and sank my teeth into its crusty top. In a way it was symbolic. I had taken something that was Mother's. Now it was mine.

A sudden rattle of crates outside the house and the rumble of carts along the waterfront in the darkness sent the fear rippling through me again, and my eyes flew to the bedroom door. Despite all my resolve, my nerves were still at breaking point. She was still in there. She still unnerved me.

I looked about me with almost maniacal anxiety until my eyes fastened on the blue silk at the end of the table. It was neatly folded into its various shapes, awaiting tacking. Mother would never finish it now. But I should. Anything would be better than sitting bolt upright on the hard wooden chair listening for the slightest sound from the other side of the door.

I snatched up my thimble and the box of threads and needles and began stitching. Jerkily at first, jabbing the needle into my finger so many times my skin was soon pricked and sore.

But gradually the task had a kind of therapeutic effect. I worked on through the night in the hiss of the flickering gas-light, as Mother had done so many times while I lay sleeping, and when I finally shook out the shimmering folds of the blue silk gown I felt a sense of immense satisfaction, knowing it was ready for a first fitting. If I did nothing more towards it, the client could show some other dressmaker the way it was intended to look, and I knew Mother would have been pleased at my diligence.

When I finally eased my aching back and looked about me I saw that it was approaching daylight. The morning activity was already beginning. Barrows and carts were being wheeled noisily over the cobblestones to and from shops and warehouses and sheds in an endless procession. I turned off the gas-light and flexed my stiff fingers. Outside, a smoky yellow haze lit the cold waters of the Avon, and across the river the cool green of Ashton Meadows stretched eerily into the distance.

An odd sense of calm was filling me. I was no longer

afraid of Mother's cold form laid out in the next room now that the darkness had passed and no spectre had materialised in front of me. The hypnotic stitching of the blue silk had restored something of my sanity, almost as if I had taken on Mother's role and something of her strength in the long hours of the night. Maybe even something of her character. I shivered suddenly and turned away from the window, dressing hurriedly in my normal, everyday clothes.

A sharp tap on the outer door made me jump. My mind winged back at once to Ruskin, but it was Mrs Ruskin's voice I heard calling me, and I opened the door thankfully.

'I've brought some breakfast for you, my dear,' she said with rough kindness. 'You'll be too upset to think of it yourself, I daresay, and you must keep up your strength. Poor girl, you do look poorly. You should have stayed downstairs with us last night instead of brooding here all alone.'

Odd that she should have used the same words as her husband. That I needed to keep up my strength.

'I'm all right really, Mrs Ruskin,' I said huskily. 'But I'm grateful to you for the tray of food. It was thoughtful of you. Perhaps you'd ask young Jim to come up in a little while, and let him run some messages for me as well?'

'Of course, lovey. You just take your time and enjoy the victuals.'

I was glad when she clumped back downstairs. She was not an attractive woman, scrawny and thin-faced, and all the time she had been standing at the doorway I had had to force myself not to stare at the flat, non-existent breasts. Remembering with painful clarity how Ruskin had cupped my own in his hands, burying his face in their fullness, muttering as if he had been given some sort of prize, 'Lovely, lovely. My big, lovely girl. Big, lovely girl. Big . . . '

He would have nothing much for his hands to grasp hold of with Mrs Ruskin. I pushed the door shut after her and put the tray on the table with trembling hands as I recalled last night. Unwillingly my eyes went down to the heavy curves that strained out against my bodice. Curves that hardened even as I remembered, the nipples pressing painfully against the coarse material of my dress, while a tingling sensation surged somewhere deep inside me.

Oh God, I didn't want to remember it with pleasure; it was anything but pleasurable at the time. It was hateful, shaming, degrading, but my own body betrayed me. My own physical desires told me this was what I wanted and needed, only never again with Ruskin. Not with the bastard who had raped me.

I ate the cold toast and honey Mrs Ruskin had brought me and drained the cup of tea. I caught sight of myself in the mirror as I washed up the crockery and was shocked by my appearance. No wonder she had thought I looked ill.

My hair was a tangled dark mass where I had neglected to comb it after washing it. My eyes were reddened by the strain of sewing by gas-light all night and the ordeals that preceded it. There was a feverish colour in my face that alarmed me most. I suddenly realised too that my limbs ached down to my toes, and there was a strange light-headedness about me as if I were intoxicated, but with none of the exhilaration of that state.

I turned quickly and wrote the message for Jim to take for me. One to Mr Higgins, informing him of Mother's death and requesting him to tell my grandfather I wished to go to Blackmaddie as soon as possible. And a brief note to William, asking him to let the school know my circumstances. I wrote the envelopes and sealed them as Jim Ruskin arrived at my door. I instructed him where to go and gave him a few coppers for his trouble. Then I almost staggered across the room, registering the huge frightened look in the boy's eyes as I fell to the floor with a crash.

I was aware of noise and movement, of men's voices mingling with Mrs Ruskin's, of being lifted and carried downstairs to another room. Of the dull thud, thud, thud of something heavy and angled and awkward being shifted out of the house. Once I thought I heard William's voice. Often I smelt Ruskin. I felt his touch, his fingers, his slobbering mouth. In my nightmares I often cried out to him to get away from me.

'There now, lovey, try to eat, there's a good girl. You

35

must take some of this broth, or you'll not be fit to travel.'

Mrs Ruskin forced the feeding-cup into my mouth and tipped it towards me. It almost made me retch, but the broth tasted good and I made myself swallow. I could not understand her words at first.

'That's better,' she went on with satisfaction. 'Now you'll start to mend. We thought at one time you were on your way to join your mother.'

Recollection rushed back at me like a cloudburst. Everything was suddenly crystal clear, except where I was and what I was doing here. I must be ill. My hands were so thin and white and trembling, I had to be. I turned my head slightly, though it swam alarmingly to do so, and realised I must be in the Ruskins' parlour, lying on their couch in front of the fire and covered by a mound of blankets that stifled me. I struggled to sit up and asked thinly what had happened to me.

'You collapsed, lovey, that's what. Right in front of our Jim's eyes. Frightened him to death for a minute. He shouted for Ruskin, and he carried you down here and sent Jim off for the doctor at once. He took your messages for you, too. Don't be worrying about them, it was all seen to.'

So Ruskin had carried me down. It hadn't all been dreaming then.

'The doctor said you'd caught a severe chill with your wet hair and then the shock of your mother's death. It's a good thing you sent for that Mr Higgins. He's seen to everything, and tells us you'll be travelling as soon as you're well. We'll be sorry to see you go, lovey, me and Ruskin will.'

I closed my eyes for a minute.

'If you tell . . . I'll see you're all right, and we'll have some more of the same.' I could hear his wheezing, coarse voice all over again. I gave a soft moan and Mrs Ruskin clicked her teeth sympathetically, misunderstanding my reason.

'There, lovey, it must have been an ordeal for you. But you're young, and the memory won't last for ever.'

My eyes glazed at her words, and then she remembered something else to tell me. 'Oh – a young man called to see you while you were ill. He said he'd be coming back this afternoon. That should cheer you up.'

'Mr Derry?' I said dully, for of course it could be no one else. Yesterday it would have cheered me. The yesterday I remembered, before Mother died and left me alone with Ruskin. Now, the thought of William's visit made me uncomfortable and guilty, as if he could read in my face and my eyes that I had given his privilege to another man. No, not *given*, I amended. I had had it wrenched from me. Even William would not deny that, if he were ever told. But he would not be told, ever. No one would.

I began to feel slightly better as the broth warmed me. And there were things I needed to know.

'About my mother, Mrs Ruskin. There are – arrangements to be made. The – the burial – ' my breath became short, my voice agitated as the horror of the scene at the waterfront and Mother gasping like a fish out of water swept through me again. 'We – we have no money for a burial plot.'

'Calm yourself, Miss Brodie,' the woman said soothingly. 'It was all taken care of yesterday. Mr Higgins saw to everything as you would have wished. It was necessary for the burial to take place, and you being insensible for four days, it had to go on without you, dearie. Mr Higgins was insistent I should tell you as soon as you awoke that it was all carried out tastefully, as he was instructed.'

Why was she speaking in that deferential tone? I suddenly realised. She knew very well that there was something going on, even if the dry-lipped Higgins had not divulged anything. Clearly, Grandfather had been informed of Mother's death and had instructed the solicitor to see to everything with no expense spared.

'Mr Higgins will be here this afternoon too, and the doctor is due at any time,' Mrs Ruskin went on. 'He'll be glad to see you looking rosier.'

I supposed I had no need to concern myself with the cost of these visits. It was a new and unreal experience. But I was aware of a terrible sense of guilt that I had lain unconscious while Mother was being buried, as if I had let her down in the final, ultimate way. And even more guilty because of the enormous sense of relief that she was no longer in our bedroom upstairs.

Ruskin suddenly strode into the room, exuding a smell of the river and the fish market. My stomach lurched as I saw him, and I had a job not to shrink back against the pillow. To my horror Mrs Ruskin slammed her hat on to her head, pinning it with a fierce hat-pin that reminded me of Mother's, and said that Ruskin would sit with me until the doctor came as she had another call on her services that day.

'Dying like flies with the influenza,' Ruskin said irreverently as she went out of the door. 'Keeps Mother in work though.'

He drew a stool beneath him and sat close beside me while I tried not to look at him. But out of the corner of my eye I could see how his great bloated stomach overhung his thighs on the short stool, and his grubby shirt popped open where the buttons were strained taut, revealing the matted hair inside. A sudden image of him grunting and thrusting into me came vividly into my mind and I felt my face grow hot with shame. This – this uncouth lout had known me more intimately than anyone else in the world, save William. I suppressed a shudder with great difficulty. The very last thing I wanted was to be left alone with him, and I willed the doctor to arrive soon. I edged the blankets up under my chin and he gave a soft, guttural laugh as he saw what I was doing.

'There's no need to be shy with me, girlie. We know each other too well, don't we? Though you've surprised us all these last nights with your babblings about your fine castle, my pretty Charlotte. I'm fair sorry you're thinking of leaving us just when you and I were beginning to get so well acquainted and all.'

'Don't, please.' I could not stand hearing him talk like this. And I was horrified to think I had rambled on about my private affairs, and that the Ruskins knew all about Blackmaddie. I licked my dry lips. What if I had said anything about the night Mother had died? But I couldn't have, otherwise Mrs Ruskin could never have acted so hospitably towards me. The horror of it had no doubt been too great to let my mind relive it, thank God.

Ruskin suddenly leaned towards me, his hot eyes burning with the lust I remembered.

'I'm real sad we won't be able to repeat the performance much more, girlie. You have a real talent for making a man randy. All that cool, stand-offish look, and yet the sparkle in them pretty blue eyes, and that lovely response despite the haughty maiden look. But you ain't a maiden, are you, my pretty? Had it before and plenty, I reckon, from the way we clicked. Yes, a real talent for it, and all the equipment so generously shaped.'

I was so mesmerised by his leering face and his coarse words I had not even realised his hand was under the blankets feeling for me. It forced itself between my legs, but I closed them together like a vice so that no more than the tip of his fat finger touched me. He laughed softly, wriggling it to and fro.

'Get out of me,' I said, between clenched teeth. 'You sick, loathsome man!'

The tone of my voice made him stop his movements and a surprised, almost hurt look came into his face, as if he really couldn't believe I would not welcome his heaving onslaught again. But then his hand grasped my breast, pushing into my cotton nightgown and exposing it. A mocking laugh rose from his throat.

'Don't try the proud lady with me now, my pretty Charlotte. Not when this little rosebud is telling me different!'

He tweaked at my nipple, twirling it round in his fingers, and for one horrified moment I thought he was going to throw the blankets aside and mount me there and then in his own parlour. I heard somebody knock at the door and I went weak with relief as he gave a muttered oath and moved to answer it.

It was the doctor, and he was agreeably surprised to see my warm, healthy colour. I could have told him it was not due entirely to my recovery, but I was so anxious to get away from Ruskin and his groping fingers, I begged the doctor to pronounce me well and say that I could travel at once.

He was extremely doubtful, but I insisted that I would go in any case. So at last he reluctantly agreed that I would probably come to no great harm if I wrapped up well, and admonished me for being a wilful young lady, allowing that no doubt my spirit would aid my recuperation.

I almost wept as I thanked him. I noticed that he stayed quite a long time fussing over me. Longer than he had ever stayed before on his few visits to either Mother or me. Then of course we had no money to spare for doctors' visits. I assumed Mr Higgins had told him I was now to be given every care and consideration.

I was almost glad to see Mr Higgins this time, and to tell him I was impatient now to leave Bristol, and that the doctor said I was well enough to travel. I would leave tomorrow, I told him imperiously, and he could inform my grandfather I was on my way. I surprised myself and Higgins with my new air of authority, and it pleased rather than irritated me to see he thought I was acting like a *nouveau riche* already. Let him think what he liked. I had a right to go to Blackmaddie.

I was just as anxious to be rid of this house. Here, one floor below the attic, all the river smells and noises were much nearer, and I longed for sweet clean mountain air and the space to breathe. I longed too for my first sight of Blackmaddie. She called me with an insistent voice.

I asked Higgins to take me to see Mother's grave. I did not wish to linger, merely to look. I owed her that much, to see where she was buried, and as I had expected it was in the best corner of a pleasant churchyard, with a damp mound of earth to mark the spot and a spray of flowers sent on my behalf lying across it, already wilting. Poor Mother. More elegantly placed in death than she ever was in life, and unable to appreciate it. I could not conjure up a tear for the irony of it all, but I was glad to turn away and be taken back to the waterfront house.

I enlisted Higgins' help in my preparations. His manner

towards me had markedly changed now, and I guessed Grandfather had given him instructions to give me every assistance. He agreed to see that the blue silk dress was duly delivered, and the few bits of furniture we possessed were disposed of. The proceeds were to provide a headstone for Mother. That much I wanted to do myself without any of Grandfather's money. I saved nothing of hers except her wedding ring and a few family pictures she had kept by her bed. Mrs Ruskin helped me to pack up Mother's clothes and send them off to the poor-house.

I was not afraid to sleep in our bedroom that night. By the time Mrs Ruskin and I had finished working, Mother's bed had been stripped and the bed springs doused with disinfectant for the next occupant of the lodgings. It was completely impersonal now. I kept the window open all night – something Mother had never allowed – and a breeze blew through the lace curtains.

Once during the night I was certain I heard the outer door handle rattle, and a steady low knocking on the door. I was sure it was Ruskin, come for more of the same, as he put it, but I had locked the door securely, and I did not stir from my bed.

I was jumpy long after the knocking stopped, but gradually my nerves relaxed and I breathed in the fresh clean smell from the disinfectant and revelled in the cool night breeze. It was heady, making me think of heather and bracken and the babble of mountain streams, and waterfalls rushing into deep glens. All the forgotten images of Blackmaddie my father had imparted to me years ago came back to my mind, and I found I was fitting them all together in my head like the interlocking pieces of a jig-saw puzzle. I was quite sure that when I finally saw the castle, it would be like coming home.

Tomorrow I would leave here for ever and begin the long journey north. Mr Higgins was to take me to the station at Temple Meads and see me to the train, and he had urged me to cover myself at all times with a travelling rug as the doctor had instructed. He was so determined to see that I arrived safely and intact that I guessed Grandfather was paying him a good fee. It was agreeable to think I warranted so much attention.

'The trains are draughty and uncomfortable over long distances, I am afraid, Miss Brodie,' Higgins had informed me sorrowfully, as if he would personally seal up every chink if he could. 'I am sure you will be glad of some reading material to take your mind off the journey and some food to sustain you. Mrs Ruskin will be only too pleased to see to the food and I will arrange that you have some books to take with you.'

His tone implied that a woman of Mrs Ruskin's station would not be acquainted with the kind of suitable reading for a young lady and a teacher at that. My mouth twisted into a wry smile. He also made it sound as if a terrible ordeal was facing me, but I was so thankful to leave the tall, ugly house on the waterfront and all its unpleasant memories that I did not feel the slightest anxiety about my comfort.

I was eager to feel the power of the great train beneath me, moving slowly in a huge cloudburst of steam away from the intricate glass and stone façade of Temple Meads station, and then to feel it gathering speed until it seemed to whisper her name with every rhythmic thundering of wheels along the track.

'*Blackmaddie, Blackmaddie, Blackmaddie . . .*'

4

As Higgins had warned me, the train journey was interminably long and every bit as uncomfortable as he had suggested. Mrs Ruskin had packed me some cake and sandwiches to take with me, and she had felt obliged to clasp me to her flat bosom in a falsely emotional farewell. This left Ruskin free to do the same, and while he pressed against me I felt his chest move from side to side against my breasts as a little reminder, and his leg tried to force itself between mine. But I had anticipated this and held myself rigid.

He smiled his farewell with a gleam in his little black eyes, and I could tell that my rebuff had only served to excite him. But it was too late for him to get at me again, I thought, with an enormous sense of relief, and I could only pity Mrs Ruskin when he turned his attention to her to effect his relief.

I was touched that William came to the station to see me off as well. He was so indiscreet as to kiss me in full view of all the other passengers on the platform, and he wished me well and urged me to write and tell him about the beauties of Scotland.

Mr Higgins had been solicitous enough to see that I was seated in a carriage with a middle-aged couple and their daughter who were also travelling to Scotland. They were a family by the name of Waverley, and from the little cough the daughter gave quite frequently and the anxious looks from her parents every time she did so, I surmised they were travelling for her health. By the time we had been in close proximity for the whole day and into the evening, we had struck up something of a friendship, and confided some personal details.

'I do hope we shall see something of you while we are in the North, Miss Brodie,' Mrs Waverley said. 'We shall be staying not far from Blackmaddie, in a hotel near the mountains. I have not seen your grandfather's home, but everyone has heard of it, of course. Everyone thereabouts, that is. We have stayed in the district before, but we never venture far from the hotel except for short walks, because of Agnes and her wretched cough. While the clear air is so beneficial, we do not like to do too much walking and overtire her.'

'I think Mother makes too much of my cough,' Agnes put in with a smile. 'It affects my chest, but not my legs!'

Her mother's words confirmed my suspicions, however. I felt a wave of sympathy for the girl as a sudden fit of coughing overtook her, as if to remind her that she was far from well. It was tragic for her to be so frail, for she was incredibly beautiful, with honey-coloured hair and a creamy-white skin. She had startling brown eyes, so dark as to be almost black. She made me feel my black hair and blue eyes and rosy complexion were almost rudely healthy and robust by comparison; we must make a strikingly noticeable couple, being so completely opposite in colouring.

'Perhaps your parents would allow you to visit me at Blackmaddie,' I said impulsively to Agnes. 'I have not met my cousins yet, and it would be most agreeable to hear another English accent among all the Scots ones, I am sure. It has occurred to me more than once that I shall feel very much the outsider there. Please say you'll come if you can. I'm sure my grandfather will make you most welcome.'

'I should dearly love to see Blackmaddie, and you too, Miss Brodie,' she smiled delightedly. 'Thank you for asking me.'

'Charlotte, please,' I said quickly.

It seemed silly to stand on ceremony when we still had so many hours to travel together.

I glanced out of the window to see how the landscape was changing, and looked back in time to see a little look of satisfaction pass between the older Waverleys after our little interchange. No doubt they too would be pleased that Agnes was not going to find the mountains boring and cold and dull, even though I had been assured by William of their immense beauty and magnitude. But Agnes would have seen it all before, and I was sure her parents would be relieved she was going to have a young companion to visit.

We settled down to sleep for part of the night, and while the others were still sleeping I awoke and felt in need of a wash. It was not as cold as I had imagined it would be in the train, perhaps because so many bodies were packed quite tightly together. I felt grubby and sticky, and slipped along the corridor to the toilet compartment. No one else seemed to be stirring in our part of the train yet, so I could take my time over my toilet, and on impulse I slipped the top half of my dress and undergarments from my shoulders and washed all the top half of my body to freshen myself up before I made my way back to the compartment I shared with the Waverleys. Agnes was awake now, smiling at me as I re-entered.

'Charlotte, you did mean what you said about letting me come and visit you, didn't you?' she said with a sudden dubious note in her voice. I looked at her in surprise and said that of course I meant it. Why shouldn't I have?

'It's just that, well, some of the Scots are none too friendly towards us, that's all, and I thought – maybe your grand-father – ' she floundered on, and I looked at her with a strange sense of alarm mounting inside me.

'Towards us? Who do you mean by us? Not your family, surely.' I glanced towards her parents, a perfectly nice, ordinary, respectable English couple.

'Us. The English.' Agnes gave a small uncertain laugh. 'It seems ridiculous, doesn't it, after all these years, but some of them still haven't forgotten. Nor, it seems, have some of them forgiven.'

'I'm sorry, but I don't understand you, Agnes. Forgiven what?'

'The massacre. That's their name for it. We know of it as the Battle of Culloden, but to the Scots it was a massacre, and though Blackmaddie castle and village is a good way from the Moor, on the other side of the country, in fact, it was still a strong centre of sympathisers for the Prince. And there are those who are still bitter towards the English.'

I listened in amazement. 'But surely the '45 uprising was over a hundred years ago. I'm not much of a student of history, I'm afraid, but I can't believe that people are still brooding over something that happened so long ago.'

Agnes shrugged her slender shoulders. 'I'm only telling you what I know and believe, Charlotte. There are those around Blackmaddie who don't like the English and will do anything to be rid of any who dare to cross the Border. And we are going right into the heart of the old sympathisers.'

A cold shiver ran through me, even though I could hardly credit what she was saying. Agnes spoke with such conviction and sincerity, and she made me feel I was stepping back into history. As if once we crossed the Border I would be one of the aliens, the hated English. It was ridiculous to feel that way, but I could not help it. I tried to force a laugh, but it was not very successful.

'You'll be quite all right with me anyway, Agnes. I'm a Brodie, and half-Scot, so I don't suppose I shall be threatened.'

She refused to smile back at my flippancy, her dark eyes shadowed and troubled. They made my heart give a little lurch of unease.

'Some say a Scotsman who marries into the English has betrayed them,' she said haltingly. 'Don't be too complacent about your position, Charlotte, I beg you. I don't mean to frighten you ... '

'Well, you're succeeding quite well,' I said, half in anger. I was beginning to wish I had not come at all.

'The massacre meant the breaking up of the clans,' Agnes went on. 'The Highlander ceased to exist as a man of action and as someone to be feared and instead became part of a legend. I have had plenty of lonely hours to study the history of Scotland when I was too unwell to do anything else, and in some places it seems as if the legend still has a hard core of reality, especially for the Stewarts and in intensely loyal regions where time has virtually stood still for the last hundred years.'

'Such as Blackmaddie village, I suppose,' I added for her.

'I appreciate that you have absorbed much of the local history, Agnes, but are you quite sure you haven't been reading too many romantic tales and letting your imagination run amok as well?'

Her father suddenly leaned towards us from the opposite seat in the compartment. I had thought he was asleep, but he had clearly been listening to part of our conversation.

'Miss Brodie, I beg you not to scoff at the things my daughter tells you. Do not be unduly afraid, because I am sure that you have the protection of your family, otherwise you would not be welcomed to Blackmaddie in the first place. But just be a little cautious if need be, and on your guard.'

Blackmaddie wanted me. Not Mother. She had spat Mother out like a maggot from a rotten apple; I remembered vividly how the simile had sprung to my mind before. Blackmaddie wanted *me*. I took feverish comfort from the thought. But suddenly I missed Mother more than I had at any time since her death. Too much had happened in too short a time for me to begin to mourn her properly, if mourn I could for such an unaffectionate woman.

But all the same, I missed her strength of character, her forthrightness. She would have dismissed at once Agnes' warning that a piece of history could possibly harm me, could possibly have anything at all to do with me. I wished Agnes had not started on this tale. I would rather have arrived at Blackmaddie in ignorance of any undercurrents against me than be on constant watch for every movement that might be construed as a danger.

Mrs Waverley stirred in her seat and began composing herself. She gestured to me to look through the window at the cold grey dawn outside. Long fingers of gold and pink streaked across the pale sky, giving it an ethereal beauty.

'We are nearing our destination, Charlotte. Can you feel the change in atmosphere?'

I admitted that I could now. There was a sharp coolness in the air, and the country outside seemed to be undulating and hilly in the early light, though I could see no visible signs of mountains. I felt a small shock of disappointment and said so, and was glad that my pouting remark lightened the conversation in the compartment, and Mr Waverley's eyes teased me.

'There is far more of Scotland than what is just over the Border, Miss Brodie. We still have more than two hours' travelling before we reach the end of the railway line. Are you being met at the station?'

'I certainly hope so,' I said fervently. 'Mr Higgins assured me that a message had been sent and that no doubt one of my cousins would be there for the last part of the journey by road.'

'What a pity we had not met before, Charlotte. We could have gone all the way together,' Agnes said.

I would have liked that. I was growing more and more apprehensive as the hours passed. Not merely because of the disturbing conversation I had had with Agnes and her father either, but because of the enormity of what I was undertaking. My mouth began to dry up and conversation with it. So much had changed in my life in rapid succession, and now that I was almost there I wanted to turn and run. If only Mother had been here, she would have been a buffer between me and the strangers who called me their kinswoman. I had never lacked spirit, but I admitted that I needed her badly now, and I had never felt so alone and afraid. I tried to smother the feeling, but it was always there whenever I let myself relax. Blackmaddie was suddenly the strange and frightening place of my worst nightmares, and not the fairy-tale castle of a child's imaginings.

'My cousin Robert is the eldest.' I forced myself to speak with as much confidence as possible. 'I daresay he will be there to meet me.'

My cousin Robert. I might as well have been talking about a creature from another world for all that the name meant anything to me. I wondered what he would be like. What all of them would be like. I knew nothing of Scotsmen, except for my own father, and he had seemed completely anglicised to me, apart from his accent. He had a fierce temper, but I never heard it directed on my mother or myself. I vividly remembered Mother telling me of a fight

Father had been involved in, and that he had won handsomely. And that he was a true Scot, dour on the surface, but with hot passions and a scalding fury when roused. I shivered, remembering.

Agnes went along to the toilet compartment some while later to prepare herself for leaving the train and refresh herself.

'I think I'll watch the scenery for a while,' I informed the Waverleys, and went into the corridor to lean against the window glass and let my face cool down.

Away in the far distance I suddenly realised that what I had thought were grey clouds on the horizon were in reality a great blue-white mountainous mass, so vast it made my heart give a great lurch, frightening to my English eyes that had seen nothing more spectacular than the drop down to the river Avon from the Downs at Bristol. This was something so different, so awe-inspiring it made me afraid, insignificant. I turned quickly and went back inside the compartment.

'Are you feeling all right, Charlotte? You look quite pale. Has the journey upset your stomach, my dear?' Mrs Waverley was all consideration, and I murmured that I did indeed have a headache, but that it would surely pass as soon as I was out in the fresh air.

I closed my eyes, but to my distress a picture of Ruskin came into my mind. I had thought I was rid of him for ever, but his presence was still here. I could smell the stench of him in my nostrils. I could feel him, pushing against me, touching the secret parts of me, feeling me. Thrusting into me with savage strokes, like a stallion riding a mare. He was a nightmare that never left me, coming back into my mind with all the suddenness and shock of his attack on my body.

'Lovely. Lovely. My big, lovely girl . . . '

Those slobbering words seemed to be stamped into my brain. I always heard them, in that coarse, thick voice whenever the memory of Ruskin's attack filled my senses with renewed horror. The memory of them made me want to retch, and I was never more thankful to hear Mr Waverley

49

say the train was slowing down and we had better gather all our belongings together.

He started lifting down his family's baggage from the rack, and then mine, and stacked them all together. The Waverley family were the only people I knew in the whole of this vast new country, and the thought of losing them terrified me.

'Don't forget to come and visit me, Agnes,' I said in a little rush. 'I shall look forward to seeing you, and as soon as I am settled I will send a note round to your hotel to invite you.'

'I shall be waiting impatiently, Charlotte,' she told me. We hugged each other on the station platform as if we had known each other a lifetime, and I looked around me in growing dismay and alarm as no one came forward to claim me.

'I do not care to leave you here alone, Charlotte,' Mr Waverley said. 'We could still take you in the conveyance with us if you wish, but if you think someone is coming to collect you at any minute . . . '

'Thank you again, but I had better wait,' I answered quickly. It was a hard job not to let the sting of tears show in my eyes, and there was a great lump in my throat as I urged them to go to the hotel, for I could see that Agnes looked suddenly very fatigued.

They left reluctantly, and when all the passengers had gone and I was the solitary figure left standing there, the station master ambled up to me and asked if I was Miss Brodie.

'Yes, I am Miss Brodie,' I said between cold lips.

'A message came for you that you're to wait here and you'll be fetched within half an hour, Missie,' he said in a broad accent that was almost incomprehensible to me.

I knew if I was feeling more myself I would not have morbid fancies. But I *was* alone. The station master had disappeared somewhere in the recesses of his hut, and I was overtaken by a great wave of homesickness. And of fear. Supposing no one did come to fetch me after all? Supposing Grandfather regretted his whim to send for me and had decided to ignore me as he had done all these years? What would I do? I knew no one, except the Waverleys. Were they the kind of people who would thank a penniless sewing-mistress for turning up on their doorstep at the hotel?

I jumped half out of my skin as I suddenly heard my name spoken. My eyes had been glazing over as I pondered the insecurity of my position, and I had heard no one approach. Now I realised the immediate area in front of me was blocked by a huge figure of a man whose violent red hair was echoed by a thick red beard, his eyes dark and hard and unwelcoming in his angular face. My eyes travelled incredulously over his figure, resplendent in cloak and kilt of some woven material, a tam-o'-shanter barely covering the red hair. In his thick woollen socks I could see the hilt of a knife of some sort. The sight of him frightened me out of my wits.

'Yes,' I stammered. 'I am Charlotte Brodie.'

He did not offer his hand, nor comment at all for several seconds, merely stood and stared at me. I felt as if I wanted to wrap my arms round myself in protection from his insolent gaze, when suddenly he nodded his head.

'Aye, so you are,' he said finally. His voice was grudging and oddly grim. Who was he? Perhaps some servant sent to collect me, but it was a faint hope. No servant would stand there with legs astride looking as if he owned the whole of the Highlands and clearly thinking impatiently that the last place he wished to be was meeting an English girl from a train. I lifted my chin. I was a Brodie and I had better start acting like one. I opened my mouth to speak as imperiously as I could, when his next words took all the spirit out of me.

'You'll no doubt have heard of me. My name is Robert. Robert Stewart.'

Black dots danced in front of my eyes. Stewart? *Stewart?* A hundred years of hatred flashed out of his eyes as he informed me of the fact. I had the dizziest feeling that at any minute he would not be above pulling the dagger from his sock and plunging it into my heart as some small retribution for his ancestors.

I heard the warning tone of Agnes' voice telling me that some never forgot, that they couldn't forgive. I knew I was letting myself be swept along on a hysterical wave, but hadn't she also said that a Scot who married into the English betrayed them, as my father had done.

The black dots cleared a little as Robert Stewart picked up my baggage as if it weighed nothing and strode with it along the platform. I had no choice but to hurry after him.

5

It was an uncomfortable ride in the covered gig to Black-maddie, made even more unpleasant by Robert Stewart's obvious dislike of me and his resentment that he had been sent to fetch me. He answered my questions abruptly or angrily, offering little himself unless I made the first approach to conversation. Long before we got anywhere near the first sight of Blackmaddie, I found myself wishing guiltily that Grandfather had died peacefully in his sleep in the course of time without ever having taken it into his head to see me.

'You *are* my cousin, I take it?' I asked Robert directly, once we had left the station and were on our way. 'I had thought you would be a Brodie.'

My voice trailed away at his scornful look. I had only meant it curiously, but from the look on his face I was adding yet one more insult to my presence here.

'My mother married a Brodie,' his voice was clipped. 'We were all quite young at the time, my brothers and myself when she married your Uncle Andrew, but the marriage did not necessitate our relinquishing our name. Family names hereabouts are a matter of pride and not to be exchanged lightly.'

'Of course not,' I said quickly. 'It was just that no one had told me.'

I could not be expected to know every detail of family history, I thought angrily.

'My youngest brother, Ian, toyed with the idea of taking the new family name some while back,' Robert went on in a suddenly tight voice. 'But I doubt that anything will come of it. If it does, Neil and I will break his head.'

I caught my breath at the way his tone changed with that last sentence. One minute he was merely annoyed, the next the hot passion was barely hidden beneath the surface of his words.

'Neil is your other brother,' I stated, for want of something to say as he stared broodingly ahead towards the white mountains. Not all white, I noticed briefly, only the tips were sparkling in the early morning sunlight. Sparkling like diamonds and just as cold and hard.

'Aye, Neil is my other brother,' Robert grunted as the gig lurched over the rutted track and he had to grasp the reins more tightly.

I looked away from him, from the huge hands holding on tightly to the reins and the hard set of his features. If Robert was a sample of my family's hospitality, I would begin to think twice about staying here, even though I had no money at all, and the thought was enough to send my spirits sinking. But I could still teach. I could sew and mend, and earn an honest living if I had to. I was not entirely destitute as long as my fingers were nimble. The realisation encouraged me.

'And my cousin Katrina . . . '

'Katrina's dead,' he said shortly.

'I do know that.' I tried to be patient but I could feel my temper rising. He had no right to treat me as though I were nothing more than a nuisance. Whatever I had expected, it had not been indifference, especially from a man who fascinated me despite his dourness. What had Mother said? That Father was a typical Scot – dour on the outside, but with hot passions beneath. I could well fit Robert into that description, even if the hot passions at this moment seemed centred on an unreasonable dislike of the Brodies.

I tried again to be as friendly as I could.

'I was merely trying to acquaint myself with the various people at Blackmaddie, if you will only listen. Katrina was your step-sister, I believe? Uncle Andrew's daughter?'

'Aye. She was a Brodie.' He suddenly turned and looked at me. His gaze was dark and direct and for some reason made my heart turn over.

'You'll be a shock to him,' he said flatly.

'Why?' I felt my heart begin to beat faster. I felt uneasy all over again. Why should I be a shock? Grandfather was expecting me, wasn't he? I knew Robert could be referring to no one else.

'You could be her,' my cousin said grudgingly. 'Same colour hair. Same eyes, mouth, shape.' His eyes flicked down to my bodice beneath the thin cloak I had pulled tightly round myself. His eyes stayed there too long. Insolent eyes, assessing me, stripping me naked. I was suddenly angry with him.

'I can't possibly resemble Katrina,' I snapped. 'I don't even have the same colouring as my father. He was more like you, strangely enough, with that reddish hair. Maybe not so fiery in colouring, but just as volatile!'

A glimmer of a smile touched his lips behind the red beard, but it was quickly gone.

'I didn't say you resembled her,' Robert said grimly. 'I said you could be her. When he sees you, you'll know it by the expression on his face. He worshipped her. It'll be as if she's come back from the dead.'

'Stop it,' I said shrilly. 'I'm myself. Charlotte. Not some reincarnation of somebody else! I won't be made to feel frightened in this way before I've even stepped across the threshold of Blackmaddie!'

Robert laughed shortly.

'You'll find plenty to frighten you there, my fine Charlotte, if you've been used to teaching little girls to sew samplers all day long and nothing else.'

So they knew all about me. His words stopped me for a few minutes. Of course, Mr Higgins would have reported everything, including how poor Mother and I had been. I was doubly humiliated. I wished feverishly I hadn't come. I wished I had thrown myself on William's warm affection and taken second-best. I did not even stop to consider that that was how I rated him, or why, since I had nothing else with which to compare him, except Ruskin. My mind veered away quickly.

'What of Kirsty?' I said evenly. 'I'm looking forward to meeting her.'

Robert burst out laughing. I looked at him in astonishment, wondering what I had said that was so funny.

'Oh, Kirsty's looking forward to meeting you too, Charlotte. With about as much enthusiasm as she would welcome a nest of hornets in her bed.'

I felt myself redden with chagrin and embarrassment and dismay. I had pinned all my hopes of settling down at Blackmaddie on the friendship of this female cousin of mine, but if Robert was to be believed, she did not want me here. And he made it plain that neither did he. And probably neither of his brothers did either. Who did then? I could have wept as the question surged through me. Only Grandfather of all the Brodie family? But he was old and sick. Supposing he should die? What would become of me then?

'You have no right to make me feel so unwelcome,' I burst out, suddenly filled with a red rage at his mocking tone. 'I did not ask to come here, as you're probably well aware, since you seem to know everything about me.'

'Not everything, Charlotte. Not *yet*.' He was smiling broadly now, as if he enjoyed my outburst, and I could not fail to understand the meaning behind his words. My father's hot temper exploded inside me, and I would have struck out at him if he had not read my intention and grasped hold of my arm with one hand.

'There's a fire within you that will complement Blackmaddie,' he said, in a suddenly mellower tone. 'It will be interesting to see which one of you will win when it comes to a battle.'

He said 'when', not 'if', I noted. I rubbed my arm where he had held it.

'She won't keep me here against my will,' I muttered, unconsciously using my father's female reference to the castle. Robert laughed.

'A minute ago you were telling me you did not ask to come, but you came, did you not?' he observed.

He seemed to have enjoyed our little brush, I thought. Perhaps he had thought I would be timid and overawed and tearful and was relieved to see that I was not – at least, not so that anyone could see. All my tears were kept locked inside my head. But from then on Robert was almost affable towards me in contrast to his earlier mood of dislike. Maybe it was natural suspicion of my motives for coming here, I thought suddenly, and now he could dismiss them as mere curiosity.

Whatever the reason, I was forced to admit that he was a splendid figure of a man when he threw back his glowing red head and laughed from somewhere deep in his throat, with his dark eyes gleaming and a wide, sensuous smile revealing white teeth in sharp contrast to the bushy red beard. A giant of a man. He caught me staring at him.

'Well, cousin,' he said softly, 'does that appraising look mean you are deciding whether or not we shall get to know one another better? Because I have already made up my mind about that. I like a woman with fire in her loins.'

I gasped at the crudity of him. But whatever I was going to say scathingly to him was lost in my throat as Robert reined the horse to a halt when we topped a high ridge in the uneven track, and pointed far below.

'Blackmaddie,' he said simply.

To be a child and listen with wonder and awe to tales told by a loving father of a fairy-tale castle in the mists and glens of a faraway land, dappled in the sunlight with the deep blue waters of a loch surrounding and protecting it, was one thing.

To be suddenly confronted with the reality, a thousand times more beautiful, more magnificent, was another. The turrets reared high into the autumn sky, thin shafts of sunlight striking fire from mullioned windows and throwing sharp reflections on the clear blue water. Hazy blue-white mountains formed an awesome backcloth. Dark green pine forests contrasted with the trees in the surrounding countryside that were turning every autumn hue, from russet to yellow and gold and fiery red.

'She's breathtaking,' I managed to whisper.

I found it impossible to say another word at that moment. My throat was thick, my mind stunned with beauty in front of me. I could only sit and clasp my hands tightly together, drinking in the peace and tranquillity, and yet fully conscious of the power such a castle's background could hold, in siege and battle. It was a silent world for me as yet, unpeopled by those who welcomed me, or sought to harm me, or hated me. There was only this lovely place that was part of my heritage. Mine, *mine*.

I felt a tingling sensation run through me. I belonged here; in that instant I was sure of it. I turned my head slowly to find Robert watching me intently, a strange look on his face. I realised my lips were parted and my eyes misty, and that I must have been embracing Blackmaddie with my emotions the way one would have embraced a lover. And he knew it.

'Welcome home, Charlotte Brodie,' he said softly, and the simple words brought a sting of tears to my eyes. I felt as if I had fought a battle and won, though for the life of me I could not think why. 'And as you are my cousin, I claim the right to greet you as my kinswoman.'

Before I could think to stop him, he had put his powerful arms round me and pressed his sensuous mouth to mine in a long hard kiss. It took me by surprise but it was far from unpleasant, even with the strangeness of the red beard tickling me. I found myself kissing him back, unconsciously winding my arms round his neck, feeling the blood within me stir as his hands moved slowly up and down my back caressingly. Almost clumsily, I pushed him away.

'I think that was welcome enough, cousin,' I said shakily.

'For the time being,' he said laughingly. 'But I promise you I shall want to warm myself at your fire, and before very much longer, Charlotte.'

I saw his eyes linger on the fullness of my breasts, the outline of them clearly visible beneath the thin cloak, and his tongue ran round his top lip before he urged the horse on down the steep slope to Blackmaddie. And the blood was suddenly pounding in my veins at his words. A short time ago I had not even known him, and in those first awkward moments with him I was positive we hated each other. Now, the look he gave me was filled with desire, the way William had looked. Not quite like Ruskin; I shuddered, just thinking of his name. But a terrible unease filled me all the same.

58

Was I somehow marked out because of – of *Ruskin*? Was it written on my face that my body could be brought to life and respond instantly by the caressing touch of a man's hands, by the thrusting into me?

Was this the price I was going to pay for those shocked, silent moments after Mother's death when I had lain like a puppet under Ruskin's writhing body. Yet not quite still, I remembered shamefully. There had been small, involuntary movements I was unable to prevent, when my body had arched towards his, despite my horror. Small, throaty noises that had escaped my parched throat.

At that moment, Mother's voice spun into my mind. With her clumsy yet vivid tales of Father and his lusty welcomes when he came home from the sea, sweeping her up in his arms. For all Mother's later tetchiness with me, she had known real love. As yet, I had not. With William it had been more a need for us both, pleasant and uncomplicated, with gentle affection added for good measure. With Ruskin, it had been hateful. Lust. Rape. The next time any man touched me, I vowed, it would be with love.

Robert was too busy negotiating the last steep descent of the hill to notice my preoccupation. But at last we were on a long stretch of flat terrain, and he pointed out the various parts of the estate – the deer forest and hunting park, the little boats tied up at the loch, the huts high on the side of the mountain that were barely discernible to me, but which I was assured were of tremendous necessity should anyone walking there be caught in a sudden blizzard.

'And does all that belong to Blackmaddie too?' I said disbelievingly. 'Not the mountains, surely?'

'Not the mountains, just the huts,' he told me. 'I'll take you walking up there one fine morning and show you the view. You'll think you're at the top of the world. There is always a dram of whisky or brandy kept there to revive you from the exertion of the climb, or from other exertions.'

He was smiling broadly at me again now, and I told myself swiftly it would not do to be alone too long with Robert Stewart. He was a woman's man as far as animal attraction went, and yet a man's man too – strong, muscular, aggressive. I turned away again, lest he should misinterpret my gaze.

Robert told me that Blackmaddie was not all that large, compared with some, more a fortress than a full-blown castle, but to me she was magnificent. As we drew nearer I could hardly count the number of tiny windows in her walls, the rounded turrets and long flat stretches of stone with the sun glinting on them. The points of the turrets were of a dull grey sheen, reaching for the sky like spears in battle. Their reflection in the loch was so perfect it seemed that the spires went down into the blue water into infinity. The castle was built right over the loch, and I assumed that this was some kind of defence. I shivered, wondering just how lusty and bloodthirsty my ancestors had been.

But rounding the northern side of the castle, I could see that she was built on a kind of promontory jutting out into the loch, and that on the southern side she was surrounded by trees that almost hid the lower part of her, and creepers that wound about her like clutching fingers. We entered through a gatehouse consisting of two round towers with a portcullis between. As we rode through I felt that Blackmaddie was truly sucking me in. Despite her beauty and the emotions I had felt at my first sight of her, as the horse's hooves rang on the cobbled stone it was like a death knell. I was terrified at the thought of actually going inside the castle and meeting all the relatives who had only been shadowy figures until now. With every second that passed I was more certain I should not have come. The sense of belonging had evaporated. I had no place here. I was a little sewing-mistress at a Bristol school. I did not belong at Blackmaddie, and I had no desire to be here. Blind panic was throbbing in my breast now, and Robert suddenly put a large comforting hand over mine.

'You're home, Charlotte. No one will harm you.'

He smiled sympathetically into my eyes as if he knew just how my stomach was churning. I remembered again Agnes Waverley's warnings about the Scots who still brooded over the English violation of their soil, and of the Stewarts' lasting resentment. But Robert was a Stewart, and there was no antagonism in his eyes now. Very much the reverse. I was angry with Agnes for filling my head with such alarm, and with myself for being so foolish as to believe every word she said. Perhaps it was her family that had managed to antagonise people here, I thought, and for that reason they themselves were none too popular. It did not mean that it would be the same for me, with my own family already solidly entrenched.

Slightly reassured, I gave Robert my hand and he helped me down. He shouted for someone called Duncan to bring my baggage, and a swarthy man wearing the same strange garb as Robert appeared from nowhere and grunted something in a foreign tongue.

'Ignore Duncan's grumblings,' Robert said curtly. 'When he wants to rebel, he lapses into the Gaelic, and it's as well to keep out of his way for a time.'

I would wish to keep out of his way at all times, I thought, as he gave me a piercing, somewhat startled look from under bushy brows. I followed Robert up the wide stone steps that were bowed in the middle with the weight of many generations of feet, and in through the door. Immediately the chill of cold stone struck my bones. I looked around me with a sinking sensation. I knew now just what my father had meant by calling Blackmaddie a great tomb of a place.

The house on the waterfront at Bristol was small and cramped and mean, but Blackmaddie dwarfed me. It was indeed a vast tomb, austere in its furnishings and so unwelcoming as to be hostile, and almost screaming at me to get out. I shook myself as I seemed to hear echoes of voices rattling round the stone walls, as if in protest at my arrival, muttering and menacing. Robert looked at me sharply and caught my arm.

'Are you all right, Charlotte? You look as if you've seen a ghost. Don't collapse now when you have still to meet the others.'

The way he spoke told me I would need to keep my wits about me if I did not want to feel crushed at once, and I gathered up every bit of courage as I nodded, with a determined upward thrust of my chin.

'I'm fine, thank you. A trifle weary after the journey,' I told him resolutely. I had not seen a ghost, but I had heard one, or more than one – all my Brodie ancestors. But in my confused state of mind I could not have told if they were greeting me or warning me.

'Bed is the place for you after such a wearisome journey,' Robert's voice lingered over the words. 'But not just yet, I fancy. Come and meet your family.'

He drew me through passages and corners that seemed like a maze. Once inside, I should never find my way out, I thought dizzily. Father had never described it quite like this. A door opened and a woman stood there, a grey-haired woman with a tight smile on her face. It seemed cordial enough, even if her hand was cold as ice as she held it out for me to shake and did not offer to kiss me.

'Charlotte, my dear, we have been waiting impatiently. I am your Aunt Morag, as you'll have guessed. What have you been doing with her all this time, Robert? Not playing any of your tricks already, I hope, and showing her the whole of Scotland in one day – or trying to!'

Her voice was teasing, but with an edge to it. Her welcome was normal on the surface and yet as I looked at my Aunt Morag, my father's sister, I was conscious of a thrill of danger running through me. I knew I was allowing myself to be overwhelmed by the sight of the castle and these people, but I had always believed in the power of first impressions, and now I felt instantly, instinctively, that Aunt Morag was in some way against me. But I forced myself to answer naturally as far as possible, and to look around the room we entered.

For some reason I had expected the room to be full of people, but it was not. There were only two other occupants, besides Aunt Morag. A young man, Robert's brother I guessed from the similarity of features and colouring, lounged against the great stone fireplace, above which hung a wicked-looking claymore and a collection of hunting trophies and deers' antlers. He apparently did not have

Robert's flair for words, and said very little when Aunt Morag introduced him as Neil.

'I am afraid you will have to wait to meet Ian and Kirsty,' she went on in her velvet-toned voice. 'They went out riding today to visit some friends and have not yet returned. I expect them later in the morning.'

Robert gave an angry exclamation.

'They were told to be here. It was the least they could do.'

Aunt Morag's eyes stopped him with one glance. I felt uncomfortable, knowing I was the cause of this little exchange and realising with a sinking feeling that Robert's reference to Kirsty's attitude towards me seemed to be confirmed. But Ian too? Did it mean that two of my cousins did not want me here? I turned quickly to the last occupant of the room as Aunt Morag drew my attention to him. This could not be Grandfather; he was not old enough for that. He sat in the depths of a hard wooden chair that did not look as if it held any comfort at all, and he glowered up at me.

'You must excuse me for not rising to greet you, girl. I've an attack of the gout that's giving me all kinds of hell. I'm Andrew, as you'll have guessed. Your father's brother. You're not much like him, are you?'

'I'm surprised you remember what he looked like, since it's so many years since you saw him,' I heard myself reply spiritedly, to my own and everybody else's surprise. My uncle continued to glare at me for several seconds, and then he gave a great guffaw of laughter that echoed all around the stone walls.

'You've got some Brodie spirit in you though, for all that your mother was a namby-pamby Englishwoman!'

Reference to my mother brought a sudden lump to my throat. I glanced at Aunt Morag, expecting to see some sympathy in her eyes, but they were like grey chips of ice, and they chilled me. She did not like the little exchange between Uncle Andrew and me, I realised in amazement. She had *wanted* me to appear as the frightened little English girl, and my reaction to his abruptness had thwarted her for some reason I could not begin to fathom.

'I had expected you to be in mourning, Charlotte,' Aunt Morag said suddenly as she bade me sit down. The voice was almost accusing, as if I had committed an unpardonable sin by not wearing deepest black. 'Were we not given to understand that your mother has just died?'

I lifted my chin. She sounded almost as if she did not believe it. A sudden vision of Mother lying there in the greyness of death, with the pennies poised over her eyes and clenched between her teeth, made me swallow hard. I would not tell this hard-eyed woman we did not have the money to spend on mourning clothes, or that we barely scratched a living to pay for the meagre lodgings in which we lived. It was bad enough that she probably guessed as much anyway, but I wouldn't give her the satisfaction of knowing it was so.

'Mother hated to see me in dark colours,' I said instead. 'With my black hair, they do not suit me. She always said when she died I was not to wear black, but to appear as cheerful as possible under the circumstances. She always said mourning should come from the heart, and not from external trappings.'

'Well said.' Robert smiled his agreement. 'And it would be a pity to hide such a lovely face and shape beneath doleful garments, though I fancy it would be striking for all that, don't you, Father?'

'I do that,' Uncle Andrew agreed sagely. The two of them looked me up and down as if I were a piece of merchandise. I was unused to this kind of scrutiny and angered by it. Aunt Morag did not look too pleased either, but clearly for some reason of her own. I glanced at Neil, who said nothing at all but looked bored by the whole thing, standing with an odd look on his face as if he had no part of the scene at all and wished to be somewhere else. He unnerved me with his silence, and Robert followed my glance and grinned.

'Take no heed of Neil, Charlotte. He'll be away in his head, composing some poem or other and on a different plane from the rest of us.'

So Neil was a poet. I had never met one before. I felt both awed and impressed, but as he barely acknowledged my existence, I assumed that Robert was right in his remarks.

'You'll want to see your room,' Aunt Morag stated rather than asked. 'Duncan will have put your baggage in there by now, so you'd best follow me. There's no use expecting any of the servants to come running as they'll all be away at their tasks.'

It seemed a strange household if servants could be so busy they could not attend to visitors. But I was family, I reminded myself, and in a place of this size, it was probably quicker for Aunt Morag to take me to my room herself than to summon someone from the depths of the servants' quarters, wherever they were. I had seen no servants as yet, except Duncan and several lads outside who had taken little notice of our arrival.

I followed Aunt Morag up twisting stairs and dark narrow corridors, and always the chill of old stone surrounded me. I could still hear the mutterings and mumblings of voices that were either coming at me from the very walls or from inside my own head. I told myself I must be so overtired I was beginning to hallucinate. At last my aunt stopped and took a huge ornate key from a pocket somewhere in her attire. She unlocked a door and threw it open, standing back for me to enter.

It was not a particularly comfortable room, though the furnishings were attractive enough after the austerity down below and the large bed looked inviting with its canopied head after my narrow one in the cramped room I had shared with Mother. But it was so large for one person that its very size unnerved me slightly. There were wall hangings and panelled cupboards in a dark heavy wood. I crossed quickly to the windows, thinking to make some remark about the view.

It was truly magnificent, as I had expected, with the great soaring mass of the mountains rearing ahead of my gaze, and the dark green forest below. I gazed out at the panorama in front of me in awe-inspired silence, leaning forward through the slightly open window. To my surprise, my room was directly over the loch. I felt a wild dizziness take hold of me as I stared down for what seemed like miles to the water far below. It seemed even farther away because of the dazzling brightness of the sun glinting on it. I felt Aunt Morag's fingers grip my arm.

'You'd best not lean too far, Charlotte. We don't want to lose you the minute you arrive. Well then, does it suit your requirements?'

I could not tell if there was sarcasm in her voice or not, for she must surely know this was not what I was used to at all, but I decided I was being unduly suspicious, and smiled warmly at my aunt.

'It's a truly splendid room, Aunt Morag, and I'm sure I shall be happy here.'

She turned away abruptly. 'I'll send one of the maids up directly to help you unpack.'

'Oh, but I can do that . . . '

'It's not your job,' she said shortly, and I fell silent, feeling it was a rebuff. Clearly I had a lot to learn in the ways of living at Blackmaddie. I wished I could have asked for her help, but she seemed completely unapproachable.

'When will I meet my grandfather?' I said instead.

'Later. He was obliged to go out on a matter of business.'

'He's not so ill as to be confined to bed then?' I tried to sound pleased at the fact, but I was piqued that he had not been here to greet me.

'That one?' Aunt Morag laughed shortly. 'He'll still be ordering folk about with his dying breath. Even his gout is not so severe as Andrew's. You'll be seeing him soon enough.'

She left me then, and I sat down heavily on the great bed, wondering what on earth to do with myself now. It seemed sensible to begin unpacking my baggage, but if I did that I would probably offend Aunt Morag and outrage the maid. I could not find my way back downstairs through the maze of passages and staircases, I was sure, and I began to panic. Blackmaddie had surely got me in her clutches, as surely as if the ancient portcullis had come crashing down on my head. I suddenly longed for William Derry and the easy companionship we had shared, and the familiar smells of home, no matter how nauseating. In retrospect, they were sweeter than wine.

A tapping at my door made me jump, and I just managed to stop myself rushing to answer it. Presumably it was the maid, and I would be expected to sit still and summon her inside.

'Come in,' I croaked.

The door opened and Robert stood there. My heart lurched at the sight of his broad figure filling up the doorway, his fiery red beard and hair almost black in the dimness of the passage. Like a demon, the wild thought flitted through my head, and then he entered, and my heart settled down again at the smile on his face. At least there was one friendly person who had not spent the first few minutes of my arrival mocking me. I had already forgotten the antagonism between us at the station, and my answering smile was warmer than I had intended in consequence, my words teasing.

'Is it the usual practice in Scotland for a gentleman to walk right into a lady's bedroom, cousin?'

'I was under the impression I had been invited,' he answered, and I suddenly saw there was a hotness in his look. I rose to my feet as a small gesture of defence, and Robert laughed softly as if he could read my mind quite clearly.

'You'll be glad of a friend here, Charlotte,' he said softly. 'Make the most of the one you have already, and as for invitations – you should learn to control those beautifully expressive eyes of yours if you don't want a man to get the wrong idea. We're two of a kind, though. I felt it from the moment you saw Blackmaddie, even if I did not recognise it before. And so, I wager, did you. Come now, admit it.'

I ignored his words and the sensual way he was saying them, even if it was impossible to ignore the effect his very presence was having on me. I stared boldly at him.

'You had a very strange way of showing friendship in those first minutes after meeting me. You made my blood turn cold with your frosty reception and the sharp reminder that I was a foreigner here.'

'A Sassenach,' he said with a grin.

'Don't dazzle me with Scottish words,' I said angrily. 'You

67

could have been more welcoming on the platform.'

He was suddenly across the room in a few long strides, and pulling me towards him. He was a good deal taller than me, and I was very conscious of the hardness in his body as it pressed close to mine.

'You rouse my blood even more when you're angered, Charlotte Brodie.' His lips were against mine as he spoke. 'You had best lock your door this night unless you're looking for a real Scottish welcome, for I warn you I shall come rattling it every night until I find it unlocked.'

His mouth was hard on mine then, his tongue probing between my teeth, his red beard tickling my chin and my throat. His hands were on my buttocks, squeezing gently, pulling me into him, and I could feel only too well the effect I was having on him, however unintentional. A hot thrill ran over me, and then I pushed him away as a strange voice spoke from the doorway.

'I'm to help ye unpack, Miss Brodie, if it's convenient.'

I sprang away from Robert with my face flaming, realising the maid had tapped and opened the door without either of us even hearing her. But if I was discomfited, Robert was not. He laughed loudly and pinched the girl on the cheek as he passed her, telling her to be sure and ask Cook to give him an extra portion of red meat that night to keep his blood hot and strong. My cheeks burned with mortification, knowing the maid could be surmising only one thing from his words. In that instant I was still the waterfront Charlotte, I thought miserably, more in tune with the reactions of this maid than with my fine relations at Blackmaddie, because surely I should be able to shrug off the episode as a mere dalliance and nothing more.

To my surprise, though, I saw the maid was smiling, her plump pink cheeks as rosy as a ripe apple. And just as suddenly I realised that she was a simple girl, and probably thought nothing at all of what had just passed. I breathed easier and smiled back at her, once Robert was out of earshot.

'What do they call you?' I asked.

'Vinny,' she said. Her eyes looked at my baggage. 'Is that all, Miss?'

'That's all.'

Vinny opened the panelled wall cupboard and showed me where my things would be stored. I would not use half of one of them, I thought wistfully, suddenly realising how shabby I was going to appear in comparison with the rest of my family. And then my thoughts hardened.

If Grandfather wanted me here so badly, the least he could do was to let me appear in a presentable manner. If he gave me a little money, I could purchase some material and occupy myself making some new clothes. There would seem to be little else for me to do, and it was the one thing I was good at. I resolved to put the matter to him at the first suitable opportunity. The thought of doing something positive eased my ragged nerves a little, and I handed Vinny the clothes for her to hang.

She was a big, buxom girl, the way simple girls often were, and not averse to chattering as she worked, telling me cheerfully that this room had once been known to have a ghost in it, but that no one had heard it for some long time now.

'Of course, no one has slept here for a long time, either, Miss,' she went on, merely making idle conversation and not realising how her words were chilling me. 'But then, there are often odd moanings and squeakings to be heard in old castles and the meanest of crofts alike, and not all of them can be put down to ghostly happenings, can they?'

She grinned cheekily, clearly seeing in me a kindred spirit rather than a grand lady. But I did not feel like smiling back at that moment. And suddenly there was a thin wailing sound right outside my door that drew a gasp from my lips. I stared in terror, half expecting an apparition to walk through the door. But Vinny looked at me apologetically.

'I'm sorry about that, Miss, but he was making such a racket downstairs. Cook told me to bring him up with me. It's his feed time, ye see, and he'll scream now until he gets the tit.'

I gaped at her as she went out of the room and came back

with a wicker basket, inside which was the ugliest baby I had ever seen. Not that I had seen many so small. This one was three months old, Vinny told me, and when she lifted him out I could see he had coppery hair down to his neck and a face roaring red with anger. To my startled horror Vinny flopped down on the bed with him as if she was prepared to stay all day, with my clothes still strewn all about.

'Ye don't mind, do you, Miss? Only if I take him back down and he's still screaming, Cook will lay one on me.'

She lay the baby on her lap while she unloosened her bodice and pulled out an enormous, blue-veined breast the size of a ripe melon. The nipple was wet, standing out as hard as a bullet, and she pulled the screaming baby to it. He proceeded to guzzle noisily for the next ten minutes, with his little fist waving about and his fingers occasionally digging into the soft flesh. The procedure was then repeated with the other breast, only by this time the baby had nearly had enough and kept twisting his head round to look at me, and each time he did a fine stream of milk spurted from Vinny's breast all over herself and sometimes the baby's head.

I had never seen a baby being fed before, nor expected to find it so sensual. It made my own breasts tingle, just watching the unembarrassed way Vinny crooned to the baby, squeezing herself so that the nipple filled the eager little mouth until he was satisfied. When he had finished she sat there smiling down at him as he lay with eyes blissfully closed and the blue-white film of milk on his lips.

'He's an ugly one,' she said softly. 'But I love him, so I do.' She pressed her full mouth to his forehead and laid him back in the basket while she re-fastened her bodice. 'I'm sorry about the interruption, Miss, and I'll get on with putting these clothes away for ye now.'

'Does your husband work at the castle, Vinny?' I was careful not to sound too prying, but she threw back her head and laughed.

'I dinna have a husband, Miss. What man do ye think would want to take a lass like me to kirk? There's no been one born yet, according to Cook. All they want is for me to lift my skirts and give them a good time, and I know how to do that all right. And they like these, 'specially now I've had the bairn there. Bigger than ever, they are.' She looked down at her huge breasts with pride.

'Does the father help you then?'

'Oh yes, he helps,' Vinny grinned wickedly. 'Helps me make beds when he's hereabouts, or should I say helps me unmake them?'

'He works here in the castle too then, does he?'

I couldn't stop my voice sounding indignant. But a sudden guarded look came into Vinny's eyes and she slammed the cupboard door shut as she finished with my clothes.

'I'll have to go now, Miss, or Cook will be bawling for me. If there's anything else ye need, there's a bell-pull near the bed.'

She picked up the baby basket and scuttled out, but not before a deep, dark suspicion had begun to form in my mind. Vinny was a pretty, uncomplicated girl, clearly not disposed to insist on marriage whatever befell her, adept at keeping a secret if necessary. What could be easier than for a lusty, persuasive man who knew every inch of the castle to bed her where and when he chose? With such an eager, willing partner as Vinny, he would not even need to seek his pleasure outside.

There was only one I knew so far who fitted every bit of that description, and he fitted it perfectly.

I thought back to the intense looks Robert Stewart had given me ever since my arrival. I recalled the moments just before she had come into my room, when Robert had pressed me tight against him, and I had felt a certain part of his body probe into mine even through the clothes I wore. He was a man of strong passions. Vinny had not even seemed disturbed at seeing us so close together, in her simple way probably not questioning it between her betters. Was he indeed the man who had fathered her child? And if he was, I began to wonder just what other secrets Blackmaddie held inside her walls.

6

I could not stay in my bedroom twiddling my thumbs any longer. I had looked in every cupboard and bounced on the bed and tidied my hair at the dressing-table mirror. There seemed nothing else to do. Eventually I squared my shoulders and decided to explore a little and see if I could find my way back downstairs. Presumably I was not to be offered any refreshment as it was halfway to luncheon-time, and anyway I was too keyed-up to want to eat or drink.

I told myself I had every right to explore the castle. I was a Brodie of Blackmaddie, and this was my home. I tried not to let myself lose sight of that fact in the maze of passages that scared me half to death. I was quite sure that once locked in my room at night and in the darkness, I should not stir until morning. And remembering Robert Stewart's hot eyes, locked in I should certainly be.

'Were ye wanting something, Miss?'

I gave a little cry as I poked my head in one of the lower rooms and Duncan appeared in front of me. He was like a stocky little gnome, and his appearance unnerved me.

'I-I-I-no, thank you,' I stuttered like a half-wit. 'I am just finding my way about the castle.'

His wizened old face suddenly creased into a smile.

'It's fair pleased I am to welcome ye here, Miss Charlotte, if ye'll forgive an old man the liberty of making so bold. I was very attached to yer father, ye ken, and I know ye'll bring a breath of fresh air to these musty old walls.'

I could only stare at the old man for some seconds, a great lump blocking my throat and a rush of tears to the backs of my eyes. This rather repulsive figure that I would have counted least among my friends was the first person here to offer me any real warmth of greeting – save Robert, and his, I was beginning to suspect, was entirely for his own desires. I relaxed my tense shoulders and walked into the room, speaking with a catch in my voice.

'Thank you, Duncan.' I hesitated. 'Tell me – were they so very angry when my father married my mother?'

If it was indiscreet to question a servant so, I consoled myself that Duncan was surely more than a servant. He was the old family retainer, and had been a friend of Father's; I hoped therefore he would be a friend of mine. His old eyes looked at me sorrowfully.

'Anger did not really come into it, lassie. It was an outrage, do ye see, to head south for England and then to go to sea. The Brodies have always been soldiers and a lusty lot too. But ye'll know all about their hot tempers if I remember yer father at all. I'll wager ye've inherited some of his spirit too.'

'I hope so. But did he never want to come back and bring Mother with him? I thought the family would have wanted him back if they were so angry to see him go.'

'Yer grandfather is an unforgiving man, lassie, though I'm willing to bet his eyes will soften when they alight on ye.'

His simple trust was reassuring. I glanced about me. 'What is this room, Duncan? It strikes as cold as ice.'

I suddenly realised I was surrounded by glass cases containing weapons of every description, of suits of armour resting against the cold stone walls, of fierce-looking claymores and pikes and flintlock pistols adorning them. I moved to the shadow of the far wall to examine some of them.

' 'Tis the armoury, lassie, yer grandfather's pride and joy. 'Tis part of my duties to see that all the weapons are kept gleaming and sharp. In times past, all these weapons were used in the heat of battle and in the defence of Blackmaddie, but they are mere mementoes now of a bloody past.'

I shivered at his words. 'Were there many battles, Duncan?'

'Oh aye, and some that still go on, at least in the men's minds. And Blackmaddie had her share of bloodletting.'

'Duncan!' A sudden roar from the passageway made me gasp, and I shrank back behind a glass case. Seconds later an overpowering figure appeared in the armoury. Beside Duncan he seemed even larger than he really was, with grey-white hair almost bristling with rage as he sought out the retainer, his beard still as bushy as Robert's. 'What's the man about? And is that a wench you've got there? Are you taking to fumbling skirts at your age, you old rogue?'

His old eyes suddenly gleamed, while I seethed with fury. This then, must be my grandfather, who presumably could not even remember who I was.

I stepped out of the shadows with my head held high as I heard Duncan's low chuckle.

'I, Sir, am your grand-daughter, if you are Malcolm Brodie,' I said haughtily, though my heart hammered in my chest at facing him like this. 'My name is . . . '

'I know well who you are, Charlotte Brodie!' His voice had changed as he moved nearer to see me better. It was almost disbelieving, and his eyes suddenly widened and stared into mine, and in an instant recalled Robert's words that my appearance would shock him.

And indeed it had. He ran a huge gnarled hand through the grey-white hair until it stood on end, but even this did not detract from the impression of the man himself: powerful, arrogant, master of all he surveyed.

'By God, do ye not see it, man?' he said in a hoarse voice at last, speaking to Duncan about me as if I were a piece of furniture. 'The likeness? The fine, proud tilt to the head, the black mane of hair, the flashing blue eyes, 'tis Katrina to the life. My bonnie, bonnie Katrina come back to me!'

He suddenly strode towards me and enveloped me in a great emotional hug that left me reeling as I pushed away from him. For it was not *me* he hugged.

'I'm not Katrina,' I said shrilly. 'It's Charlotte, Grandfather. The daughter of your son, James.'

'Jamie?' the voice was still thick, even muddled, and then it hardened as he looked at me again, and all the gladness had gone out of it. 'I have no son of that name, but I welcome you, Charlotte. One look at you confirms the fact that you belong here and as such you are welcome. And now I've completely forgotten what it was I wanted Duncan for, the old fool, so I'll away and think on it some more.'

He stamped out of the armoury, leaving me to stare after him in speechless anger, all my feathers ruffled. How *dare* he speak so of my father? How dare he order me about, getting me here and then dismissing me almost as a servant? I was trembling all over after this first meeting, and Duncan laid a sympathetic hand on my arm.

'Be patient with him, lassie. He's an old man and Katrina was the very light of his life. 'Tis true that ye bear an uncanny resemblance to her, and – ' he hesitated, 'and to the other one.'

'The other one?' I echoed.

A sudden crawling sensation I couldn't explain filled every part of me. What other one was this? Was there another death I hadn't heard about as well as Katrina's? A feeling of foreboding enveloped me and I almost begged Duncan to tell me what he meant by those words. I did not want to know, and yet I had to.

'We don't talk of her, lassie, and if ye hadn't looked so much like her, ye'd most likely never have heard of her at all. But since I'd told ye this much, mebbe it's as well that ye know all there is to know. Follow me and I'll show ye.'

I followed him along the passages until we reached a heavy door, for which Duncan produced a key from the huge bunch dangling about his waist. I did not know what I expected to see inside, but there was nothing fearsome at all. It was merely a store-room of sorts, larger than most, where every conceivable unused object was evidently kept: old trunks, some falling to bits with age; a blaze of tartan in one corner in a pile of cloth perhaps for future use; toys; picture frames; forgotten furniture . . . all overhung with the smell of decay. I shuddered at the mustiness that pervaded the room.

Duncan, foraging behind a pile of stacked-up portraits, motioned to me to come forward and look at the face and form smiling up at us from a canvas. I felt my heart give a huge lurch of shock.

The girl in the portrait was young. She had a mane of black hair cascading down her back. Her eyes were startlingly blue, with a blatant invitation in them that was echoed by the full red mouth, its lips parted with the gleam of saliva on them. The full creamy breasts rose voluptuously from the extremely low-necked gown she wore, so that the dark circle of the areolas surrounding the nipples were clearly visible. A very sensual young lady, was my first impression. The second, almost instantaneous, was that it was like a mirror-image of myself.

'My God,' I whispered. 'Who is she? Is this Katrina? Is this why Grandfather . . . ?'

To my surprise Duncan shook his head.

'This is the original lady of the castle, my lassie. This is Maddie, as black-hearted a creature as ever walked this earth. Because of her battles were fought and won or lost, and always there was blood spilled in her name, even long after she perished. Though there are some that say she never did perish, and that through time immemorial her spirit will rise again and a young woman will appear in her likeness. It was thought to have happened with Miss Katrina. She could have been the twin of this Black Maddie, as she was known.'

We looked at each other. My mouth was dry with the weight of all he was telling me. I felt there was so much more left unsaid. I felt he was sorrowing for me because of his allegiance to my father, and because of the certainty in his own mind that I was the reincarnation not only of Katrina, but of this blackhearted Maddie, who, it did not need him to tell me, had driven men wild with lust for her and killed because of it. I was shaken to the depths of my soul.

'Let's get out of this room, Duncan.' I shivered, because the voices were suddenly there again, clamouring and insistent and they terrified me.

'Aye. It would not do for us to be found in here,' he agreed. 'And – I wouldna let on about what I've told ye, lassie. Just remember this – if ye ever need a friend, my shoulder is strong.'

* * *

I was to keep reminding myself of the old man's words during the rest of that day. It was an uneasy lunch, with Ian and Kirsty staying away at their friends' house and sending a message to that effect, so that Aunt Morag was furious. They did not come back until late afternoon, and I kept out of the way as I heard raised voices from one of the downstairs rooms, and guessed that they were being chastised none too gently for their blatant show of bad manners.

I slipped outside the castle while the tirade was going on, not wishing anyone to think I was eavesdropping, and wandered about the grounds. They were so extensive it would be easy to get lost, and once away from the gardens and shrubberies, I was soon enveloped in trees. But never truly lost, of course, for the turrets of Blackmaddie rose up into the sky as a landmark

The dry autumn leaves crackled under my feet as I strolled through the woods, feeling my nerves relax a little in the sudden peace and seclusion of the shade offered there. And yet, despite the tranquillity of the woods and the sudden breathtaking glimpses I saw through gaps in the foliage of lochs and mountains, there was always the brooding shadow of a bloody past lurking near. Right here in these woods, much Brodie blood had been spilled in the past and many heads broken, if I was to believe all that Duncan had told me. And there was no reason not to believe him.

Eventually I decided I had better go back. Someone might even have missed me, I thought with a wry twist to my mouth, though I doubted it. Since my arrival I had been left very much to myself, and the weeks ahead seemed to stretch endlessly. I was still not convinced I had been right to come here. And yet, remembering Ruskin, it had been the only place to flee to at the time. A refuge. But now the shock of Mother's death was receding and giving way to regret that we did not understand each other better, and the memory of Ruskin's assault was not so searingly new, maybe I should think again.

I gave a little scream as a dark figure suddenly stepped out of a thicket of trees right in front of me, and then laughed shakily as I saw that it was Neil.

'My goodness, you gave me a fright.' I tried to sound normal, though the blood felt as if it was surging through my veins. 'I didn't hear you moving about.'

It struck me that that was odd when my own feet made so much noise among the crackling leaves and twigs. Had he been stalking me, this strange, quiet cousin of mine? I wished he would say something and not stand there with brows drawn together and an expression of doom on his face.

'Watch out for Kirsty,' he said suddenly. He twisted past me and would have gone striding on, when I found my wits and raced after him.

'What do you mean?' I demanded. 'You cannot give me that kind of warning and then leave me without any explanation. Why should I watch out for her? Does she wish to harm me?'

'They're children, both of them. Playing at things they don't understand.'

'Both of them? Who else?'

Neil stared at me with an intentness of expression that sent a ripple of fear through me. There was no sexuality in his face as there was in Robert's, only the sad look of the poet seeing more than normal men, yet it had the power to unnerve me and to make me wish I was away from this shadowy glade, where every glint of sunlight through the trees could be interpreted as a clash of steel on steel.

'You'll have seen Grandfather?' He ignored my last question, and I nodded impatiently. 'Then you'll know you have the likeness.'

My heart lurched and almost stopped. He spoke about it as if it was some terrible affliction, some curse. Was this the curse of Blackmaddie, I thought with a shiver?

Common sense made me suddenly angry with him. 'There's nothing unusual in members of the same family looking alike,' I retorted. 'You and Robert have the same red hair and I suppose your other brother does too?'

'Aye,' he muttered. 'But 'tis more than looks and colouring to which I'm referring, Charlotte.'

He directed his haunted eyes directly on to my mouth

then, and followed downwards to the curve of my breasts and below. But I was not like *her*, I wanted to shout aloud, not like black-hearted Maddie of the past, for whom men lusted and blood was spilled. But what of Katrina then? Had she been the same?

'Your sister, Katrina,' I said tremulously. 'Did she have the – the likeness too?'

'She was our step-sister,' he corrected. 'There is a difference. Aye, she had it. She was the most beguiling creature you ever saw.'

The haunted dark eyes glowed as if a sudden light had been lit behind them. He had loved her, I thought instantly. Now I knew why he had been so insistent about telling me she was his step-sister. It was as clear as daylight. He loved her and he was so ashamed of his feelings he had to justify them in this small way, to abolish the suggestion of incest from his own mind.

'How did she die, Neil? No one ever told me.'

I did not mean to pry. I did not mean to upset anyone. But as Katrina was my kinswoman, I thought I had a perfect right to know. To my horror, I became aware of a snuffling sound, and when I looked at Neil he was practically crying. *Crying*. In all my life I had never felt so embarrassed as I did then, standing beside this tall, broad-shouldered young man who looked as if he could take all the world's ills in his stride, and yet the tears were brimming in his eyes.

'I'm sorry, Neil,' I began in agitation. 'You don't have to tell me anything if you don't want to.'

'How can I forget? I don't want to forget, *ever*. It's like a raw, weeping wound inside me, and no one understands, no one.'

I was overcome with pity for him. I put a tentative hand on his arm. 'I think I do, Neil.'

He gazed at me abjectly for a few seconds, his eyes large and dark and still shiny with tears. He backed away from me slightly, as if not wanting me to show any understanding, and then he turned and blundered off into the thicket of trees and I was alone again.

I was more shaken than I could say. But one thing was

beginning to puzzle me. If this 'likeness' was so bad, why was it everyone appeared to have loved Katrina? She couldn't have been the reincarnation of this Black Maddie if everyone was so affected by her beauty, and distraught at her death.

Not everyone seemed to notice that I had it, I thought. Aunt Morag and Uncle Andrew did not comment; which seemed odd, especially as Katrina was Uncle Andrew's daughter. Perhaps it was only to certain eyes that the likeness was so discernible, and that made it all the more eerie. Robert had certainly seen it straight away, and Grandfather. But Neil had definitely shaken me. I had thought he was the morose one of the family, living in his own peculiar dreamworld, but I saw now he had all the emotions and the precarious knife-edge of character attributed to poets, and all the hot passions of his brother as well.

Watch Kirsty, he had said. A little thrill of fear touched me. *They're children, playing at things they don't understand.* I frowned. I did not care for riddles. I shivered again as the sun went behind a bank of cloud and the afternoon suddenly chilled. I hurried back the way I had come, pulling my woollen shawl more tightly round my shoulders.

After the warnings, from both Neil and Robert, and hearing the sound of raised voices before I left the castle, I was prepared to meet with hostility when I encountered Kirsty for the first time. But perhaps she had been told to act the part of the kinswoman and to behave herself, for she managed to greet me fairly cordially when I found my way to the drawing-room, where she and Aunt Morag were sitting together.

'We began to think you had lost yourself, Charlotte,' Aunt Morag said in her clipped voice. 'Kirsty has been impatient to meet you.'

I could hardly believe that, and I was tempted to retort that she had not been impatient enough to be here on my arrival. But I had no wish to stir things up between us. I was still apprehensive of her attitude towards me, and since I had the 'likeness', I was doubly suspicious now when people did not comment on it. And Kirsty did not. Then as I observed Uncle Andrew in the corner still nursing his gouty foot, I thought charitably that maybe Kirsty kept away from the subject in consideration of his feelings for his daughter. I hoped it was merely that anyway.

'I am so glad to meet you, Kirsty,' I said. 'I hope we shall be friends as well as cousins.'

Her smile became a little fixed.

'I doubt that,' she said sweetly, still with the frozen smile on her lips so that I wondered if I had heard aright. 'I understand you are a seamstress? I have several gowns that need some attention. Perhaps you could take a look at them and see if anything can be done?'

We stared at each other. Her mother said nothing, and I knew instantly that of these two, Kirsty would always get the better of her mother in a tussle. My face burned with resentment at being put in my place right away, as a little sewing girl. I was tempted to say I had put my sewing things away when I left Bristol and had no intention of bringing them out ever again except for myself, but in a way I felt it would be cutting off my nose to spite my face. I needed to be kept busy, to stop myself from thinking too much, and besides, I was not used to a life of inactivity. Sewing was also the most therapeutic method I knew of restoring my sanity. I had proved that the night after Mother died. After Ruskin.

'I'll take a look at them if you wish,' I said coolly, and she darted a triumphant look at her mother, as if this had been a little contest between us two, and Kirsty had already declared to her mother that she would be the winner. This time, I thought. *This* time.

'We'll go to my room now,' Kirsty decided. She led the way upstairs and I followed, feeling I was being cast inexorably into my role as part relative, part servant. It was a bitter sensation to realise it, and to feel all the same the small sense of relief at being asked to do something at which I excelled. I had been too long in the service of others, even as a teacher of small girls, to settle easily into any other way of life, and Kirsty had seen it immediately. The knowledge galled me.

'And how do you like Blackmaddie then? Is it all you expected?' Kirsty's voice was softly insulting when we reached her room and she had closed the door. I told her shortly that Blackmaddie was just as my father had described it to me, letting her know I was a Brodie too, and had every right to be here. She laughed softly and turned to the wall cupboard to throw several evening gowns on to the bed.

I took a good look around her room while she was occupied. It was just as large as mine but more cluttered, more personal. As yet I had had no time to make my room as personally mine. She had strange pictures hung on the walls, and animals seemed to be her favourite subject, but they always looked tortured and in pain. There were a few pictures of groups of naked women, which took me by surprise. And cards pinned to the wall with strange symbols on them, presumably written by Kirsty herself, though I could not tell and would not ask. I could not begin to understand them, but I had not expected her to be the studious type somehow.

'Well?' she said impatiently. 'Are you going to help me with these gowns or aren't you?'

I turned quickly. Kirsty stood in front of me without a stitch of clothing on, and I felt the hot colour rush to my cheeks as I looked at her. There was nowhere else to look when she demanded my attention, and she gave a little mocking laugh at my embarrassment. Her smooth skin was flawless, with the tawny hair like a cloud resting on her pale shoulders. Firm, rounded breasts with the pink-tipped nipples standing proud, beneath which her belly was softly rounded. It was a young girl's body without the voluptuousness of womanhood, nearly hairless, with little more than a triangle of soft golden fuzz. I turned away in embarrassment again as she held up her arms to let the first gown fall over her head and body.

It was a shimmering leaf-green, wonderful with her colouring, but a bit baggy at the waist. My seamstress's eyes took control again.

'I want it very tight-fitting,' Kirsty commanded. 'To emphasise my curves without the need of any restricting undergarments. They are worth emphasising, are they not?'

She ran her hands beneath her breasts, clearly hoping to shock me. But I was too used to some of the young lady clients of my mother's to be shocked at such a move. They too had hoped to provoke some response from the sport of being as outrageous as possible to a little seamstress. I moved forward and tweaked at the fullness of material on the bodice, knowing very well I tweaked her too. The nipples stood out in protest.

'This could do with taking in a bit,' I said coolly. 'And here, to reduce the suggestion of a bulge.'

I pressed the flat of my hand against the soft roundness of her belly. Pressed it hard, and she gave that small, mocking laugh again.

'I see you and I are going to understand each other very well, Charlotte,' she said. 'Well then, do as you think and I'll leave it all in your capable hands.'

She pulled the gown over her head and threw it on the bed. Her action and tone was so exactly like that of some of the young ladies in Bristol it brought an involuntary smile to my lips, and suddenly I was no longer affronted that she had insulted me like this. It showed me that my presence upset her for some reason, and surely that was infinitely better than being totally ignored. Besides, I would be glad of the activity to ease me into the new world at Blackmaddie.

She turned round and caught the glimmer of a smile on my lips, and suddenly she was the one to be embarrassed at her nakedness, and pulled another gown quickly over her head for me to adjust. I could sense the change in her mood. She was very transparent. A child, she was nettled that I had not been intimidated by her, nor reduced to tears or shouting. And for my part, I felt it was I who had won the first small victory after all. Until that moment I had not even realised that I was here to do battle.

7

Ian was like the sun coming out after rain.

I did not meet him until dinner that evening, but immediately I took to this youngest of my three male cousins, with sandy hair, rather than the bright red of his brothers, and an innocence of expression in his clear grey eyes that did not brood like Neil's, nor smoulder like Robert's.

I had felt nervous of appearing at the long dinner table with all these relatives of mine, and my heart was thumping as I entered the huge, austere dining-room. Aunt Morag greeted me and showed me where I was to sit, and Ian's smiling eyes were opposite me. Grandfather, of course, was at the head of the table, a vast, commanding figure of a man, the patriarch, the laird, and I wondered how anyone ever dared speak out against him.

I thought I would not dare to speak at all, but dinner was quite informal and the chatter loud and noisy, with drink flowing freely. Ian told me he was sorry not to be here when I arrived, but he and Kirsty had been visiting friends and it had been a long-standing arrangement. They did have friends then. I chided myself for the thought, but the whole lot of them seemed such a close and clannish family, I could not rid myself of the feeling that once inside Blackmaddie, you might as well be in chains.

'You must come with us next time, Charlotte,' Ian was saying generously. 'You'll like the Sinclair girls, and the boys will certainly like you!'

'Stop your blethering, Ian, and pass me the jug,' Grandfather put in at that point, and I was conscious of various reactions as I passed the jug along the table from the middle to the end. Ian's smiling, approving eyes as he gazed at my face and flickered downwards to the creamy curve of my cleavage in the evening gown I wore. Neil's brooding, morose look at his brother. Robert's mocking, intimate stare that could make my heart beat faster, and Kirsty, scowling, jealous, her piercing glare at Ian telling him and me very clearly that she did not want me included in their circle of friends.

'I do have a friend of my own staying in the neighbourhood,' I babbled nervously. 'I would very much like it if she could call and visit me, if no one objects.'

'A Sassenach?' Grandfather growled. I made a big mistake at that moment. He looked so comical with the jug half-raised to his mouth and the last dregs trickling down the grey-white beard, I allowed myself to give a small laugh.

'English, yes! But then, so am I, and I don't feel in the least foreign!'

To my dismay the jug was thumped down on the table so hard I thought it would crack, and Grandfather waved his arm imperiously at a servant to bring another full one.

'You're a Brodie, girl, and don't ever forget it. You belong here. Your mother – ' he shrugged, and muttered a few words in Gaelic that were obviously insulting, and my cheeks burned. I forgot all about being scared of him and felt my breath coming very fast in my chest, and I was clenching my fists together without realising it.

'I would remind you that my mother has just died, and that she brought me up on her own ever since Father was drowned. She was a good, honest, hard-working woman, and she and Father loved each other very much. I am not ashamed to be their daughter, by whatever name I am called.'

My voice had thickened as I spoke, to my fury, because the last thing I had intended was to break down in front of them all. But he riled me, and at that moment I came nearer to mourning and grieving and loving my hard-hearted mother than I had ever done. I would not stand by and let my grandfather demean her. What had he ever done for me in my lifetime until now?

'Well said, Charlotte.' Uncle Andrew suddenly spoke

from the other end of the table. 'It's good to hear a lassie speak well of her parents. Too many of them go the other way these days.'

I saw Kirsty toss her head, and guessed that young lady had no time for family sentimentality.

'We don't want strangers here,' she said pointedly.

Grandfather suddenly turned his wrath on her and roared, 'If Charlotte wants to bring a friend here, then she shall. Who are you to say who shall be invited to Blackmaddie? Let the friend come, Charlotte, and there's an end to it.'

I was glad to leave the table and get away from Kirsty's hostile eyes. Grandfather was clearly the type of man who had to make all the decisions here, and he was contrary enough to change his mind at a second's notice. Everyone else was obliged to dance to his tune. I decided to slip away after dinner and write a brief note to Agnes to ask her to come as soon as possible, and to ask one of the servants to deliver it for me. I was still in my room, sealing it into an envelope, when Vinny tapped on my door.

'They want ye downstairs in the music-room, Miss,' she said sullenly. 'They're putting on an entertainment for yer benefit, and if ye dinna show up it'd be taken as an insult.'

Vinny was another one who did not bother to watch her words – except in one respect. I remembered the ugly little baby I had last seen sucking furiously at her breasts, and asked after him. Her pale eyes lit up.

'Getting bonnier by the minute, Miss. I put him out in the garden in his carriage this afternoon, as it was so warm, and he gurgled and laughed at the trees till ye'd think they were talking back at him.'

It suddenly occurred to me that there were three red-haired young men who could feasibly be the father of Vinny's child, if indeed he was one of the Stewarts. It did not have to be Robert. The thought gave me an odd little glow of comfort, until I remembered the way he had told me to be sure to lock my door at night, for if he once found it unlocked . . .

'Would you see that somebody delivers this note to the

hotel in the village, Vinny?' I said quickly. She took it and stuffed it in her pocket.

'I'll see to it myself, Miss. I'm going down to the village in a few minutes.'

'Oh!' her words took me aback. Said so matter-of-factly, as if it was quite usual for a servant girl to go out whenever she wished. And such a distance too; she could hardly go there without a conveyance of some kind. I shrugged; it was no business of mine. Perhaps the sullen look on her face was because she had been delayed when she was clearly ready to go out. She wore a long skirt of some tweed material, a very low-cut blouse, so tightly-fitting as to be strained across her breasts until the buttons almost popped, and a shawl hung round her shoulders. Her hair was looser than usual, and she had a gleam in her eyes I recognised instantly. Vinny was going to meet a lover, and unexpectedly I felt a twist of envy and a longing for William Derry's warm, loving embrace that had satisfied us both. Suddenly I missed him.

I shooed her out of my room before I began to get maudlin, and went back downstairs. I was not in the least interested in whatever kind of entertainment was being arranged, and would rather have stayed in my room and slept. I was extraordinarily tired, and attributed it to the long weary hours of travelling, the strain of coming to Blackmaddie and the pure mountain air.

'Here she is at last.' Aunt Morag spoke with the smile on her lips that seemed fixed and never reached her eyes. It had taken me long enough to find my way, and she looked impatient. 'Do you play the piano at all, Charlotte?'

Her eyes were innocent, for of course she knew I did not play. How could I ever have learned, with no money for such extravagances, and hardly room in our lodgings for ourselves let alone a pianoforte.

'I'm afraid I do not have a very musical ear.' I lifted my head and stared back defiantly. Aunt Morag gave a sympathetic little smirk.

'What a pity. It's such an accomplishment to be able to play. Kirsty excels at the instrument and has a clear soprano voice too. Do you not sing either, Charlotte?'

She would not demoralise me, I thought. 'I do not,' I answered. 'I do have other accomplishments, but musical ability is not one of them, though I can still appreciate it in others.'

Ian gave a wicked little laugh as he sidled past my chair. 'I have no doubt if Robert were here that he'd be hinting at what those other accomplishments might be, Charlotte,' he whispered in my ear. He said it so artlessly I could not be affronted, and no one else heard, and I knew my eyes were twinkling as I smiled back at him. Kirsty did not miss the little intimacy, though, and her eyes flashed dangerously as she said sharply that if anyone was prepared to listen, she would play.

She had a pleasing enough voice, I conceded, as she proceeded to go through her repertoire of Scottish ditties and ballads, but I found the whole thing tedious. I was not used to sitting still listening to someone sing and play, and my hands were restless, wishing I had some sewing to do or a book to read. I could not help wondering too where Robert had gone. The rest of them were all here in the music-room.

Inevitably my thoughts strayed. Remembering that Vinny had gone out too and how strange I had thought it. The two of them had made their escape, perhaps together. I found I was clenching my hands more tightly, not wanting to think of them together, not wanting to think of Robert's hot eyes smiling down into the willing little servant girl's as he loosened the buttons on that tight-fitting blouse until the large breasts lay heavy in his hands, not wanting to think of Robert's body covering hers in some secret rendezvous and bringing her to an ecstasy of delight. I was suddenly hot and perspiring with a sweet heaviness in my loins, knowing I wanted him for myself.

And then I remembered the arrogance of him, the certainty that he had only to lift his little finger and I would lie down for him, and told myself firmly that whatever the attraction between us he would not have me that easily.

I realised to my relief that the singing had stopped, and

that Grandfather was groaning as Neil prepared to read some of his poetry.

'I'll not stop for this. I'll be away to my room if ye'll all excuse me,' he said gruffly. 'Goodnight to every one of ye.'

He may not be as young as the rest of them by far, but the room was suddenly empty without his presence, I thought with a little start of surprise. King of his castle. Neil stared round irritably, asking if anyone else wanted to leave.

'There's no use getting ruffled because your grandfather won't listen to you,' Uncle Andrew placated him. 'He's no one for listening to poetry and you know it well enough.'

I was quite interested to listen to Neil's poems, and at last he started reading them. He was instantly transformed from the rather tragic, insipid cousin to one of greater stature, of stronger voice and more ruthless character. Though I grew more and more disturbed as the poems unfolded, for their content was not what I had expected. I had thought they would be sad, soulful little pieces without much depth. Instead they were full of an arrogance Neil himself did not possess. They were passionate and hot-blooded, both in describing relationships between man and woman and in his vivid descriptions of violence and death. When he was finished I was almost embarrassed to see his brooding eyes watching me.

'That was – quite an experience, Neil,' I said at last, hardly knowing whether one complimented a poet in the ordinary way or not.

Kirsty and Ian were whispering together at the back of the room, and Ian looked up and chuckled at my careful comment.

'That's a new word for it, isn't it, brother?'

'You've no soul, Ian,' Neil snapped, shuffling all his papers together in a fit of temper.

'I'd rather have no soul than no . . .'

'Ian, that's enough,' Uncle Andrew suddenly thundered at him, and I was horrified to see the sudden look of hatred in Neil's haunted eyes. Hatred directed at his brother. He stamped out of the room and slammed the door behind him. Nobody seemed in the least embarrassed by this, and Kirsty and Ian laughed out loud while Uncle Andrew and Aunt Morag rose to leave the music-room together.

'It's his compensation, Charlotte,' Ian grinned at me.

'What are you talking about?'

'Our literary brother. He pours all his passion on to those bits of paper because nobody loves him, you see. Or rather, *he* doesn't love anyone – or can't. Kirsty tried to find out for certain once, didn't you?'

I still wasn't quite sure what he meant, though I had an uneasy suspicion. 'Tried to find out what?'

Kirsty looked at me coldly. 'If all his passion had any foundation in truth or if it was all in his imagination,' she informed me. 'And I'm afraid our Neil was sadly lacking when it came to the reality, and quite unable to fulfil the promise of his tantalising verses. The passion is all in his head and nowhere else.'

I felt my cheeks go a fiery red as I interpreted her words. Her eyes mocked me, as if determined to make me feel uncomfortable, a namby-pamby English girl. I resented it furiously and gazed back at her more calmly than I felt.

'He should have tried a spell of living near the waterfront to know about the passion that flames a man's senses,' I remarked. 'I'll wager I learned more about it in one precarious walk along Bristol's dockland than ever came out of fine verses, however well told.'

I was suddenly aware that Kirsty's expression had changed and that she looked at me with a blaze of excitement on her face. Ian too was leaning forward with a sudden rapt attention. They reminded me instantly of the children I had taught when they were about to hear an exciting new story.

'What was it like, Charlotte?' Kirsty spoke quickly, before Ian got the chance. 'Were there ships of all nationalities there? What were their cargoes? Did you ever get into conversation with any of the crews?'

'I'll wager she did. I'll bet she was in great demand, with those teasing eyes and that swaying walk.'

'Will you both stop talking about me as if I wasn't here?' I was half-angry, half-amused. 'I was not a waterfront whore, if that's what you're thinking, and my mother was very strict about letting me go out after sunset with all the un-savoury characters there were about. It wasn't the glamorous vista you seem to imagine. As for cargoes and crews, I only remember the cobbles usually reeked with the stench of rotting food and the crews frightened me half to death with their sweating bodies and coarse talk. And whether they were British or foreign the crudity could still be understood readily enough.'

I shivered, remembering vividly how I had hated it at close quarters, even though it had had a certain glamour for me seen from high in the waterfront house. But the nearer one got to the cobbles, the more overpowering the stench. I remember, too, how I had felt trapped in that environment with an unloving woman my closest companion and an endless round of sewing garments more beautiful than I would ever own.

'You don't make it sound very attractive,' Kirsty said.

'It was *not* attractive. Not my life anyway. Cooped up in two attic rooms in a miserable house full of people I didn't like very much.' I stopped suddenly, remembering Ruskin. To say I didn't like him very much was such an understate-ment as to be laughable. I loathed him with everything that was in me.

'You must have had some attachments though, Charlotte.' Kirsty was persistent, her smile persuasive. Trying to probe my secrets, if I had any. I did, of course. Didn't everyone have a dark side that they wished to conceal from the rest of the world? Mine was the memory of Ruskin. I wondered briefly what Kirsty and Ian had to conceal, if anything. Or were they really as artless as they appeared to be this even-ing? I had drunk far more wine at the table than I was used to, and my thoughts were beginning to feel muddled.

'I was quite fond of a young tutor at the school where I taught,' I said quickly, hoping this small confidence would satisfy her, but instead it seemed to excite her and her eyes glowed as she and Ian laughed at my flushed face.

'I knew it. We both made a bet about you, Charlotte. Ian said you would only have had one lover up to now, but I said there would be many. As another woman I know all the

91

signs, you see. Now tell us which of us was right!'

They *were* children, I thought, in a kind of bewilderment. Both leaning forward, lips parted almost lasciviously in the innocent way of children – or simpletons – and yet I knew them both to be almost adult. I sensed that they were playing with me, leading me on for some silly amusement of their own, and I too felt a sudden reckless desire to shock, to stun the laughing faces in front of me into appalled silence. The wine was making me overfree with my speech already, and I forgot my vow to myself that I would never divulge the horror of Ruskin's attack to a living soul.

'Oh yes, William was my lover,' I told them quite calmly. 'In a way, Ian was quite right about him being my only one, because that was the case until a short while ago.'

'What happened then? Did your attention wander? Did he not satisfy you?' Kirsty was eager to have all the details.

'I was taken by force,' I said bluntly. 'Raped, while my mother lay on her death-bed in the next room. By the most loathsome creature you can imagine.'

If I had hoped to shock them I had certainly done so. The two of them looked at me in stunned silence, but then I found I had made my second mistake in saying anything about Ruskin, because they clamoured to know more.

'I've told you enough,' I said, my palms beginning to sweat at being asked to relive the nightmare of his body grinding into mine.

'But what was it *like*?' Kirsty insisted petulantly. 'Did he throw you on the bed and leap on you with a knife at your throat?'

'He leaped on me all right,' I shuddered. 'Not on any bed, but on the floor, and I was bruised all over at the end of it. He was like someone demented. He didn't have a knife, just his great fat body.'

'You could have fought him off if he wasn't armed, surely?' Ian put in.

'I could not! Believe me, I tried hard enough. Anyway, I've told you I don't wish to discuss it any more. It's over, and I want to forget it ever happened.'

'They say a woman always stays a little in love with the

man who rapes her,' Ian said softly, watching my reaction.

'What rubbish!' I cried. The very idea was an insult, an obscenity.

'Don't you even remember one little bit of it with pleasure?' Kirsty asked curiously.

I remembered the low, throaty moans that escaped from my throat, the involuntary arching of my back, the small, pulsating movements.

'Absolutely not.' I rose furiously to my feet. 'I think we've talked quite enough about a subject I find most distasteful, and I hope neither of you will refer to it again. Now if I can find my way around this tomb of a place I will go to my room and see you both in the morning. Good night.'

I swept across the room with my legs trembling beneath me, as much from the stupid way I had let them bait me and the effect it had on my senses as from the reaction to too much wine. I wondered how on earth I had let this conversation begin, and was thankful I had ended it on a note of authority.

That authority had evidently reached Ian, though not quite how I had intended. 'Good night, school-marm.' I could hear the gurgle of laughter in his voice, and I knew that as soon as I was out of the room the two of them would be discussing my disclosure with great glee.

I was still trembling as I reached the door of the music-room, and the traumatic memories they had goaded me into remembering were spinning round in my head. I realised the door was slightly open and as I walked through as steadily as I could, I saw that Robert was on the other side. My face flamed instantly, wondering just how much of our conversation he had overheard.

'You had better let me show you the way to your room, Charlotte.' He spoke in a level voice and I could not see the expression on his face in the dim lighting of the corridor. 'Those two ninnies will be chortling together for hours without ever thinking to wonder if you'd get lost.'

It seemed churlish to refuse, and besides I thought I very

probably would get lost if I started wandering about the corridors of Blackmaddie alone late at night. The thought of it sent the blood racing in my veins, and I knew I should never dare to venture from my bedroom once I reached it safely.

'Did you enjoy the entertainment the family provided?' Robert asked. 'Did Neil surprise you?'

I thought back briefly to Neil's sudden emotional outburst in the woods when we had spoken about Katrina, and knew that nothing about this pale, intriguing young man would surprise me now. There was far more to him than he showed to the world, as his poems revealed for all who took the trouble to listen seriously. Apparently his family regarded him as something of a buffoon.

'I enjoyed listening to him,' I said honestly. 'I have never heard a poet perform before.'

'And I suppose Kirsty had to sing and play until Grandfather stamped out of the room in sheer boredom?'

We had climbed endless staircases, it seemed to me, and I had to pause for breath. I looked at the arrogant, handsome face of my cousin with its flamboyant red beard, and thought that he was far more a Brodie of my grandfather's ilk than could be expected in a relative not of his blood. It was uncanny how much alike they were in stature and manner.

'You don't like each other much, do you – you and your brothers?' I ignored his jibe and answered with a question of my own.

'Tolerate would be the better word, dear Charlotte. We tolerate each other.'

'What of Katrina? Was she tolerated too?'

I almost felt the warmth seep out of him. It was as if a sheet of ice had suddenly surrounded him, and he almost pushed me along in front of him.

'Katrina was loved,' he said stonily. 'Loved by all.'

'How did she die?' I asked.

It was an innocent question, and surely one that I was entitled to ask. She was my kin as much as his, and I had a right to know. Robert thrust past me and opened a door, and I found we had reached my room. A pale, full moon threw beams of light through the windows that struck eerily on floor and furnishings alike. I was glad when he lit my candles for me. And then I got a good look at his face.

It was anguished and white, contrasting violently with the fierce red of his hair and beard. I was shocked by the pain in his eyes as much as I had been afraid of him at the station. But it was a very different emotion running through me at the tormented expression I glimpsed on his face. It made me want to run to him and pull him close the way he'd pulled me close earlier. To comfort and hold him and love him.

I hardly knew him, and yet I loved him, I realised instantly. Deeply and passionately and for all time. And I couldn't reach him, because at that moment he was as remote from me as the blue-white mountains towering up into the night sky outside my window. As remote as eternity, and I could hardly believe he had told me he would want to warm himself at my fire, and had warned me to keep my door locked against him. But what had I done? What had I said but to enquire about my dead cousin? I licked my dry lips.

Robert suddenly strode across the room and stared out through the curtainless windows into the vast mountainous mass that reared up all around Blackmaddie.

'She died up there on the mountain,' he said, in a voice held taut. 'Waiting for a lover who never came because he was prevented by some stupid sailors in a tavern who got him roaring drunk and too insensible to reach her. Stupid sailors who beguiled him with tales of crossing the sea to America and the fortunes waiting to be made there. And for this she died, waiting and waiting, not heeding the first soft fall of snow. She loved the snow. She always said it felt like a lover's caress on her cheeks, soft and tender. So she just waited in the little hut. When the snowfall became a blizzard she must have got frightened and instead of staying where she was, she tried to find her way down. The blizzards up here develop very quickly, blinding and freezing. We found her the next morning, like a little frozen statue, her fingers still clawing to get a hold on the mountainside.'

'My God!' I could only stare at him in horror as I whispered the words. Robert seemed to have forgotten I was there. He was the image of Neil at that moment, off somewhere in his head, alone with his memories of Katrina, and I was the intruder. I, who loved him. I must have made a sudden sound in my throat, because he suddenly remembered me. He came slowly away from the window and stood in front of me. Towered over me, his face still tight with the pain of remembering, and I grieved that I had been the one to revive the memories with a thoughtless remark.

'It seems we both have a lot to forget, Charlotte Brodie,' he said slowly, and I knew then that he had heard me talking about Ruskin downstairs. My face burned with the knowledge, but suddenly he pulled me into his arms with a roughness that was almost desperation.

'You're so like her – so like her. My Katrina, my love, my darling.'

His hands were caressing me, fumbling inside my bodice, his mouth bruising mine with his kisses. For an exquisite moment I responded, for what did it matter what name he called me as long as he wanted me? But just as suddenly humiliation washed over me, for I could never be his fantasy lover, nor lie in his arms in ecstasy beneath him while he thought of somebody else.

I pushed him away from me. 'I am not Katrina,' I almost sobbed for the second time that day. 'Katrina is dead. I am Charlotte – *Charlotte!*'

He muttered strong oaths as he crossed the room in several great strides, but at the door he turned and looked at me, his breathing heavy as his eyes undressed me where I stood.

'And you are very much alive, so remember what I told you and keep this door locked, for I shall return.'

I stumbled across the room as soon as he had gone and fumbled with the heavy key in the lock. My hands were shaking and my reflection in the dressing-table mirror was white against the blackness of my hair. I couldn't think straight. I couldn't think whether his words were a threat.

Did they mean he resented my very existence because I resembled his lovely Katrina? Or did he really desire me? Me or Katrina? I was dizzy with the effect of too much wine and the unhealthy disclosures of my family. They were all mad! I had come to a madhouse, and if I stayed here among them I should be as mad as any of them.

I undressed quickly and crawled inside the unfamiliar sheets. I knew I wouldn't sleep. It was as light as day from the moonlight and the reflected whiteness of the mountains. Presumably castles did not have curtains at the upper windows. There was certainly no chance of being over-looked at this height, and the thought of that long vertical drop into the loch below my window made goose-flesh stand out all over me. It was quiet with an unearthly silence. I was used to the noise and bustle of the waterfront at Bristol, the sound of river traffic hardly ceasing day and night, the voices and laughter and the milling about of all the human flotsam that made it familiar to me.

At Blackmaddie there were no late-night revellers to make me grumble or smile in the darkness according to my mood. There was nothing but the silence. I might be the only person alive in the whole world, and blind panic ran over me like crawling fingers. I would even have welcomed the rat-tling at the door that told me Robert was keeping true to his promise. I heard nothing at all that night, though if I had done I would probably have died with fright. Hadn't Vinny said there had once been a ghost in this very room? Why once? If it had haunted here in the past, it wasn't likely to change its domain, was it? My teeth were chattering so much as my thoughts spun about that I doubted if I'd have heard anything else anyway.

I tried to think sensibly and to make sleep come to me. I had always been sensible until now. After all, everything was bound to feel strange here at first. It would be an unusual person who could walk straight into such a different kind of life and not be affected by it. For myself, I had met four people around my own age that day and been violently affected by each of them. No, perhaps not violently by Ian. He was the least complex of my cousins, but he and Kirsty together were an implacable duo I did not understand.

Kirsty alone was all too obvious. She resented my arrival and my very existence, and had no intention of letting me assume my status as a Brodie of Blackmaddie if she could prevent it. But that was exactly what I was, and she could do nothing to change it. I had something she did not, which was the Brodie name. I realised for the first time that none of them had that but me. The boys were Stewarts, and Kirsty was a Morrison. The realisation sent a shiver of excitement through me.

I thought I definitely had the measure of Kirsty, as long as she was on her own. I could cope with her then, but not with Ian. They were the kind of children who were impossible to control. But I knew I must stop thinking of them as children. Even though Kirsty's pouts and sulks could be excused that way, there was nothing childish about the way she had flaunted herself naked in front of me when I had adjusted her gowns to a better fit.

I let my thoughts veer towards Neil, the withdrawn one, the unexpected one. I felt a strange sort of disquiet about him and yet a rush of pity too, for from the taunts of the other two, I presumed him to be impotent. Kirsty had a cruel streak about her, again reminiscent of a child, to have tormented him in the way Ian had suggested, and then to laugh about it with his brother.

That left Robert.

The bedcovers had warmed slightly by this time and I uncurled myself from my foetal position and lay on my back. I looked through half-closed eyes at the high, unfamiliar ceiling and the shifting patterns cast on to its surface by the clouds scudding across the sky. And thought of him. And all I could see was his face, as if it were right there above me, warm, sensual, demanding. I could almost hear him breathing.

I blinked my eyes wide open but the room was empty except for myself. Yet I felt as if I only had to stretch out my hand and he'd be there. My imagination raced on, fed by the wine that intoxicated my senses, feeling in my waking dreams the tickle of that red beard that was such a new and exciting sensation. Hearing his deep voice in the strange accent I was beginning to comprehend slowly, hearing him say my name. *My* name, not hers, not Katrina's. I pushed the thought of that moment away from me as if it had never happened and let the sweet sensations fill my mind. Knowing from some deep hidden well of knowledge how it would be to feel his body enveloping mine. He was the gentleness of William and the brutality of Ruskin all mixed up into one, an exquisite delight. I could feel him there already as my hand brushed the fleshy mound below the luxuriant black triangle of hair at my groin. I jerked it away as I began to tingle all over, burning with a fever that was part-shame at my own desires, part-longing to have them satiated. My only consolation was the certainty that it *would* happen. With the sudden blaze of desire between Robert and myself, the outcome was inevitable.

8

'This used to be Katrina's room, you know,' Kirsty informed me a few days later when I took the altered gowns back to her. I looked at her in surprise at the conversational tone. She changed like the weather, another of her unstable characteristics. She was studying one of the pictures on her wall which I found so objectionable. 'These were hers – Katrina's, I mean. She was very interested in the occult. I wish I knew what it all meant. Ian and I have been trying to find out.'

'It seems a very unwise thing to do,' I said.

Kirsty laughed. 'Why unwise? Is it unwise to thirst after knowledge? I'm surprised a school-marm thinks so. Exciting perhaps, and mysterious. There are some books in the library on the subject, but Ian and I have discovered someone not too far from here who can tell us much more about it than old books.'

A sudden unease caught hold of me as I saw the gleam of excitement in her eyes. Thoughts of covens and chantings and rituals flashed into my mind, and I had a sudden suspicion that Katrina's involvement with such things had gone too far. Kirsty was no more than a foolish young girl swept along by the thrill of discovering something out of the ordinary, but I felt I had to warn her. She and the others might be allowed to run wild at Blackmaddie in a way I had never expected, but in some ways I felt I was infinitely more worldly-wise than Kirsty.

'I think you'd do better to forget about such things,' I said positively. 'I'm quite sure your mother and grandfather wouldn't approve.'

'Do you think it your business to tell them, school-marm?'

she suddenly hissed at me. She snatched the gown I was holding out of my hands and said she would see her mother gave me something for my trouble. I flew into a temper just as quickly.

'Don't treat me as a servant, Kirsty. I have as much right here as any of you, and I'd ask you not to forget it.'

I flounced out of her room before we both started haranguing each other like a couple of fish-wives, heedless that I was acting as childishly as she at that moment. Since Ian had called me school-marm in that insulting way they had seized on the term at every opportunity. I had tried to ignore it, thinking it the best way to make them tire of it, but it wasn't working very quickly. She irritated me so much at times I felt the need to be by myself to get over her jibes. I was sorry it was so, because I'd really wanted to make a friend of Kirsty. Somehow I had the feeling it would never be possible.

I wandered through the maze of corridors. The castle was still an alien place to me. Beautiful and magnificent on the outside, surrounded by such splendidly awesome surroundings, from the tranquil loch to the vast mountains. But inside, Blackmaddie seethed with undercurrents of feelings and old hatreds that went back into history and yet were ever-present. Perhaps not everyone felt it, but I did. I was a true Brodie, and the shadow of my ancestors brooded over me as surely as if its seed had been sown by the other one – Maddie, from whom I had inherited the likeness.

Had she been interested in the occult or even in black magic, I wondered suddenly? I most certainly was not. It was a subject that had always chilled me, with its dark obscenities and bloody rituals. I knew a little, a very little, and I did not wish to know more. But it troubled me to think that Kirsty and Ian wanted to probe its dark secrets. It was unhealthy.

It was quite amazing how the picture of Katrina was building up in my mind. Not just the physical picture – I knew well enough by now that she could be my twin – but her character. I knew she was wilful and reckless enough to meet a lover on the mountain, and to stay in the little hut until all hope of his arrival was gone, even at such great risk to herself; that she'd loved him so much, in that respect we were alike, for I too could love deeply. One thing I would not let myself do was speculate on the identity of the lover. If it was Robert I did not want to know. If it was any other, it was nothing to do with me. But this new revelation of a dark side to her nature that peopled her bedroom walls with those obscene pictures – we were totally different there, and I thanked heaven for it.

My steps took me outside the castle walls into the grounds, where the last of the summer flowers were dying rapidly and autumn was truly in the air. I had fretted for news of Agnes. Vinny had taken my note and reported back with a casual message that the young lady was unwell after her travelling and confined to bed for several days. But this afternoon she was coming to tea at Blackmaddie, now she was well again. How she would love to see all this, I thought. The foliage of trees and shrubs was turning a deep russet and bronze, and I marvelled at how quickly the seasons were merging.

In the short time I had been at Blackmaddie I felt I both knew the inhabitants of the castle quite intimately, and at the same time that I did not know them at all. Truly, I thought, with a glimmer of amusement, my mother would be outraged if she knew what a strange family resided at Blackmaddie, despite all her romantic ideas about them. Today, here in the sharp sunlight that glittered like needle-points on the waters of the loch as the light breeze rippled its surface, I was going to forget the peculiarities of my cousins and my grandfather's blasphemous complaints about his gout. I had arranged for Duncan to take us down to Blackmaddie village in the gig before we had tea; it would be the first time I had left the castle since my arrival. I was as excited at the prospect as if I were meeting a lover at some secret rendezvous.

If only I were! If only Robert had not left Blackmaddie for several days on estate business before we had really found our way back to the easy relationship I had begun to cherish. He had not forgiven me, it seemed, for wrenching

the story of Katrina's death out of him, though when I
questioned Vinny about it at the earliest opportunity, I discovered that none of the family or servants cared to discuss
it.

'The Master said we'd all be sent packing if we went on
about it,' she told me, round-eyed and apprehensive, as if
the very walls of my room were going to scream that she had
mentioned it to me.

'But surely he meant you were not to gossip about the
tragedy with village people,' I said in exasperation. 'It's
different with me because I'm one of the family. You know
all about *your* family, don't you? And they like to know all
about you, too.'

I was explaining as if she were a backward child, when
really I'd like to have shaken her into telling me what I
wanted to know.

'My family don't want me any more,' she said sullenly.
'Because of the bairn. My family's here now, and I was told
to say nothing about Miss Katrina.'

Her lips clamped together.

I wished I could needle her into disclosing the identity of
the baby's father, but when Vinny got that mutinous look on
her face I might as well ask the moon not to rise. At least the
Brodies could be sure of one servant's loyalty, and I learned
nothing more from her about Katrina.

The pony and trap approached the gatehouse of the castle
soon after lunch. I raised my hand in greeting as soon as
Agnes was near enough, and I could see the look on her face
as her eyes took in all that was slowly becoming familiar to
me. Astonishment and apprehension registered together,
and I could appreciate those feelings only too well.

I was conscious, too, of a feeling of pride as she alighted
from the trap and we fell into each other's arms as if we had
been parted for months instead of a few days. I was so
thankful to see her, and to see she had some colour in her
previously porcelain-pale cheeks.

She was my friend, my confidante, my link with home. I
realised at that moment that, humble though it was, as yet

the waterfront house at Bristol was home and still had a tenuous hold on my heart. Magnificent and awesome and ancestral Blackmaddie might be, but she did not own me. The thought was strangely comforting, and I hugged Agnes warmly, which served to cover the small awkwardness that she appeared to feel, though I did not.

'I can't tell you how pleased I am to see you again,' I told her huskily, 'nor how wonderful it is to hear an English accent again. I feel as if I am surrounded by foreigners, and have to keep reminding myself that I am the foreigner! But are you quite well, Agnes?'

She assured me that she was, and though I had made light of feeling foreign with all the strange tongues around me, Agnes gave an answering laugh and told me that I would soon get used to it. 'I find it quite a pleasing accent,' Agnes went on, as we strolled arm in arm on the soft carpet of grass between the gardens. 'Especially among the gentlemen. But Charlotte, let me catch my breath a moment and try to take in all this magnificence. I had no idea it was so beautiful. My parents and I have never ventured far from our hotel on our visits, and my short walks were confined to level country. To think that such a short drive away Blackmaddie was nestling among the mountains like a priceless jewel!'

She stood and gazed all around her, and I felt a warm glow at her poetic phrase. She was absolutely right. On that afternoon the castle was perfection in its setting of mountain and pines and mirrored blue water. She *was* like a priceless jewel, a focal point in a perfect circlet of all the best that nature could provide. I had been just as overawed when Robert had first pointed her out to me, but now I was seeing her anew through Agnes' eyes, and the stirrings of pride were strong within me. Pride of possession, of belonging, of being part of something steeped in history, no matter how bloody and stormy.

'Come along,' I said, as Agnes gave a small cough to remind me that she was not as robust as I was. 'The breeze is quite cool unless you keep moving, and I want you to meet my family.'

I hoped she did not notice my small hesitation over my

description of the inmates of Blackmaddie. I wished fervently that Robert were here; thinking of his broad shoulders and towering figure and the commanding presence he brought with him whenever he stepped into a room sent a little thrill coursing through me. I wished Agnes could meet him, then just as suddenly did not. I was becoming as perverse as Kirsty, the thought fluttered through me, but I knew I did not want Robert's dark eyes to linger too long on Agnes' ethereal golden beauty and find her pleasing. I wanted him for myself.

'How many of them do I have to meet?' Agnes sounded alarmed. 'I had not expected to be on exhibition when I accepted your invitation, Charlotte.'

'They are not all here today,' I said soothingly. 'Uncle Andrew and Ian will be away all afternoon, and Robert does not come back until tomorrow from his business affairs. Grandfather will join us for afternoon tea when we have taken our trip to the village, but for the present there is only Aunt Morag and Kirsty and Neil.'

I could see she wanted to ask something about them before we entered the castle, but at that moment Neil appeared from the direction of the stables with the usual sad, enigmatic look on his face that meant he was composing one of his poems. He stopped as soon as he saw us, his expression suddenly flickering into an awareness that surprised me. But he was not looking at me. It was Agnes who held all his attention, and I found myself hoping desperately that this intriguing cousin of mine would not stammer and stutter and show himself up for the fool he was not. I felt a strangely protective fondness for Neil as he looked at Agnes for the first time, a beautiful pale goddess with sunlight striking pure gold through the strands of her honey-coloured hair. And an infinite pity too, for Neil looked quite stunned by the vision in front of him, as if instantly smitten. If the tales about him that Kirsty and Ian had maliciously told me were true, then he would be even more tormented by the anguish of love that could not be fulfilled.

'Agnes, this is my cousin, Neil,' I said quickly. 'He is a poet – the first poet I have ever met. Neil, my friend and travelling companion, Miss Agnes Waverley.'

He stepped nearer and took her proffered hand in his. I could see Agnes' reaction to Neil's intense gaze and the small flush in her cheeks as her white hand rested against Neil's long, sensitive fingers; as if she too were taken aback by the sight of him, tall, red-haired, kilted. Too late, I heard Agnes' murmuring answer as he said how delighted he was to make her acquaintance.

'I am very pleased to meet you, Mr Brodie.'

Brodie . . . and Neil was a Stewart. I had not thought to warn her. The memory of how violently Robert had reacted when I had made the same mistake soared into my mind. Robert said that Ian had once wanted to change his family name, but that if he mentioned it again he and Neil would break his head. Underneath the enigmatic expression Neil habitually wore, I knew that strong passions smouldered; I had heard it in his poetry and in the way his emotions had overtaken him when we had met in the woods. I held my breath in astonishment as I heard him laugh.

'My name is Stewart, Miss Waverley. I am a step-cousin to Charlotte, in actual fact.'

Now I found my breath coming fast on Agnes' account. Remembering her warnings about the Stewarts in the train, and the way she had unwittingly frightened me with references to Culloden, and that there were still those who thought a Scot who married into the English was a traitor – would she now snatch her hand away from Neil's and betray the anxiety she had instilled in me?

She did not. Rather did her fingers curl round Neil's for a lingering moment and her breathy apology appeared to be like music in his ears and as we went indoors it was obvious that Agnes reciprocated Neil's feelings.

He went to great pains to show her the best view from the windows in the great hall, and to explain the intricacies of the huge family tree which hung on one wall. I had not even studied it myself as yet, but promised to do so at some time in the future. Nor had I had such an extensive tour of the lower part of the castle before, I thought, with some amusement, and listened with interest as Neil knowledgeably told

Agnes some of the Brodie history. I would find out more from the great tomes in the library, I promised myself, for it would be an occupation for the solitary hours when I did not have Agnes' delightful company.

During the next half-hour, however, I began to wonder just who she had come here to visit, as she and my cousin laughed and talked together, sometimes hardly remembering my presence, it seemed to me. I could not be cross about it though, for happiness sparkled from each of them, and Neil was more animated than I had seen him before. He resembled Robert more closely when he was so enlivened by Agnes, and I warmed towards them both because of it, and could not find it in my heart to be angry with them for unintentionally shutting me out.

Aunt Morag was in a reasonably sociable frame of mind that afternoon, and Kirsty seemed so surprised by Neil's sudden flair for words in speech instead of merely on paper that she resisted the usual sarcastic tone of voice she reserved for him. I was relieved to see it, for I could not have borne to see the fragile attraction between the two of them reduced to humiliation for Neil and embarrassment for Agnes by any of Kirsty's thoughtless taunts. Even the uneasy remembrance of the hints she had made about Neil's manhood I would not allow to dampen the afternoon, and when Duncan appeared to ask if the young lady and myself were ready to make the trip to the village, it was Neil who said he would escort us, as he was sure Duncan had plenty of duties to attend to.

Whether he did or not, he acquiesced immediately, and there was no arguing with the radiance in Agnes' face at the unexpectedness of the afternoon. I knew she would mark it up in her memory as one of the special days in her life, the way I notched up my meeting with Robert. Knowing so well how it felt to be in love, I could see it all happening in front of me for these two, like a flower unfolding in the warmth of the sun, and it was beautiful.

'What would you like to see?' Neil asked us both, once we were seated in the gig with him.

'Everything!' Agnes said expansively, and they both laughed like two conspirators. I joined in the laughter, for it was suddenly good to be alive, and the sun was sparkling like diamonds on the snow-tipped mountains and touching everything with its warmth. The snow stayed on the summits all the year round, Aunt Morag had informed me, and now I could appreciate the extra dimension it gave to a mellow autumn afternoon.

Neil didn't hurry us to the village. Instead we stopped frequently while he pointed out various landmarks, many of which I discovered to be on Brodie land. Agnes was very impressed, but there was no hint of speculation in her eyes or voice. She was just overawed and interested, and my heart was happier for knowing it. Whatever she felt for Neil, now or in the future, she felt for the man and not for his family connections.

It suddenly struck me to wonder just where Neil came into the family inheritance. He was the second brother, but he was not a Brodie, I reminded myself, and neither was Robert. Uncle Andrew was the natural successor, of course, but he had only step-sons. So then it would be – my heart started beating painfully fast – did that mean that I . . . ?

'There is Blackmaddie village, Agnes.'

I heard Neil say the words, hardly realising that they had gone beyond the niceties of formally addressing each other in the short space of time I had been dreaming, and looked to where Neil was pointing, and gasped with pleasure and surprise.

The village nestled in the shadow of the mountains, a sprawling huddle of cottages and gardens in a maze of narrow streets, with the tall spire of the kirk rising above them all. It was a fairy-tale village, seen from the sparse stretch of scrubland above where we were now pausing, perched like an afterthought on the hillside above a short stretch of winding river that ran straight out to sea. And there within sight of us, vast areas of ocean frothed against a harbour wall, where tall ships strained and jostled against each other and the squalling sea-birds transported me instantly, nostalgically home.

I cried out in delight and stood up in the gig to see more clearly, and would almost have tipped us all out in my exuberance.

'Why did nobody tell me we were so near the sea?' I exclaimed. 'You must have known of it, Agnes!'

'I suppose I did, but I had not thought it would be of such importance to you,' she said. 'The hotel where I stay with my parents is well away from the village and I have never seen it before because of the steepness of the incline leading down to it.'

She sounded mildly affronted, and I apologised at once. She was practically a captive in the hotel with her consumptive chest, and I knew that her excursions were limited. The idea of being near the mountains was in the nature of a cure, not an expedition. But looking at her now, the exhilaration in her face matched my own; it would be hard to imagine that she was ill at all. If I had not heard her bouts of coughing in the train as we headed north, I would have doubted it myself. It was a pity she ever had to return south when the Scottish air was clearly so beneficial to her.

'Can we go down to the village?' I said eagerly. 'I am anxious to walk around the harbour wall and breathe in the heady ocean scents!'

Neil laughed outright as he jerked the reins and we jogged forward.

'You and I must put our heads together some time, Charlotte, and compose an ode to the sea. I did not realise I had such a poetic cousin to rival my humble talents.'

'I cannot imagine I am anyone's rival in that respect,' I smiled at him. 'And Agnes here is more poetic than I! But I do love to be near the water. The loch is a delight to my eyes and a poem in itself, but there is something about the sea that fascinates me and draws me. It's probably something to do with the sea being in my father's blood as well. When he came home from his travels, he would delight me with tales of faraway places and his exciting adventures in my formative years. I always yearned to see them for myself and cross some vast expanse of water. Childish dreams, of course.'

Until then Neil had seemed interested and indulgent, though I suspected he was happy to let me prattle on while he occasionally exchanged a happy smile with Agnes at every opportunity. But now his smile had vanished, and he gripped the reins more tightly. I could not think why. I had been merely making bantering remarks.

'You share something else with Katrina then, beside your looks,' he spoke reluctantly, as if he had to tell me. 'She had the same urge to travel across water. It was almost an obsession with her, though of course her dreams were never to be fulfilled.'

Because Blackmaddie would rather have her dead than let her go. The words spun into my mind, unbidden, unwanted.

I told myself later that days did not change from warm to chilled in an instant. The sun did not ride high in the sky at one moment, a golden globe of warmth, and sink behind a cloud to reappear with the hint of twilight turning it to red, so that its rays spread out across the great expanse of water below me until they resembled streaks of blood.

It was an illusion, a blurring of the senses, a warning. I blinked rapidly, glancing at the other two. Agnes was leaning forward to point out the course of a fleet of fishing-boats coming into harbour, smiling happily at the ordinary, tranquil scene in front of her, and everything was as it had been before.

There was no violent past rearing its bloody head in the shape of the sun's transition, no magician's hand casting a veil in front of me to hide the obvious and create an illusion of wonder, of terror, of things unseen and unknown. There was still warmth surrounding us, and the chill was only inside me. If I had not seen the knuckles standing out so sharply on Neil's hands as he drove the gig carefully down the rutted track towards the village, I might have thought I had imagined the moment. But I had not, I had not.

It was the weirdest sensation I had ever experienced. It spread right through me, exciting, chilling, as wildly erotic as a sexual arousal. I could not explain it, nor did I want to. It frightened me, as if I could see things others could not. I *had* seen something, because here were Agnes and Neil talking amicably about fishing-boats and the way the sea could be whipped up in an instant to a frenzied tornado with a strong wind behind it, while my stomach churned and frothed inside me. I had a knowledge I did not understand, that I was unable to harness. But I knew in that instant when I had seen the red streaks like blood on the water that there was danger for me here at Blackmaddie, and that I was connected in some way with Katrina. Not only because of the likeness we both inherited from Maddie, our black-hearted ancestor, but from something more basic that had somehow crystallised for me. As if we both wanted to escape. And yet that was foolish; I had only just come here, and I could leave any time I chose. I gave a sudden involuntary shudder.

'Are you quite sure you want to wander around the harbour, Charlotte? You don't have to see everything at once, no matter how attractive it looks,' Neil was saying, his voice quite normal now. 'It's much cooler by the sea, and you both have flimsy gowns, and Agnes should not risk catching cold.'

'Perhaps not then, but could we just drive round it?' I conceded.

Next time I would stay much longer, if it meant coming here by myself. In fact, it would be most enjoyable to be here alone.

That afternoon I was content to be refreshed by the smells of fish and ozone that might be repugnant to some, but were peculiarly nostalgic to me, of course. I never thought I should feel that way about the tawdry waterfront at Bristol, but I was learning more about myself since coming to Blackmaddie than I had ever expected. It was as if she was opening my eyes and my mind to a world outside the familiar one.

Was I *psychic*? The thought hurtled into my mind. I did not want to be, did not choose to be, but what choice did I have if it was so? If I thought back carefully, there were things my father had said to me, impossible for me to understand when I was a child, but which could be interpreted

111

more fully now. Maybe he too had had this insight, this extra perception of which my two companions seemed blissfully and totally unaware. Even Neil, with his sensitive and poetic nature.

One sentence of my father's would be for ever indelibly imprinted on my mind: *Blackmaddie has an aura about her as destructive as a possessive woman, and just as captivating, and she puts a curse on all those who try to escape from her clutches.*

Yes, I thought, my father had seen it too, as others did not. He had called the castle huge, when in terms of stone and metal it was not terribly large, according to Robert. But I understood exactly what Father had said. In terms of power, whether for good or evil, Blackmaddie was huge. She was vast, all-consuming, everything that was monstrous and seductively beautiful, like a black-hearted woman with the looks of an angel.

'Are you feeling unwell, Charlotte? You've gone quite pale, and almost as if you're in some kind of trance.'

I became aware that Agnes was talking to me. Her face hovered in front of my eyes, moon-white in her anxiety. I forced a smile to my lips, though they felt as cold as ice at the experience I had undergone, which I now firmly believed to be a psychic one. I had been lifted on to an astral plane and given a warning, which I had every intention of heeding, and I vowed to keep my wits about me.

'I do feel rather chilled,' I admitted. 'I did not realise how quickly the air cooled as the afternoon passed.'

'It is colder,' Neil agreed. 'And you will both be used to mellower climes in the south. We had better be getting back anyway, or Aunt Morag will be complaining about our being late for tea. We should not have stopped so many times to admire the scenery. Or else we should have arranged to take tea in the village tea-rooms. They do an excellent oat-cake there, but maybe another time.'

His mention of tea-rooms took me instantly back to the lace-covered table-cloths of the tea-rooms on Bristol Downs and William Derry gazing earnestly into my eyes. And my own remark that suddenly had more ominous meaning now

than when I had spoken it to William: *It seems my grandfather wishes to gather us all in to Blackmaddie like a
spider catching flies, before it is too late!*

Or was Grandfather merely the instrument? For it was
Blackmaddie herself who wanted us all, who was too greedy
to let any of her possessions go. Oh William, how I ached
at that moment to return to our uncomplicated relationship,
to feel pleasurably aroused by him, ready and willing to lie
beneath him and feel his hands and body caress me and to
respond to his excitement while still in control of my senses,
with no indication of the violent storm of passion ready to
be unleashed inside me. I had not known myself fully then,
but I had been satisfied with the shadowy knowledge that
love-making was a very pleasurable activity. The awakening
sensations that had been fanned by Ruskin's lust were ready
to burst into flames, and Robert was waiting to warm himself at my fire.

'You look better now we've turned away from the village,
Charlotte,' Agnes said in a relieved voice as we jogged back
along the rising track. 'It was a keen wind back there, and
you have more colour in your cheeks now.'

I could have told her I burned with the sudden heat of
desire, but instead I said I was quite all right and merely
overcome by the unexpected change of scenery and the
delight of realising we were so near to the coast. Yes, I
would return by myself, and soon, I vowed. I had not
appreciated the luxury of being alone with my thoughts until
now, when they were constantly interrupted by the concern
of these two. And yet I could not be unaffected by the very
fact that they noticed and cared about me when it was clear
they only wished to be with each other.

'How long are you to stay in Scotland, Agnes?' Neil
asked, almost as if his thoughts carried on from my own.

'It cannot be for too long. Father's business commitments
will not allow it, and I expect it will only be for another two
weeks at the most.'

Neil's face had a stricken look about it. He had only just
found her and already she was slipping away from him. I
could imagine his withdrawal back into his secret self after

Agnes went away, and I did not want him to retreat there. I had had a glimpse of the whole person Neil could be, despite the derogatory remarks of Kirsty and Ian, and I spoke impulsively.

'Would your parents allow you to stay on at Blackmaddie if I asked Grandfather about it, Agnes? It would be so good for your health, and it would mean a lot to me to have a friend of my own for a short-term visit, or even indefinitely.'

It would mean a lot to someone else too, I saw immediately. Neil's dark eyes suddenly glowed, and were so exactly like Robert's at that moment it made me almost ache with longing for him.

'That's a marvellous idea, Charlotte,' he said eagerly. 'Well, Agnes? Would your parents agree, do you think? Would *you* agree?'

She was as ecstatic as Neil at the idea, and hugged me effusively for thinking of it. At least, her arms hugged me, but her spirit was engulfing Neil and we all three knew it. Her little cough reminded us that we had been in the fresh air for long enough, and Neil urged the horses on to greater speed to take us back to Blackmaddie.

'I'll choose the right moment to ask Grandfather about your visit,' I told her hurriedly just before we entered the castle. 'He is extremely tetchy at the moment with his gout, and I'll wait until he is in a happier frame of mind. But I shall be in touch with you immediately I have any news.'

It was as well I had warned Agnes, for Grandfather was humping himself about as if he was in excruciating pain and roaring at family and servants alike. I wondered if this would make Agnes change her mind about wanting to stay here, but I guessed nothing would have deterred her from the chance to be so near Neil. And after all, Grandfather made only a cursory appearance for afternoon tea, and went stamping off to his study as soon as possible.

So Agnes met Ian for the first time, and though she chatted quite amiably with him and I could see he thought her a very comely young lady, he seemed surprised that she did not respond to his usual flirtatious manner. I was not surprised at all, only relieved that no one else seemed aware of the strong undercurrents of feeling between Neil and Agnes, because Ian and Kirsty would have teased Neil later on and I was not sure how his volatile temperament would have stood up to it.

Agnes did not outstay her welcome on that first visit, and Neil announced that he would ride alongside Agnes to see her on her way. When they left I marvelled that though not one word of love had passed between them the entire afternoon, it pulsated between them like a living thing. I wondered fleetingly about Neil's strange confession of love for Katrina, but pushed it out of my mind; Katrina was dead. I felt sure that he and Agnes could blossom and grow together and that only good could come from their relationship. Providing the taunts Kirsty and Ian had made about him were unfounded.

But that was something I could hardly ask him about. I could not go to his room one night and demand that he prove his virility to me on my friend's account! Nor could I breathe a word about my uncertainty to Agnes. It was something she would have to discover for herself, if ever ...

I kissed Agnes good-bye quickly as she left in the pony and trap, knowing that Neil would never do the same on so short an acquaintance in full view of myself and any on-lookers, but wondering if this was the reason he had elected to ride with her. I promised her I would speak to my grandfather at the earliest opportunity about her coming to stay at Blackmaddie, and waved until they were out of sight.

I saw Neil ride back some time later when I was seated at the drawing-room window with some sewing, but he went off at once to the stables with his horse and did not return. I imagined he had gone off into the woods in that dream-world of his, but now it would consist entirely of poems about honey-coloured hair and clear, velvet-brown eyes and a flawless figure. Agnes was a poem in herself, I thought.

Kirsty and Ian came into the room, eagerly discussing a visit to their friends, the Sinclairs, in several days' time, for the evening.

'You can come if you wish, Charlotte,' Kirsty said grudgingly. 'We are all invited, and I daresay the Sinclair boys will want to look you over. Neil may not bother to come, but Robert certainly will. He is very fond of Helen Sinclair.'

The earth shifted under my feet at that moment. Well, what had I expected? That such an arrogant, masculine, sensual man as Robert should have been waiting all these years at Blackmaddie for Charlotte Brodie to arrive as if it had been predestined, with no other feminine diversions to attract him?

Yes, my new inner self answered me. *Yes, yes, yes.* That is exactly what I had expected. For he was mine. I wanted him and I would have him. I never paused to think that in that instant of self-revelation, Blackmaddie and I were one and the same.

9

I did not get the chance to ask Grandfather about Agnes' proposed visit, for he decided to stay in bed and nurse his gouty foot and demanded no visitors until he appeared downstairs.

'And you'd do well to heed his request, Charlotte,' Aunt Morag warned me. 'He's as irascible as can be, and wants no one but Duncan to listen to his curses. They are not fit for young ladies' ears, at any rate.'

I decided against mentioning Agnes to her or anyone save my grandfather, as the final decision would have to come from him. He stayed in his bed all the next day as well. I had to amuse myself, since none of the others seemed to be around. I discovered that Neil was very taken up in training a hawk. I admired him for his patience, having heard somewhere of the difficulty and danger in such a proceeding. Kirsty had been scathing about it, saying it was a new game to him, but surely a game with a difference, for did not hawks have great talons and vicious beaks? It was not a game I would care to have joined in, to train such a bird.

'He may let you watch some time,' Kirsty said carelessly, 'though I doubt it. He never lets Ian and me see what he does with the thing. Ian can't be bothered with it anyway. He's too busy getting himself ready.'

'Ready for what?'

Kirsty scowled, her dark brows almost joining together in the middle of her forehead.

'Of course, you wouldn't know, would you? He goes away to the University at Edinburgh next week, so the ceilidh at the Sinclairs' will be by way of being a farewell occasion as well.'

I was taken by surprise. I had not thought of anyone leaving Blackmaddie. But then, Ian was not a Brodie.

'Does he want to go?'

'Of course, *he* wants it. But I do not!' Kirsty's eyes had filled with tears of frustration at losing her playmate, for I could not think of them as anything else. Maybe when Ian had left the castle, she and I could become better friends, but there was a coldness in Kirsty that would never stretch out the hand of friendship to me and I knew it. She flounced out of the room and I was left to myself.

I would go down to the village, I decided. By myself. If they did not want my company here, I did not want theirs either. Only Robert's, and it seemed I was still to be denied that, as he had not returned to Blackmaddie yet. I went outside and round to the stables, where Duncan and several stable-lads were about their business, and asked if I might use the pony and trap that morning.

In ten minutes' time the castle was behind me and I was setting out on the road I had last taken with Neil and Agnes, with the wind blowing gently in my hair and the sudden excitement of discovery in my bones. I would explore the little streets and harbour alone and forget I was Miss Brodie of Blackmaddie, for there was nothing about my garb or bearing to mark me out as anyone of consequence, and I was unknown to the villagers.

Yet not altogether unknown, it seemed. I was forgetting my likeness to Katrina, and more than one pair of eyes looked at me curiously, and I saw heads nodding together behind the lace curtains of cottages. Was it that obvious? I thought angrily. I was myself, my own person. I tied up the pony near the harbour. The salt breeze was tangy and strong, and I gloried in its aroma. I watched the little boats busily coming and going, and the fishermen with their catch. Not such little boats as I had thought, I saw when I neared them. They were double-ended craft, curved at both ends and with a full deck, and I kept hearing the men refer to them as 'skaffies'. They seemed to be alive with the slippery glint of herring, and I watched them for a long while until I realised some of the comments and grinning glances in my direction were not altogether ladylike. I moved on round the harbour, my eyes on the glittering water as it rushed against the harbour wall, and on the tall masts of larger ships being dressed with billowing sails ready to get underway.

I felt a tug inside me, thinking how my father must have loved these last moments when his ship was getting ready to set sail, and feeling a sharp affinity with him at that moment. I wished I had been born a man, I thought passionately, to sail the seas and battle against the elements.

Suddenly my heart gave a great lurch. I was not sure whether it was a mirage or not, but there walking towards me, in deep conversation with several sailors from one of the ships, was Robert. I did not know where his business took him, or the nature of it, but the unexpectedness of seeing him here was enough to make the blood surge in my veins. He caught sight of me then and excused himself from the men. He was unsmiling as he strode towards me.

'What are you doing here by yourself?' he said angrily. 'Have you no more sense than to flaunt yourself in front of these men, some of whom have not seen a woman these several months?'

My face coloured at his words. Did he think I was trying to set myself up as a waterfront whore, or was he merely worrying about my safety? Either way, he did not have to catch hold of my arm so roughly and hurry me away as if I were a wayward child, as if I were Kirsty.

'I have seen sailors before,' I snapped. 'You forget my father was one, and that I lived by the waterfront at Bristol.'

'Then you should know better than to lounge about,' he snapped back. 'Is there no one with you? Neil or Ian or Kirsty?'

'No one.' I stared at him defiantly. 'I prefer my own company at times, strange though it may seem to you.'

His dark eyes raked over me till I felt he could see right through the soft warm dress I wore and the shawl round my shoulders. His gaze affected me the way it always did, sending little shivers through me until I had to put my hand on his arm and bring back the smile to his lips that warmed me so.

'I'm not a fool, Robert,' I said softly. 'There are plenty of others around here to come to my assistance if need be, and it is broad daylight. What can happen to me that I cannot handle in the middle of the morning?'

The smile appeared as I had known it would. 'If you and I were in some secret place, I would soon show you.' His voice was intimate. 'But I have work to attend to, and you may accompany me if you wish.'

'Work?' I said in surprise. What work could he have here?

'Blackmaddie village is my last call before going home,' he said. 'I still have to visit the tenants and collect the dues. Have you ever seen inside one of these cottages, Charlotte?'

Of course I had not, and I was pleased that he asked me. I would like to have asked him about his business with the sailors, but something told me this was not the moment for too many confidences, when he was still half-annoyed with me for venturing here alone. He rode alongside me once I was seated in the trap and led the way up the steep hill out of the village to the straggle of cottages at the top, where he dismounted and helped me down.

'There are a dozen cottages here that belong to the Blackmaddie estate,' he told me, 'and various crofts on the way back. They may surprise you.'

They did indeed. The cottages were small, so small and dark that I could almost appreciate the two rooms my mother and I had shared in Bristol. Most of the inhabitants looked poor but reasonably well-fed, and as most of them had a cow or chickens or a goat tethered in the back patch of land that served for a garden, I assumed they were at least partly self-sufficient. I was urged to take a warm brown egg for my tea, or accept a cup of still-warm, frothing milk, or eat some crowdie – a soft Highland cheese that had a peculiar taste of its own I wasn't too sure I liked. I was made welcome because of Robert, and it was clear that he was respected and liked. Even though it was morning, several of the cottages had their cruisie lamps lit while the woman of the house got on with her work of knitting away every spare minute. I was extremely interested in the intricate patterns the women knitted at great speed, and though the stench in some places was indescribable, from animals and the spluttering oil lamps and the mass of humanity such small hovels seemed to house, yet I was quite sorry to come out into the sunlight again and find that our task was over. I had enjoyed my unusual morning more than I had expected.

I thanked Robert for taking me with him.

'I wish I could take you right away,' he said suddenly. 'So far that there would be no need to fret over the effect you have on poor unsuspecting sailors. Though to go where I would wish, you would be forced to see them, and for them to ogle you, my sweet Charlotte!'

I had never heard him talk quite this way before. And take me away? Surely Robert was not thinking of leaving Blackmaddie? I felt a surge of alarm. I would not want to stay without him. It would be like the sun going out of my life if he went. I demanded to know what he meant, and he smiled teasingly.

'My heart is set on sailing for America one of these fine days,' he told me. 'One day when the time is right. I may even take you with me if you can tear yourself away from Blackmaddie.'

Or if she would let me go. But to America?

'What would you do there?' I exclaimed.

Robert smiled. 'The world does not begin and end at Blackmaddie, Charlotte. There is a whole, exciting new world across the ocean, with fortunes to be gained by hard work and a canny mind. People everywhere have to eat and wear clothes. They need wool, the same as they do here, and wool means sheep. The Blackmaddie shepherds are a skilful breed, and Grandfather has seen to it that my brothers and myself are not lacking in these skills. Neil may go his own way more than myself, but that is because Grandfather indulges him, and Ian still has his education to complete, but if the worst came to the worst, I wager I could earn a pretty penny as a sheep farmer on the prairies of America.'

I could hear the sudden enthusiasm in his voice, and I was filled with sudden alarm. 'You are not thinking of emigrating this very day, by any chance?' I tried to make a joke of it though my heart was churning, because I did not want him to leave at all.

Robert laughed. 'Things cannot be accomplished that quickly,' he said, 'but when the time is right I shall turn my back on this place for ever.'

I was shocked to hear him speak so.

'I thought you loved Blackmaddie. How can you bear to leave it? It's your home!' My voice was thick and choked.

'So it is, but not of my own making.' His voice was low, passionate. 'I want to build my own roots, Charlotte, not step into somebody else's shoes that are not even of my own kin. I am not a Brodie, remember, and it's a matter of pride with me.'

But you would be closer to the Brodies if you married one. The thought sprang into my head. But I knew Robert's pride would dismiss the idea of making Blackmaddie his own because of the ties of marriage. He was too fiercely independent for that. His disclosure about his future disturbed me more than I let him know. I could see now why he too had been so interested in the knitting the women at the cottages did, for he told me the wool they used was Blackmaddie wool from Blackmaddie sheep. There was much I still had to learn about my family, I realised.

'Can I see the farms some time?' I asked. 'And learn something about the sheep and how the wool is obtained?'

'Some time,' he agreed. 'But not today. I will be shut up in Grandfather's study all afternoon, going over the tenants' accounts and reporting on my last few days' work. Grandfather is an exacting laird, but one who is highly respected for the reason that he is totally fair and honest, and expects everyone about him to be the same.'

We were nearing the castle again now, and nothing could stop the thrill of pride I felt when we topped the high ridge to see it shimmering in the sunlight, as I had done on that first day of my arrival when Robert had looked deep into my eyes and welcomed me home, and I had been overcome with emotion on seeing all that my father had described to me so beautifully and awesomely displayed, as if nature had bestowed all that was most infinitely lovely on the scene spread out in front of my eyes. I would never tire of seeing it so.

I spent the afternoon wandering around the gardens and shrubberies until the sun began to get lower in the sky and the air cooled. I could not be happier that Robert and I had resumed our friendship with one another, and I had enjoyed this day immensely, more than any day since coming to Scotland. And that evening at dinner, I resolved, I would ask Grandfather about Agnes coming to stay. I was in an optimistic mood by the time I went to my room to change for dinner.

I knew Grandfather liked me to look pretty in clear, bright colours. He had annoyed Aunt Morag when she had hinted once again about my lack of respect for my mother by not wearing sombre black, roaring at her not to bother wearing black for him when he went, because he'd come back and haunt her if she did for her hypocrisy. She had flushed a dull red and snapped back at him that she'd wear white if it pleased him. Upon which, he'd told her it was a bit late to act the part of the straight-laced virgin, and to wear whatever she damn well pleased. Grandfather did not mince his words when anyone annoyed him, as I was learning very quickly.

On that particular evening I chose my attire for dinner with great care. I favoured blue, as it accentuated my blue eyes and rosy complexion, and suited my black hair, but I decided it was a night for seeking compliments and for putting him into a genial mood. I had only one rich-looking dress, a deep ruby red moire that Mother had brought home in triumph from one of her young lady clients who had tired of it. It suited me to perfection, giving me a gypsyish yet elegant look, and I decided that would be the dress to put a gleam in Grandfather's eyes. He still made me feel more like a possession than somebody who was wanted for herself, a possession that had somehow slipped out of his grasp and was now safely recovered. The satisfaction that I was back where I belonged was enough, so I was accorded no more attention. That was his way, and he had lived too long to change.

Vinny brought me my washing water and exclaimed with delight when she saw the stiff, crackling folds of the red moire as I brought it out from the closet and removed the cotton protective sheet with which I had covered it. She helped me into it and adjusted the revealing neckline to its best advantage. It was *very* low, I thought dubiously. It reminded me suddenly of the portrait of Maddie I had seen, when Duncan had told me I had the likeness. I certainly had it now, I thought uneasily, as I pulled down several tendrils of hair to frame my cheeks, I could *be* her. I wished I had never seen the portrait.

Vinny was bustling about tidying up my room. She had formed a rough attachment to me and on my part I had grown quite fond of the wizened little red-haired baby whom she called Luke. She often brought him to my room when he was howling, and it was a strange sensation to bounce him on my knee and stop his shuddering sobs with a few cuddles and kisses, for I had never held a baby before in my life. But I could never quieten him as successfully as when Vinny suckled him.

'Ye'll be wanting one of yer own, Miss,' Vinny had laughed, her voice cheeky and friendly and most unservant-like. 'Though I sometimes wonder if the pleasure of getting them's worth all this yelling and sleepless nights.'

'Especially with no husband to take a turn,' I put in, but as usual she would not be drawn into any mention of the baby's father, save to say tartly that men were more interested in the fun than the work, and she just hoped she wouldn't get caught again too quickly. She'd held up two podgy crossed fingers and grinned again, and I knew she too thought the fun better than the work, for all that she doted on Luke.

But that conversation had set me wondering. All the times William and I had threshed about in his studio, and that other time when Ruskin had forced his way into me and stayed there until he had finished jerking and throbbing, there had been no babies for me, thank heaven. I had hardly considered the possibility, until now. I had assumed William and I were being watched over by a lucky star and that I would conceive within the bonds of marriage and not before. Such naïvety turned my stomach now when I saw Vinny with Luke, but there was also the uneasy feeling that maybe I was barren. I did not want a child until I had a wedding-ring on my finger, but what if I could never have one? It made me chilled to think about it, knowing there was no way to prove or disprove it.

I finished pulling at my hair now, and gave a final tweak to my bodice. There was no time to change my mind about the dress, because the big gong was ringing out downstairs and Grandfather did not like to be kept waiting for a meal.

'Ye look a real picture, Miss,' Vinny said encouragingly as I reached the door. 'Red was Miss Katrina's favourite colour as well.'

It was stupid to let the coldness seep into me again, or to imagine I could hear those clamouring voices through the very stonework as I made my way down to the dining-room. It was just a thoughtless remark made by a servant. A piece of flattery maybe, in the hope that some trinket or other would be her reward. I was foolish to take any notice of it or to let my heart race so unevenly as I reached the door. There was unlikely to be any reaction from my family other than a possible compliment on my appearance.

The moment I stepped into the room I knew it was a false hope. It was a moment out of time, I thought dizzily, when everything seemed suspended as I absorbed the expressions in front of me with a kind of frozen horror.

Aunt Morag looked furious, as if I had transgressed so far beyond the modesty of mourning as to be past help. Uncle Andrew merely looked startled and drank deeply of his claret. Neil smiled vaguely, appreciating my décolleté, but hardly noticing anything else, and I knew his thoughts were still with Agnes. Kirsty gave a gasp and exchanged a look with Ian that seemed full of venom, and it was all directed towards me. She had been in the act of passing a glass of claret to Grandfather, but as he turned to greet me his face paled and then flushed, and the glass slipped out of his fingers to shatter on the edge of the table.

The red liquid spread across the tablecloth and into the

splintered fragments of glass. Grandfather's eyes had a glazed look in them as he came towards me with outstretched hands while Aunt Morag shouted furiously for a servant to come and clear up the mess.

'Katrina, my love . . . ' His voice was thick with emotion and yet querulous, an old man's voice, and though wild anger and the urge to cry out in frustration nearly overcame me, I was filled too with a feeling of infinite pity for him. I stepped forward and caught hold of his hands, trying to stop my own from shaking.

'Not Katrina, Grandfather,' I told him as I had done once before, and as evenly as possible considering the churning inside me. 'It is Charlotte. Charlotte Brodie.'

His hands dropped. His eyes clouded and he turned abruptly away from me. I wanted to weep. He had commanded me to come here, yet time and again he rejected me. But he would not turn me out. Of that I was certain. It would be like rejecting Katrina and Blackmaddie herself, and I knew he would never do that. The knowledge did not give me one vestige of comfort. It only angered and frightened me. I lifted my head high and walked across to take my place at the table. As I did so a side door opened and Robert appeared. There was a sharp tightening in my throat as he looked over me, slowly, without expression. *Please don't do as Grandfather did*, I begged silently, *I could not bear it*. He suddenly moved swiftly towards me and kissed my lips in full view of everyone.

'You are magnificent,' he said softly, so that only I could hear the words. I saw his eyes linger on the swell of my breasts in the ruby red moire. His eyes were dark and hot and the moment was so intimate I had to turn away quickly, knowing my cheeks matched my gown. But I was filled with an excitement that could not be dampened as Robert sat across the table from me at dinner and we faced each other through the soft glow of candlelight. I was exhilarated each time our eyes met and his eyes told me I was beautiful and desirable. I knew too, without a word passing between us, that he would come to my room that night, and that the door would not be locked.

126

I was so fired with my own emotions I almost forgot I had intended asking Grandfather about Agnes coming to stay at Blackmaddie until I caught the look in Neil's eye. I had meant to choose my moment, and it would have been better if I had waited until the gout did not roughen his temper as much as Aunt Morag's constant grumbling about the broken wine glass on the table. But instead of heeding any of the warning signs, I burst right in with my request.

'Grandfather, you remember my friend, Agnes Waverley? Her parents will probably be going home to Bristol very shortly and taking Agnes with them. I would very much like it if she could stay here at Blackmaddie for a few weeks if you are agreeable. It would be so pleasant to have a female companion.'

I stopped, realising I was talking too shrilly and too fast, and that Kirsty was glaring at me.

'You have your cousin.' Grandfather echoed her thoughts. 'And three young men to dance attendance on you. Most young women would be happy enough with that arrangement.'

But Kirsty was not my friend and never would be. I was annoyed at the finality in Grandfather's voice.

'I would like Agnes to stay here,' I said deliberately. 'You seem to forget that I am still feeling like a stranger here myself, and the days are long after my busy life in Bristol. Kirsty has her own friends and does not always want to be bothered with me.'

'Then she *will* be bothered with you,' he roared out. 'You belong here and I'll have no more talk about you feeling like a stranger. How can a Brodie be a stranger at Blackmaddie?'

'Watch your blood-pressure, Father, or I shall have to send for Doctor Fraser,' Aunt Morag said tetchily. I could see she did not care for the way Kirsty was being put in her place. Grandfather rounded on her at once.

'My blood-pressure can take care of itself, woman. Why have you all let Charlotte feel so unwelcome?'

Aunt Morag's face burned with rage at this, and it was ill-concealed.

'We have not let her feel unwelcome,' Kirsty stormed. 'We've already invited her to the Sinclairs for their ceilidh on Friday evening. Why should she want her English friend? We don't want any more of them here.'

'You are beginning to sound like a shrew, Kirsty! If Charlotte wants Agnes to stay, then I say let her come!' A sudden outburst from Neil as he thumped the table with unaccustomed fury was enough to make Kirsty look at him in astonishment. And then the sudden taunting look was back on her face, and I knew she was about to make some scathing remark about his virility, or lack of it, and I could not bear to see him humiliated in front of them all. I was appalled at the passions that had erupted from my harmless request, but suddenly I found my courage and scrambled to my feet, my hands flat on the table to stop them from shaking.

'I want Agnes here,' I repeated in a clear, determined voice. 'And if she does not come, then I will not stay either. I am sure her parents will allow me to travel back to Bristol with them.'

'By thunder, you will not!' Grandfather stood up too, and faced me so quickly his chair rocked back and forth. 'Your place is here, and if you want your Sassenach friend to stay, then so be it, but let's have no more nonsense about your leaving!'

He stamped out of the dining-room while everyone else was still bristling. I was still stunned by all that had happened. Still conscious of that strange feeling of a light going out whenever he left a room. I sat down heavily again and tried not to cry. I had won another round of the battle, but it was a bitter victory for I felt as if I had alienated almost everyone in the room. Ian, of course, would agree with Kirsty in the strange bond they seemed to share. Neil looked withdrawn again and he probably thought I had handled the whole scene very clumsily. Aunt Morag and Uncle Andrew avoided looking at me and discussed people of whom I had never heard, effectively shutting me out.

Only Robert seemed unperturbed by my clash with the family, though I could not read by his expression whether he was admiring or censorious. But at least I would have my own way, I consoled myself, and Agnes would not have to return to Bristol so soon. Perhaps never, if Grandfather was agreeable, and it was what she wished.

I realised that Robert was pouring wine from the decanter and pushing a glass towards me. He raised his own glass in a small salute and I smiled tremulously back. At least I had one friend here, and one whom I hoped would be more than a friend. But my nerves were still shaky, and it soon became obvious that Kirsty was going to ignore me for the rest of the evening. She and Ian got their heads together in a huddle and pored over a book on the sofa. Neil went off on his own pursuits, a solitary figure as usual, and I guessed that he was going to tend his hawk. It no longer seemed so strange a companion for him.

Eventually I could stand the atmosphere downstairs no longer and bade the family goodnight. Robert's answer was as cool as the rest of them, and I began to wonder if I had imagined the look of desire on his face when he had first seen me that evening wearing the gown the colour of rubies.

I went upstairs and closed my door. I did not need to light any candles, for the moon lit the room as bright as day with a white clear light that was thrown back from the mountain tops. I stared at my reflection in the mirror as I had done earlier. And despite the upsetting events, my eyes sparkled and my cheeks glowed. My lips were parted as if they had just kissed a lover, and I knew the feeling of exhilaration was still with me. I *had* won, and Agnes would come to Blackmaddie, an ally against the rest of them. I kicked off my shoes and lay full-length on the bed, uncaring that the red moire would be crushed. I did not have to iron it. Vinny or some other maid would see to it. I was Miss Brodie of Blackmaddie, the *only* Miss Brodie, and I was no longer content to be treated as the poor relation.

I threw my arms above my head on to the pillow and gazed up at the ceiling through half-closed eyes, and I was absolutely at one with my father's sentiments about Blackmaddie. She *was* beautiful, I conceded. And perhaps she possessed me a little, but she was not going to destroy me.

I heard the click of my door handle as someone entered and turned the key in the lock, imprisoning us both.

I knew I should be afraid. I should leap off the bed and heave on the bell-pull for someone to come. I should be thinking of the ghost who was supposed to haunt this room, or of Kirsty coming to rail at me with more vindictiveness. My heart should be pounding, and so it was – but not with fear. It pounded with a sudden elation, and there was fire running through my veins as a shadowy figure approached the bed. I knew it would be Robert.

My eyes opened slowly. In the white moonlight I saw him untie the cord from the waist of his dressing-robe. It dropped to the floor and he was naked beneath it. I caught my breath as my eyes took in his muscular body. He had told me earlier that evening that I was magnificent, but so was he, so was he. His shoulders were broad and taut, his chest covered in robust red hair like his beard, tailing down over the flatness of his belly to the proud protuberance below. I had never studied a man's body so freely before, and I could see the curve of a smile on Robert's face as he watched me. My whole being was suffused with a kind of lethargic yet tingling heat, and I was aware of the shallowness of my breath.

'I thought you'd be ready for me,' Robert said softly. 'Why aren't you?'

'I am ready,' I said tremulously. I had never been more ready or eager or aching to receive a man's body into mine. He moved swiftly towards the bed and lifted me to a sitting position while his hands dealt quickly with the fastenings of the red moire. It rustled to the floor, and the undergarments followed in feverish haste as I helped him. Finally I lay as naked as he, and I heard his intake of breath as his lips brushed my nipples. His tongue circled them slowly and they hardened at once into cool damp pellets. He laughed softly, and my own laughter bubbled up in my throat. I had deter· mined that the next time I lay with a man it would be with love, and I had so much love for Robert. I could hardly believe it was possible to love a man so much.

I thrilled to the feel of his body next to mine, the strength and the tenderness and the hardness of him. His beard tickled me deliciously, and he was kissing every inch of me, starting at my eyes and then down, down, over my breasts that strained towards his touch, his tongue teasing and tantalising until it reached the warm secret places of my body. I could hear the soft moaning in my throat and it seemed to delight him and spur him on to bring me to heights of pleasure I had never known before.

Then, when I felt the abandonment of desire was blurring my senses, the real ecstasy began, with the weight of him warm and heavy above me, and his sensual, vibrant body pulsating into mine. I felt my limbs relax as if they melted into the bed as Robert thrust against me slowly and exquisitely, and I thought there could surely be nothing on God's earth to match this. It was beautiful, beautiful.

He buried his face between my breasts, cupping them together so that his beard created yet another tingling new sensation. I felt as if every one of my senses was alive for the first time, knowing he evoked responses in me I hadn't known I was capable of giving. I was part of him and he of me, and I felt my body arch towards him time and again so that the movements were mutual, rhythmic, hypnotic. I was living a dream that was a thousand times more exciting, more brilliantly-coloured, more heaven-sent than any I had ever known in sleep. He was the dominant male, and yet his very maleness needed fulfilment, and he had chosen me for his mate. Or rather, we had come together, fused together, closer than blood ties could ever make two people.

And Robert was seemingly as insatiable as I. We lost all sense of time for it was only the present that mattered here in my turret room at Blackmaddie. If I had never known the meaning of possession before, I knew it now when he possessed me and I him, and I wished this night could go on for ever. At one point he withdrew from me for a brief moment, rolled over on to his back and pulled me over him. So now I was the dominant one, and after· the first few hesitant moments, I discovered it was something new and wild and erotic. My hair had loosened and fell in a tangled black curtain around my shoulders. Robert curled the tendrils around his fingers and held me captive by it. It was as if I were in the hold of some hallucinatory drug, oblivious to who or what I was, in command astride my willing horse, riding in wild abandonment, gloriously aware of Robert urging me on.

There was a sudden exquisite sensation in my loins. A heaviness that spread like honey through every part of me and took me so much by surprise that I gasped and stayed motionless while the secret part of me that held him tight jerked and pulsated against him as if it had a mind of its own. It was an explosive sensation, making my eyelids flicker and my breath quicken, and the soft moaning became a series of sharp gasps in my throat. *Oh Robert, Robert, my beloved.* I heard him give a low, delighted laugh, and with a sudden swift movement our positions were reversed again, but now it was his hands that caressed me, pushing and kneading the fleshy part of my lower abdomen above the black triangle of hair. Soothing, calming, lulling the wild, sharp sensations until the gentle probing and searching began again, and with it a renewed surge of desire.

And then he was inside me again, slippery and warm. I wanted to keep him there for ever. He thrust home harder and faster until I could smell the animal sweat on his body and see it glistening on his skin. It exalted me, and finally he gripped me very tightly and pressed his mouth on mine. I felt his teeth cut into my lips but nothing mattered as long as he loved me.

'Hold me, hold me,' he said urgently against my mouth, and I strained against him as I felt his seed exploding inside me as he writhed and twisted to release it.

'Dearest one,' he mumbled incoherently. 'My lovely, lovely Katrina.'

In one horrified instant all sensation ceased for me. I froze, unable to credit my own hearing as I heard him mumble her name as if it was wrenched out of him. After all this, after so much intimacy had merged us together until I had felt our very souls were united as well as our bodies, I could not believe that all this time he had been thinking of

132

her! Using me as a substitute while all his senses cried out to Katrina, who was dead, as if he could conjure up her spirit out of the intimacy between him and me. It sickened and revolted me. It was obscene. It was lust and rape and Ruskin all over again.

'Charlotte, for God's sake forgive me!' he whispered, agonised, into my neck now, his body still covering me, but with no more passion in it. I knew that he was appalled at his indiscretion, but nothing he ever did or said could excuse it or blot it out. He had lain with me, wanted and desired me ever since the day I arrived, me, *me*. He had warned me teasingly against leaving my door unlocked when we both knew it was inevitable, and now, when I loved him so much, when I had abandoned myself more freely with him than any tavern whore, it had been *her* name that was wrung from his lips.

'Get out of here,' I moaned. 'Get out, before I die of shame and humiliation with you right here in my bed. How would you find the words to explain that away, cousin? Or would you leave me here for the servants to find in the morning, and disclaim all knowledge? All *carnal* knowledge! That's the biblical name for it, isn't it?'

I heard my voice rise shrilly. And though I shrieked for Robert to get out, I still clutched him to me, my fingers digging into him so that my nails must have felt like needle-points in his neck. I hoped they did. Maybe he had seen me merely as a little sewing-mistress with a voluptuous body and had thought to make me his mistress, and it was nothing more than that. He had never said he loved me. The realisation choked me as I felt the dampness of his skin against my own clammy body. Suddenly I felt imprisoned by him and Katrina, both pressing down on me and stifling the life out of me. My head twisted frantically from side to side and I could hardly breathe until I felt the sharp sting of Robert's hand on my cheek. I gasped with shock and pain, but the rigidity of my body relaxed and he moved swiftly away from me. It was like the finality of death. I felt the tears running down my face as he cupped my chin and placed his lips gently on my mouth.

'It was only your sweet self in my arms and in my heart just now, Charlotte.' His voice was low and intense. 'You must believe that. Tell me you believe it, *please!*'

His voice begged for forgiveness, but I could no longer bear to look at him or to have him touching me. I was too humiliated.

'Just *go*. For pity's sake leave me,' I told him harshly.

He knelt by the side of my bed, his hands smoothing my hair back from my forehead as if I were a child. But I was not a child. I was a woman, with all a woman's hurt and disillusion burning like a fever inside me. I jerked my head away from his hand and turned away from him. I heard him rise to his feet and knew he was donning his dressing-robe. I lay curled up on top of the bed in a foetal position as if seeking comfort from a non-existent womb, and Robert put a bedcover over my nakedness as I started shivering. He hesitated a moment longer, and then with a sudden explicit oath he turned and left me. I heard the door open and shut and I was alone.

And then the shivering became racking sobs. I wanted to die. I wished the power of Blackmaddie, whatever it was, would come to my aid so that I never had to wake up to face another day. Never had to sit across the table from Robert and see the dark desire in his eyes and on his sensual mouth and know it was all meaningless. I did not want to see his fingers curl round the stem of a wine-glass in the characteristic way he had and know they had probed my body and brought my tingling senses to life. Nor to watch his proud, muscular body stride about the estate and relive the way it had been tender and hard and pulsating into mine, nor to remember the wild delight he had brought me. I did not want to guess at how humiliated he himself would feel tomorrow and all the other tomorrows, knowing how Katrina's name had been almost torn out of him and the perfection between us had been shattered in an instant. Robert would not be able to forgive himself any more than I could forgive him.

It did not bring me any kind of comfort. The closeness between us was finished. I had found the love I had been searching for and it was all in ruins, for I could never, ever risk the same thing happening again. A feeling of blind p nic rose nauseatingly through every part of me. I was alternately hot and cold, and those weird mumbling voices I had imagined earlier through the stonework were becoming louder. They were filling my head.

It was her, of course. Katrina. Or Maddie. Or both of them. Katrina and Maddie in league together to get rid of me by driving me mad. Because I had the likeness. I had thought Maddie would want someone to carry on, but perhaps I did not fit the mould. Perhaps I was to be rejected after all, and because they were dead, they wanted me dead too. I could not bear the sound of the voices, but it was impossible to shut them out. They were inside me. They *were* me. I thrust my hands over my ears and my sobs changed to screams in an attempt to shut them out. Screams of terror. Louder and louder. There were more sounds. The sounds of running feet and hammering on my door. The door opening again and human voices shouting at me. Human voices, and not those in my waking nightmare. And another stinging blow to my face to bring me back to reality.

10

The room seemed to be full of people. Aunt Morag held a candle above her head so that her features appeared grotesque and distorted in its yellow glow. Neil hovered anxiously near the door with the artist's reluctance to become involved in anything that might be repugnant. Grandfather, a night-cap perched ludicrously on his grey head, bellowed to know what the dickens was happening in here and if demons were attacking me, while Uncle Andrew suggested tersely that we either send for Doctor Fraser or get Cook to mix me a herbal sedative. Their vociferations made me dizzy.

But it was Kirsty and Ian who drew my attention from the vortex into which my emotions had plummeted me. Perhaps it was because of my own recent experience of intimacy, but I knew as soon as I looked at them that they had been together. They were both flushed of face, their eyes sparkling, hands not quite steady. And yet not with the fever of lovers. It was something else that these two had been engaged upon, I was sure of it. And when Kirsty came nearer the bed with false solicitude all over her face, a strong sweet odour wafted round the room with her. Herbal, perhaps. Or incense of some kind such as I had noticed when I passed certain churches in Bristol on Sunday mornings. I could not identify it and yet I was afraid of it and repelled by it.

'I am sorry you have all been disturbed,' I forced myself to say through chattering teeth. They all crowded round me as if surrounding a death-bed, I thought hysterically. 'I was having some kind of nightmare, about – about my mother,' I invented quickly. 'I quite thought I was back in Bristol, and I do apologise for shrieking out the way I did, but I assure you I do not need a doctor, Uncle Andrew. Nor a sleeping-draught.'

Ruskin had brought me a sleeping-draught, I recalled. Forcing his way into my room with insidious concern for my well-being, when all the time . . . .

I suddenly remembered I was naked beneath the one woollen bedcover, and it was beginning to feel scratchy on my skin as my thoughts ran away with me, and these people continued to stand around me and argue over me as if I had no mind of my own. I pulled the bedcover more tightly round me with one arm, and saw Kirsty and Ian exchange a glance as my bare shoulder was exposed for a moment. They knew I was naked, even if none of the others had noticed anything, and the stain of colour in my cheeks probably told them why.

'I will see to it that you are given a hot drink, and I do think a sleeping-draught is necessary, Charlotte,' Aunt Morag said firmly, in a voice that allowed for no further argument. 'We cannot have our nights disturbed like this. It must have been a bad nightmare, for you look as if you are still not in command of your senses and as if someone had been wringing the life out of you.'

She dragged at the bell-pull near the bed, and I saw the smirk on Kirsty's face. She had guessed, I thought immediately. The stain on my cheeks deepened and I felt as if the blush was continuing right through my body.

'Where's Robert, I wonder?' Kirsty asked innocently, in a smooth voice that did not fool me for an instant. I was on the alert at once. 'I'm surprised he has not come to see what all the commotion is about, since you and he seem to get along so extraordinarily well together, Charlotte. He must be sleeping the sleep of the blessed.'

Aunt Morag was fussing about now, picking up the ruby red dress that I had abandoned so feverishly, collecting up my undergarments from the floor where they were scattered, trying to keep them away from the men's eyes and grumbling about my untidiness as she laid them over a chair. But these actions too brought a knowing smile to Kirsty's face, and to Ian's, I saw to my acute embarrassment.

'Perhaps you would all leave me now?' I mumbled, trying not to sound too ungracious. Neil said goodnight at once, and hoped I would feel better in the morning. Grandfather and Uncle Andrew followed a few minutes later, complaining about all the fuss. I felt guilty at wakening everyone and wished the others could go as well, but Aunt Morag said she had no intention of leaving until one of the servants had arrived and she had seen that I was safely taken care of. Kirsty and Ian seemed disinclined to leave as well, and I knew that they had not been disturbed from sleep, for I was quite sure neither of them had reached that state yet, for all that it was well into the early hours of the morning. Kirsty's room was next to mine, though along the passage a short distance, and the walls were thick, so I had heard nothing from there, and yet there was this certain feeling that they had been there together. Kirsty sat on the end of my bed, her eyes innocent and round.

'Why don't you tell us what your nightmare was about, Charlotte?' she said persuasively. 'It often helps to dispel a bad dream to talk about it. Sharing the experience serves to halve its horror.'

She knew very well it had been no nightmare. At least, not to begin with.

'We could try to analyse it for you,' Ian added, goaded on by Kirsty. 'It was something to do with your mother, you said. Was she perhaps trying to come back to life on the night she died while you were so agitated in the next room? They do say that's the weirdest time when the spirit hasn't fully departed, and if the closest survivor needs help they'll reappear.'

'Stop that kind of talk, Ian,' Aunt Morag snapped. 'It's blasphemous.'

'No it's not, Mother!' Kirsty interrupted. 'I think it's very interesting, don't you, Charlotte? Did you need your mother to help you on the night she died? Do you remember being particularly in need of a visitation?'

Mother's ghostly fingers clawing Ruskin away from me might have been worse than the reality. No, they would not. In retrospect, even that would have been preferable to his assault. I glared at Kirsty through feverish eyes.

'I don't want to talk about it,' I muttered. 'It's over, and I want to try to forget it. I want to try and get some sleep with however much of the night remains, and I should have thought you'd want to do the same.'

Aunt Morag looked at her daughter sharply.

'A sleeping-draught might be good for you too, Kirsty. Your eyes are too bright and excited by the story of Charlotte's nightmare. Get off with you before I insist on it – and you too, Ian. I shall stay until the servant arrives. What in heaven's name can be keeping her?' she said irritably.

Almost as she spoke the door opened after a cursory tap and Vinny stood there sullenly, hair awry and spiky with curling rags, a voluminous night-shirt hardly able to disguise the unrestricted breasts beneath it, with the nipples standing out against the coarse cotton material in the chill night air. The thin shawl around her shoulders was doing no good at all, and my aunt tut-tutted at the sight of her, though I saw Ian's eyes roam over Vinny with a barely restrained smile on his lips. Vinny started at the sight of so many people in my room.

'Will you ask Cook to prepare a sleeping-draught for Miss Charlotte immediately, and bring it back here as fast as you can?' Aunt Morag commanded. 'Stop gaping, and move yourself, girl. Oh – and a glass of warm milk as well.'

Vinny disappeared. I was putting so many people to such a lot of trouble, and all I wanted was to be left alone. I purposely would not think of Robert, and despite Kirsty's sly enquiry as to why he hadn't appeared on the scene, I was desperately thankful that he had not. I could not have borne the mockery of seeing his supposed concern for my pretended nightmare when we both knew painfully well the true cause of my anguish.

Kirsty still lingered with Ian, and I could see they were itching to goad me into some revelation about this night, but for once I was glad of Aunt Morag's forthright insistence, and at last they reluctantly left my room. My aunt still stood by my bed like a watchful angel, lighting my candles for me from the one she had brought, all solicitude, but she

made me feel uncomfortable for all that. I would like to
have got into bed properly, but my nightgown was still under
my pillow and I could not wriggle down under the bedclothes without her seeing my unclothed state. It seemed
an interminable time that she stood there waiting for Vinny
to reappear.

At last the maid arrived with the medicine and warm milk.
I hated warm milk, but I promised Aunt Morag I would
drink every drop and would not disturb her again.

'Very well, then I shall leave you, Charlotte. But see to it
that you stay in bed for a while in the morning. There is no
need at all for you to present yourself for breakfast until
you are quite yourself again. Vinny can bring you a tray in
bed. And now I'll bid you goodnight.'

I was enormously relieved when she left the room and Vinny
came across to the bed with the two glasses. She was wide
awake now after the two long excursions up the winding
stairs from the kitchens far below, and full of curiosity.

'Are ye ill, Miss?' she asked at once. 'Cook says ye'll most
likely have caught a cold because the climate's that much
chillier than what ye're used to.'

She seated herself on the edge of the bed much as Kirsty
had done, clearly feeling that a meeting like this in the
middle of the night was of sufficient strangeness to warrant
such familiarity. And I did not care. She was the only person
with whom I felt reasonably comfortable out of all those
who had come running to my room that night. She was like
a child as she sat there, expectantly waiting to be told a tale;
a child in facial expression, but not in form, as she folded
her podgy arms in readiness and the large breasts spilled out
over them behind the cambric night-shift.

I took the glass of medicine from my side table and
wrinkled my nose as I sniffed it, but I knew I had better take
it all. My mother used to say that the nastier a medicine
smelled, the more good it did a person. I sat up to drink it,
forgetting I wore nothing at all, but it was too late to try
and disguise the fact as I saw Vinny's grin as I drained the
glass quickly and shuddered violently, grabbing at the glass

140

of warm milk to take some of the taste away. Even warm milk was preferable to the mixture, with its sharp, bitter taste, somewhat salty. I asked her what on earth was in it and if someone was trying to poison me.

'It's a mixture of Cook's own making,' Vinny told me. 'Made from the leaves of the henbane plant, and perhaps it's as well ye didn't take it earlier on, Miss Charlotte, or that it wasn't slipped into someone else's drink!'

Vinny was laughing as she spoke. I reached quickly under my pillow for my night-gown and then slid out of bed to put it on properly, not caring now that her interested eyes were on me. All I wanted was for the sleeping-draught to bring me oblivion quickly, to blot out the traumatic events of the night.

'And just what do you mean about slipping the sleeping-draught into somebody's drink, Vinny?' I snapped.

Her eyes still laughed knowingly as she held out her hand to take the garment from me to help slip it over my head.

'The henbane, Miss,' she said cheekily. 'It acts very well as a sleeping-draught, but Cook's always threatening me she'll give a large dose to me some time because it suppresses certain desires, if ye follow my meaning. Perhaps if ye – and another person – had taken a large dose ye'd not be showing the signs of love so clearly. Here, look – and here!'

I looked down at myself to where her fingers pointed, and on my breasts I could see large red marks like bruises, and others on my abdomen. I remembered throwing my head back in ecstasy as Robert's mouth drew at my skin, his teeth tingling rather than hurting, his tongue tantalising, and this was the result. I snatched my night-gown from Vinny and almost threw it over my head to cover myself, my face burning to think Vinny had seen the evidence of our desire.

'It's all right, Miss, I willna tell,' she said generously as I climbed back into bed. 'It's no the first time I've seen love-bites by a long chalk. Anyways, ye're all right. There's none on yer neck to show when ye wear yer low dresses to tease the menfolk.'

Love-bites, there could not be a more descriptive phrase for the red bruises. Had Robert also distributed them on

Vinny's body? I thought agonisingly. I knew I shouldn't care, particularly after all that had happened, but I did care. I cared for him as passionately as any woman had ever cared about a man. He was my lover, husband, friend; everything and nothing, because it had all been a terrible farce and his love-making all a fantasy on his part. And a tragedy, because I would always love him, always want him, even though I had no intention of ever letting him use me like that again. But nothing could stop the wanting, and I couldn't bear to think of him lying with Vinny in some sweet love-nest.

My eyes were beginning to feel heavy and my body languorous. I began to experience a light, floating feeling of detachment and I welcomed it because it stopped me thinking too deeply about anything at all. I could pretend the clamouring voices that still plagued me were no longer reaching out to me from the stonework. My head was heavy to turn, but my eyes swivelled enough to let me look at Vinny. She was hugging herself at the foot of my bed, rocking back and forth slightly, the way country-folk did as if in some ancient ritual of self-preservation, humming in a softly crooning voice as if it were Luke she held there. But even as the noise of it soothed me, the humming stopped and I sensed that she was listening, head cocked to one side, her eyes suddenly gleaming, mouth parted in a sort of smile. And then I knew the voices weren't all in my head. Vinny heard them too.

I summoned up my faculties to demand to know what they were, for through my glazed eyes I could see that Vinny didn't appear to fear them as I did. Perhaps she had heard them before. She looked excited more than anything.

'What is it, Vinny?' I mumbled, but the words hardly seemed to come out intelligibly. My tongue seemed too big for my mouth to hold any more.

I could no longer see her clearly as she moved about my room. The white cambric of her night-shirt was blurred at the edges and her face was indistinct. I knew vaguely that she had moved towards the closet where my clothes were hung, and that she was carefully arranging the red moire on a hanger. As she carried it from the chair where Aunt Morag had put it, a red cloud seemed to move across the room. She was a long time in the closet, a ridiculously long time. And the voices were buzzing in my head now. I could almost imagine Vinny's crooning voice was joining in the chanting, but that was even more ridiculous, of course.

I wished I could tell her to go and leave me to sleep, for I felt as if I was beginning to drop into a deep black velvet vacuum. It was deliciously inviting and I wanted to enter it alone. I was too tired to try to speak any more and my arms felt too heavy to wave her away. The voices were beginning to blur at last. They were still there, but no more than a low drone, not unpleasant, not anything, just a background humming in keeping with Vinny's own humming.

It seemed as if I lay there for an eternity in a kind of stupefied lethargy, half-sleeping, half-conscious. Finally Vinny closed the closet door and moved towards me. I was strangely aware of all that was happening, and yet it was as if it all happened to someone else and I was detached, watching the whole proceedings. It was very odd. I only knew Vinny was there by the vague white shape that seemed to undulate rather than walk, her bouncing breasts helping to create the illusion of constant movement. And the pink blob above the white shape was circular, so it must be her face. I heard her voice then, soft, still treating me to the same tones she used for Luke for some reason. Faraway tones, insidious, mesmeric.

'There now, my pretty one. Ye'll sleep the clock round and be better for it. There's no use lying awake trying to ferret out things ye canna understand. It's time wasted, and time's precious. A moment lost never comes again.'

Through the muddle of my thoughts, I remembered thinking that the words seemed extraordinarily deep for someone of Vinny's nature. I could make out her pale eyes staring down at me from the blur of her face. They shone like candle flames, not dense, but wavering like the rest of her. And then her spectral shape moved out of my line of vision and I heard the click of my door. I should get out of bed and lock it, I thought vaguely, but I would never be able to walk that far. I raised my head an inch and the whole room undulated like waves on the sea, and a sudden nausea engulfed me and made me sink back quickly on to the pillow and close my eyes tightly. I would have to leave the door unlocked. It didn't really matter. No one would disturb me. And if they did I wouldn't care. They could have their fill of me. I was not capable of resisting or co-operating. I was floating somewhere in space, a child of the universe, lost, in a deep black velvet vacuum and it was devouring me.

When I awoke I had the most terrible headache. I could hardly think above it. Vinny was still there, which was odd, for I was sure she had left during the night. It took a few minutes to realise that the spiky hair rags were gone from her head and that she was dressed in her normal, everyday clothes, that she held a tray of breakfast in her hands and that outside my windows the day was a sparkling gold and blue. I struggled to sit up but it hurt my head too much and I just eased myself slightly on the pillow and ran my tongue round the roof of my mouth. It tasted awful, as if full of sand. I drank deeply of the tea Vinny handed me before I was able to speak a single word.

'Is everyone else up?' I managed to ask huskily.

Vinny laughed, the insidiousness of last night gone, her usual cheerful energy showing through as she looked down at me.

'Bless my bonnets, I should just think they are, Miss. It's well past eleven o'clock, but the Missus said ye were to be left undisturbed after your bad turn last night.'

Bad turn? Oh yes. The nightmare I had invented for the family's benefit to cover the true nightmare of Robert's rejection of me. That was what it was, of course. He had pretended to love me, used my body while it suited him, pretending a passion . . . no, the passion had been real. No man could have faked that. But it was only my body that had lain beneath his. His mind, his soul, the essence of him had been already given to Katrina, and it was something I couldn't fight. How could anyone fight a dead woman? I felt my throat constrict as I faced the futility of it.

'I think I will stay here a while longer,' I said listlessly. My mind was still dulled with last night's drug. Whatever it was, I would not wish to try it again. 'Will you tell my aunt, Vinny? I'd rather get rid of my headache lying here alone, and I'll join the family in time for luncheon.'

'Yes, Miss. Do you want a powder for your headache? I could ask Cook ... '

'No, thank you! No more of Cook's potions,' I told her. I wanted to keep my wits about me and have no more of those nauseating floating sensations of last night.

'It was a mite strong for ye, mebbe,' Vinny said sympathetically. 'But ye looked so wild-eyed if ye'll pardon me for saying so, Miss Charlotte, it was me that told Cook to give ye an extra good helping of the henbane. Ye'd not be used to such medication, I daresay.'

'No I would not.' I pushed away the tray after managing to eat half a piece of toast. 'I can't get this food down. I shall be sick if I try. Take it away, will you, please?'

I lay back and closed my eyes again until I heard her leave my room. So I had been wild-eyed, had I? So would anybody have been. So would *she* have been, though perhaps a little country girl like Vinny had a simple acceptance of whatever life had to offer, and would not trouble overmuch about being called by someone else's name by a man making love to her. Especially if it was one of the gentry, someone like Robert Stewart, who dallied with her for an hour's amusement when it suited him. She'd probably be so gratified by his attentions that a small detail like another girl's name being blurted out would be of no consequence. But I was not a simple girl, and I had no intention of being used.

But did Robert still see me as the poor relation and someone to be dallied with as he chose, the way Vinny was? I had more or less convinced myself by now that he had to be the father of the ugly little baby. I couldn't imagine it being Ian, who seemed so obsessively wrapped up in the childish antics he and Kirsty indulged in. And Neil, apart from the implied impotency which I was not altogether sure I believed, he was too head-in-the-clouds with his poetry, and too sensitive to lift the skirts of a generous servant girl. So ruling out my grandfather and Uncle Andrew, that left Robert. It always came back to Robert. I hated him even while my soul yearned for him, and I grieved for the loss of something wonderful between us that had been there for a brief moment and then snatched away. It was like seeing a glimpse of heaven through a grey mist, but now the mist had closed in on me again, never to be lifted.

I suddenly couldn't lie inactive any longer. I put my feet out of bed and sat up carefully, experimentally, and the room did not spin too badly. Maybe fresh air was what I needed after all. My room was unbearably cloying, and I fancied I could still smell the sickly sweet odour Kirsty and Ian had brought in with them last night. At least I assumed it had been them; it could have been any of the people who had crowded into my room. But I didn't want to think of that now. I sponged my face and hands quickly and dressed in a warm tweed dress. I felt the need to wrap myself up a little, to cosset myself as if I had been ill for a long time.

No one seemed to be about when I went downstairs and I slipped outside unnoticed. I wanted no one's company, least of all Robert's. I had no idea how we were going to face each other the next time we met. I wandered about the grounds of Blackmaddie, trying to draw comfort from her beauty, but there was none. I was still detached from it all, still in a kind of dream-world, but the clear mountain air and balmy autumn sunshine helped. Though my nerve-ends were still raw and unrelaxed, the tension in my head was lifting slightly and I strolled past the sheds and low buildings behind the stables, out of sight of curious eyes from the castle. I needed to be alone.

'Charlotte.'

The voice made me jump. I paused and looked all around. Then Neil emerged at the doorway of one of the sheds. He was still in shadow as yet, and one hand looked enormous and ugly and different from the sensitive hands I knew. Was I still in a half-drugged state? I wondered bemused. He came fully into the sunlight and I saw he wore a huge thick leather gauntlet, and he beckoned me inside. I went because I was

146

instructed, as if I had no will of my own.

I blinked at the darkness inside the shed. For a ridiculous moment I wondered just what Neil wanted of me.

'Look,' he said softly. 'Over here. Don't make any sudden movements.'

I followed the line of his pointing finger. I caught my breath. His hawk sat on its perch, seeming to watch me with suspicious, menacing, jewelled eyes and jerky head movements. I felt a stab of alarm. I had never been fond of birds, nor for the fashion of caging them, but this was not just a bird. It exuded power and strength, from the grip of its great talons around the wooden perch to the half-spread wing-span as it sensed a stranger and held itself in readiness for flight or attack. Its plumage gleamed dully in the light from the small window. So this was the hawk that Neil cared for so deeply. It was not a pet I would have chosen.

'Do you have a name for it?' I whispered, for I could think of nothing else to say.

'She,' he corrected. 'I call her Boucca, which is a Celtic name for spirit. In the literal sense it's the god-like spirit, but I named her because of her own spirit. She's a great fighter, my Boucca, a killer, of course, but then she is a bird of prey, and it's her nature to kill.'

I shivered at his words. I realised it was great honour for Neil to show me his hawk, but there was something about the way he referred to Boucca that unsettled me. I tried to be interested when he told me of her habits and how she was gradually becoming tamed, but that it was a long, hard struggle against the bird's natural inclinations.

I stayed as long as was polite but I was glad to be out in the sunlight again. I saw Duncan near the stables and requested the use of the trap that afternoon. He was glad to acquiesce, and I warmed again to the unexpected friendship he showed me. I decided to go to the hotel myself to ask Agnes and her parents about her coming to stay at Blackmaddie. I had almost forgotten about Grandfather's agreement.

Luncheon was a strain, with everyone being over-polite or wrapped up in private thoughts. There seemed to be an air of secrecy surrounding each of us, as if we had all retreated into a little world of our own making. Robert did not appear at all, and I did not ask where he had gone.

The afternoon was beautiful, the trees surrounding the loch a mass of colour, from russet-red to the bright sheen of gold, to deep burnished copper, and the dark evergreen pines soaring skywards in search of the sun. The mountains still dominated, but on such an afternoon their presence was benevolent rather than frightening, their slopes subtly indistinct in the blurring haze of sunlight, less menacing without the stark outline of crag and spur and chasm.

When I reached the ridge before the descent into the small glen where the hotel was situated, I looked back towards Blackmaddie as I had done on the day I arrived with Robert at my side. She was just as beautiful and awesome. But her inmates were as complex as she. There were things here I did not understand and was almost too afraid to discover. But discover them I must.

I had been so intent on my scrutiny of the castle that I did not know a rider was approaching until I heard the soft whinny of a horse. My face flamed with colour as I saw Robert mounted on the great black stallion that so complemented his personality. He sat proudly erect, hair and beard a fiery red in the sunlight, a magnificent sight to behold, unsmiling as he looked down at me. As stern as when we had met at the station and sparked off an instant antagonism between us.

Had he really lain between my breasts last night? I thought bemusedly. Taken everything I had to give and more, while my body and soul exalted in his dominance? Had I really eased myself over him and abandoned myself in a frenzy of indulgence, astride my willing horse? I swallowed quickly and averted my eyes from his unsmiling gaze. I burned with embarrassment, knowing how differently I would react if he slid from his stallion and took me in his arms, and despising myself for my weakness. But I knew I would always be weak where he was concerned.

'I shall not see you again for several weeks, Charlotte,' he said evenly. 'I have business to attend to in Edinburgh, and then I am going on to visit some of my mother's relatives. It's a kind of yearly pilgrimage, and since neither of my brothers is willing to do it, I undertake it myself. I fancy you will not be too displeased to see me go.'

What could I say? I would not ask him to stay, nor plead with him not to look at me with such cold indifference. I was learning more about myself as well as all my family, for at that moment I wanted nothing more than to throw myself into Robert Stewart's arms and beg him to love me again and again and again. But the shame of knowing it restored my pride.

'You must do as you wish. It is nothing to me. I am the stranger here and I don't expect life at Blackmaddie to alter one jot because I have arrived among you. I hope you enjoy your visit.'

I wondered if it had been a hastily arranged visit because of what happened last night. But I doubted it. I doubted whether he cared about me that much after all. As he turned away from me abruptly, from the place where I had believed we had given each other an unspoken promise on that first day, I felt now that this was an ending to something that had hardly begun.

11

Robert had made no attempt to kiss me good-bye. I would have liked to think there was pain in his eyes, and that he remembered as I did, that he was holding himself tightly in check for fear of offending me again. I would have liked to know that he still yearned for me as I yearned for him, but the chasm between us was too great and too new for either of us to cross at that moment. I watched as he rode furiously away from me, and it was as if a light had gone out of my life. I had found him too late, I thought tragically, and *she* had been the one to capture his heart. She. Katrina. Maddie. One and the same.

I jerked at the reins and urged my pony on towards the hotel, refusing to let myself get morbid again. I remembered my mission, and the joy I would see on Agnes' face when I explained why I had come. I was not disappointed. She fell upon me with cries of delight when I told her Grandfather had extended his hospitality to her if she wished to stay at Blackmaddie and if her parents would allow it.

There were tears in her beautiful, doe-like eyes as she hugged me and confessed that her doctor in Bristol had been urging her father for some time to send her to Scotland on a prolonged visit, if not for good.

'But it was not possible, Charlotte,' she said huskily. 'Father is not a wealthy man, and he would not let me stay here alone without the protection of himself and my mother. The doctor thought I had every chance of a complete recovery if only I could stay near the mountains and my lungs were given a chance to breathe good pure air. Father has been so torn, not knowing what to do about it.'

'Well, now you can stay,' I told her warmly. 'As long as I

am at Blackmaddie, it is your home too, Agnes. I can't tell you how glad I am at the prospect. My cousins are agreeable for the most part, but you are more like a sister to me.'

More than Kirsty would ever be, I felt with swift regret. I had not known Agnes very long, but I had felt drawn to her from the beginning, and it was not at all strange to think of her as my confidante.

'I shall be interested to meet the other cousin – Robert,' Agnes said suddenly.

'I'm afraid he'll be away for several weeks.' I felt a pang as I said the words. 'Though I fancy you'll be happy enough to get to know Neil a little better!'

A rosy flush filled her cheeks, and her eyes were like stars. If she could look like that just by the mention of his name . . . But I felt uneasy. Hadn't she been the one to warn me against the Stewarts? To suggest that marriage between the Scots and English was unwise? Perhaps I was letting my imagination run away with me again, but I did not want Agnes getting hurt. Nor Neil. I was fond of my creative cousin and thought him rather a special kind of person, and I did not want to see him humiliated in any way.

'He is training a hawk,' I said quickly, before she wondered why the frown had replaced the smile on my face. 'A dangerous occupation, I'd have thought, but an interesting one for all that. He showed it to me today, so I feel quite honoured. I'm sure he'll want to show it to you too, Agnes.'

'I shall be very interested!'

I felt she would be interested in anything, no matter what it was, as long as it concerned Neil. I wished I knew how to warn her about Kirsty's hinting, but it seemed a hateful thing to do when I couldn't be sure. I was glad when her parents arrived in the hotel lounge at that moment and we intimated the news to them about Agnes' invitation.

As I saw mother and daughter embrace, I noticed things I had not done before. A threadbare cuff on Mr Waverley's jacket; the thin clothes Mrs Waverley wore when one would have expected warmer garments for a northern visit, especially when Agnes seemed more suitably attired; the lack of jewellery and pretty accessories. Most of all I noticed the genuine affection between them all. Yes, they were a loving family. Mrs Waverley thanked me with a small catch in her voice, and I could see how much they would miss Agnes, but her health was all-important to them. It made me wish I had someone to care for me like that, and I regretted the cool relationship between my own mother and myself that had always kept affection at arm's length.

I suggested they should all come for afternoon tea one day to meet my family, and they accepted gratefully. It was a new role for me to play at benefactor, but why should I not enjoy it? Blackmaddie was my home, and I fancied I knew how to handle my grandfather now when it came to getting my own way. Agnes and I took a short stroll outside before I returned to the castle. I was almost reluctant to go back, because my nerves were beginning to relax comfortably in Agnes' company. I could even remember the delightful moments of last night without the horror of what followed crowding into my mind.

'The hotel manager, Mr Ferguson, has been quite entertaining on this visit, Charlotte,' Agnes told me as we strolled arm in arm in the hotel gardens. 'He knows us quite well by now, of course, and has been telling us about some of the village characters, past and present. Did you know there's a woman still living there who is reported to have magical powers? He says she's quite harmless and a bit weak in the head at times, though she fancies herself as a witch. Can you imagine a witch who's slightly weak in the head? It might be quite disastrous if she were to get her spells mixed!'

Agnes was laughing, clearly finding the whole idea quite comical. But I found I could not join in the laughter, though I tried not to let my body tense against hers nor my senses to run riot as I wondered if this was the woman Kirsty and Ian had referred to when they said they were finding out about the occult. Someone who knew, they had said mysteriously.

My thoughts ran on. There were the pictures in Kirsty's room that used to be Katrina's; the voices; the chanting; the sweet sickly odour about Kirsty and Ian last night and the high light of excitement in their eyes; the power of Blackmaddie and the likeness passed on through Maddie to Katrina to me . . . I caught my breath in my throat and almost stumbled over a rutted piece of ground.

There was a roaring in my ears like the sound of the sea heard through a shell when it was pressed close to the head. The mysterious aura of the unknown, impenetrable. The pieces began to move slightly together. They didn't fit yet. Maybe I didn't really want them to fit too soon, because when they did I would know it all, and I was still afraid. Afraid to know something terrible and evil that involved some or all of my family at Blackmaddie. My family, into whose filial circle I was about to draw this lovely golden girl at my side. I hoped I was not doing her a terrible mischief by my innocent invitation.

'Have you ricked your ankle, Charlotte?' Agnes was all concern, and held tightly to my arm as I stumbled. The mist cleared a little as I smiled reassuringly at her.

'No, I'm quite all right, thank you. But I suppose I had better be getting back. I had a nightmare last night and kept half the family awake, so I do not want them thinking I have got lost and sending search parties out after me. They'll start believing that old woman of yours in the village has put the devil into me and made me contrary.'

Agnes laughed, thinking I was jesting. But why had I said that? It had come glibly to my tongue, and I clearly remembered Grandfather grumbling that it sounded as if I had demons in my room last night with all the hullaballoo. The afternoon chilled for me.

'Our Mr Ferguson was full of the old folk-lore,' Agnes prattled on, not realising what uncertainties she was stirring up. 'Did you know, for instance, that folk around here will never dare to kill a swan because it's considered to be the reincarnation of a dead woman? A fascinating story, but one I was ridiculously pleased to hear, for I'd hate to think of anyone killing such beautiful, elegant creatures, wouldn't you?'

I agreed, but all the way back to Blackmaddie in the trap I was mulling over our conversation, and the white swan became Katrina lying cold and white on the mountainside, waiting eternally for a lover who never came. The reincarnation of a dead woman: a romantic enough piece of folk-lore unless the imagination was vivid enough to connect it with the present, as mine was. I seemed to imagine evil in every innocent conversation just lately, I thought in some agitation. Since arriving at Blackmaddie every one of my senses seemed to have sharpened, making me suspicious, aware of atmosphere, receptive to nuances of voice and look in a way I had never been before.

I reminded myself that I had three great upheavals in my life very recently that must have contributed greatly to my new perception. The shock of Mother's death, followed so savagely and swiftly by Ruskin, and then the complete change in coming to Blackmaddie. Such things could not be expected to have no effect at all. I tried to console myself that time would repair the damage to my emotions, and that I was behaving no less rationally than any other young lady would in the same set of circumstances.

All the same, I had been intrigued by Agnes' chatter. I resolved to take a look in the library when I reached Blackmaddie and see just what I could discover about the strange pictures in Kirsty/Katrina's room, and maybe about the story of the swan, which I took to be merely folk-lore told to Sassenachs to give more colour to a romantic country steeped in history.

My interest had been caught now, despite Kirsty's disclosure of Katrina's involvement with the occult. I had no wish to be anything like Katrina in character; the precise reason evaded me, perhaps it was the revulsion I had experienced last night when Robert had called me by her name. Perhaps it was a natural desire to be myself, and not a reincarnation or replica of somebody else.

I really knew very little about Katrina. It struck me, not for the first time, that she was rarely mentioned at Blackmaddie, except by those who chose to mistake me for her – Grandfather and Robert. Neil had given me the impression that he loved her, but now I wasn't so sure. Perhaps it had been merely the shock of seeing me so suddenly in the thicket of trees, and the remembered circumstances of her death that had made him so emotional at that moment. I still wondered who the lover had been who never arrived at their tryst on the mountain. I wished I dared to ask.

I returned the pony and trap to the stables, and Duncan told me my aunt and Kirsty had gone over to the Sinclair house and that I had missed them by quite a while. I tried not to show that I was glad. I still felt I had greatly displeased Aunt Morag by the fuss I had made last night. How much more horrified she would have been if she had known the true reason for my pretended nightmare, and seen Robert and me in our wild abandonment.

'The young men have gone riding,' Duncan grunted now. 'Except for Mister Robert. Your uncle took him off to the station some time ago, lassie.'

I stared in sick dismay. So soon? So it had been good-bye up there on the ridge, without a last chance to repair the shattered remnants of our relationship. I had not really expected to come home and find he had already gone. I bent my head and left the stables hurriedly before Duncan should see the tell-tale shine of tears in my eyes. I was being completely perverse and I knew it, but it seemed that the moment Robert was beyond reach I longed for his presence. I wanted to touch him, to hold and caress and feel the warmth of him. I wanted the ecstasy of his body enveloping mine. I wanted him.

There was no use in wishing for the moon, I told myself. I went inside Blackmaddie. She closed around me, unwelcoming, silent. There was no one about. I shrugged off the feeling of disquiet that I was the only person alive in this vast tomb of a place, and made my way to the library. Its shelves were stacked with tomes and it smelled of the peculiar mustiness of non-use. It took me quite a while before I found the volume I was searching for. I took it to my room, seating myself on the window-seat, and began to thumb through the pages. For all my reluctance to delve into such matters, I was soon completely absorbed in the content, even though much of it was incomprehensible. Witchcraft was an interesting subject, seen purely from an academic viewpoint, and far more erotic than I had ever supposed.

I had not realised that it was a fertility cult, deriving much of its customs and rituals from the natural cycle of seed-time and harvest-time and from animal procreation. It was very much of the earth. I blinked my eyes as I reached one page, and my face felt suffused with colour so that I had to read again to make sure I had seen aright. For one of the ancient charges made against witches in the days where it was so feared and so rife was that they stole men's penises or rendered them useless. Rendered them useless, impotent.

Kirsty tried to find out for certain once . . . but the passion is all in his head and nowhere else. That was what Ian had said about Neil. Just what had she tried? I wondered. The possibility was too horrifying to contemplate. I had assumed at the time she had tried to seduce him, but suddenly I wondered if there was something infinitely more sinister behind that remark of Ian's.

I turned the pages of the book quickly, learning about meeting-places that did not have to be out in the open. Though the most popularly-accepted venue for a coven was a wooded glen or moonlit shore, for reasons of comfort a large parlour, draped in black with doors and windows tightly shuttered and lighted with wax candles, was often used for the weekly esbat or business meeting. I shivered, but I was compelled to read on now I had started. A sabbat was a more impressive occasion, I discovered, coinciding with feast days when covens joined together for homage or sacrifice, for renewing promises of fidelity to the devil by kissing him where he chose. And there were 'witch-mark' ceremonies for new initiates. I was chilled all over, and yet the fascination was so great that I could not deny it. Then I read that meetings should be beside water when possible, because of the perennially magical powers of water.

I love to be near the water, I had told Neil.

So had Katrina. And she had introduced those strange pictures into her room that was now Kirsty's, and the drawings with the peculiar symbols – they were all here in the book, the pentagons, the six-pointed star – the Magan David. She had clearly thirsted for knowledge the way I was doing now, and gone even farther. But how far? How far did one have to search before there was no turning back? How far had Katrina been involved – and Kirsty, who seemed to me to be trying to emulate her, I realised without needing to be told. Maybe that was one reason why she disliked me, because I had the likeness and she did not. To her I was Katrina all over again when it was what *she* wanted to be.

I snapped the book shut, my mind refusing to accept what everything around me was suggesting. Maybe Katrina had bewitched everyone around her – Neil, Robert, Grandfather, Kirsty – but only in the fanciful sense which made her an enchanting, captivating young woman. Not in the dark, evil sense from which the world recoiled. That was too monstrous to contemplate.

The glint of sunlight on the water of the loch drew my eyes outside. Pale sunlight now without the warmth of summer to enliven it, and the breeze that soughed through trees and rippled the dark water moaned and sighed as if mourning something lost for ever. I shivered again and got to my feet, having had quite enough of my own company for now. I needed to find someone to talk to, though after a moment's hesitation I left the book on my window-seat, knowing that when Agnes arrived she would want to peruse it too, and that probably reading it together would allow me to smile and see it all in a more harmless light. A horror shared was a horror halved. Someone had said something of the same to me quite recently, but for the moment I was unable to recall whose voice it was.

Kirsty and Aunt Morag had returned when I went downstairs. I was so relieved to see another living person I greeted them more warmly than usual.

'I've seen Agnes, and she is happy to accept my invitation to stay here,' I informed them. Kirsty's raised eyebrows said that who would not be happy to live in such a place? I ploughed on. 'I do hope we shall have some enjoyable times together, Kirsty. Agnes is such a darling. I'm sure you will like her when you get to know her properly.'

'I doubt it,' she snapped. 'I don't like to have my friends chosen for me, or strangers thrust upon me.'

I gaped at such rudeness, and even Aunt Morag could not let this go by. 'I think that was an unnecessary remark, Kirsty,' she told her daughter keenly. 'And deserving of an apology.'

For a minute I thought Kirsty was going to refuse, and I was going to be the unwitting cause of yet another hassle in the household. But my cousin shrugged her shoulders.

'Then I apologise,' she said coolly.

Her mother nodded, and swept out.

But I knew Kirsty's words were meaningless, almost insulting, because they implied it did not matter to her whether I believed them or not. I still could not understand why she hated me so much. It *was* hate. There was no mistaking it. I had done nothing at all to deserve it, and yet when I looked into her eyes it spat at me. Unless, unless it was Katrina at whom the hate was directed. The thought disturbed me greatly, but even more than that it angered me on my own account, because I was Charlotte and no one else. Nor ever had been, no matter how far back into history one delved. The thought sparked off a remembered curiosity.

'If you've nothing else to do, Kirsty.' I spoke just as coolly as if I had never noticed any insult. 'I would love to take a good look at the family tree and have it all explained to me.'

The dark eyes flashed. 'Trying to calculate just when Blackmaddie will be yours?'

'Not at all.'

'Good. Because it never will be. It cannot be claimed by a female, so if anyone came here with the idea of becoming an heiress, she had better think again,' Kirsty said spitefully.

I tried not to show my surprise at this piece of information, nor my anger at her insinuation. Instead, I countered it with a barb of my own. 'But any woman in the world could become its mistress through marriage,' I reminded her.

'Providing Blackmaddie wanted her.'

Kirsty's voice was soft, insidious, totally believing her own words and the power of Blackmaddie, as my father had done.

'Are you going to show me this family tree or aren't you?' I said irritably.

'All right.' Kirsty suddenly smiled more naturally. She was always pleased when she got me riled, and again I thought it a pity that we were never going to be friends. She was so much the perverse child, like some of those I had taught, so much in tune with Ian I knew she was going to miss him when he went away to university. I wondered how he would fare there, but had no doubt he would charm everyone as he did here.

Kirsty led the way to the huge collage of the family tree where it hung on the wall. At its head was the name of Maddie as I had expected, and fanned out below were strange medieval names that meant nothing to me. Maddie had been as procreative as her voluptuous looks had promised in the portrait. I had the same looks, and I scanned the various branches of the tree quickly, wondering why my curiosity had got the better of me. There was nothing here to understand. It was just a collection of old names out of history. I looked at the bottom, where there were more familiar ones: my grandfather and my dead grandmother, and below theirs, Uncle Andrew and my father. There was nothing beyond them.

'Intriguing, isn't it?' Kirsty's voice was right at my cheek. 'After those – who? After only one of them really, since your father's dead. My mother doesn't count, so she's not on it.'

There was a world of bitterness in her voice that worried me. I stared at the haphazard pattern of names, noting the absence of women, except in marriage, the necessary instruments for providing Blackmaddie with more sons. More sons . . . if Maddie had wanted men so much why had she wanted me? Unless it was that her spirit had so exalted in the likeness coming out in Katrina that when Katrina died she had brought someone else with the likeness, myself, a woman in her own image who was more acceptable to her than any other. I felt suddenly as if I was grappling with an unknown assailant, a loving, smothering assailant whose arms sought to hold me fast like clutching tentacles, and they were choking me, choking me.

'I don't want to see any more,' I said quickly. I was letting myself be carried away on flights of fancy again, and it wouldn't take much more to reduce me to a quivering jelly.

'They won't let Blackmaddie pass to a Stewart, you know,' Kirsty went on relentlessly. 'There are documents about it in trust with Grandfather's solicitor. Nobody's seen them except himself and Uncle Andrew, being the next to inherit. The documents are so old they'd probably crumble if they were handled too much. But it's all there and can't be refuted. It goes back farther than Culloden, back to Maddie herself. Perhaps it was a Stewart who rejected her – who knows? It's too far back in time to discover the truth of it. But none of them will own her – not Robert or Neil or Ian.'

Her voice stopped, and I knew she was hoping to see some violent reaction from me, and I purposely made my features blank, as if I were still absorbed in tracing back this family of mine. But in reality I was thinking it was unfair to the Stewart boys who had grown up here and looked on it as their home, and yet there was no chance of any of them ever becoming laird. Maddie, reaching out from whatever grisly grave she slumbered in, was controlling men's lives even now.

'So the only female who could be mistress of Blackmaddie would have to marry Grandfather or Uncle Andrew!' I had to say something to cover my bewildered thoughts, and I tried to sound amused. 'But if Maddie was so against men, why did she insist that the castle always went to one of them?'

I glanced at Kirsty. Her face was contorted. 'Who'd want to marry old men?' she snapped. 'They have nothing to offer a woman except decay. And Maddie wasn't against men, you fool. She worshipped them and lusted after them the way a man is supposed to lust after a woman. But because a man dared to reject her she decided never to let another woman have as much power as she had, or so the legend goes. She was so vain, so beautiful, having everything she wanted, except that one man, that she could not believe

160

it had happened. Despite her beauty, she could be hurt. I suppose she didn't want to think of any other woman owning her castle and having the love she couldn't keep for herself.'

Her voice shook with rage and she glared at me, as if I had forced her to say things that were private. But I had a right to know as well as she.

'Kirsty,' I said distinctly. 'There's no reason to hate me. I'm not Maddie. I'm not a threat to anybody.'

'You are. You *are*!'

She twisted away from me and ran through the old stone corridors until I could no longer hear her footsteps, leaving me shocked and disbelieving. She was deranged. She must be. I couldn't believe that she could be so vindictive unless her mind was disturbed. And she had certainly disturbed me. Of course I wasn't Maddie or Katrina or anybody but Charlotte Brodie, sewing-mistress and distant relative of the Brodies of Blackmaddie.

No, not so distant, I amended. A direct descendant of James Brodie, son of Malcolm. My eyes were drawn back to the family tree, moving upwards to all those Brodies and sons of Brodies. I would never want to own all this, any more than I wanted Blackmaddie to own me. In fact the knowledge that I never could gave me an odd sense of freedom. I gave an involuntary sigh and turned away from the family tree. I was sorry for Kirsty because I was certain her feelings were very different from mine on that score – and she could not even marry into the inheritance because the only two Brodie males were her grandfather and her uncle.

Somehow I could see neither one of them marrying again, even to secure the succession of the line. And yet it was always possible, I reasoned. Especially for Uncle Andrew. Not Grandfather, for even with his blustering ways and vociferous presence, his ardour was surely long since spent. But my uncle, though certainly not a young girl's ideal suitor, was not beyond marriage. Still capable of producing children.

My mind suddenly caught hold of a possibility so fantastic, so undesirable as to be almost immediately rejected. But it would not be pushed away from me.

Vinny's child. The ugly little red-haired baby she called Luke. The baby whose father's identity she guarded so jealously. I had assumed it must be one of the Stewart boys, with Robert the most likely candidate, as if to torture myself. But it was not beyond the realms of credibility that it was Uncle Andrew's child. He had the dark hair of the Brodies, though not so black as mine. Vinny was of light brown colouring with pale eyes. The two of them could easily mix to produce a red-haired child.

There was every opportunity. Even if the idea was so unlikely as to stretch the imagination to its limits, Uncle Andrew was still a commanding enough figure of a man, and presumably virile enough for a pretty girl to put a gleam in his eye. And Vinny was alluring and willing, as I knew only too well from her own admission. Willing and eager to lift her skirts, and if she had done so for Uncle Andrew and Luke was the result, it could only mean that the servant girl's baby was the natural heir to Blackmaddie.

12

It was a suspicion I knew I must keep to myself, too awful to share; degrading. In that moment I was no longer Miss Brodie, sewing-mistress of humble environment, but Charlotte Brodie of Blackmaddie, and if what I suspected was true, I knew I would hate and despise Uncle Andrew for the rest of my life for his weakness in putting Blackmaddie in the hands of a servant's baby. I did *not* know, of course, not for certain, but from that day on I could no longer feel the same attachment to little Luke, and I felt a shuddering whenever Vinny asked if I wanted to hold him. I told myself that he was only a child, an innocent child, no matter what his parentage, but it altered nothing. I avoided touching him as much as possible, and to try to put the idea of his fathering away from my mind.

Fortunately, there was the ceilidh at the Sinclairs' on Friday evening to take up my attention, and Kirsty and Ian were full of chatter about it. Perhaps I was feeling particularly vulnerable where Kirsty was concerned these days, but it seemed to me she was deliberately malicious towards me on every possible occasion, and no longer made any pretence at friendship except when the older members of the family were present. At dinner that evening she was busily deciding what she would wear.

'It will certainly be one of the gowns Charlotte altered for me,' she commented. 'You are so clever with your hands, Charlotte, I really am pleased with the result. You have a real talent for dressmaking.'

Her words were complimentary, but the intended slight was there, and I did not miss it if the others did. I lifted my head.

'I think I shall wear my red moire again, since everyone seemed to like it. Especially Robert, and it's a pity he's not here to see it again. I remember reading somewhere that red is the colour of desire. Had you heard that, Kirsty?'

I looked innocently across the dinner table, hoping no one was going to take offence at my remark. Kirsty's eyes glittered. She knew exactly what I meant by it. I was telling her that Robert had desired me and that his desires had been fulfilled, and when I wore the red moire again she and I would both remember it. Although she had never seemed particularly attached to Robert, and yet I could see it annoyed her to think he wanted me, she was jealous of another woman's attractiveness. *She* was like Maddie in that respect, I thought suddenly, not me.

Before she could put in any more little barbs I turned to my grandfather. 'May I please purchase some material to make myself a warm cloak, Grandfather? There is a place in the village that has all that I require.'

'Of course you can, lass, but why bother yourself with such jobs? Let someone else do it for you.' He dismissed the occupation as menial and I bristled at once.

'I choose to do it myself because I am an expert, and pride myself on getting a better result than anyone else can give me,' I said spiritedly. Grandfather laughed.

'Aye, you probably would at that, Charlotte Brodie,' he growled with sudden good-natured affection in his voice that pleased me ridiculously. 'I'd wager anything you did would be done to perfection and give excellent results. As you please then. Charge whatever you wish to my account.'

I thanked him, avoiding Ian's eyes that were full of mischief. He was like a cheeky imp at times, and I could guess what he was thinking when Grandfather said anything I did would be done to perfection. Robert had thought so too, and nothing that had happened since could change it.

'Did you see Agnes, Charlotte?' Neil said suddenly. 'Has she decided to stay in Scotland when her parents return to Bristol?'

'Yes she has.' I smiled at him, sensing that he strove not to appear too eager in his questioning. 'She will come here at the end of next week, if that is all right, Grandfather?'

'Oh aye, aye, whenever it suits.' He had already lost interest in me, and I could see he was anxious to get away from the dining-table and the women's talk. He and Uncle Andrew were in the middle of a lengthy and determined game of chess and both of them were eager to return to it.

For my part, I decided to have an early night. I was beginning to feel very tired. Last night's excitement – the thrill of Robert's loving and the events that followed – had kept my nerves taut and jumping. Then the unnatural sleep induced by the henbane had left me feeling dull-witted, and as soon as I could I left the others and went back to my room.

As soon as I entered, I knew something was different. It was a feeling more than anything, a feeling that someone had been here, touching my bed, moving the things on my dressing-table, perhaps looking in my closet and pressing strange hands over my clothes. For some inexplicable reason I felt unclean at the thought, and suddenly cold, and I hurried over to the windows to close them. I had a shock that almost made my heart stop as I looked out.

The mountains were obscured by thick cloud at their summits, and around the ground a soft grey mist swirled back and forth like a floating shroud. It covered the loch, and I felt the castle was suspended on a cloud. Father had warned me about the suddenness of the mist around Blackmaddie, colouring his tales with an eerie drop in his voice as he did so. I wished then that he had not been so eloquent in his descriptions, and yet those deliciously creepy tales had been less frightening than the reality. Then I had been able to snuggle down between the warm bedcovers with Father's gentle hand on my forehead soothing me to sleep, and Blackmaddie had only been a dream.

I turned away from the shrouded night to the comparative warmth of my room, and immediately my eyes were drawn to the book on the window-seat, the book I had slammed shut when its contents began to frighten me.

It was open now, its pages riffling slightly in the breeze from the windows where I had pulled them shut, as if ghostly fingers still turned them. It was closed when I left, I was positive of that. It could not have opened itself, so someone had been looking at it since I had. Someone else with an interest in witchcraft. I felt the pounding in my heart, the clutch of unease. My cousins had been downstairs for dinner, but either of the boys could have come in here while I was with Kirsty. Neil or Ian. I licked my dry lips, trying to tell myself it meant nothing. If I had an interest, why shouldn't someone else? It could have been anyone, not necessarily the boys. One of the other members of the family; one of the servants. I picked up the book mechanically. It was open at a section I had not read. It dealt with sacrifice – and babies. The skin crawled on the back of my neck.

A baby for a sacrifice. That was what it said. The idea was so ghoulish as to make the bile rise in my mouth. An unbaptised child, being outside Christian help, often a stillborn child of a witch, otherwise stolen from a grave. Or even a living child if there was no other readily available. And, I felt my stomach turn, they were sometimes eaten. Oh God! My horrified eyes would not move away from the page. I was compelled to read on as if some devil made me. This last was for very special magic, more often the sacrifice – animal or child – was consumed by fire and the ashes sprinkled over land or water. A fertility charm: ashes returning to the earth so that the spirit could rise again. The cycle repeated. Indestructible. Oh God, oh God! It was *horrible*.

I heard a small movement outside. I ran across and wrenched open the door. Vinny was just coming out of Kirsty's room, where she had presumably had some domestic task to perform. I almost pulled her inside my room and pointed to the book with trembling hands.

'Have you seen this, Vinny?'

'It's a book, Miss,' she said wonderingly.

'I know it's a book. Have you been reading it?'

'I can't read, Miss.'

I stared at her. Of course she wouldn't be able to read. She was a simple village girl who would have had no education. But she could have been curious about the pictures in the book, some of which were very erotic.

'Have you been looking through it though? Opening the pages?' I almost begged her to admit it. She shook her head vehemently.

'No, Miss.' She began to sound affronted. 'What would I want with books? I learned all I need to know without book-reading.'

And mostly on her back, I thought instantly. My thoughts veered off in another direction.

'Vinny, have you ever had Luke baptised?'

Her face suddenly paled and she flinched away from me. 'No, Miss,' she said sullenly. 'And if there's nothing else I can do for ye, I'd best be getting back downstairs or Cook will be yelling for me again. There's all the clearing away to be done from dinner yet.'

She was edging away from me all the time she was talking. I wanted to urge her to get Luke baptised because of the new fear that was filling me, instilled by the book I held in my hand. Maybe I was being irrational, imagining that there was witchcraft at Blackmaddie, with no evidence other than a feeling deep inside me that something evil was all around, that it was still rife and throbbing with life, perhaps touching people who were close. But it was a feeling I could not dismiss.

I had to let Vinny go without pressing her any more about Luke. I could guess the reason for her sharp reaction to my question about having the baby baptised, and for the odd look of fear in her eyes. She would doubtless be required to give the father's name to the minister. And Vinny might easily be put under pressure to produce him at the ceremony. Which of the Blackmaddie men would be willing to stand beside a servant girl in the kirk and declare that her bastard was his child? Every one of them was too proud for that.

I was far less sleepy now than when I had first come upstairs, and although Vinny had denied it, I decided she was the one who had opened the book. She had probably been too ashamed to admit that she had been looking at the pictures. I locked my door securely, undressed and got into bed, trying not to remember that it was only last night that I had lain here in the red moire dress, waiting for Robert, waiting for my life to begin, knowing he'd come to me. Then seeing him naked and magnificent in the moonlight as if this had all been predestined, touching and holding and feeling him, wanting him, the way I did now, with the spreading ache in my loins I was beginning to know so well. I sighed, picked up the book and began to turn the pages to glance at the pictures myself before I went to sleep, avoiding the text as much as possible.

Such pictures! I had never seen their like before. Orgy pictures. Naked men and women in all attitudes of copulation, some so tortuous that the expressions on the faces looked more agonised than ecstatic. But I had not expected to find them so exciting. They sent little quivers of pleasure running through me until I ached for Robert to come to me and bring me fulfilment as he had done last night. But he was far away by now, probably making polite conversation in some respectable drawing-room and never giving a thought to me, never dreaming that among the mist-shrouded mountains at Blackmaddie a woman ached with desire for him as she dropped the book to the floor, blew out her candle and turned face-down on her cool pillow, wishing passionately her body held him captive beneath her again.

Next morning I hid the book in my closet. I was somewhat ashamed of the effect such an inanimate object had had on me and determined not to give Vinny the chance to look at it again. Agnes and I would peruse it some time perhaps. I wondered if Agnes had ever had a lover. I thought not; she was like a beautiful golden flower, untouched by any bee as yet, but infinitely ripe for the plucking.

It was the day of the Sinclairs' ceilidh. Kirsty and I spent the afternoon having our hair put in curling rags and resting. She was going to wear the cream shot gown I had altered. I would definitely wear the red moire, not only because I had sweet memories of it, but because it was the only gown suitable. When I went to the village for some warm woollen cloth for my cloak I would purchase some silk for several new gowns as well. Grandfather had told me to charge whatever I wanted to his account, so I would do so. Agnes and I could make an excursion to the village once she came to stay. My spirits lifted at the thought just as the mist and cloud lifted outside. The weather was on the turn but it was not winter yet. There were still mellow days ahead.

Kirsty came into my room to ask me to fasten the back of her gown. It fitted her to perfection now, and I felt a glow of pride knowing I had improved the style considerably. She preened herself in my mirror.

'You'll be able to meet Helen Sinclair tonight.' Her eyes watched me in the mirror, and I hoped I did not betray how my heart jolted. Robert was very fond of Helen Sinclair, Kirsty had not been slow to tell me.

'And the others,' I said steadily. 'There are others in the family, I believe?'

Kirsty's eyes lost their sharp watchfulness and she teased the dark tendrils of hair to frame her face.

'Oh yes. There are five of them. Helen, her two sisters, Isabel and Mairi, and the boys, Jimmy and Alex. They're a lively crowd.'

'Parents too?' I asked. For once Kirsty's voice was fairly normal without the usual bitchiness, and I thought how different she could be when she wasn't seeing me as a rival.

'One parent. Mrs Sinclair died last year. But there's a grandmother, also Mrs Sinclair. She's a grand wee lady for her years, and she'll be dancing into the small hours with the best of them.'

Her eyes were suddenly shining and I could see how much she was looking forward to the evening. So was I – except for a natural nervousness at meeting another set of strangers. I wished Robert was going to be there. Or perhaps I didn't, if I had to watch him being sweet and attentive to Helen Sinclair all evening. I recognised a searing jealousy that flooded through me whenever I thought of him with any-body else. A jealousy that was possessive and unfeminine maybe, but I just couldn't stop it. It was agonising to think of him wanting anyone else now I had had him for myself and known the sweetness of his love. And for all that he had hurt me beyond measure when he had called me Katrina, the pain of it was already diminishing a little. In its place there was the determination to make him love me for myself. To have him back with me again on any terms, belonging to me, for I knew I couldn't live without him.

'Are you ready?' I said quickly to Kirsty in case my mouth had softened and my cheeks reddened, and the tell-tale glow of remembered passion shone in my eyes.

Grandfather had decided to accompany us to the Sinclairs as well as my aunt and uncle, so there were two carriages that left Blackmaddie that evening, with all the younger people in one and the elders in the other. Kirsty was in a sparkling mood, considering this occasion was almost like a farewell party for Ian, since he would be leaving for Edinburgh on Monday, and I knew she did not relish the thought. I hoped that she would not be plunged into gloom and despondency after he left, making me bear the brunt of her waspish remarks. I brushed aside the thought, for tonight I was going to enjoy her unaccustomed cheerfulness.

It was a fairly long drive to the Sinclairs, through striking scenery that was clearly well-known and commonplace to the others, but which almost took my breath away as we rode through a deep glen guarded at either side by lofty mountains that soared away into the night. The light of the moon gave strange life and form to shadows and crags and tree-stumps. It would have been frightening to be here alone, but with my cousins to accompany me, I could marvel at the picture nature had painted for our delight.

Ian too was in great form tonight, but Neil was dreaming in his usual way. Perhaps not so much of his poetry as of Agnes, I thought, catching a gleam in his eye at times that was more alive than haunted. I did not think this ceilidh was altogether to his liking, but perhaps next time anything of this nature happened, Agnes would be coming with us, and that should put the smile back on his face.

I wished again that Robert were here. I couldn't help the feeling of being shut out. Kirsty and Ian had so much of their past to share and were a complete unit in themselves, like two happy children who needed no other playmate. Neil had his thoughts. But I – I needed Robert.

'Look, Charlotte, there's the Sinclair house, over there, among the trees.' I looked to where Ian was pointing, and saw a sprawling stone building, well-lighted with lamps and candles, and felt a surge of nervousness. How many other strangers would be there I had no idea, but I was suddenly very conscious of being the outsider again. The English girl, attending an occasion among strangers that was essentially Scottish. The fact that I was part of the Brodie family meant nothing at all at that moment, and I wished I was anywhere but here as the carriages drew up at the front of the house, where the door was open wide in welcome. Kirsty and Ian alighted eagerly. As I started to rise, Neil's hand closed over mine.

'Don't worry, Charlotte. None of them can match you here tonight. And as Robert is not here, I shall take charge of you. Perhaps we can both make believe a little, eh?'

His smile was genuine and warm, and I wasn't sure whether he guessed how I felt about his brother, or if he merely meant that as the second brother he was taking on his family duty in looking after a stranger. I knew that he was happy to be with me because I was a link with Agnes. I smiled back at him gratefully, and he helped me out of the carriage.

The others had already gone inside and we followed. The house seemed to be full of people. I had not expected there to be so many. Names were told to me that I would instantly forget, and compliments flowed as I was handed from one person to another with the briefest of hand-shakes. Formality was not the order of the day at a ceilidh, Neil informed me. It was a festive evening, and there would be eating and drinking and entertainment and dancing and the skirl of the pipes.

I had never in my life heard the pipes, I realised suddenly, and it seemed such an admission to make in the company here that I kept it to myself. The Sinclair house was not as splendid as Blackmaddie, but neither was it such an austere place. It was lavishly furnished and carpeted, with great jungle-like areas of plants which the Sinclair family clearly liked very much. The air was quite oppressive with the

171

scent of them, but it wasn't unpleasant, and mingling with the candles and the oil from so many lamps it seemed to create a very mellow atmosphere. The whole place seemed to dazzle with light and colour, from the elegant gowns of the ladies that were like a summer garden of colour, to the splendid attire of the men. Every one wearing the kilt and dark velvet jacket atop a shirt so white it was almost startling. There was never such a splendid sight as a company of Scotsmen, I thought, and if Robert were here he would be the most magnificent of them all.

'Charlotte, you must come and meet Helen.' Kirsty's voice rang out right behind me as I was commenting to a lady whose name I couldn't even pronounce about how awe-inspiring I found the mountain scenery. I felt my heart give a lurch, hardly able to refuse to turn round, and yet I did not want to face someone of whom Robert was very fond. But I had to, of course.

And then I stared in disbelief, aware that Kirsty was smiling gloatingly behind Helen's head, perfectly aware that she had been putting the wrong idea in my mind all this time. Because Helen Sinclair was only a child. She was about twelve years old, dark and vivacious, and she would one day be beautiful, but right now she represented no more threat to me as a woman than any one of the children I had taught in Bristol.

'I told Kirsty to bring you to see us before now, Charlotte.' Helen was pouting with the unconscious provocativeness of children. 'I've never heard anybody speak English before. Not real English with that funny accent that sounds as if they've got a plum in their cheek. Say something, won't you?'

She would have been extraordinarily rude if she had not had such unconscious charm, but instead of being affronted I burst out laughing.

'I'm afraid not everyone has that kind of accent, Helen,' I told her with a twinkle in my eye. 'I used to live in Bristol, and I suppose if I have any accent it is more of a West Country one.'

'Oh, you do have an accent.' Helen's eyes were sparkling.

172

'It's funny, but it's nice, isn't it, Kirsty? Does Robert like it? I bet he does. He's met English people before when he's been on his visits to his mother's family as they live quite near the Border! It's not fair that he couldn't be here tonight. He always dances with me when a lot of the other young men think I'm too young, and he never minds when I insist on playing party games as well as just silly old dancing.'

'I'll dance with you, Helen,' Neil put in.

'Will you really? But you don't like dancing! Oh well, never mind, if you step on my feet I shall just have to give you lessons, Neil.'

She was like quicksilver, artlessly darting from one thought to another and enchanting everyone around her. No wonder Robert was fond of her, I thought indulgently. It was very easy to be charmed by such an elfin child. And apparently Neil was being more outgoing than usual at one of these affairs. I hoped it was on my account – or rather, Agnes'. Whatever the reason, he was a delight to be with, and Helen had recognised it at once. The fact that we all got along so well, Helen, Neil and I, seemed to annoy Kirsty. Perhaps it was usually she and Ian who commanded most attention. I could well imagine it was so, but tonight Neil and I were beginning to enjoy ourselves. It was a lovely feeling to think I was accepted here and that people smiled at me and knew who I was, and enquired after my health and seemed to be anxious for my well-being. If Kirsty was chagrined about my success, I ignored it. I had no intention of living in her shadow at Blackmaddie, and she had better recognise it.

The other young Sinclairs were a friendly crowd too. The girls, Isabel and Mairi, were much less exuberant than Helen. They were in their mid-teens and more aware of themselves as adolescents. The boys, Jimmy and Alex, were fine young men with whom I danced frequently; there always seemed to be a young man at my side, which I could see was also annoying Kirsty. The red moire, I thought, wondering if she had the same idea in her head, the colour of desire. Whatever the truth in that, it certainly had the effect of keeping my spirits high that night.

When the entertainment began I was further absorbed,

remembering that my father would have watched similar occasions many times in his youth. It was beyond nostalgia, it must be in my blood, I thought, for I had seen nothing to resemble sword dances with kilts flying, or reels so intricate they left me gasping, and the lone piper standing proudly aloof playing haunting, plaintive airs to a hushed audience brought a lump to my throat and made me want to cry. I had never expected it to be so beautifully evocative of a proud race, a bloody past and a passionate nature. I wanted Robert there to share these moment with me, and I willed my thoughts to reach out and touch him, wherever he was at this moment.

I gave a long-drawn-out sigh as the piper ended, too emotional to join in the applause. The Sinclair boys were at my shoulder, urging me to come and have some hot punch to get the blood singing in my veins for some more dancing.

'I have had too much already,' I protested laughingly. 'Something to eat might be better for my digestion, I think. I do not care for my head to swim too much.'

It was doing so already, and the colourful gowns of the ladies were beginning to kaleidoscope together in front of my eyes. I did not want to disgrace myself in this company, and Neil took my arm and said we had better make our way to the dining-room, where the food was all laid out for whenever it was required. I was grateful to him for being so solicitous towards me.

'I have not seen Grandfather for ages,' I commented.

'He'll not be where the dancing is,' Neil smiled at me. 'He and the older men will be getting their heads together in the Sinclair study and putting the world to rights. It's their favourite pastime, and I'll wager Grandfather will be lairding it over them all as usual.'

Helen and her sisters were already loading their plates with food when we arrived.

'Hurry up and eat, Charlotte, for we are having party games soon,' Helen said in a shrill excited voice. The young men around us groaned in an exaggerated manner, but I could see that it was done purposely, and that this young

174

lady was quite used to having her own way and even delighted in the mock grumblings of the guests. I was not used to party games, except on very rare occasions at school, and was not sure I wanted to make an exhibition of myself, but there was no arguing with Helen, and eventually we all crowded back into the big hall where her father and brothers were trying to keep order among the merriment.

It wasn't too bad, I admitted later. In fact, it was a great deal of fun to join in guessing games and hunt-the-thimble and Helen's favourite game of charades. Some of the miming was so awful the participants almost collapsed with laughter in the process.

'The next game is one of Helen's own making,' Mr Sinclair announced and there were loud groans again, to which the child responded with delighted squeals.

'At least, that's what she says,' her father smiled indulgently. 'It sounds very much like blind man's bluff to me! Anyway, we're to have a lot of the candles blown out . . . '

'All of them! All of them!' Helen insisted.

'All right, all of them. Someone is blindfolded and wanders among the rest of you, trying to find someone to replace him as seeker. The seeker asks the person to speak as soon as he touches him, and that person can disguise his voice, but if guessed correctly he must take over as seeker. The difference is that everyone has to be blindfolded in this game, so I don't think it had better last too long or there'll be no ornaments left in the house. All those willing and foolish enough to participate are to come along to the green drawing-room, where there's less likelihood of accidents.'

It sounded a bit hazardous to me, and I'd have willingly declined, especially if I became seeker, for I would know few people to identify by their voices. But Kirsty was pulling me with her and telling me it would be easy enough as only the younger guests would join in, and I'd met most of them during the evening. So amid the general laughter I let myself be propelled along to the green drawing-room, where the blindfolds were being handed out. Wearing one with no candles lit, it certainly would be blind man's bluff, I

175

thought, and I took a good look around the room before I tied the blindfold around my eyes.

It was a large room of uneven shape. There were pillars here and there and several windows with balconies outside. The windows were floor-length and open, because the number of people in the house had made it very stuffy. I noted their positions carefully before the general laughter and baiting began and Helen crept about the room as seeker.

It seemed a silly game, because everyone kept blundering into one another, and I suspected some of the young men and girls were taking advantage of the darkness for sport of their own, from the giggling that came from various parts of the room. In any case, they all indulged Helen, and I could hear the shouts of laughter when someone was identified and a new seeker prowled the room. It was a weird feeling, stealthily moving about with arms outstretched, wondering when one would encounter another human hand doing the same thing, and it was easy to become completely disorientated in the darkness. I usually knew when I was near the windows, though, because of the welcome freshness of the cool night air after the cloying scents of mingled perfume and human bodies and snuffed candles.

Suddenly a hand touched my outstretched fingers. My heartbeats quickened as I tried to join in the spirit of the game. After all it was harmless. The fingers left my own and reached down over my shoulders while the laughter gurgled up in my throat. I didn't think this was part of the game, but perhaps it was someone who was stumbling about and needing support. The hands moved down, circling my breasts, and I caught my breath in my throat as I moved away backwards. But the hands pressed me and their owner followed my movements.

'Is that you, Charlotte Brodie?' a hoarse, disguised voice said, very close to my face. I felt the smile on my lips. The seeker wasn't supposed to disguise his voice, I thought, only the person who was caught. But one of the rules of the game was that you admitted your identity when you were captured and called by name.

'Yes it is,' I began reluctantly, and lifted my hand to remove my blindfold and become the seeker. But before I could do so the hands started pushing me more violently so that I staggered backwards, and then I felt something hard against my back and I was being pushed against it. The hands were fastening around my neck, tightening just enough to stop me from screaming while trying to make me lose my balance and fall. I realised I had my back to the railings of the balcony outside the green drawing-room, and there was a drop of about sixty feet below to stone steps. If I fell I would be killed or end up with terrible injuries. I struggled with my unknown assailant with every bit of strength that was in me, while my senses were reeling and I felt as if the breath was being choked out of me.

Suddenly I managed to bring my knee up into the person's groin and lunged forward. He grunted furiously and swore under his breath, but he relaxed his hold for an instant, and it was enough for me to wriggle away from those clutching hands and tear the blindfold from my eyes as I moved swiftly back into the room. I was gasping and almost sobbing with fear and relief that I had not gone over the balcony, but the room was dim and the rest of the guests were blundering about in their blindfolds with arms outstretched, filling in the distance between me and the window, so that I could not tell which one of them had attacked me.

I leaned against a wall to stop my wild heartbeats, trying not to scream out loud in panic. Perhaps it had all been accidental, and someone had really been trying to save me, thinking I was falling. I was a little muzzy with the punch, and it could have been that I had lurched too far over the balcony. I touched my fingers to my throat. It was sore, but not so sore as to be very bruised, I fancied. Was that done by design so that there would be little proof that I had not fallen by accident? But who would want to kill *me*?

The idea was horrifying, and yet the longer I stood there, recovering my breath and my composure, the less likely it became. I must have imagined it, despite the tenderness of my throat and the pressure of those hands pushing me. Everything in me wanted to believe it was a mistake on my part. I didn't want to throw this evening into utter confusion and ruin the Sinclairs' ceilidh by demanding they stop the music in the great hall and the general merriment and start an investigation.

By the time Mr Sinclair and some of the older men arrived in the green drawing-room with lighted candles and smiling faces and announced that the young people had been on their own long enough and we were to re-join the others, I had convinced myself that I had got carried away with the general pushing and shoving, of which there had been a great deal, and that nothing had happened which could not be explained away in general boisterousness. It was a long time later that I remembered the hoarse, disguised voice that asked if I was Charlotte Brodie and that I had told my assailant exactly what he wanted to know.

13

Everyone slept late the next morning. I hardly remembered the journey back to Blackmaddie, for I was dozing in the carriage with my head against Neil's shoulder. Kirsty and Ian seemed to have talked themselves out, and sat silently on the other side of the carriage, to my relief, for I could not have listened to any more chatter that night. I climbed out of my clothes half in a daze and left them on my chair for Vinny to put away when she came to attend me in the morning. I remembered to lock my door, then knew nothing more until I heard her calling me. I struggled to open my eyes and stumbled across to the door and opened it, and staggered immediately back to bed.

'Well, I'd say there was someone here who had a good time last night.' Her saucy voice held a smile. She had brought me some water to wash and put it on the marble stand, then stood scrutinising me. Suddenly her mouth twitched. I groaned, hardly awake, and not really ready to listen to any of her arch comments this morning. 'I'd say you had a *very* good time, Miss, if the evidence on ycr neck is anything to go by. I didna think the respectable Sinclairs went in for that kind of party. Was it someone very handsome, and will ye be seeing him again? I'll wager ye are, after that amount of attention. He must have been fair taken with ye, but I dinna doubt it in that red dress.'

'Vinny, what on earth are you going on about?' I grumbled sleepily, wishing her prattling voice would stop and that she would not stand by my bed with arms folded under her huge breasts in that way, expecting me to share some sort of confidence with her. She had a lascivious gleam in her eyes, and she was not in the least put out by my apparent disinclination to talk. Instead she went over to the dressing-table and brought a hand-mirror for me to look into. I flinched at the sight of my tumbled hair and sleep-filled eyes, but then I looked lower, to where the marks of someone's fingers on my throat were visible if anyone cared to look for them. Not so visible as to look like ugly weals though, and Vinny could be mistaken for thinking someone had held me ardently in his arms and given me a series of love-bites all round my neck, for that was exactly how it looked. I shuddered, knowing the truth of it, that I hadn't been mistaken last night. Someone *had* been trying to kill me.

I touched my fingers carefully to the marks on my throat, reliving the horror of those silent moments when I had been unable to see or speak. My throat constricted, remembering how the hands had first circled my breasts, as if determined to have his moment of pleasure before disposing of me.

'Was he good, Miss?' Vinny's voice was thick with excitement as she watched my face and mistook my emotion for something else.

I pushed the mirror away from me, knowing I couldn't tell her the real cause of the marks or it would be all around the castle in no time, and it was too late to try to denounce somebody for suspected murder. Who would believe me now? I should have done it last night, not now, when everyone would think, as Vinny had, that I had had a lover and was covering up the reason for the bruises by some ludicrous tale. I could have wept, seeing the foolishness of my action in not coming forward, for if there was a dangerous man about, he should be apprehended as soon as possible, and I had done nothing to stop him acting again. And to add to it all, I had this stupid, simpering servant girl leering at me and expecting me to tell her of some young man's amorous attentions.

'Mind your own business, Vinny,' I told her haughtily, and she could make what she liked of that remark.

She chose to be offended, and clattered about the room without another word, banging things about in a way that rocked my delicate nerves, until I had to beg her to be quieter for my head ached shockingly.

'I'd best leave ye then, Miss,' she said sulkily. 'Luke's needing a feed anyway, and he's not one who likes to be kept waiting. He's like all the men, greedy for the tit.'

She marched out, her words as forthright as always, but instead of making me smile they somehow sickened me. I really was in a delicate state of health, I realised, and the thought of that ugly little baby, noisily guzzling away at the great exposed breast of Vinny's, as if he was trying to devour her, made me shudder, and I buried myself back beneath the bedcovers. I was not ready to face the morning yet.

Aunt Morag was the next to arrive at my room, telling me shortly that if I wanted breakfast I had better come down soon or it would all be cleared away. I could see that I was not the only one in poor spirits, and answered that I would come down right away, being careful not to raise my head too far above the pillow for fear of her seeing the bruises on my neck. I washed and dressed as quickly as my throbbing head would allow, putting on a high-necked blouse and woollen skirt. Fortunately most of my clothes were high-necked, so I should be able to cover my neck and throat until the bruises faded. I hoped it would be soon, for every time I looked at them in the mirror it would be a reminder of how they had got there.

Uncle Andrew was the only person still in the dining-room. He asked me how I had enjoyed the Sinclairs' hospitality last night, and I told him it had been a most unusual evening. *More unusual than anyone of my family could guess*, I added silently. Or did one of them know all too well what had happened to me? I paused with my hand over the big porridge spoon as I helped myself to breakfast. Someone had tried to kill me, but I had not thought to ask myself why. Who could hate me that much, and for what reason? I knew none of those people at the Sinclairs' last night – none except my own family. It was a frightening and repugnant thought that one of them could have designs on my life, and one that I tried to dismiss at once, for how could I stay here in constant fear for my safety? I could hear the sound of my own heartbeats, loud in my ears.

'I said, what was your impression of our dancing, Charlotte? Are you quite awake this morning, my dear?' Uncle Andrew repeated patiently.

'Oh – I'm sorry, my mind was wandering, Uncle! I enjoyed all the entertainment very much indeed.' I could at least put some enthusiasm into my voice on that account. 'And the piper too – it was so beautiful – I had no idea it would sound like that.'

'Aye, to a true Scot there's nothing so fine.' He was well pleased at my response, and after draining his cup he asked me to excuse him as he had business to attend to. 'I'd suggest you get some fresh air, lass, for you're looking a mite pale this morning. The head not as strong as the grape, mebbe?'

I smilingly agreed with him. He could be very pleasant to me when he chose, and considering that I resembled Katrina so closely, he might very well have resented the very fact of my being alive when his only daughter was dead.

The moment the thought spun into my mind, I could feel the dryness in my mouth, but why could it not have been Uncle Andrew last night? Who was to know the identity of anyone in the green drawing-room, once the candles were snuffed and the blindfolds on? Anyone from outside could have come in on a pretext of his own. My uncle's mind could easily have been twisted since the shock of Katrina's death and then seeing me, so like her . . . he had never shown any such shock, but that signified nothing. A man with murder on his mind had to be of a devious nature.

I stood up jerkily from the breakfast table. I must be wrong, of course, and the vivid imagination with which I was cursed was leaping ahead of me. I willed it to be quiet, but the inside of the castle was beginning to oppress me, and I had to get outside. At least that suggestion of Uncle Andrew's was a sensible one. I needed space and fresh air to clear my head and to try to think things out more logically. I sped back to my room to fetch a shawl, glad I saw no one on my way. I did not want to talk to anyone.

Once outside, I left the grounds and struck out for the wooded copse where I had first encountered Neil. It was cool and shady among the trees and my feet made no noise on the soft damp carpet of leaves. I had to think, and the members of my family were uppermost in my mind. If what I suspected was true, one of them had grasped me round the throat last night and tried to push me over the balcony at the Sinclairs'. I fought against rising panic, against the incredibility of such a situation, and tried to detach myself from too personal a view, trying to see it all as if through a professional investigator's eyes.

There was Grandfather; I could surely dismiss him from suspicion, for he had brought me to Blackmaddie, and I could not believe he would willingly hurt a Brodie for any reason at all. Uncle Andrew; I glossed over his name in my mind. I was too uneasy to consider him further for the moment. Aunt Morag? She was kind enough in her own way, and I could think of nothing I had done to annoy her, let alone instil hate in her sufficient to want me dead! I shook my head. Surely not Aunt Morag.

That left my three cousins: Kirsty, Ian and Neil. I thought of Neil first. No – not Neil. Complex and creative and temperamental – passionate and emotional too, as I knew him to be – But not a murderer. Besides, he wanted me at Blackmaddie, if only for the reason that if I was not here, Agnes would not come either, and I believed them to be half in love with each other already. I was positive it had not been Neil's hands round my throat last night.

Ian I dismissed almost at once. Impish, wickedly childish at times, but with an open nature that surely had no dark side to it. I would never believe it of Ian. So that left Kirsty.

She certainly did not like me, nor did she want me here. She was put out by the attentions I received from young men when she wanted them for herself and made it obvious to me, if to no one else. But she was a young girl, and surely those were the hands of a man last night? And the voice of a man? I could not be sure. A husky voice, heavy with disguise could have been either, and the hands of a killer could surely gain strength at the moment of attack whether they belonged to a man or a woman. I had thrust my knee into the assailant's groin – but I still could not have told whether it was a man or woman.

Uncle Andrew seemed to be the most likely. And yet it

was preposterous. My father's brother – a man who had shown me bluff kindliness since my arrival – no, it had to be someone else. Perhaps this was another of the Sinclair party tricks, and I had unwittingly spoiled it by not going screaming out of the green dining-room in a fright. I forced myself to believe that it had merely been a childish prank after all, for anything was preferable to believing that someone at Blackmaddie was trying to harm me.

But whoever that person might have been, it could not have been Robert. The realisation flooded into my mind like the warmth of the noonday sun.

A sudden movement away to the right of me stopped my silent footsteps and I stood quite still. Was Neil suddenly going to appear in front of me again as he had that other time? There was a crackling of twigs and a thin, plaintive cry of a bird as it flew skywards out of a tree, and my heart settled down again. But there was something else too. Voices speaking very low in a mumbling monotone I couldn't quite hear. I didn't want to hear them anyway, because I would be eavesdropping if I continued standing perfectly still. I turned swiftly and walked back the way I had come. It was only later that I realised the mumbling monotone was vividly reminiscent of the clamouring voices I felt rather than heard through the stonework of my room.

At least my head was clearing. I decided not to wait for Agnes to come to Blackmaddie, but to go down to the village that afternoon to purchase some woollen cloth for a cloak. Autumn was chilling the air, and I needed warmer garments. Besides, I needed something to do *now*, to stop my thoughts taking me into the realms of nightmare. I had been so late getting up that morning it was nearing time for luncheon when I returned to the castle, and as I had eaten hardly anything, I was feeling quite ravenous. I hurried back to my room to leave my shawl and to freshen my face and hands. Inside my room I stopped quite still, disbelieving and horrified.

The red moire dress lay across my bed, though I distinctly remembered Vinny hanging it up that morning. Someone had hacked it to shreds, and it lay like streaks of blood on the white fabric of the bedcover. My chest was tight with the pain of holding my breath and my fingers dug into my palms where I clenched them together. It was such a senseless, cruel thing to do, but instead of making me afraid, as someone had probably had in mind, anger was boiling up inside me.

Someone was trying very badly to unnerve me. If they had wanted to kill me, surely they could have done it last night instead of half-heartedly pressing my throat. There had been ample opportunities. Uncle Andrew could have cut my dress, I thought suddenly. He had suggested I had some fresh air. Or Kirsty, for I had taunted her about red being the colour of desire. Even Vinny, affronted because I had snubbed her that morning. Someone wanted to make me so afraid of staying I would leave. But weren't they forgetting that Blackmaddie wanted me? I was a true daughter of Blackmaddie, and she would protect me. They would not get the better of me, nor would I say anything about the red moire. I would let whoever had done this be as puzzled and agitated as he or she thought they had me, by keeping perfectly quiet about it. And that afternoon I would buy as much red fabric as I could find in the village. I would make not one, but two, three, four new dresses in as brilliant a colour as I could, and as quickly as I could, and flaunt myself in them in defiance of whatever devious tricks were being hatched up against me.

I bundled the red moire dress together and stuffed it in the back of my clothes closet. When I went downstairs to luncheon I purposely mentioned that I had just come from my room, to watch the reactions of the others seated round the dining-table, hoping to find a tell-tale flush on someone's face; but the faces were as blank as if I had not spoken at all.

'I am going to the village this afternoon, Kirsty,' I said at once. 'To look for some material for a cloak and some new dresses. Do you want to come as well? Maybe there's something you need as well.'

'No, thank you,' she said. Was her voice more clipped than usual? I looked at Ian.

'I thought I'd make another red dress, since my other one wa₋ so well admired.'

'A good idea,' he said enthusiastically. 'Robert will be pleased to hear it, I'm sure. I shall look forward to seeing it when I come back from university in a few weeks' time. I don't intend being incarcerated there any longer at a stretch than needs be. I shall be back for All Hallows.'

Not a response that led me to think he had cut the red moire so savagely. He and Kirsty were chattering again and leaving me out in the cold, and I shrugged. No one else seemed to be taking the slightest notice of my remarks, and I surmised that they were all feeling a little liverish after the festivities of last night, as I was myself.

'You'd best ask Duncan to accompany you to the village, Charlotte,' my grandfather said suddenly. 'There's plenty strange folk about at this time of year with all the rowdies flocking in for the fair and the games.'

'What's all this, then?' I felt a stirring of excitement. Kirsty echoed it as she glanced at me and answered my question.

'The annual fair up on the waste land above the village. It's always held in the last week of October, just before All Hallows. The idea is that people are so full of merrymaking by then, they don't notice anything weird happening when all the witches are abroad. They're too full of smugglers' brandy and moonshine whisky.'

'I'll have no talk of witches at this table,' Grandfather suddenly roared out. 'You know well my feelings on that subject, Kirsty, and ye'll respect my wishes or have your meals sent to your room. Is it understood?'

I gaped in amazement. He really was the most volatile man; it had appeared to me to be just a harmless remark. I was suddenly sorry for Kirsty at that moment, sitting red-faced and humiliated in front of the rest of the family. But I knew better than to interfere and I held my tongue as she acquiesced sullenly.

'Tell me more about the fair,' I urged her instead. But she shrugged her shoulders and muttered that she wasn't in the mood for chattering, since every word was likely to be taken as having an ulterior meaning. 'You can find out about it from anybody.'

I was exasperated. I wanted to find out about it here and now. My interest had been captured, and Kirsty was glaring at her plate as if at a dish of poison. I turned to Neil.

'You'll tell me, won't you, Neil?'

'It's the usual kind of thing,' he said carelessly. 'Stalls set up for a week with the most terrible trash for sale. Fortune tellers who couldn't foresee the afternoon's weather if a storm cloud hung over their tents. Animals for sale – some so obviously caught wild or stolen it's an outrage that they appear at all, but it's a week when everybody is slightly moon-drunk, and folk get away with murder.'

I wished he hadn't used those exact words, but the excitement was too much for me to worry unduly.

'And the games? What are those?'

'That's the best part,' Grandfather put in indulgently, since I seemed to be showing so much curiosity, 'when the young men show their strength with the caber and the weights. Robert will be showing his skills I daresay. He usually takes off a prize or two.'

I felt a swell of pride at hearing his name. My beautiful, magnificent Robert with the strength of ten men and yet all the tenderness of a kitten.

'And you as well?' I asked Ian and Neil. Ian guffawed.

'Not me. Not the heavyweight stuff anyway. I usually enter for the running as I'm pretty swift on my feet. But our Neil would rather sit and compose a poem to the swinging motion of the kilts, wouldn't you, brother?'

'We all have our own talents,' Neil said evenly. 'I prefer to watch everybody else displaying their muscles and showing off, but never fear that I lack them, brother.'

The tension between the two of them was unmistakable. Ian made it perfectly plain that he despised Neil for his womanly occupation of sitting and dreaming while he composed his verses, violent though those verses emerged, and Neil resented Ian's attitude. But there was nothing womanly about Neil's temper or his physique, and if it ever came to a

187

physical confrontation between the two of them, I shouldn't like to take bets on the winner.

As soon as I left the luncheon table I went off in search of Duncan. He was only too pleased to take me down to the village in the gig, and half an hour later we were on our way. I sat companionably beside the gnarled old man, feeling more comfortable with him than any of my family, save one.

'This puts me so much in mind of the old times when I had your father here with me, Miss Charlotte,' he said suddenly. 'A strong, eager lad he was, always alert and lively. A joy to be in his company for any length of time.'

It delighted me to hear him speak like this. 'Did they have this annual fair in those days, Duncan?' I asked.

'Oh aye, it's been going for nigh on a couple of centuries, I should think, lassie. Old traditions die slowly, and your daddy was always in on the games. He was only a wee lad compared to some of the village boys, but he'd always enter for the next class of race than his age warranted, just to prove to himself that a Brodie was capable of anything he put his mind to. A rare one, was your daddy.'

I felt the sting of tears behind my eyelids at the rough affection in the old man's voice.

'And my cousin Neil says everyone gets slightly moon-drunk during the week. Is that right too?' It sounded such a romantic, yet slightly wicked phrase.

'Oh aye,' Duncan chuckled. 'Ye'll need to keep yer wits about you, lassie, if you're not to lose a few kisses and cuddles to the village lads. It's a week when near everything is permissible and the local lads take full advantage of the mixing of classes. And by All Hallows half of them are in a fine old stupor. They'd notice nothing if it was all happening right under their noses.'

'If what was happening?'

Duncan glanced at me, sensing my sudden intent expression. The book I had found in the library had dealt with All Hallows at some length, but I hadn't paid too much attention to it. It was all written in a rather technical way anyway, and there were only a few passages that could be readily understood; such as the baby business. I shivered.

'Oh, nothing for you to worry your head about, my dear. It's just that some say the witches still ride their broomsticks on that night, and that the fair was first started so that the witches could get new initiates to join while they were only half-sensible and didn't really know what was happening to them. Anybody who joins a coven is supposed to do it of their own free will – did you know that? But with the whisky swilling about inside a body, who's to know how much is his own free will?'

'You can't be serious, Duncan,' I exclaimed, feeling a coldness on my face. 'Not nowadays, surely? There's no truth in it, is there? Covens and witches, I mean. Not around *here*?' I glanced about me as if I expected to see a horde of them suddenly flying right up in front of me, black cloaks flying, pointed hats and all. 'I mean, it was all wiped out a century ago, wasn't it, when they stopped persecuting them?'

'They stopped persecuting them,' he agreed. 'But does a plant stop growing because its flower is plucked?'

His words frightened me. I wasn't sure how this conversation had started, but I wanted it to end right now.

'Please talk about something else,' I said quickly. 'I don't like to think about such things. Tell me more about the games.'

'I'm sorry, lassie.' There was genuine distress in Duncan's voice now. 'I didn't think it would upset you, and of course it's all fairy-tales. Well then, the games.' He stopped the gig for a few minutes, and pointed. 'It's just around here where it's all held. A few weeks from now and you won't see a bare patch of ground for stalls and practising runners and sportsmen and the air will be filled with a caterwauling from the pipers.'

'Oh Duncan, you disappoint me.' I started to laugh, my mind lulled by this blasphemy. 'And you a Scot! I thought you were all supposed to love the skirl of the pipes?'

He grinned back from his wizened face.

'I'll tell you a secret, Miss Charlotte. I'm tone-deaf, the doctor once told me, and it all sounds the same to me. I can still appreciate a reasonable tune, but you just wait till you hear a couple of score or more all rambling about, each practising his own special tune, and then tell me you like the noise!'

We were both laughing then, and I looked around me with interest. There was a large expanse of scrubland here above the village of Blackmaddie, with wooded areas stretching back towards the shelter of the mountains. A clear burn bubbled somewhere to our left, and a sheer fall of water shimmered down the mountainside to meet it. It was a place of beauty and delight, and such things as witches and the dark side of life had no meaning here. And yet, even as I thought so I experienced again that weird sensation of my mind opening out to receive an image I didn't want to see. A sudden hazing of the sun as a cloud passed in front of it. A shifting shadow on the ground thrown by the mountain so that it became grotesque like a crouching figure. A sharpening of the senses so that the sound of rushing water became more shrill, like a woman's scream.

'We've lingered long enough, lassie,' I heard Duncan say. 'You're beginning to look pinched, and we'll want to get back before dusk. If I know anything about young ladies you'll be taking long enough in this fancy furbelow establishment of yours.'

'I hope you're feeling strong, Duncan,' I told him quickly, glad to be thinking of more normal matters. 'I intend to buy bales and bales of material and I'll need a helping hand to carry it all out to the gig!'

If I sounded extravagant, it was a new and heady feeling. Always before, buying fabric in any quantity had been for others, never for myself.

Duncan laughed. 'You'll not need me for that. As soon as they see who you are and know it'll be going to Blackmaddie, you'll have a string of minions scurrying about to carry your purchases. You'll see.'

It would be the first time in my life if it really happened, I thought with sudden amusement. I had a small wager with myself that instinctively the proprietors of the sewing emporium, as the little shop was so grandly called, would see me still as a sewing-mistress and nothing more. But Duncan

190

had been right. Whether it was my face or my name, I was treated with all the deferential manner I could ever desire, and it instilled in me a wild desire to laugh and skip and sing. Oh, I was becoming accustomed to the high life, I thought gleefully, half-ashamed of the pleasure it gave me.

I spent a very pleasurable hour inside the sewing emporium. They did not have as much red material as I would have liked, but there was enough for two dresses, a shot silk of a similar colour to the red moire, and a dazzling scarlet taffeta. I bought them both for evening gowns, and besides them I chose a rich sea-green silk, a blue wool for a day dress, and some plaid for a long skirt to wear with the blouses I already possessed. Besides all this, there was the deep blue woollen that would make an admirable warm cloak for when winter came. I was delighted with everything, and my happiness must have shown in my face, for the lady and her assistants could not have been more obliging, and I was sure it was not merely for the size of the sale. I felt a glow of pride as I told them to charge it to my grandfather's account and signed the chit: *Charlotte Brodie, Blackmaddie,* and I almost skipped out to the gig to where Duncan was waiting, only resisting the impulse by reminding myself of my status in the eyes of the shop ladies, who were all hovering behind the leaded windows to peer at me.

But once back on the road for the castle I let my feelings show and hugged Duncan's arm in ecstatic delight. Perhaps it was not the done thing to be so free with a servant, but he was more than that to me. He was my father's friend and therefore mine too and I wanted so much for someone to share these moments of pleasure with me.

Once back at the castle he carried the bales of cloth inside for me. We met Grandfather inside the door, and he stopped in astonishment at the sight of Duncan, weighted down with bright shimmering material that was already poking out through the brown paper, as I hadn't been able to resist taking a look at it every five minutes of the journey back.

'What's all this?' he exclaimed. 'Are we having a fancy-dress ball?'

191

I suddenly felt a brief embarrassment, hoping my enthusiasm hadn't got the better of me and made me take advantage of his generosity.

'Grandfather, it's the material I told you I wanted to buy, to make myself some new clothes,' I said, my head high though I quaked a little inside at his frown. 'I hope you don't mind that I bought a little more than I mentioned.'

'A little more!' he bellowed in those familiar ringing tones that echoed all round the stone walls. 'I should think you've bought up the entire shop and put the owner in easy street for the rest of the year. And quite right too. If a Brodie woman can't be extravagant then I don't know who can. I've no doubt you'll do it all justice.'

Before he'd finished speaking I had thrown my arms round his neck and hugged him. He was so dour and yet so unexpectedly sweet at times, and he looked ridiculously pleased and surprised at this rush of affection although he quickly disentangled my arms from his neck.

'You'd best let Duncan get it all upstairs before he expires from the weight,' he said gruffly, and strode away from me to be about his business. But I felt a wild happiness in my heart at having felt a brief affinity with him that was between him and me alone, with no shadows of Katrina intruding. I knew it as surely as I breathed.

Upstairs in my room I spread all the material out on my bed, admiring it and touching it, feeling the old sensuous pleasure I used to know from the smell of new fabric and its clean, virgin state before my expert hands got to work on it. I held each one up against myself, smiling at my reflection, knowing I had chosen well; seeing myself in each new colour and texture through Robert's eyes; knowing he would appreciate what he saw; and setting myself a target, to get at least some of it finished before he came home.

I was eager to begin, even though I knew there was no time until after dinner that evening. But once the meal was over, I would come back here and start cutting out. It was nothing new to me to cut and sew by candle-light, for it was what I had always been used to, and in far less congenial surroundings than this. I glanced around me, glad that my room was so large and that I would have none of the cramped conditions I had had in Bristol. I rang my bell for Vinny, while I rummaged in my closet for my sewing-box.

By the time she arrived I had all my things spread out on the bed: my thimbles, measuring tapes, sewing threads, cutting-out scissors, tiny scissors for snicking loose threads, tailor's chalk. The familiar smells of it all were like balm to my senses.

Vinny tapped at the door and came inside. She had Luke perched over her arm. She stared in amazement at the sight of the material and sewing implements spread out over my bed.

'Vinny, can you find out if there's a good-sized table I can have sent up here, please? And an upright chair so that I can sit at it when I need to? I daresay Duncan or one of the younger servants will carry it up for me. As soon as you can, please, because I want to cut out some material after dinner.' I suddenly smiled at her wide-eyed face as I fingered the soft folds of the red shot silk in my hands, and it flitted through me that she certainly hadn't hacked up the red moire, because there was only an innocent envy in her look. 'Isn't this gorgeous? I'm going to trim it with white lace.'

'Oh, not red and white, Miss. That's a sign of blood,' she said, involuntarily enough to make my heart lurch.

'All right then. Cream lace,' I said quickly, though I told myself it was only a silly country superstition. But I persuaded myself that cream lace would probably look better anyway, and white would be too stark against the red. I managed to cluck at the angry-looking Luke, his face almost as red as his hair as he hooked his tiny fingers over Vinny's bodice in an attempt to get at her breasts, and sent her on her way.

I would start on the red, I thought. Though probably it should be the blue wool or the plaid for some day clothes, and of course the dark blue for the cloak. That was what I had gone for in the first place. Perhaps I would have an evening of cutting out so that the pieces were all prepared ready for tacking. Then if I was not too tired, I could begin on whichever garment took my fancy. My heart was definitely lighter now that I had a definite plan in mind and I was singing by the time I heard the noisy arrival of Duncan and several lads with a table and chair for me, which they had great difficulty in getting inside the room. But at last it was there, and my mouth seemed to be fixed in a permanent smile as I pictured the happy hours ahead of me, doing the job I liked best of all.

All my fears of someone trying to kill me had receded. I had been nervous of the occasion at the Sinclairs' and allowed my imagination to play havoc with my reason. I had convinced myself of that now. What other explanation could there be? I was here at Blackmaddie, back where I belonged, and in a short time my dearest friend would be staying here on an extended visit, and my beloved would be back. There was everything in the world to live for.

'Oh, Vinny.' I caught hold of her on the stairs as I was going down to dinner. 'Would you ask if anyone in the kitchen has any pins to spare? I seem to have mislaid my large box of them and have only a few. I can probably manage for tonight, but the shop will be closed tomorrow and I shall be busy with my sewing by then.'

'I'll ask, Miss.' She whirled away from me in her usual hurry, late for her duties as always from her attentions to the baby. She was definitely indulged in that respect, I thought, as she would be if the baby was a natural child of someone here. I pushed the thought out of my head. I had no wish to go over unwelcome ideas when my mind was so taken up with the style of my new red gown and which patterns I would use, and the pleasure I always got out of the spread of fabric and the anticipation of beginning.

And no one was going to diminish my high spirits that evening. Grandfather laughed teasingly at me, and told Kirsty it was going to be a hive of industry in our passage of the castle and why couldn't she find some interesting occupation to do while Ian was away at university instead of mooning about the way she always did whenever he was away?

She glared at me, annoyed at being put in the role of idler, though Grandfather had not meant it in that respect.

'It will be useful to have a handy dressmaker so close at hand,' she said sweetly. 'Will you run something up for me when you have a spare moment, Charlotte?'

'Of course. And I daresay Agnes will be glad of my expertise as well. Not all of us are gifted with the ability to turn a useless piece of cloth into something beautiful, and even then its beauty all depends on the wearer.'

I stared pointedly at her bodice, which was rather clumsily caught together as if it had been torn and then hastily cobbled. I was getting as adept at veiled sarcasm as she, I realised, and not always so veiled either, as I witnessed by Grandfather's guffaw, and his comment that that certainly put Kirsty in her place. I did not mean to ruffle her feelings, but at this she flounced her shoulders away from me and concentrated on talking to Ian as usual. Neil caught my eye and smiled, though whether he was feeling cheerful from my getting the better of Kirsty or the mere mention of Agnes, I didn't know and cared less. I was anxious to be upstairs on my own again, and I excused myself as soon as the meal was over and shut myself in my room.

It had to be the red shot silk first, I thought lovingly. It was so beautiful. I threw the bale across my table and it gleamed in the candle-light, reminding me of that other time, when I had done the same with the bale of blue silk on the night Mother died. I had felt the same sense of detachment from my surroundings then as I did now as my creative eye studied the delicate self-patterning of the material and decided on the cutting for a long time before I took up my scissors and pins. And once again I was back in my familiar role, snip-snip-snipping the way Mother had done, exhilarated by creating something from nothing by the skill of my own hands.

Those hands seemed extra sensitive tonight, as if I had been away from my craft for too long and they were compelling me to make the best effort I had ever done. And of course, I was making this gown for Robert's benefit. I was never in any doubt about that. I wanted him to look at the finished creation with the eyes of love, seeing in every line an invitation for him alone, and a warm glow filled my cheeks as I remembered the way his eyes had lingered on my breasts the night I had first worn the red moire, lingered and travelled over me in that sensuous way of his. And then his lips had told me I was magnificent, before he kissed me. I caught sight of my face reflected in the mirror now, and the same air of excitement I had felt that night was written in my face, the night that Robert had come to me and slipped the red moire from my shoulders until it fell to the floor in a rustle of silk. I refused to let my mind go beyond those first trembling moments, for they were infinitely precious to me and I wanted no other memories to spoil them.

Finally, when I had finished cutting all the pieces of the red shot silk, I started on the other materials. The woollens took longer, being thicker to cut through, though my scissors were good and sharp, the best we could afford, for if Mother spent our hard-earned money on anything, it was to provide the best tools for us both, and I appreciated it now. I worked on, oblivious of time or the lowering of the candle-flames, absorbed in my task, when suddenly I heard a movement outside my door. A sort of scratching movement, and my hands paused in mid-snipping, my fingers rigid, my ears listening.

And unreasonably all the fears were suddenly back with me: the notion that there was danger here for me; the weird sensations I had had on my trips to the village; the imagined attempt to push me over the balcony at the Sinclairs' that suddenly didn't seem imaginary at all; the evil, real or fancied, at Blackmaddie and in the old book on witchcraft I had so foolishly read in an impressionable state.

My mouth was dry, my heart pounding as I stared at my door. Was the handle slowly beginning to turn? Remembering I hadn't thought to lock it, I stumbled across the room to turn the key, hardly realising that I clutched my sharp dressmaking scissors in my hands, blades out in a desperate gesture of self-preservation from whatever might open the door before I reached it.

The handle turned and Vinny's face appeared. We both stopped at the same instant, her face a picture as she saw the scissors in my hands, the knuckles standing out bone-white. And I felt foolish, with a wild desire to laugh hysterically, when I saw the box of pins she held in her hand as she stepped a very little way into the room, her eyes still on those sharp points of the scissors.

'I'm sorry it's so late, Miss,' she said quickly. 'Cook's only just managed to find them, and I thought you might be needing them tonight.'

'Thank you, Vinny, and thank Cook too – and next time don't creep about the castle at all hours of the night to bring me pins! It could have waited until morning and you wouldn't have given me the fright of my life!'

'You gave me a bit of a fright too, Miss,' she said in her usual spirited manner. 'I'll be getting off to my bed now then. Goodnight.'

I said goodnight and turned the key behind her, feeling infinitely safer once I had done so. I looked down at the box of pins she had brought me and my hands were shaking. I walked back across the room to my table, trying to breathe more slowly and to stop my heart from pounding so much, and I brushed my right hand over my forehead, feeling it damp. The gleam of the scissors I still held caught my eyes in the reflection of myself in the mirror. They stuck up alongside my ear, half-open, sinister, like devil's horns. The sound of muffled voices was clamouring through the wall again. Maybe it had been there all the time and I had been too absorbed to hear it before. But I heard it now.

14

The next week was a strange one. Ian left for Edinburgh on Monday and Kirsty mooned about, being as irritating as possible and determined to bait me whenever she could. She taunted me about making the new red dress because of Robert, but never by a whisper did she betray whether she was the one who slashed the red moire. I thought I would probably never get to the truth of it, and once again I had left matters too late to make proper enquiries. Just as at the Sinclairs' when I had persuaded myself not to make a fuss about the attack during the game of Blind Man's Bluff, it was too late now to complain about something that was past history, and I tried to shrug it off as an act of simple maliciousness on someone's part with no sinister undertones.

Agnes and her parents came for afternoon tea the next day, and Mr and Mrs Waverley were obviously impressed and awed at the magnificence of Blackmaddie. So much so that they appeared to find conversation difficult, and this in itself made everyone slightly embarrassed, so it was rather a stilted hour, and we were all thankful when it was over. I walked to the hired carriage with the three of them before they went back to the hotel.

'I know Agnes will be very happy with you, Charlotte.' Mrs Waverley was more eloquent away from my grandfather and aunt and uncle. 'Though I confess I should not like to spend my time wandering about the great corridors finding where things belonged. You seem to have settled in to it remarkably well, dear, if I may say so.'

'It's her home, isn't it?' Mr Waverley stated. 'Blood will always tell, whether it's good or bad. Not that I'm suggesting yours is bad, Charlotte, my dear! But you have an air of belonging about you.' He smiled at me benevolently, clearly well satisfied that his daughter was happily settled now, though I knew it would be a wrench for them to leave her.

'I shall see you on Friday then, Charlotte,' Agnes said now, and there was a slight tremble in her voice. It was an upheaval for her too, I thought, but she would have me here, and Neil, and surely that alone was enough to warm her heart. I hugged her impulsively as we said good-bye, and then I bade her parents a safe journey back to Bristol.

I waved until they were out of sight, thinking that I, at least, did not have the remotest desire to go back there, so I supposed I must be settling down in my new environment, even though it didn't always feel like it.

'Have they gone?' Kirsty's voice spoke sulkily behind me, and I turned with a start. 'I'm not sure I like that friend of yours, Charlotte, with her simpering ways and those cow-like eyes.'

I gasped at such rudeness, and I could feel the fury rising inside me.

'Perhaps I don't like your friends either,' I snapped, though that was not true, because I did indeed like the Sinclair family. But she stung me into retaliation. 'Agnes is a charming girl, and I won't have you making her feel uncomfortable here.'

'I shall do as I please.'

'You'll be agreeable to Agnes and not make her life a misery,' I retorted, knowing too well that she could do that very easily if she tried.

'Who are you to tell me what to do?' Kirsty almost hissed the words.

'Charlotte Brodie,' I said calmly and stalked away from her.

But though I held myself with dignity and marched round the shrubberies as if I had some definite purpose in mind, inside I was trembling with rage. She would not make life unbearable for Agnes or me, I thought, and together we would put up a solid front against her bitchiness. I did not feel like going indoors yet. I had intended getting on with my sewing, but I knew if I attempted it at the moment I

199

would stab the needle into my fingers and make a cobble of the fine stitching needed to put the finishing touches to the red dress.

I frowned, remembering that in a rare moment of generosity Kirsty had promised me a length of delicate cream lace that would do beautifully for my trimming. She had said carelessly it was on her dressing-table and that I could go and fetch it if I wanted to. I would have to do just that, because if I asked her again for it now she'd probably change her mind just for spite. I was under no illusions about my cousin Kirsty.

I was at the side of the castle now, near the servants' quarters, and Vinny's baby was in his perambulator under a tree. He was squalling as usual in that thin, petulant whine of his, and I turned to go around to the front, not wanting to see Vinny come out and scoop him up in her arms and ask me to look at him and see what a fine boy he was becoming. He still looked an ugly miserable little thing to me, and somehow I just couldn't take to him. I slipped around a clump of shrubs and was about to emerge when I caught a glimpse of a green plaid skirt bending over the perambulator. Kirsty's skirt!

I could hardly believe it when I heard the soft crooning way she spoke to the baby at that minute, and saw her rocking the handle of the perambulator. It was unexpected to see her acting as any normal young woman would towards a baby, and even more extraordinary that it was a servant's baby. I had never seen her pay any particular attention to Luke before. The next minute Vinny came out from the side door, her face wreathed in smiles, and picked the squalling baby out of the perambulator. She held him aloft, gently shaking him to make him laugh and then she offered him to Kirsty to do the same.

'He's a lovely boy,' I heard Kirsty say. 'A credit to you, Vinny.'

'Oh aye, he'll do fine,' Vinny answered complacently. 'The master's fair pleased with him, Miss. Try putting the tip of your finger in his mouth, just there, look. I declare he's cutting a tooth already, and not four months old yet.

He's well ahead of his days, but I'm thinking he'll have to stop guzzling me so often if he's going to have sharp teeth to nip me. Not that it's aught but a pleasurable sensation, for all that.'

I could hear the laughter in her voice but I wasn't listening to the two of them prattling on about Luke's virtues any longer. I was struck by Vinny's remark about the master being fair pleased with the child. The master – which one of the Blackmaddie men was that, the one who was obviously the father of the child? And another thing was obvious, that Kirsty knew his identity. It struck me as very odd, for I would not have guessed that these two were confidantes.

It was an intriguing puzzle and I wished I knew the answer. I wanted to know the father's identity on several counts. I badly wanted to eliminate Robert from being a candidate. I wanted the same thing for Neil because of Agnes. Ian – I still couldn't think of it as being Ian. Grandfather – it was distasteful to think of Grandfather cavorting with a girl such as Vinny. That left Uncle Andrew, and if he was the father, Luke was the heir to Blackmaddie, if he was ever recognised. I shuddered, thinking that was the most distasteful thought of all, not merely because of the connection between my uncle and Vinny, but because of Luke himself. He was evil – the thought was formed in my mind before I could stop it, and immediately I was horrified at myself.

Luke was an innocent baby, born out of wedlock to a servant girl, and that was not his crime, but Vinny's. If he was more miserable than some, it was probably due to the fact that he was teething early, as Vinny had just suggested, and any child's face would be contorted into angry rages if he was in constant pain. I should be able to make allowances. I was a woman, supposedly endowed with maternal instincts, but it seemed that in this instance Vinny and Kirsty were both more normal than I, for I could feel nothing but revulsion for Luke no matter how hard I tried to change. I was the unnatural one.

I sped away silently and returned to the castle, to take up my sewing again and try to restore my jittery nerves by the use of needle and thread. I had finished the dark blue cloak and it hung in my closet, and I was well pleased with the result. I had worked on it and the red dress simultaneously, alternating the fine stitching of the red shot silk with the bolder stitching needed on the woollen cloth, to give both my eyes and my fingers a change. But now I needed the cream lace Kirsty had promised me. I hesitated, and I decided to fetch it for myself before she had a chance to change her mind. Once sewn on the red dress, it would be safe.

I went along the passage to Kirsty's room. If it was locked I would have no choice but to wait and ask her for the lace. But it was not locked and I slipped inside and went straight to the box on her dressing-table where she kept all sorts of trimmings and hair tidies and other little bits of nonsense she seemed to collect. I didn't look at Katrina's pictures, for I knew now that they were similar to those in the old book I had found in the library. Perhaps she had used the same book to study, and this had stirred her interest in the occult.

I didn't want to stay long in Kirsty's room. It was cold. Colder than mine, as if the sun rarely warmed it, and yet it must receive as much sunlight. She had one less window, though. It was a gloomier room than mine, and I was surprised that Kirsty had wanted it after Katrina died. It seemed a morbid thing to do, unless she was strong-willed enough not to sense any kind of atmosphere the way I invariably did. It was here now, the coldness that sent a chill right through me, an abnormal lowering of temperature. I tried to think prosaically that I should want several warming-pans in this bed if I had to sleep here. Involuntarily my eyes went to the bed.

On top of the bedcover was the old book I had got from the library. It had been in my closet, pushed in at the back, out of sight of Vinny or anyone else, behind the hacked-up red moire dress. My heartbeats were drumming in my chest staccato fast. And then I heard the click of the door.

Kirsty stood there glaring at me. 'What are you doing in here?' she spoke shrilly.

I held out my hand, the cream lace spilling out. 'You said I could have it,' I reminded her as steadily as I could. I was suddenly very afraid and yet I did not know why. She would probably snatch it out of my hands and say I could not have it after all. But she merely shrugged.

'I suppose you can. It's no use to me.'

'May I – may I borrow that book too, please?' I hardly knew I was saying the words. They were saying themselves, my lips moving of their own volition, but my eyes stayed unwaveringly on her face. Kirsty's eyes flickered for a moment, and then she laughed and tossed it to me.

'Are you thinking of casting a spell on me, cousin?' she said in a taunting voice. 'Or maybe you're searching for a love potion to put into Robert's drink when he returns. Does he need it to make him forget Katrina?'

The shock of her words made me forget whatever else I was going to say. Until that moment I had thought she only guessed at what had gone on between Robert and me on the night he came to my room. But now I wondered agonisingly if she could possibly have overheard. But how could she? The walls of the castle were thick, even the connecting ones between the rooms. Although . . . I glanced sideways for an instant. There was a closet on the wall in her room that would be directly against the one in mine, and they were deep, going right back into the wall. Deep enough for a person to hide inside, as I had no doubt the younger Brodie children had done out of mischief for generations. But perhaps if the closet one side was open and someone pressed their ear against the connecting wall, it was thin enough to hear sounds from next door. The thought sent burning colour to my face as I remembered the sounds Robert and I had made. The sounds of love – moaning with pleasure and delight; the words of love we had both spoken; the way he had referred to my body and the act we were performing to such perfection in words that would have been crude and basic if they had been used in any other circumstances; the way he had had Katrina's name torn out of him as if it was something beyond his control. Oh God, had Kirsty heard all of *that*?

She still stood there with a mocking smile on her lips, waiting for my reply. But there was no reply. All I wanted to do was to rush back to my own room and be alone, much as a wounded animal returned home to lick its wounds. I twisted on my heel and left her, with the book in one hand and the cream lace in the other, but all my interest in one and my pleasure in the other was gone.

I trembled as I leaned against my door and turned the key. My instinct was to rush to the closet and step inside, to press my ear against the connecting wall and see if I could hear Kirsty moving about. But I was so afraid I would hear the sound of mocking laughter if she guessed what I was about, and so I resisted the temptation. All the same, through the mists of my senses, I realised one thing. The mysterious voices that came to me so often through the stonework were probably of a more down-to-earth nature after all, and not the ghostly clamouring of some evil presence in my room. It was probably Kirsty and Ian and whoever else she was in the habit of chattering with nocturnally. No doubt the sound became distorted considerably through the stones and was no more than several voices all talking at once.

I made myself return to my sewing, pinning on the strips of delicate cream lace and taking great care over mitring corners and ruching where necessary. I wanted the finished dress to be magnificent. Of course, if I wore it on the night Robert came home Kirsty would know why, but no matter.

My fingers stopped pinning and strayed to the old book that was now safely back on my own bed. A frown creased my forehead. Just how had it got into Kirsty's room anyway? Either she was a clever actress hiding that she had been caught stealing something from my room – or someone else had taken it. The crawling sensation ran up and down my back. I remembered the other time when I felt someone had been in my room. That time I had found the book open when I had left it closed. But I had hidden it carefully. Someone had searched hard and long enough to find it – and it had ended up in Kirsty's room. Whoever took it must have seen the remnants of the red moire too.

I brushed my hand across my forehead in perplexity. I did

not like mysteries and there were too many of them at Blackmaddie. The doors of the rooms all had ornate keys in the locks that were seldom used by other members of the family as far as I knew, but from then on I locked my room every time I left it and carried the key about with me, making sure I was there each time Vinny arrived to make the bed or any of the other servants wanted to clean the room. I was watchful from that day on as I had never been before.

It was a great relief to me when Agnes finally arrived to stay, for I had to confide in someone. Her wide-eyed stares when I showed her the shredded dress and the book I now kept tucked beneath my underwear in a dressing-table drawer, were disbelieving, almost comical.

'But who on earth would want to do such a thing, Charlotte?' she exclaimed. 'It must have been one of the servants, doing it for spite, I should think, or envy, because you must have looked very grand in it. How upset you must have been to find it – and frightened too.'

'Yes I was,' I admitted. 'But I'm over it now.' I tried to make myself believe it, and I didn't tell Agnes about the book turning up in Kirsty's room either, for fear it would throw suspicion on my cousin, and I was not sure she was to blame for either happening. 'Anyway, come and have a look at some of the things in here. It's fascinating, providing one keeps a level head and doesn't get too petrified. Oh – and some of the pictures are a bit – well, lurid. If you'd rather not see them . . . '

'Oh, why not? I'm not so narrow-minded as all that,' Agnes said quickly, but all the same her cheeks were very pink as she looked at some of the pictures, and I still thought my guess was right, and that she had not known the touch of a man yet.

Agnes now looked as well as I, and the little cough that had plagued her so much when I first knew her was far less in evidence now that the mountain air was doing its work. Her eyes sparkled and her face was quite radiant at times, mostly when Neil was around.

I felt a little as if I was Agnes' protector – and Neil's too, in a way. I always seemed to be on my guard when Kirsty was near us all, for fear she would say something unpleasant about Neil and shake the tremulous love that was blossoming so quickly between them. I still wondered if I should say something to Agnes about Kirsty's suggestion of Neil's impotence, but again I decided it was best left to fate to sort out.

In that first week I began to wonder just who Agnes had come to visit, though, for she spent so much time with Neil. Often the three of us would go walking together, but whereas Neil used to be preoccupied, now I felt as if I might as well be composing verses or something, for all the notice they took of me. They didn't shut me out deliberately, and often one or other of them would suddenly include me in the conversation with an embarrassed flush on their cheeks, as if they had genuinely forgotten I was there. But I couldn't find it in my heart to censure them when they were so wrapped up in each other.

Agnes was allowed the privilege of visiting Neil in the little shed where he kept his hawk. She hadn't been too happy about the prospect at first, but he assured her the bird was kept chained while indoors, and that she would come to no harm. I suspected the little sojourns to the shed were not entirely because of Boucca, the hawk, from the way Agnes came out looking as if she had stars in her eyes.

'I fear Kirsty does not like me,' Agnes said to me a little sorrowfully one evening when we were sitting alone in the drawing-room. Kirsty had been gone all afternoon to visit the Sinclairs and had not yet returned, and though I should not think it, it was refreshingly calm without her.

'Kirsty doesn't like anyone very much,' I answered. 'Except Ian, of course. Presumably she'll be in a happier frame of mind when he comes back for the week of the fair.'

'It's a pity he's not here all the time then,' Agnes sighed.

It was. The atmosphere always seemed lighter when Ian was around, with his uncomplicated sense of fun, but by now I was impatiently counting the days and wondering when Robert would be back. Agnes still had not met him, though

I had described him to her. Not too glowingly, I admitted shame-facedly to myself, for I did not want her to feel too intrigued by the thought of him, nor him by the sight of her. If there was any dark streak of Maddie's that I had inherited, it must surely be the one of jealousy, I thought.

'Do you want to see something very strange?' I said to Agnes, the sudden excitement springing to my voice.

'As long as it's not a ghost or anything,' she smiled back.

'Not a live one anyway,' I assured her. 'Come along, while everyone seems to be busy with their own amusements. Grandfather and Uncle Andrew will be playing their chess game all night and Aunt Morag has a headache and won't come out of her room until morning. I don't know where Neil is...'

'Gone to see someone about buying a new horse,' Agnes put in at once, and I hid a smile, thinking that of course she would know his whereabouts.

We picked up our candles and I bade her follow me through the maze of passages and corridors that I knew would finish up at the room where Duncan had taken me on my first day at Blackmaddie. The room where the portrait of Maddie was stored. I had already coaxed Duncan into letting me have the key, ready for an opportunity when I could show my friend the curious likeness I shared with my ancestor. When we reached the room I inserted the key in the lock and we went inside. I could not help my own shock when Duncan had shown me the portrait, and when I had found it and held my candle aloft to show it to Agnes, I was prepared for her gasp of surprise.

'Is it you, Charlotte?' she said hesitantly. 'It's so like you, and yet it's as if the artist has captured something not quite – not quite – '

'Wholesome?' I asked quietly. 'That is exactly how it appears to me, so I must thank you for thinking it is not quite identical to my features. There's something evil in her, isn't there?'

'But who is she?' Agnes said at last, when she had stared at the portrait for several minutes.

I told her the story of Maddie as Duncan had told it to

me, and that the likeness came out in other young women on infrequent occasions, but quite close together in the case of Katrina and myself. I had always thought that strange, since there were no records of another, as far as Duncan knew, for over a century.

'Perhaps it was destined that Katrina would die and you were to come here in her place.' Agnes' voice was hushed and dry with excitement. 'Perhaps somewhere in the ether this Maddie had seen you – and you wouldn't even have been invited to Blackmaddie if you hadn't looked so much like her!'

'That's nonsense,' I said sharply. 'We'd better get out of here before somebody hears us and we get into trouble. Nobody's supposed to come up here, so don't say anything about my showing you the portrait, will you? And Black Maddie is looked upon as being a very wicked lady, so don't even breathe her name at the dinner table, Agnes!'

We left the room and re-locked the door and hurried back downstairs to the drawing-room, where we amused ourselves while we waited for the dinner gong. There was a scrawled note on a side table that said *Come to the shed where the hawk is kept.*

I smiled teasingly at Agnes. 'Well, it certainly isn't meant for me, is it? Perhaps Neil has trained Boucca to do something extra clever and wants to show her off to you. I'll go on up to my room and start getting ready for dinner, so don't let Neil keep you too long, Agnes.'

She was smiling as she left the drawing-room, and I smiled too at the glow of happiness on her face. Those two had a rare affection for each other as tender and unspoiled as a young green plant.

I was still halfway up the stairs to my room when I heard the shrill screams that chilled the blood in my veins and stopped me rigid. My heart gave a great lurch of fear as the screaming went on and on and on, and I was suddenly flying back down the stairs again and flinging open the great front door of the castle, leaving it open wide so that the candle-light streamed out as my footsteps carried me down the stone steps with fear pushing me on towards the shed, Neil's shed.

'Agnes!' I was screaming and sobbing myself, and before I reached it I could hear other sounds. A terrible flapping of wings as they beat against the wooden walls of the shed. The shrill screech of anger that was Boucca's. The flailing of horses' hooves and the shouting that was Neil's coming towards me from the other direction. *Neil* – but he should be inside with Agnes. Oh God, what was happening in there?

'It's Agnes,' I shrieked at him. 'In there. With Boucca.'

I could only seem to get two words out at a time because my heart was banging so painfully in my chest. Neil slid from the horse and rushed to the door to open it, shouting at me to keep clear in case the hawk flew out. I shrank back, not wanting those cruel claws digging into my flesh or the powerful wings lashing out at me. But what had they done to Agnes?

It seemed an eternity before Neil brought her out, but it could only have been minutes. By then Grandfather and Uncle Andrew had appeared, wanting to know if devils had taken possession of the castle, and that was truly how it was beginning to seem to me. Aunt Morag, too, arrived, white-faced, and Kirsty came from the direction of the stables, demanding to know what all the excitement was about. Excitement! I took one look at Agnes' scratched and bleeding face and could have wept for her. She looked so shocked she wasn't really aware of what was happening. Her clothes were torn, and there were ugly red weals on her shoulders and throat and on the curve of her breasts. I had to swallow back the lump in my throat as I looked at the terrified expression in her eyes and took her in my arms. The others crowded round us, demanding to know what had happened, with Aunt Morag trying to shut them all up and telling Kirsty to run and ask Duncan to go for Doctor Fraser at once. Neil had shut the door of the shed behind him once he had handed Agnes over to me and was now inside, presumably trying to quieten the hawk, which had reverted to all its natural wildness as soon as Agnes had opened the door.

Suddenly, as we were starting to walk slowly back to the castle, with Uncle Andrew helping me to support Agnes, the struggling and squalling inside the shed stopped. There seemed to be a horrible silence in contrast with the *mêlée* that had been going on before, and then the door of the shed opened, and Neil's hands and arms were covered in blood. It had spattered all over his chest and face and it was the most gruesome sight I had ever seen. His face was filled with pain as he looked at Agnes and me.

'She'll not hurt anyone again,' he said chokingly, and then blundered off in the direction of the stables.

'Good God, man, you've left the door open,' Grandfather roared after him, and strode across to close it for fear of Boucca swooping out. But as he looked inside I could swear his face turned pale in the twilight, and for a moment he looked as if he was about to retch. He glanced back at the rest of us, his voice hoarse when he spoke again.

'He's killed it,' he said slowly. 'Snapped its neck with his bare hands. By God, I didn't know he had the strength or the guts.'

There was rough admiration in his voice even while he was shocked, but I felt a growing horror creeping over me. If it took strength and guts, it also took ruthlessness to do what Neil had done, a ruthlessness I for one hadn't suspected he was capable of showing.

But there were other things to think about. It was obvious Neil hadn't sent the note for Agnes to come out here after all. Whoever had sent it had freed Boucca somehow, so that she was no longer chained and would fly at a strange person going into the shed without any warning. And Agnes' screams would have been enough to inflame her into panic and self-defence. Hawks were meant to kill, but kill whom? There was no name on the note, and why should anyone want to harm Agnes? Wasn't it much more likely I should have been the intended victim? After all, Neil had shown me Boucca several times since I had arrived at Blackmaddie, and Agnes' visits had been kept quiet from the rest of the family. So the trap had been set for me, only it had been Agnes who had walked into it.

Agnes was now sobbing in my arms as I helped lead her back indoors, while my blood ran cold as the suspicion that my life was in danger became a certainty. Uncle Andrew carefully placed a cushion behind Agnes' head on the long sofa and Aunt Morag fussed around bringing her a glass of brandy, and Kirsty hung about at a complete loss for once. Instinctively my eyes went to the side table where the note had been left, but it was no longer there. Someone had removed the evidence.

15

By the time Doctor Fraser arrived Agnes was lying on her bed and holding on to my hand. People kept looking in and enquiring after her but of Neil there was no sign at all. I could imagine him blundering off into the wood with his lonely grief at feeling forced to kill his beloved Boucca, but I felt a deep resentment towards him for not being with Agnes now, when I was sure he loved her very much. How much was that love worth if he couldn't be by her side when she needed him? And yet I wondered if she did need him or anyone as she lay and whimpered silently, and I tried to give her what comfort I could.

'Neil must have gone out of the shed for a few minutes,' she whispered huskily, 'and not realised that I would arrive so soon, or he'd never have left Boucca unchained. He's told me before that it would be dangerous for anyone but himself to walk in while the hawk was free. I should have waited outside until I heard him tell me to come in, instead of opening the door the way I did. But I was so eager to see him.'

She bit her lip as it trembled, and I could see it was a job for her not to cry. But I could imagine how the salt tears would sting the scratches on her face, and I told her quickly to lie still and that I would bathe her face. Vinny had brought a bowl of warm water and some soft cotton, and I did it as gently as I could, knowing I was hurting her, but realising that she would rather I did it than anyone else.

When the scratches were cleaned, they didn't look quite so bad, though there were deeper ones on her throat, and I shuddered at how much worse it could have been. I had decided to say nothing about my suspicions to Agnes, at least while she was still in a shocked state, but she would be bound to find out the truth from Neil when he asked her why she had gone to Boucca's shed. Then she would know he hadn't sent the note, and he would discover what I already knew in my heart, that there was danger here. Not for Agnes, but for me. I grieved that she had been the one to receive the fury of the hawk's attack and shivered, wondering if the pursuer of my well-being would try again. I was certain he – or she – would.

Aunt Morag tapped at the door and appeared with the doctor. She looked as agitated as anyone, I thought, perhaps wondering if Agnes' parents would come storming up here and demand compensation for their daughter's attack. But I could not be bothered to think about that. I was too anxious to hear what Doctor Fraser had to say. He examined the scratches and weals carefully, while Agnes tried not to cry out at his touch.

'Well, young lady, it's not too bad,' he said heartily. 'It could have been a whole lot worse if those talons had gone deep, but I don't think there's too much damage done. You're young and your skin will heal quite soon. What I'm more concerned about is the damage to your nervous system. You've had a nasty shock and I must insist you stay in bed for several days to get over it. Now I'll leave you some salve to put on those scratches and they'll be better in no time at all.'

He talked to her as if she were a child, but Agnes did not seem to mind. She just looked at him with those big, trusting brown eyes of hers, and I believe if he'd said she had to run around the castle five times a day she'd have done it. All she wanted at that moment was for someone to tell her what to do, and she would obey implicitly. It disturbed me slightly, as if she had had all her own will wiped clean and was content to be like a leaf in the wind. As the doctor rose he told her to try and eat some dinner that evening even if she did not feel like it.

'I couldn't,' she began. 'The thought of it makes me sick ...'

'Yes you can,' I said firmly. 'I shall have mine sent up

here with you, Agnes, and I shan't leave you or eat a mouthful of mine unless you do the same.'

'Good lass,' the doctor said to me. I hardly felt like eating either, but if the doctor thought Agnes should eat, then I must see to it that she did. He rose to go, saying he would come back the next morning to take another look at her, and telling me to ensure that plenty of the soothing salve was applied to her skin.

Aunt Morag came back as soon as he'd gone and said she would have two trays sent up at once. I fancied she was somewhat relieved that I was staying with Agnes, thus removing the embarrassment of making conversation with me downstairs after what had happened to my friend. The thought flitted through my head that she could have written the note, but I dismissed it at once. Cold and unfriendly she might be, but she was my father's sister, and I still could not imagine she would try to kill me.

'Oh, and Aunt Morag – is there a small bed that can be shifted in here for a night or two, please?' I went on. 'I would prefer to stay with Agnes until she is feeling better in case she needs anything during the night.'

My eyes challenged her to argue with me, and she said shortly that she would see that it was attended to after dinner. When she had gone, Agnes protested that it wasn't necessary, but that she was glad I'd thought of it all the same. I could have told her that if she had had a shock that night, so had I, and I too would feel happier to have some company. I would not leave her until she was more her old self again.

'I wish Neil would come to see me,' Agnes said in a small voice. 'Though I can understand his need to be alone for a while. Did he – did he really kill the hawk, Charlotte?'

I nodded, the horror of the moment when he had come out of the shed spattered with blood rising like bile in my mouth again.

'To do that for me.' Agnes' voice was still soft and far-away, and I knew she was off in a dream-world somewhere, for it was so much like the look I'd seen so often on Neil's face. The attack had not altered Agnes' feelings, that was

214

clear. But Neil was such a complex character, once he fully realised he had killed his beloved Boucca, he might turn against Agnes. But that was a bridge to cross if need be, and there was no sense in worrying about it now. The first priority was to put the salve on the scratches, and though I shrank from the task, Agnes assured me that it did not hurt too badly, and once the greasy substance had covered the broken skin it felt a lot easier.

The trays of dinner arrived shortly afterwards. Vinny bobbed up and down as she fussed around us, her eyes full of interest at this excitement. I was glad to shoo her out of the room, though she appeared again with Duncan and one of the lads to bring in a narrow bed for me. The men tried to avert their eyes from Agnes' face, which was swelling around the scratches now, but I could see Duncan's troubled look. He guessed, I knew at once, guessed that this was meant for me, and I resolved to seek him out as soon as I could and find out if he was aware who had arranged this.

Agnes picked at her food, but I cajoled and threatened, putting in mouthful for mouthful of my own food, and telling her that if she did not want to see me fade away she had better eat something, even if her mouthfuls were about a quarter as much as my own. She did quite well, and when finally she said she could eat no more, I was relieved to see the haunted look had gone from her eyes now and the colour was coming back into her cheeks. I put the trays on a table ready for Vinny to collect, picked up a comb from the dressing-table and began to smooth out the tangled honey-gold hair to make her look and feel better, until it lay spread around her head like spun gold on the white pillow. She looked like a broken doll, I thought, with a catch in my throat. Anyone who looked at her now could still see the beauty of her, and must surely condemn whoever had cold-bloodedly arranged Boucca's attack.

There was a knock on the door. I smiled at Agnes. At least the family were being conciliatory in their wishes for her speedy recovery, which pleased me. Even Kirsty had looked shocked and disbelieving when she saw the state Agnes was in. Perhaps she had come to sit with her for a few minutes. I called out 'come in', but there was no reply.

'Someone's too shy to enter a lady's bedroom,' I said teasingly, though the Blackmaddie men had not displayed any signs of shyness in their characters. I walked across and opened the door, and as I did it felt as if all the blood in my body surged into my cheeks and my heart pounded so fast it made me dizzy, for Robert had come home. And whatever reaction he had expected from me the next time he saw me, I knew it was impossible for me to hide the love in my eyes. He must see it, feel it, know it. I took a half-step towards him and then his arms were opening to crush me close to him and I could feel the response of his body against mine at once as my arms wound themselves around his neck and I was giving him back kiss for kiss as if everything in life had been leading up to this moment. All the black times were momentarily forgotten, and all I could think about was that he was here, my love, my darling, my own beloved Robert.

There was a sudden cough beside us, and I almost had to drag my eyes open to glare at this intruder into our private moments. Vinny glared back, though whether resentful at having to keep coming up and down with trays or because she was jealous at seeing Robert and me in such an intimate embrace I neither knew nor cared. But we moved aside to let her go into the bedroom, and the spell was broken.

'I hear we have a casualty among us,' his fingers still caressed the back of my neck and it was enough to send the delicious tingling running through me. 'Everything was so much at sixes and sevens downstairs when I arrived, I couldn't make sense of it all. I thought at first it had been you the hawk attacked.'

'It could have been,' I told him, 'if I had been the one to go to the shed. I'd become quite interested in Neil's hawk.' Some instinct told me to say nothing about the note Agnes and I had read.

'But no longer, I understand. My brother has the strength of ten when the power moves him.' Robert spoke lightly, but I wondered about his choice of words. They could have been meaningless. Or they could have referred to the power of Blackmaddie that was inexplicable and total. I shivered, knowing I was letting the hysteria take hold of me again, and I wanted no such fancies to cloud my joy at seeing him. Vinny came out of the room with the trays, and I led Robert inside to meet my friend.

She looked so fragile lying there. And yet not even the scratches and the shock of her attack could take away the golden beauty of her. It was an ethereal kind of beauty that would always appeal to men, and I saw the way Robert looked at her as his eyes took in the spread of golden hair against the pillow and her abnormally flushed cheeks in the porcelain-fair oval of her face. And the way his gaze travelled lower to the nightgown into which I had helped her, and which was carefully open as wide as it would go at the neck, so that the pressure of it would not touch the broken skin. I saw how he gazed at the white swell of her breasts and felt a searing jealousy of which I was instantly ashamed, even though I could do nothing to stop it.

'Robert, this is my friend, Agnes Waverley,' I said in a voice that sounded jerky to me. 'And Agnes, you have heard me speak of my cousin Robert, Neil's older brother.'

Their hands touched in a gesture of meeting, and I felt as if I wanted to snatch them apart. What on earth was wrong with me? I thought in bewilderment. I had not felt any kind of jealousy in Bristol when other female teachers had had occasion to be in close contact with William Derry. I hated the sensation for I felt as if it was controlling me, instead of the other way around. But the hands broke apart and I was conscious of breathing more easily.

'It's a pretty damnable business to have to meet you for the first time like this, Agnes,' Robert was saying agreeably. 'And you'll not be thinking too much of Scottish hospitality if we can let such an accident happen.'

'It was my own fault,' she demurred. 'I had expected Neil to be there and I did not stop to knock before I opened the shed door.'

She was so anxious to absolve Neil from all blame, I thought fondly. The eyes of love were truly blind. Not that I

217

believed for one moment that Neil had been responsible for the note being delivered, but even if he had, I think Agnes would still have blamed herself for walking into the shed without waiting to be admitted.

I was aware of Robert glancing at me from time to time, and I knew he had not missed my eyes lowering as he called the affair an accident. It was no accident, of that I was certain. He suddenly caught sight of the extra bed in Agnes' room.

'Are you to have a nurse to stay with you, Agnes?' he asked. 'I hope your wounds are not too severe.'

'I am staying in here with Agnes until she is fully recovered.' I could not stop the little tremor in my voice, remembering sharply the night he had come to my room. The sudden click of the door and the certainty that it was him; the sight of him standing there, naked and magnificent; the urgency with which our bodies had melted together. The remembered intimacy made the colour stain my cheeks, and Robert saw, and knew.

'The doctor says the scratches will heal quite quickly,' Agnes was saying to him, 'but I did have a terrible shock, and it will be very comforting to know Charlotte is close at hand during the long hours of the night.'

'I am quite sure Charlotte would be a comfort to anyone during the long hours of the night.' Robert's voice was dry, but before Agnes could begin to ponder that remark, he said that Neil had come in and when he had cleaned himself up he too was coming to see her. Anything else in Agnes' mind was forgotten, and Robert could surely see that there was something between her and Neil. Agnes' face shouted it more eloquently than any words. I supposed I should stay in the room when he came, but I did not want to chaperon them. They were both adult and in love, and my presence would be an embarrassment to all three of us, though I wasn't too sure what the older members of my family might think about it.

'Would you like me to bring you some lavender water to refresh you, Agnes?' I said quickly, as I heard Neil's footsteps.

'That would be lovely,' she replied, and I went along the

passage to my own room to fetch it. I passed Neil, clean and presentable now, though he hardly seemed to notice me as he went into Agnes' room without even the pretence of a knock on the door. Strangely, even though it meant the end of Boucca, I had the feeling that what had happened was going to bring them even closer together. I suddenly envied them for being on the brink of something wonderful.

I entered my own room and rummaged in my box for the lavender water, knowing I wouldn't hurry back with it. I knew the moment Robert came in behind me. Within three strides he was across the room and I was in his arms again.

'Why did you say you'd sleep in her room?' His voice was arrogant, aggressive, the way it had been on the day we first met. Demanding, sure of me. 'Couldn't one of the servants have seen to anything she needed? Vinny could have stayed there.'

'And her baby?' I could feel a hot anger rising at his assumption that I would be here waiting for him even after the episode when he had called out Katrina's name. Suddenly she was there between us again, even if he did not seem to realise it. But I did; her spirit seemed to jeer and mock me, telling me he was still hers and I could not have him.

'That bawling brat,' Robert dismissed Luke. Surely he would not have spoken quite so scathingly if Luke had been his child? 'One of the other servants then. Why you, when you must know how impatient I am to lie with you again.'

I would not let myself be stirred by him. I made myself stay angry.

'And am I supposed to hold myself in readiness for every occasion when it suits you?' I cried. He tipped my chin up to his face, and his eyes were full of mischief now, his mouth very near to mine.

'Yes,' he said arrogantly, 'because I know you, Charlotte Brodie, as I know myself. Our needs are the same and without each other we are only half alive. Deny it if you can.'

I realised one hand was caressing my breast, kneading it gently to a point, and I could not have denied him anything if he had asked for it there and then. But he gave a soft laugh and said Grandfather was expecting him in the study to give him a report of his doings while he had been away, and he had better show his face before somebody came to investigate.

'Perhaps it will be all the sweeter for waiting, Charlotte,' he said softly. 'Like an apple ripening for the first succulent sweet taste. I look forward to my next taste of you.'

He bent and kissed me roughly, and then he went away. As always I was left trembling, half angry that he could be so sure of me, half knowing that I could as easily call him back to me, for he was right: my needs and my wanting were a match for his, and yet, I was only half alive without him. I had been half-alive for all my life until I met him. It was almost frightening to know how completely I depended on him for my happiness, and it was humiliating that my revulsion at his indiscretion could so easily be overcome by the desire he roused in me. I had always believed lust was something only in men's minds, but if this longing to hold him and touch him and kiss him was lust, then I knew women were capable of lustful feelings as well.

I left Agnes and Neil alone as long as I dared and then I went back to her room with the lavender water. I called out softly that it was me, but the two of them made no attempt to move out of each other's arms when I went into the room. Neil was sitting on the bed just holding her, though I would have thought the scratches made it extremely painful. She did not seem to notice it, and I sat by the window and looked outside at the dark mass of the mountains and the even darker water of the loch far below, feeling as if I was intruding on something very intimate, even though they did nothing more than hold each other.

At last I heard Neil moving about, and he told her he would come back to see her in the morning. I glanced at them both, and I could see that they were both in that special world of their own making, and Boucca was a thing of the past. The love between them here and now was all that was important. It took my breath away to see it so palpable between them. It humbled and softened me, and if that was how it made me look too, then by whatever name it was called, love or lust, desire or tenderness, it was something infinitely good and beautiful.

'Goodnight, Charlotte.' Neil remembered me. 'Take care of her.'

'Of course,' I murmured.

He gave her a last long searching look as if he could not get his fill of looking at her, and then he went out and shut the door behind him. Agnes was somewhere out of this world but she smiled at me and told me what I already knew.

'He loves me, Charlotte, and I love him. Don't say it's too soon, because if we knew each other a day or a lifetime I couldn't love him more. Would you – would you have any objection to our becoming related by marriage?'

'Has he asked you to marry him?' I exclaimed.

'Not yet. At least, not with words,' she laughed softly. 'Oh, Charlotte, it's so strange to think such a terrible evening could end up so happily, isn't it? But I can forget all about the terror of Boucca's attack now I know Neil really loves me!'

I went across and hugged her quickly, glad she was so happy again. But there was still the question of the note nagging away at me, and I was a little perturbed in view of Kirsty's scathing remarks about Neil. I did not want Agnes to be bitterly disappointed. She was such a lovely golden girl, the type who inspired a man to offer his heart and soul, a man like Neil, who lived half his life on a higher plane anyway. I was suddenly afraid for the two of them, hoping they weren't heading for disaster.

'Did Neil ask you why you went to the shed in the first place?' I said quickly.

'Yes.' Her brow puckered. 'He didn't know anything about the note, Charlotte, though he thought it might have been one of the stable lads leaving a note for one of the young servant girls. And that the meeting-place wasn't inside the shed at all, but near to it, as it's quite near the start of the woods.'

It sounded feasible enough, I suppose, but it still didn't explain how the note had disappeared. Anyway, I thought it unwise to start stirring up doubt in Agnes' mind, and told her I had better apply some more salve to her skin since Neil had probably got more on his shirt than she had on her body by this time, and then we might as well try to get some sleep. We were both exhausted by the evening's happenings, and Agnes agreed at once. The doctor had left a sedative for her to be taken each night, and in a very little while I could hear her breathing become regular and even and knew that she was asleep.

It was a different story for me. I lay awakè in the darkness, watching the shifting patterns on the ceiling thrown by the moonlight passing over the clouds, remembering that other time when I had done the same thing, the night Robert had come to me. Since then I had managed to let the image dull a little unless I deliberately conjured it up, but now that he was back, here in the castle, the images wouldn't be dulled. They clamoured to be present with me making me remember, until I hardly realised I was twisting my head back and forth on the pillow and unconsciously arching my back and feeling my muscles twitch convulsively. I felt the heat inside me, the spreading ache of desire, the longing to touch and be touched. I buried my face in my pillow and tried not to think of him.

I must have slept because the next thing I remembered was Vinny knocking at the bedroom door with breakfast for Agnes and myself. I leaned up on one elbow and asked Agnes how she felt.

'A bit sore, but not as bad as I'd expected,' she told me. 'Doctor Fraser's magic salve seems to have worked very well.'

'I'll put some more on for you when you've had a wash,' I promised. The scratches certainly didn't look so bad this morning and the swelling on her face had gone down considerably. I was very relieved. The thought of that flawless face being permanently scarred was too horrible to think about. I was suddenly hungry, and Agnes had recovered her appetite as well. Within an hour we had both eaten and washed and dressed ourselves. Agnes refused to spend all day in a night-gown, and she was impatient for the doctor to arrive and tell her she didn't have to stay in bed after all.

Neil came to see her even before the doctor.

'You look much better.' He sounded relieved, too. 'Perhaps the doctor will let you come out in the gig for a while.'

'I doubt that, Neil,' I said. 'The wind in her face will make the scratches sting.'

'I suppose you're right. Well, if you can't come outside, I'll have to sit with you and read you some of my poems.'

'That would be lovely,' Agnes said eagerly. I might as well not be in the room at all, I thought with amusement. But the doctor echoed my comments about the wind, though he said if Agnes promised to sit in a sheltered corner of the garden if the sun came out, it wouldn't do her any harm for a short space of time. He seemed surprised at her sudden improvement, but I wasn't. Love was the best healer of all.

But the sun refused to shine that day. Instead the mist gathered Blackmaddie up in its clutches and blotted out everything farther away than the shrubberies. The trees loomed up like huge grey shapes, and the loch and the mountains might have been non-existent. It was early October now, and the warning of what a winter at Blackmaddie might be like was instilled in me as I tried to force my gaze through the white shroud outside my own window. It was silent and frightening, I thought. I hated it.

I had come here ostensibly to do some sewing because the light was better in my own room, and to give Agnes a chance of seeing other faces besides mine. But of course there was only one face she wanted to see, and he was there now, reading his poetry to her and transporting her to his own private world of the imagination. Before Neil had arrived with his poems, Aunt Morag had looked in to see how she was, and Grandfather and Uncle Andrew had each made a brief enquiry from the doorway. It angered me that Kirsty had not bothered to visit Agnes, and I considered it a slight. I had her very much on my mind, and when she poked her head in at my bedroom door, I felt almost as if I had willed her to come up here.

'Charlotte, have you a minute to put a few stitches in the

back of this dress?' she said imperiously. 'I've just caught it on something, and Mother says it's only the seam. Can it be done without my taking it off?'

I examined the tear. It wasn't much, and though it would have been easier to do it without Kirsty inside it, I had no wish to see her flaunting herself about in front of me as she had on that other occasion, so I said I thought I could manage it if she stood near the window and kept quite still.

'I thought you might have been going to see how Agnes was feeling,' I said pointedly.

'Oh I will. It's just that – well, I don't like seeing people ill in bed. Illness makes me uncomfortable.'

'That's rather an uncharitable attitude, isn't it?' I said curtly. 'You'd expect people to sit with you if you were ill.'

'I'm never ill. I don't believe in it. Not like Katrina. She spent half her time in bed with some imaginary ailment or other.'

I paused in my threading of the needle. This was a new aspect of Katrina. I had been sure she would be as robust and healthy as myself, since we looked so much alike.

'What was wrong with her?' I asked.

Kirsty shrugged. 'Nothing usually, except the desire to have attention all the time. And of course she got plenty of that. All the men used to dance to her tune when she lay in her bed with those great blue eyes wistful and begging for sympathy, and her black hair loose and flowing. She knew how to make the best of herself, even when she was supposedly suffering with stomach-ache or pains in the head.'

'Did she have many such attacks?' I spoke evenly, though my heart was beginning to beat uncomfortably fast.

'Some,' Kirsty said carelessly. 'Finished? Thank you. I'll just look in on your friend for a minute, since you think I should, though I'm not the best of sick-room visitors.'

She went out as imperiously as she had entered, but I couldn't be bothered to think about her attitude to me now. I was intrigued by the little conversation we had just had, wondering about Katrina's illnesses, and if they had really been imagined, or if the stomach-aches and pains in the head had been all too real; and wondering if someone had been trying to get rid of Katrina, too. It was all wild conjecture and I knew it, but here, today, with the knowledge that someone was trying to kill me, and with my friend lying injured along the passage in an attack that I was sure had been meant for me, anything was believable.

Robert had said Katrina died on the mountainside, waiting for a lover who never turned up, a lover who had been too busy in a village tavern with tales of the fortunes to be won in America across the water. And hadn't Robert himself told me in a moment of confidence that one day he'd like to leave Blackmaddie and seek his fortunes in America in the great sheeplands over there? Until that moment it seemed incredible that I had not connected the two items, and perhaps it had been a slip on his part to include that piece of information about Katrina's would-be lover. Perhaps he had never thought I would suspect him, but of course he had loved her. I had thought he was devastated because she had waited for someone else until she froze. But if he was the one, it made the episode in my bed even more degrading. There was no way he was going to stir me into submission again. When I left Agnes' room to return to my own bed, the door would be securely locked every night.

I couldn't help wondering, too, if Kirsty's remarks about Katrina had been meant as a warning for me, and if Kirsty had been involved in Katrina's 'illnesses', and in my own recent experiences. She had had ample opportunity to try to push me over the balcony at the Sinclairs', and she had certainly shown me no love since my arrival. She could have left the note last night, asking me to go to Boucca's shed. It would explain Kirsty's nonplussed look when she returned home from the Sinclairs, and her reluctance to visit Agnes. But I did not want to believe it of her.

It could have been anyone who left the note. I had not thought to examine the hand-writing, and if I had, I could not have said whose it was. I had only ever seen Grandfather's and it certainly wasn't his. It could even have been Robert. He was not at the Sinclairs', though knowing Helen so well, he could have put the idea for the game into her head and arranged for someone else to push me. And he had appeared last night. How long had he been back before I saw him?

But why? I assumed he loved me, though he never said so. Surely he could not have lain with me and not loved me; unless he was really lying with Katrina, and I was merely her shape and form. Oh, it was too hideous, and my imagination was running riot again, but I couldn't stop it. I could believe anything of anyone here. There was something treacherous about every one of them.

Blackmaddie had an aura about her as destructive as a beautiful and possessive woman, my father had said. But it wasn't Blackmaddie; it was the people inside her.

I got up from my window-seat, spilling my pins all over the floor. Suddenly I didn't want Kirsty sitting with Agnes, pretending to be her friend, and perhaps gaining her confidence so that Agnes confessed the fragile love she and Neil shared. I didn't want the burst of laughter coming from Kirsty's cruel lips, and the insulting words that would demean Neil as a man in front of Agnes and destroy all that was between them before it had a chance to reach fruition. I had to make sure there was no chance of that. I sped along the passage to Agnes' room. Kirsty was there, wandering about, picking up a hair-tidy from the dressing-table, examining a hair ribbon, being companionable. I knew it was all pretence, if Agnes did not. I would never trust Kirsty.

'Kirsty's been telling me more about this October fair,' Agnes said as soon as she saw me. 'It sounds very exciting, Charlotte. I shall have to make sure I'm fully recovered by then.'

Kirsty laughed teasingly. 'It might be better if you still had some scars to show, Agnes. There will be plenty of village lads well in their cups that week, and all bent on making the most of every pretty girl they can lay their hands on. And not only their hands, if you follow my meaning.'

I saw Agnes blush. We'd do well to keep in a party whenever we visited the fair, I thought instantly, and I had no doubt all my cousins would make a point of visiting it every evening.

226

'It's an old custom,' Kirsty went on. 'Everything culminates on All Hallows' Eve, so the merrymaking gets wilder as the week goes by. By the end of the week some folk can barely recognise whether their bedmate is their original one or not. I'm sorry if I'm shocking you, Agnes, but it's best to know what to expect.'

'I'm not that easily shocked,' she murmured, but I was not so sure of that.

'Anyway,' Kirsty said lightly, 'the fair starts first thing every morning. As soon as it gets dark, flares and lanterns are set all around the place, and every stall has its own lights, so we shan't all be groping about in the dark. At least, not everyone will.'

She gave a little laugh, and I could see the sparkling excitement in her eyes. The fair certainly seemed to excite Kirsty, and at least it had drawn the conversation well away from Neil.

However, Kirsty soon got bored with sitting around and said she was going downstairs. This hateful mist was making her feel claustrophobic, she added. If it were not so thick she'd go out riding for an hour or so.

'You must come with me some time, Agnes,' she said generously. 'I can teach you if you haven't ridden before.'

She darted a little glance at me. She had never asked me to accompany her riding, nor offered to teach me. Agnes smiled with pleasure at the offer, though I thought she'd prefer it to be Neil who taught her anything. But she thanked Kirsty prettily, and I breathed a sigh of relief when we were alone.

I slept in Agnes' room for a week, though it wasn't strictly necessary. At least I was saved the unease of listening for the voices that seemed to grow out of the stonework so often, and saved from the knowledge that I was locking my door against Robert. I neither wanted to know that he was trying the handle and getting angry at finding it constantly locked, nor continually being frustrated because I was willingly denying myself of something I badly wanted.

When I returned to my room, I locked the door firmly every night and buried my head beneath the bedclothes to shut out the voices if they were there, and the sound of a door handle rattling entreatingly, angrily and finally never at all.

Agnes' scratches healed remarkably quickly. The salve and the constant attention I gave her certainly helped to save the skin from permanent blemish. Neil complimented me on my nursing ability one evening at dinner, and Agnes on her return to radiant beauty. It was a rare moment of unguardedness on Neil's part to let the compliments flow so freely, and Kirsty looked at him in astonishment. His words were usually best on paper, but these were most eloquent, and I saw the gleam of mischief in her eyes.

'What's all this then, Neil? Complimenting two young ladies at the same time? Do you think there's safety in numbers then? Not so likely for one of them to get any designs on you that won't be . . . ?'

'Kirsty, have you heard from Ian?' Uncle Andrew's voice was harsh and threatening as he glowered at his niece. But to my amazement Neil's face went a furious red and he rounded on his father.

'No, don't shut her up, Father. Let her go on making a fool of herself if that's what she wants to do. She seems remarkably good at it.'

'And what are you good at, Neil?' Kirsty was as red as he now. I wished myself anywhere but here as I saw Agnes look from one to the other of them in absolute bewilderment, for it was the first time she had been present at any of my family's sudden explosive temperamental outbursts.

'Leave it, Neil.' Robert shot out a hand as Neil got to his feet and for one minute it looked as if he was going to knock Kirsty about the head.

'She has the devil inside her sometimes,' Neil said between clenched teeth, and I saw Kirsty's hands tighten on her table napkin, though she still stared him boldly in the eye.

'And are you the little angel?' she said sweetly. 'It's not a bad name for you, is it?'

'Must we always have these upsets at the meal table?' Grandfather suddenly roared out, banging his fist on the table to create a louder disturbance than anyone else had

228

done. 'God knows what the young woman must think of you all. She'll think she's come to live among a lot of savages.'

Kirsty tossed her head. She clearly wasn't going to be put off and she bristled at Grandfather's tone.

'Well, it's just so unusual to hear Neil say all the right things to a lady, especially two of them,' she went on. 'I just can't help wondering what's behind it all. Are you changing spots like a leopard at this late stage, Neil? I hope Agnes knows what she's in for, that's all.'

'Shut up, Kirsty,' Neil suddenly shouted furiously. 'I've had enough. And if you must know, I have every intention of asking Agnes to marry me.'

He could not have surprised everyone more if he had jumped on the table and done a sword dance naked. Complete astonishment stunned everyone for a few moments, though Uncle Andrew's face soon registered delighted pleasure. Robert merely slapped him on the back, while Kirsty sat like a fish with her mouth open. I was sure she could not let it go past without some kind of insulting remark, so I thought frantically of something to say to cover up the small silence. But what did one say? It had not been a formal announcement of an engagement after all, and even as I sought for the right words, and Kirsty drew breath, doubtless to utter something damning, it was Agnes who stopped her. She looked straight at Kirsty for a long cool moment, and then she stretched out her hand to put it over Neil's.

'And I have every intention of accepting,' she said clearly.

16

I could only assume that after the scene at the dinner table Kirsty had been given a good talking-to, because she made no further comments about Neil, and though Agnes was curious as to what she had meant, I told her Kirsty was just jealous of Neil's poetic ability and always mocking him.

'She must have a really twisted mind if she can be so mean,' Agnes commented. I couldn't agree more, but I was relieved she did not pursue the subject and seemed to accept my explanation. Anyway, now they were officially engaged, Agnes and Neil were blissfully happy and seemed immune to anyone else's remarks. The mist lifted over the next few days, and the weather seemed set fine for the October fair, and everyone's spirits seemed to be rising because of it. Agnes wrote a long letter to her parents, telling them of the news about her and Neil, and of how exciting the fair promised to be.

'I shan't say too much about the activities going on into the evening,' she told me with a smile, 'or Father would probably think he had to catch the next train up here to try and stop me going, thinking that it would be ruinous for my health.'

'You're so much better, aren't you, Agnes?' I commented. 'The doctor was right about the mountain air. And once you and Neil are married, I presume you'll live here and you'll be completely well in time.'

'Oh Charlotte, I can't tell you how happy that makes me,' she smiled radiantly. 'Not just to be living at Blackmaddie, for I shall never get used to these kind of surroundings, but that as well as getting my heart's desire, I shall never have to move away from you, my dearest friend. I am the luckiest girl alive!'

She hugged me impulsively. I smiled back.

'Providing I am not the one to move away from Blackmaddie!' I said teasingly. I did not know why I said it. There was no likelihood of it, nor did I particularly wish it. The words just came out before I had time to think, but Agnes' face changed its expression at once.

'Oh, don't even think it, Charlotte,' she said. 'I could not imagine life here without you.'

'But when you have a husband, he'll be the one you'll confide in,' I reminded her with a little surge of jealousy. 'You won't want me so much then.'

'I shall,' she said positively. 'You'll always be my friend.'

But things were bound to change between us and we both knew it. They certainly would if I had a husband, if I had Robert . . . I pushed the thought away, and hoped instead that Agnes would not be needing my shoulder to cry on once she and Neil were married. I wondered if I would know, just by looking at her afterwards, if everything was all right between them, or if she would feel the need to tell me. In a way, I hoped not. I would prefer to think that all was well between Agnes and Neil than know for certain otherwise.

Grandfather had seemed entirely pleased at the prospect of Neil taking a wife, and said in his forthright way that it was high time the Stewart boys thought of getting themselves wed. Even to a Sassenach, he had added cheekily towards Agnes, and she had laughed, and said she'd force herself to try to speak with a Scottish accent now and then if it would please him. Those two seemed to have formed an unusual attachment, I realised, and if I had not liked Agnes so well I could have been very jealous of it.

He wanted the wedding to take place at Blackmaddie, and though Agnes half-wondered if she should not go home to Bristol, there was not really any doubt. Blackmaddie would be a perfect setting for a marriage, and I was quite sure her parents would be only too delighted to fall in with Grandfather's wishes, especially as he would be footing the bill for it all. Uncle Andrew and he had evidently got their heads together over this, and were plotting and planning like two old women, I thought with amusement. But it was so nice to have happier times to look forward to, even though the wedding was not to be until the new year.

'A new year and a new life,' Agnes said softly to me. 'Could there be anything better, Charlotte?'

She was so happy, so confident. I had a sudden shiver as if too much happiness was a precarious thing, and started talking about the October fair instead.

'Neil says Ian will be back that week,' Agnes remarked.

'I'm glad of it,' I said grimly. 'Kirsty will be in a better frame of mind then.'

Not that she'd been so bad in the past week or so, I admitted, but Ian's presence and the prospect of the fair would put her in good spirits. There would be a full moon as it approached All Hallows' Eve, giving added light for the evening entertainments and the games and pipers. I was looking forward to it immensely, and I would let no shadows of presentiment spoil it. Nor any anxieties about the way my relationship with Robert was deteriorating.

Since he realised that my door was kept locked, he had treated me more like a sister than a lover. It piqued me, particularly since he paid Agnes many little compliments and teased Kirsty outrageously, while with me he remained polite, distant, even cool. I knew he did it deliberately, but if he thought I was going to beg for his favours, then for the present he could think again. In a way it suited me, while my emotions were constantly changing about my own personal danger and which, if any, of my family meant to harm me. Loving Robert would have complicated things and clouded my judgement. It was better to keep things cool between us and not to let the wanting start again.

By the time the week of the fair arrived, Neil and Agnes and I had ridden over many times to the scrubland where it was to take place and seen the stalls being erected and the teams of village lads at work. Even though Neil was with us, I could sense the comments passed around, and the bursts of raucous laughter that followed left no doubt as to what they were discussing. I knew at once Kirsty had been right about the way some of these nights ended, and that a young girl out alone would be very foolish indeed.

Neil pointed out one large tent at the end of the piece of waste land.

'That's the drinking tent,' he grinned. 'And it's no accident that it's the largest tent of all, for it'll hold more people inside it than all the others put together. They say a piper plays a sweeter tune on a dram of whisky than all your English ale, but I've no doubt there'll be an abundance of both. Plenty of the sailors who'll come up here will be from England and other places so there'll be catering for all tastes.'

'It sounds as if it'll be a pretty wild affair,' I smiled, and he assured me it would be, but extremely interesting as well.

'It was after one of these fairs that I first took an interest in hawks,' he mused. 'There was an old Highlander with a hooded falcon on his glove, and there seemed an affinity between the two of them that was something beyond the affection of human beings, so I decided to train one for myself. But it was a long time before I found Boucca.'

I could see that Agnes did not like to hear the mention of the hawk, and Neil suddenly realised it when she put her hand in his.

'Are you very lost without her, Neil?' she said hesitantly. In answer he turned her palm over and kissed it.

'I'll never be lost, ever again, as long as I have you,' he told her, and I wished I had not been there, for it was a moment when they should have been alone. But so they were, for I did not really exist for them for a few seconds.

Then Neil said we had best be getting back, for it grew chilly and he did not want Agnes to start one of her coughing fits again now she was so much better. I was glad I had made my warm dark blue cloak, for the season warranted its use now, and Agnes was similarly attired in a dark cloak of her own. By the time we reached Blackmaddie again the air had whipped up the warm colour in our cheeks.

We were both exhilarated, and we laughed at Vinny crashing about upstairs as she tidied the bedrooms. I enquired what was going on, for she looked fit to burst a blood vessel.

'It's Cook throwing her weight about,' she informed me. 'Telling me I dinna give Luke enough fresh air and he could still be put outside in his perambulator for an airing as long as he's wrapped up, and that he'll have wheezing lungs before he's five years old without fresh air. Taking on as if he's her babby and no mine. Well I know what's best for him and it's no putting him out in the freezing cold just so she doesna have to listen to him fretting with his teeth.'

'Poor Vinny.' I grinned across at Agnes. 'How many teeth does he have now then?'

'Only one,' she grumbled. 'But that one has got an edge on it like a razor. He'll be on the bottle soon if he's not careful.'

But I doubted it. She grumbled, but I knew she got as much pleasure out of feeding Luke as he did, and I could see the little smile playing about her mouth as she bent over the bed. Still, I did think Cook probably had a point about fresh air. It certainly did Agnes a lot of good, and if the baby was well wrapped up I couldn't see what harm it would do. But it was none of my business, and Vinny would have to fight it out with Cook herself.

Robert was going to meet Ian at the railway station the following day. Kirsty was furious because she wanted to go with him, but her mother had said since she was so keen to go over to the Sinclairs at every opportunity she could accompany her there tomorrow, since old Mrs Sinclair was ill in bed and she wanted to visit her.

'You know I hate sick visiting,' Kirsty wailed petulantly.

'Then you can amuse yourself with Helen or one of the others,' her mother snapped.

'They're children.'

'And so are you, or you act so sometimes,' Aunt Morag retorted. 'I'll have no argument, Kirsty. Ian will be here for over a week, and you'll see enough of him.'

'Anyway, Charlotte can come with me to meet him,' Robert put in. I felt my heart jump at his words, and his eyes challenged me. *Come back with me to the railway station,* they said, *and see if our relationship is as platonic as you would pretend.* I lifted my chin, knowing too how it would annoy Kirsty.

'I'd like that very much,' I said. Neil and Agnes would be happy enough without me for once, and Kirsty could grumble all she liked, but I knew Aunt Morag would have her way. She was a Brodie by birth, and they could dig their heels in when necessary. And I – I felt a sudden excitement. I was going to spend an hour or so alone with Robert and I would not deny that the prospect filled me with exaltation.

I had still not entirely eliminated Robert from being the one who sought to harm me. But I preferred to think of him wanting me and loving me, and for that one hour at least, I was going to pretend Katrina had never existed, that we were starting all over again, Robert and me. After all, he had asked me to go with him, so that must mean he wanted me too.

Once we were on the road together I realised there was something special he wanted to talk to me about.

'Charlotte, I don't want to alarm you, but I would rather you kept close to me or Neil or my father during the next week and took no foolish risks.'

I stared at him. 'What kind of risks?' I demanded. 'You can't throw in a remark like that and not tell me exactly what you mean. Am I in some kind of danger this particular week? Neil has already told us about the drunkenness that goes on and we're well aware of all that.'

'I don't mean village lads and sailors,' he said evenly. 'I mean something closer to home.'

'If you'd stop talking in riddles, I'd have more idea of what to look out for,' I said in exasperation, though there was a strange feeling running through me I had experienced before, as if I knew he spoke the truth, and that I must listen, even though I did not want to hear.

'Ian and Kirsty sometimes go a little crazy, along with others of their age group.' He still spoke cautiously. 'Sometimes they organise parties in the woods and pick on somebody to tease as a kind of scapegoat. I wouldn't want you to get tangled up in any of their nonsense, Charlotte. Sometimes the jokes end up more serious than they started.'

Like the note that Agnes thought was intended for her, I thought in a startled moment. But I had a feeling he was hinting at more than that.

'You mean like this interest they have in the occult and witchcraft?' I said with sudden illumination. 'You think it may be put into practice next week?'

'I didn't realise you knew about any of that,' Robert commented.

'What is there to know?' I demanded. 'I wish somebody would tell me. I know Kirsty is sleeping in Katrina's old room and that the strange pictures on the walls that I find so objectionable were Katrina's. If I had been Kirsty, I'd have got rid of them long ago. Are they dabbling in it at too great a depth, Robert? Is that it?'

He looked at me, a helpless sort of expression on his handsome features.

'I honestly don't know. Sometimes I've suspected so, but then they act so childishly, how can one suspect them of anything evil? What I fear is that they may well be led on in spite of themselves to doing things from which there is no turning back. All I'm asking is that you be careful, Charlotte, and don't be tempted to join in any foolish games organised by those two or their friends.'

I had already had my fill of childish games at the Sinclairs'. He knew nothing of that, and neither did anyone else, but the need to confide in someone was stronger than the caution that had kept me silent so far, and I related the incident quickly to him, keeping my eyes on his face all the time. He showed nothing but concern; there was no flicker of the eye-lids that made me suspect he had arranged any of it.

'You should have said something at the time, of course,' he told me, as I already knew. 'Now that it's so long ago, I think it's best to put it out of your mind, Charlotte, and hope that it was merely a joke.'

I had the feeling that he and I both knew that it wasn't.

Our journey to meet Ian was evidently to be just that, and not a kind of assignation between us. I was disappointed and relieved at the same time. Of course it was better for the fever to burn less brightly between us, though at the moment when he lifted me down from the gig and held me close to him for an instant, it was all there, all the longing and the loving, there in his eyes and reflected in mine. It needed no words.

Ian's train came in very soon, and when he alighted I thought with a little shock how different he looked in a few short weeks. I was used to seeing him running with Kirsty, of course, boyish, teasing. Here on the station platform with his back to the light, he looked more serious, older, darker-haired, until he stepped out towards the light and I could see the friendly smile and the familiar sandy hair, and once in the gig the chatter was the same as always all the way back to Blackmaddie.

After the first greetings with the family and Kirsty's ecstatic welcome, we saw little more of him, except at meal-times, and I heard Grandfather grumbling about it to Uncle Andrew.

'You wanted the boy to go away,' Uncle Andrew said, 'whatever his own inclinations.'

'Aye, it was best.' Grandfather spoke heavily, and I wondered about that little exchange. Was Ian so much his favourite – or alternatively was he becoming anxious about Ian and Kirsty and the fondness they displayed so artlessly? It was still a fondness of children, but if it ever tipped the balance of childish affection, they were not blood-related, but perhaps it was not altogether desirable to Grandfather.

However, there were other things to think about. The excitement of the October fair gripped everyone, and on the first day we made up a complete party, the whole family from Blackmaddie, and some of the servants followed behind. Even Vinny, bringing Luke slung over her arm in a shawl in the way of countrywomen, with his coppery hair bobbing up and down against her breast, his pale greenish eyes alert and darting about. They were almost transparent, those eyes, and they made me shudder, though Kirsty and Ian clucked him under the chin a few times and made him laugh.

The piece of scrubland had been transformed. It was a whole village of stalls and tents and bustling humanity. Fortune-tellers vied with trinket sellers and gypsies, there were ponies and sheep for sale, and chickens squawking by the dozen, it seemed. There was a pressing of people and animals and a merging of smells that hung about the whole area and made it quite humid, despite the time of year. The beer tent did fine business from the moment it opened, with village lads and girls and sailors from the ships in the harbour spilling in and out of it all day long.

'Come on, Charlotte, Robert's going to try his skill with the weights,' Ian yelled in my ear above the hubbub. He dragged me by the arm from where I was watching some arm wrestlers and wondering whether the muscles were going to burst right out of the skin where they bulged and stretched so much. But I willingly let myself be steered away.

They were all large men, giants in comparison with some, and Robert was the most splendid of them all. I felt a thrill of pride as he lifted weight after weight, matching anyone else there, and finally went off with the prize to a thunderous burst of applause.

'That was wonderful, Robert.' Before I could rush up to him myself and congratulate him, Helen Sinclair had pushed through the crowd and thrown herself into his arms. The Sinclairs had arrived after us, and Helen had wormed her way to the front, to be scooped up in Robert's arms as if she were a little doll, and from then on she clung to his side adoringly.

She was only a child, I reminded myself, though when the same sort of thing happened day after day and Helen seemed to be his constant companion, I began to feel restless. I would have liked to wander about the place with Robert on my own, holding on to his arm as Agnes did with Neil, as plenty of other girls were doing.

I could see just what Duncan had meant by his expression 'moon-drunk'. By the end of the week, everyone was slightly moon-drunk, for it was an intoxicating time, with something new to see or do every day, and the never-ending pipers and dancers ready to entertain.

Agnes was enjoying it all, though she confided to me on the last day that Neil was getting a bit tired of it by then. He was not so keen on being in a crowd for long periods of time, and needed time to be on his own.

'He's going to compose a poem about the fair,' Agnes smiled. 'And he's only half here with us now, you know. In spirit he's already busy with it, juggling words and phrases.'

I had nearly had enough too. Contrary to what we had been led to believe, it was only the drinking tent that stayed open for any length of time in the evening, carrying on where the taverns left off, and one or two die-hards such as the fortune-teller, perhaps hoping that people might appear under cover of darkness where they wouldn't venture in daylight. The rest of the stalls and tents closed down, though people still milled about as if reluctant to move away back to the humdrum and ordinary.

It was All Hallows' Eve now, and the final day of the fair. Kirsty and Ian were urging Agnes and me to go with them into the woods for some sport, but I remembered what Robert had told me and declined. I couldn't think there was any danger for us, because they were so high in spirits, two children of the night, but all the same I wasn't taking any chances, and they ran off to join their other friends. Ian was no longer the serious, rather sombre young man I had seen on the station, but Kirsty's playmate again.

The moon was glorious that night, as if to complement the occasion. High and bright, a perfect yellow orb. Duncan had said it was a night when witches were expected to be abroad, but it was all nonsense, folk-lore, and how could one look at such a lovers' moon and think of broomsticks and magic and dark evil rituals? Especially with the haunting tune of a lone piper in the background like some ancient pied-piper luring and lulling.

Agnes and I had wandered a little way from the fair to the edge of the plateau. The village of Blackmaddie was spread out below, the harbour just visible by the light of the moon, the sea a dark gleaming metallic silver. It was very beautiful. We could hear the noise of the fair behind us, but it was subdued from here, less raucous and rowdy. At least, it had been. Suddenly we realised a group of sailors were lurching towards us from the direction of the beer tent. We had come too far without realising it, and they blocked our way as we would have hurried back to the fair and the safety of my family. Where was Neil, I thought frantically? Off composing his poem somewhere in a cranny on the edge of the mountain? Robert had been sitting with the young Sinclair girls the last time we saw them, listening to the piper. Ian and Kirsty were God knew where. The older members of the family weren't here tonight. Duncan was about somewhere, but he was probably in the beer tent.

I felt my mouth grow dry as the sailors suddenly saw us and paused momentarily. I felt Agnes grip my hand. There was nowhere for us to go to avoid them. If we moved backwards we were in danger of slipping down a steep incline. Forwards, we had to get through them to reach the fair. Sideways, the woods; but perhaps if we were nimble enough we could manage to get there before them. They were all drunk and lurching about, some with bottles still in their hands.

'Run, Agnes! Towards the woods, and then back to the fair as fast as possible.'

We picked up our skirts to run. But even as we took the first few steps the group of sailors began laughing and shouting and spreading out in front of us. There were half a dozen of them, and they could outrun us easily, hampered as we were by our long skirts, and drunk or not, their brains were still active enough to know when they saw a pair of pretty girls.

'What's your hurry, my pretties?' they leered. 'Hold fast now, and see what Big Jake's got for you.'

'This way, lads. Spread out. Don't let them get away. There's sport enough here for all of us.'

Oh God, oh God! The breath was a sobbing pain in my chest as I raced towards the edge of the woods, hoping to skirt round it and back to the fair, with Agnes right behind me. But it was hopeless and we both knew it.

'Robert!' I screamed, but the sound was lost on the wind, and with so much merrymaking still going on, I knew no one would hear. The men came closer, and in desperation I turned towards the woods. Maybe Kirsty and Ian would be somewhere close at hand with their friends. If we could find them, any of their foolish games would be preferable to this.

Agnes followed me blindly with the laughing sailors hard behind us. Perhaps they thought we were leading them on deliberately. I could hardly think straight for the pain in my chest. Suddenly I heard Agnes give a cry and then she fell heavily over a tree-stump. I turned to haul her to her feet, but it was too late. Rough hands grabbed me, pulling at my cloak and tearing it from my shoulders, pawing at my bodice, fondling me, ripping the material and slobbering all over me as they exposed my breasts to the cold night air. It was Ruskin all over again. I gathered up all my dignity.

'I'm warning you to leave us alone,' I said shrilly. 'My grandfather is the laird of Blackmaddie, Malcolm Brodie, and if you do anything to harm me or my friend, he won't rest until he sees you strung up from one of those trees.'

They laughed louder.

'I like a spirited piece of skirt,' one said. 'And a Brodie as well. We're coming up in the world, lads. Who's first then?'

I could see two of them struggling with Agnes, and my heart ached for her.

'Leave her alone,' I screamed. 'Take me if you must, but leave her. She's never . . . '

I bit my lip. I couldn't say it. But there was no need. They weren't so drunk that they couldn't scent a prize. One of them was lying flat on the ground in a drunken stupor and I didn't think we'd have any trouble from him. One other seemed to have disappeared, but that still left four. Two holding and groping at me, and two with Agnes. One of these was clearly Big Jake. He yelled at the rest of them, his voice guttural and jubilant, making my blood run cold.

'What's this then? A maid, is it? And just ripe for plucking by the looks. This one's mine, lads. Scouse can hold her still. And you two bide your time with Miss High and

Mighty Brodie. You'd best keep a look-out till I'm done here. Your turn will come.'

He was clearly in charge. Big Jake. I shuddered. I fought and scratched against the two who held me but it was like a caged bird fluttering uselessly against metal bars. I wanted to reach Agnes as the others pinned her to the ground, but it was hopeless. I could see her threshing about, her lovely honey-coloured hair fanned out behind her on the bed of autumn leaves as she twisted frantically from side to side. It was getting dirty, spoiled. Her screams were smothered by the one they called Scouse pushing his fist against her mouth. If anyone from the fair even heard anything they'd merely think it was village lads having a lark with their girls. The two men had her spread-eagled now, her skirts pushed up high around her waist. I sobbed helplessly because I could do nothing to stop it with the men gripping me fast, their hands groping all over me, and I didn't want to watch, to hear.

I closed my eyes tight, pushing out the sight of Agnes' un-used golden body, so pale in the moonlight, the brush of gold at her groin serving to excite these louts even more. I heard their coarse jeering comments and wanted to die for her. They were bent on wenching tonight, and they had found themselves a prize. And I knew so well how degraded Agnes would be feeling. I was experiencing the horror of Ruskin all over again; even now revulsion could still claim my senses with shocking suddenness. I swallowed dryly. I would not let myself watch, but I could still hear, for I could not free my arms to put my hands over my ears.

There was a sharp scream of pain that forced itself through the fist rammed into her mouth, and a disgusting shout of delight from Big Jack at her deflowering. And then I could hear him pumping into her, urged on by his cheering mates, while her screams died away and there was only a horrible muffled sobbing coming from Agnes' throat, echoing my own.

When Big Jake finished writhing against her, Scouse took over, grunting and growling. They were animals; worse than animals. They cared for nothing but self-gratification. The

242

two holding me shouted hoarsely for their companions to hurry up, for they were tired of keeping watch and wanted some action of their own. I could hear the ruttish note in their voices. Oh God, surely they would not want Agnes as well, not *all* of them . . . there was a sudden noise of cart-wheels and men's voices. The grip on my body slackened and they shouted hoarsely that there were people coming, and they'd better leave off and get away back to their ship.

For a moment I thought Scouse was going to refuse to pull himself off Agnes, but Big Jake hauled him away and told him not to be a bloody fool, and minutes later they were running away from us, still fastening their breeches as they ran. My knees felt so weak they almost buckled beneath me, but I sank to the ground with thankfulness.

I held my breath, but the cart slowly trundled past the spot in the woods where we were hidden by trees and bracken, and then it was gone to join the other revellers. I crawled over to where Agnes still lay as if numb with shock, her eyes tightly shut in her white face. She frightened me. For one heart-stopping moment I wondered if she was dead, for she looked as if she was carved out of marble. And then I heard a soft moan come from her lips, and I felt a lump in my throat, knowing how used she must be feeling. Like an object, a thing.

The soft honey-gold hair was a tangled mess with damp leaves clinging to it and dulling it. I pulled her clothes down over her quickly, but not before I had seen the bruises on her thighs where rough hands had pressed the soft flesh. There was blood and fluid seeping into the ground, matting the golden brush of hair. I covered her very gently and took her in my arms. There were no words to say. None that would comfort her. There was only the mute sharing of an experience more destructive to the soul than to the body, an understanding of the raw violation of self that only women who had known it could communicate.

Coming so soon after the attack on her by Boucca, the hawk, it flitted through my mind to wonder if it was all Blackmaddie's doing, after all. If, like Mother, Blackmaddie had not wanted Agnes. But I dismissed the thought angrily. I would not believe it.

Suddenly I heard the sound of wheels again, and they were coming our way, as if searching for someone.

'If we move over to the burn, we'll be out of sight of the road,' I whispered. 'And we can bathe you with the cool water. It will help to ease it, Agnes.'

I helped her the short distance to the burn and ripped a length off the bottom of my petticoat, dipping it in the cool bubbling water and bathing her face first, and then the other parts of her that had been so cruelly used. She winced a little, but I knew the act of cleansing would soothe her mind as well as her body.

The sound of wheels was approaching us again, and I felt my nerves tighten. Agnes and I shrank together, not wanting to see anyone, or for anyone to see us, wondering just who it might be. Then I heard my name being called anxiously.

'It's Duncan,' I croaked with relief. I raised my voice. 'Over here, Duncan, by the burn.'

There was the creak of someone alighting from a conveyance, and as he moved towards the sound of my voice through the undergrowth, Agnes gripped my hand tightly.

'Don't tell, Charlotte,' she whispered. 'Don't tell.'

I hushed her. Of course I shouldn't tell. I knew the shame she was feeling, an inexplicable shame, because her only fault was being born beautiful and a woman. I pulled my cloak round my neck to cover my ripped dress, and fastened Agnes' cloak for her as Duncan reached us.

'In God's name, wha's happened to ye both?' he said in alarm. 'I was sent this way to look for ye, and the young gentlemen are looking in other areas and becoming anxious for your safety. Have you been attacked?'

If we had, Duncan would take up the dirk in our defence, old man that he was. I put my hand on his arm to reassure him, grateful for his concern but anxious that he should not raise the alarm and have everyone knowing of our ordeal.

'We're all right, Duncan. Foolishly, we wandered too far into the woods because it was such a lovely night, and then we heard some revellers shouting and ran toward the burn to avoid them. I'm afraid we both went headlong over a tree-stump and have been nursing our bruises ever since.'

The lies came smoothly to my lips, knowing our dignity depended on them, and any tale was better than the truth.

I heard the relief in Duncan's voice. 'Well, that's a nice way for two lassies to end up on All Hallows, isn't it? Though I'm thinking ye should have had more sense than to come anywhere near the woods after the things I told ye, Miss Charlotte.' He spoke sternly and shook his head in exasperation. 'Ye'd best come straight back with me now, for the young gentlemen are wanting to get ye back home, and let's all be thankful nothing worse happened to ye both this night.'

'Oh, you mean, like being carried off by a witch on her broomstick?' I tried to make a joke of it, but if Duncan only knew, the very worst *had* happened to Agnes, and I put my arm round her as we walked slowly to the gig, blaming her slowness on a wrenched ankle. She hardly said a word, and as we seated ourselves in the gig, Neil came thrusting his way through the trees towards us.

Where were you? I wanted to shriek. *Where were you all when we needed you?* But it was our own fault. We had been warned and we hadn't heeded the warnings. I couldn't blame Neil for not being at Agnes' side.

'Agnes – darling – are you ill?' He rushed over to her at once, and I saw her flinch away at his touch. She murmured that she was all right, just badly shaken after falling, but that there was nothing wrong with her other than that. She insisted on it, even when he suggested bringing the doctor to her, but I knew full well she would refuse to see a doctor. Finally she almost snapped at him not to fuss so much, and if Neil was bewildered at her reaction, I was not. It was as clear to me as if it had been shouted from the tree-tops. Agnes had been raped, and at this particular moment men were the most loathsome creatures in the universe to her; when Neil wanted to take her in his arms, he was all men, coarse and lusting and abusing, Big Jake and Scouse.

I was even more afraid for their future together.

17

I decided to sleep in Agnes' room that night. The narrow bed that had been brought up after Boucca's attack was still there, and I told Aunt Morag that I would prefer it. She didn't seem to care much what I did, and was fretting that Kirsty and Ian hadn't come home from the fair yet. It was hours since I'd seen either of them, but I was more concerned with getting Agnes upstairs and into bed. I told Neil it would be best if she had a good night's rest and not to worry her with too much talking. He and Robert bade us goodnight and I closed Agnes' door thankfully behind them.

'Oh, Charlotte!' Agnes burst into tears and fell into my arms. 'It's not always like that, is it? Feeling degraded and hurt? I – I can't bear the thought of being married if I thought I had to endure . . . '

'Hush darling.' I felt tears in my own eyes, and knew I must tell her of my own experience. About Ruskin and the way I'd felt exactly the same as she did, and about Robert, and the night of love we had shared that was more wonderful than anything I had ever known, before or since. I impressed on Agnes that what had happened in the woods that night was nothing at all to do with the love between a man and a woman who wanted to share their lives together.

She listened, eyes fixed on my face, and I would have felt embarrassed at telling her so many intimate things if I had not been convinced it was the one way I could help her. I did not want the love she and Neil had found to be besmirched and spoiled by those louts in the wood. Finally, she seemed calmer, though whether my words had done any good, only time would tell. We had undressed and were in bed, still talking quietly, when Vinny tapped at the door and came in with two glasses on a tray.

'The missus thought perhaps you'd like a hot drink of milk, Miss Charlotte,' she said primly. 'Seeing as it's a cold night.'

'Thank you, Vinny. Just leave it on the table, will you?'

I was touched by Aunt Morag's thoughtfulness, and though I did not care too much for hot milk I knew it would do Agnes good, so I drained mine to encourage her to drink hers. It tasted a bit chalky, but my mouth felt so dry nothing would taste the way it should tonight. I blew out the candles and said goodnight to Agnes. I was tired and yet my nerves were still jumping, and I suspected Agnes' would be the same.

I was extraordinarily tired, I thought some while later, and yet sleep wouldn't come. It was as if I had been drugged, and yet something in me was capable of fighting it off, except for a terrible lethargy. I didn't think Agnes was sleeping either. Her breathing was still uneven, and it was very stuffy in the bedroom.

'Agnes, will it be too cold for you if I open the window a little?' I whispered.

'Please do,' she whispered back. 'I'm so hot, as if I were on fire.'

I slipped out of bed, feeling a little drunk as I moved across to the window. My arms seemed too heavy to lift them, and objects in the room seemed to swerve and blur in front of my eyes. I stumbled against a table and held on tightly to steady myself. Agnes asked if I was all right, and I realised she was getting out of bed too. She sort of floated across towards me, ghostly in her white night-shift, and I told her to get back into bed. My tongue was so thick the words hardly seemed to make sense. I opened the window and put my head out into the cool night air, hoping it would stop my head spinning round so alarmingly. Agnes was there too, both of us gulping in fresh air as if we were fish thrown high on a bank.

Agnes' room was not directly over the loch as mine was. It faced the woods. I must be hallucinating, I thought wildly, for I fancied I could see a thousand dazzling lights among the trees, dancing and flaring and making my senses swim. I fastened the window so that it was partly open and pulled Agnes back to bed, both of us staggering and needing each other to keep on our feet. I helped her into bed and fell across my own, and knew nothing more until the morning.

But when I awoke my head was crystal clear. Agnes was still sleeping, and I crept cautiously over to the window and stared down at the dark, rustling trees in the wood, seeing again in my mind's eye the dancing lights that circled frenziedly about, hidden partly by the trees. But they had not been all in my imagination, I knew. Last night had been All Hallows' Eve, traditionally the night when witches were abroad and held one of their biggest sabbats. Kirsty and Ian had been missing last night. Had they gone to watch, to participate? My skin crawled, wondering just how deeply my foolish cousins had got themselves involved. Or was I merely letting my fertile imagination get the better of me again?

I caught sight of the two glasses that had contained the hot milk last night that had tasted chalky to me. Perhaps if our nerves hadn't been so alert from the attack in the woods, the drug would have had more instant effect. I caught my breath, knowing I was fast convincing myself the milk had been drugged. But who could have administered it? Aunt Morag? Vinny? Or someone unknown, unsuspected?

Of one thing I was sure. It was no ghostly hand that administered drugs and tried to push me off balconies and sent Agnes – thinking it would be me – to Boucca's shed. It was someone very human and very determined.

'Charlotte?' Agnes whispered. 'Are you awake?'

'Yes. How do you feel this morning?'

She gave a thin smile. 'Better than I expected to. I think the burn water must have worked a small miracle. And I had a very good sleep, though I hadn't thought I'd sleep at all. But I was dreaming the strangest dreams: lights in a wood, flickering and circling. They made me dizzy as if I was being hypnotised.'

I felt a strange excitement despite my dread of the unknown. I hadn't been imagining the lights then, because Agnes had seen them too. I toyed with the idea of letting her

248

think it really was a dream, but the suspicion that was growing in my head was too big to keep to myself any longer.

'Listen, Agnes,' I said urgently. 'Those lights weren't a dream. They *were* there in the wood, and I believe I know what they were. If you feel up to it perhaps we can go for a walk this morning and see if there is any evidence.'

'Evidence of what?' Agnes sounded mystified.

I drew a deep breath. 'Of a witches' coven.'

The words had been said. Out in the open. Stark and frightening. Agnes gaped at me as if I had gone mad, but I had never felt so clear-headed, so certain that this was the evil that smouldered like the embers of a dying fire, ready to burst into flames whenever the opportunity occurred to fan it into life. And Agnes realised that I was deadly serious.

'You're frightening me,' she said at last. 'What evidence do you expect to see?'

'I don't really know. Remains of fires. Scraps of food. Empty bottles. Perhaps a smell still lingering on the air.'

Like the smell that had clung to Kirsty and Ian when they came to my room the night Robert and I . . . when I had been so sure they had been together, but engaged in something other than love-making. Something that drew them together in a wild conspiracy. I was so afraid of my two childish cousins being swept into something they couldn't control.

'Do you remember the book I showed you, Agnes?' I asked her. 'And the sabbats that were usually held on special dates – like All Hallows' Eve? And how it described what happened, with feasting and dancing in some open-air place?'

I did not need to go on any further. I could see Agnes' mind was quickly keeping pace with mine.

'Last night in the wood,' she said slowly, 'you really think that's what it was?'

'I'm convinced of it,' I said firmly. 'I'm going to fetch the book from my room and we'll take another look at it before we go down to breakfast, Agnes, and then we'll just say we're going out for a walk like any normal day.'

*   *   *

I threw my robe over my night-shift, too keyed-up to lounge about any longer. While I was in my own room I dressed into a warm skirt and blouse. By the time I took the book back to Agnes, Neil had looked in to see how she was, and though she spoke fairly normally to him, I could sense the tension in her voice, and knew the underlying fear was still there, and the memories of the rape still very much with her.

Of course I knew they would be. I knew it so well. But thinking about other things was the best way of lessening the horror, and I spoke briskly to Neil. 'We're going to have an all-girls' morning today, Neil, so you'll have to do without your Agnes for a while. After all the excitement of last week, we want to wander about on our own and renew our energies.'

'I see.' He sounded amused at my dictatorial manner. 'Well, don't alarm yourself, dear Charlotte, for I intend speaking with Father this morning on an important matter of my own. It's time he and Grandfather realised there is another Stewart capable of controlling part of the Blackmaddie estate, especially one who is to be a married man in a few months' time, and therefore responsible for a wife and family of his own. So take Agnes off with my thanks for keeping her amused.'

He smiled at Agnes, and though she smiled back there was little real warmth in her smile. At least Neil spoke in terms of a wife and family, I realised, which surely meant he considered himself capable of fathering children. Though now it was Agnes who did not appear to view the prospect with any sign of pleasure, and her hands trembled slightly against the bedcovers. I'd like to kill those louts with my bare hands, I thought savagely, for reducing her happiness to fear of something that should be beautiful.

'What's that book you've got there, Charlotte?' Neil was frowning at me. I showed him the jacket. 'I thought Grandfather had got rid of all those books,' he went on. 'Don't let him see you with it, that's all.'

'Why not? I know he doesn't like any mention of witchcraft, but it's only a book.'

'It was Katrina's,' he said shortly. 'And if you've got any

sense, you'll get rid of it. Throw it in the loch as deep as it will go and forget you ever looked in it.'

He turned on his heel and went out of the room. I was astonished at the vibrant emotion in his voice. I hadn't known the book was Katrina's. For an instant that very fact made me want to fling it away from me, but that was nonsense. What harm could a book do to anyone?

'Are we going to look at it or not, Charlotte?' Agnes said nervously. 'What did you want to find out?'

'Nothing that I don't already know,' I said slowly. I stared at it in my hands, its pages tight together. No, I didn't want to look at it. I had absorbed too much of its content already. Impulsively I went across to the window and before I could stop to think I did as Neil had suggested and threw it into the deep waters of the loch.

'Well, that was a pretty decisive thing to do,' Kirsty's voice suddenly sounded from the doorway. 'Do you always throw other people's property away, Charlotte? I wonder what Grandfather would have to say about that.'

'I should think he'd be as disturbed at discovering some-one had chopped up someone else's dress and stuffed it in a cupboard,' I whipped back at her, my heart thudding at seeing her there so unexpectedly.

She stared back, eyes narrowed. I could see she was burn-ing to ask if I was accusing her, but maybe if she did the question of the book being taken from the same cupboard and turning up in her room might have to be answered. Instead she turned on her heel and stalked away, saying angrily that wasn't it time we came down to breakfast, and muttering insultingly about guests thinking they could do as they pleased in someone else's home.

'Take no notice of her, Agnes,' I said quickly. 'She's probably got a thumping headache from all that incense stuff she's been sniffing, and a night out in the woods.'

We stared at each other. I didn't want to believe it of Kirsty, nor Ian, come to that, but too many things had happened for me to think they were entirely innocent.

We washed ourselves and Agnes dressed. She found it a little uncomfortable to walk too quickly, but we both wanted to get outside and into the fresh air and away from the castle. We ate the minimum of breakfast and left the dining-room as soon as we could. Everyone else had already gone when we got there, or else had not come down yet. Either way, I was relieved we were on our own, so no one could comment on Agnes' pallor or her unusual silence. We walked towards the wood, and I saw her give a shudder as we passed Boucca's shed.

'I begin to wonder if I should have come here at all, Charlotte,' she said slowly. 'My chest is benefiting, of course, but all these other things . . . '

'Of course you should have come!' I linked my arm through hers. 'I want you here, and so does Neil. He loves you – we both do, and Grandfather is quite taken with you.'

'I know Neil loves me, but it is that very thing that makes me afraid.' Her voice was brittle and afraid. 'After last night – '

'I told you, Agnes, last night had nothing to do with the feelings between a man and woman who care for each other deeply,' I insisted. 'It is a completely different sensation, and one to be welcomed, not feared.'

I knew I would not convince her, and it was too soon anyway. It would take time for her bruised body and spirit to heal, and I was glad the wedding was still some months away.

Once away from the castle and into the wood I tried to make her forget about last night, but the very trees and bracken were enough to stir up the memories, even though it was a different place, a different time of day. I should have thought of that. But I determinedly chattered on as if un-aware of the tensing of her hand on my arm, as if we were merely taking a stroll in the unusually fine weather for so late in the year. And then we came to a clearing and the excitement leaped in my veins again.

The signs were all there, if one looked for them. There was the smell of incense, and mixed with that the remnants of cooking – bacon or mutton smells, a bit rancid in the cool morning air. There were bits of bread and scraps of cheese that birds swooped upon, and it was almost possible to make out the scuffed circle where the ring dancing had taken place. My mind winged back to the book I had thrown in the loch. I could see the printed words as if I still held it in front of me.

'The dancing induced a light-headed ecstasy, making them believe they were spinning somewhere above the ground,' I said softly to Agnes as we examined everything around us, 'whirling around in the opposite direction to the path of the sun, after the ceremony of kissing the god/devil wherever he chose to be kissed. I wonder if there was an initiation ceremony last night, Agnes.'

I stopped, thinking she would not want to hear about the orgy that followed the witch-mark ceremony of a new initiate, after her own ordeal last night. But I could not help imagining the group of naked people, copulating under the stars, lit by moonlight, believing implicitly in the rightness of what they were doing. I shook myself. None of this was right; it was wrong, wrong.

'What happens at an initiation ceremony?' Agnes sounded as if she did not really want to know, but felt she must take some part in this conversation. I tempered my reply carefully.

'Oh, the witch-mark that was put on them by the god/ devil, supposedly a scratch from one of his claws, and the promise to devote themselves to the Master. One hand was laid on the head and the other on the sole of the foot and everything in between was dedicated to him. Perhaps being given a new name.'

I avoided all reference to the orgy, and decided that Agnes had heard enough. At least we had found out what we wanted to know. Whether it was a sabbat or not, something had taken place here last night, and I was certain in my own mind what it was.

'It sounds a terrible thing to be taken over like that,' Agnes shuddered as we started on the stroll back towards the castle.

'They aren't taken over unless they choose to be,' I informed her. 'They join of their own free will, and it can be revoked after a certain number of years. Seven, I believe. It's a magic number, seven.'

I remembered when I had first read that, it had given me a certain amount of comfort. I would have supposed one was committed for life in a coven, but apparently it was not so.

We were nearing the stables. I could hear Duncan talking with someone and seconds later Robert appeared. I was always going to be stirred by the sight of him, I thought at once, as my heart gave its familiar little leap of pleasure. He said good morning to us both, but his eyes were on my face, his look intimate, and I wondered instantly if he had tried my bedroom door last night, gone inside and found it empty. And if he had – my thoughts took another disturbing turn – he might have thought I was out here, cavorting in the woods. No, he could not think that! But even so, I had to make sure.

'I'm sorry about being so foolish last night, Robert, after you cautioned me,' I said quickly. 'Agnes and I both had a bit of a fright, and I slept in her room – supposedly to reassure her, but I don't know which one of us needed most reassuring really.'

It sounded obvious to me that I was reassuring *him* of my whereabouts, and remembering that I had told Agnes of the blissful night we had spent in each other's arms, I felt the hot blood in my cheeks. He laughed teasingly.

'As long as you came to no more harm than a fall over a tree-stump, I shall try to forgive you both.'

I laughed back, but Agnes did not.

'I have to go down to the village this afternoon,' he went on. 'Would you both care to accompany me? I know Charlotte is partial to a ride around the harbour, and I fancy some air would do you good, Agnes. You do look less cheerful than usual, if I might say so. And not quite the happy engaged young lady. What has that brother of mine been getting up to? You'll have to curb his exuberance, I can see.'

'Excuse me, Charlotte, but I think I'll go on indoors,' Agnes broke in jerkily. 'I don't feel quite myself and I think

I'll lie down before lunch. Thank you for including me in the invitation, Robert, but I think it would be best for you and Charlotte to go without me, for I'd be poor company today. I'm sorry.'

She moved away from us stiffly, and when Robert would have stopped her I put my hand on his arm and told him to let her go. He had chosen the most unfortunate moment to tease her about Neil; it was enough to set her nerves jumping again.

'What did I say?' Robert demanded. 'I did not think her to be fragile as glass, and it was a harmless remark. Does she think Neil's made of chaff, the same as the rest of them? I can assure you he is not, and he'll make her a worthy husband.'

He sounded angry, and I was sorry he should have got the wrong impression about Agnes, and I knew I had to say something to make him realise my friend would normally look forward to a rich and fulfilling marriage. I had to tell him about last night.

'Robert, can we go and sit in the shrubbery for a while?' I said. 'It's a bit cool, but I'd rather tell you why Agnes spoke like that out here.'

I didn't want to go inside yet, and feel the walls of Blackmaddie closing in around me.

'I'm never cold when you're around, my love.' He spoke softly, intimately, his anger gone, but I didn't want these moments for ourselves. I wanted to explain about Agnes.

His face hardened with contempt for the louts who had claimed her.

'Why didn't you tell us at once?' he demanded. 'We should have found them and ...'

'And what? Knocked them senseless? Killed them? What good would any of that have done for Agnes? Nothing in this world can give her back what she's lost, Robert. Maybe it's hard for a man to understand. Maybe not one of them ever could.' My voice grew thick with emotion, and his big hand closed over mine. He put his face very close to mine, his beard touching my skin, his eyes full of compassion and something else. I hoped it was love. I wanted so much for it to be love.

'Don't ever think men aren't capable of feeling emotions as deeply as women, my little Charlotte. Maybe some of them are more urgent, more basic needs, but feelings of hate and love, lust and pity are common to us all. It's merely that men are more used to hiding their sympathetic feelings, and women expected to hide their desires. But that doesn't mean they don't have them. Does it?' He bent his head and kissed me slowly, lingeringly on the lips, hardly pressing them at all, the touch of his tongue moving sensuously sideways sending a shaft of desire running through me, and I knew that he was right.

I had tried to tell Agnes that taking a woman by force was worlds apart from sharing the experience in love. There was not even the need for pounding passion, as William Derry had thought necessary, for there was more sensuality in the almost passionless kiss Robert was giving me now than in anything I had ever experienced.

'Robert.' His name was soft on my lips, my arms drawing him to me, when there was a sudden almighty scream from the direction of the castle. A scream that went on and on, and an accompanying shouting that made us jerk apart and jump to our feet.

'What the devil!' Robert was seconds ahead of me as we ran towards the noise. It came from the side where the servants' quarters were situated, and when we reached the garden Vinny was wringing her hands frantically, completely hysterical, with Cook trying to comfort her and other servants all clucking away together.

'What's happened?' Robert demanded, pushing his way through and seizing Vinny by the shoulders to shake her into silence.

'The babby, the babby . . . ' Her voice rose again, and he slapped her hard. Her eyes swivelled in her head at the shock of it, but she was still gabbling away unintelligibly and Robert turned in exasperation to Cook, who was only too ready to tell the tale.

256

'She left the bairn out here in the perambulator for some air, Master Robert, like I keep telling her she should – '

'And now he's gone!' Vinny shrieked. 'Spirited awa', and all because I listened to ye, ye old hag.'

'Stop that, Vinny,' Robert snapped. 'Nobody's spirited the child away. There's some perfectly simple explanation.'

'You tell it then!' Vinny was still screaming. 'Did you take my Luke? Because somebody did. He couldna have walked off by himself, no unless he suddenly sprouted grown-up arms and legs to make him tall enough to push the perambulator off as well! Somebody's taken him!'

All the while Robert was questioning Vinny and the other servants as to exact times and movements, I was conscious of a growing horror inside me. The book I had thrown into the loch, I wished desperately I still had it here to check, but I clearly remembered the passage about the sacrifice of a child or an animal and that sometimes it would be a stolen infant. Last night had been All Hallows, and supposedly any rituals that had occurred at the sabbat were over, but I couldn't rid myself of the fear inside me. Irrational, evil, bubbling up inside me like a gathering storm.

'We'll spread out and look for the baby,' Robert ordered, since no one else seemed to know what to do. 'Charlotte, you go inside and see if you can find any of the others and tell them what's happened. The more people alerted the better, though he can't be far. Someone's probably bouncing him up and down this minute and all this screaming is unnecessary. Knowing Vinny's scatterbrain, I shouldn't be surprised if she hadn't put him out here at all this morning and he's sleeping peacefully in his basket.'

She glared at him, but the screams had subsided to a resentful shuddering and sniffing, and everyone spread out to search the grounds while I sped indoors. Grandfather and Uncle Andrew were nowhere to be found, but Aunt Morag clucked her teeth irritably and said she'd take a turn round the shrubberies. I could have told her Luke wouldn't be found there, because Robert and I had just left, but she seemed in no mood for conversation and strode outside. Neil looked quite pale when I informed him what had happened and said he'd take a look at once, though I was not to disturb Agnes as she was resting. I assumed from his agitated look that they might have had words.

'If you see Ian or Kirsty, perhaps you'd tell them what's happening,' I said. I suddenly needed to get outside and look for myself. I didn't like Luke, but the sooner he was found safe and well the sooner I could rid myself of the hideous suspicions that were filling my mind.

I rushed past Neil and ran about the gardens, my footsteps leading me to the edge of the loch. The dark waters rippled and splashed against the bank with a menacing, smacking sound. A greedy, satisfied sound, such as Luke himself made when he sucked furiously at Vinny's breast. I stared into the loch with dilated eyes. Was he here? I thought agonisingly. Had his perambulator somehow rolled steadily down the small incline, gathering speed until it hurtled headlong into the water to be swallowed up greedily? And if it had, how had it started its journey? Not by itself, and no one would ever know. I could hear the harsh sobs in my throat, wishing desperately that I had never come to Blackmaddie, for it had opened up my mind to dark possibilities I had never dreamed of before.

I had almost convinced myself that Luke was here beneath the dark waters, and that my footsteps had been led here by someone – or something – to tell me so.

'Charlotte, we've found him!'

I suddenly heard Robert's voice calling to me, then to Neil and Aunt Morag. He didn't know where I was, and his voice receded as he went off in another direction to see where I had gone. I was stunned for a moment. I had been so sure. The tears were running down my face with wild relief that witches or demons or worse had not claimed little Luke and flung him into the waters of the loch.

I didn't want to face anyone for a few minutes until I had recovered my composure. My face might betray too many things – horror, suspicion, fear, and a wild relief that surely was exaggerated in the circumstances when no one else but me – and Vinny herself – had any doubt that the baby would be found safe and well? And her fear was a natural one. I sat quietly by the loch until my heart stopped its pounding and then began to walk slowly towards the castle.

I could hear Uncle Andrew's voice coming from the stables. There was a small group of servants with their heads bobbing together as they discussed the morning's excitement. Aunt Morag was scolding Kirsty loudly in the servants' hearing, which must have infuriated that young lady, but I gathered from her tearful expression and her snappy replies that she had merely taken Luke off for a stroll in his perambulator in an effort to stop him crying. It had been as simple as that, except that Kirsty had neglected to tell anyone, which seemed a bit foolish but typical of her impulsive ways.

I didn't want to talk to any of them. Besides, there was something else stirring inside me now. Surely after the distress Vinny had shown, and the anxiety of the baby being missing, surely it would be the most natural thing for Luke's father to go to her and see for himself that the child was all right. They would be together right now, the three of them. It would be the most reasonable thing to suppose, and I badly wanted to know.

There was no sign of any of the Blackmaddie menfolk. Uncle Andrew had disappeared again, and my three cousins were nowhere in sight. Nor Grandfather. My heart pounded again. I was going to know the truth about this, at least. I skirted round the side of the castle and slipped in the door of the servants' quarters, past the kitchens, where all the chatter was still concerned with the baby. No one bothered to look into the passage where I crept silently past and up the short flight of stairs where the bedrooms were situated. I knew Vinny had a tiny room to herself because none of the others were willing to share a room with her and a caterwauling baby, and it was right at the end of the passage, where there was a connecting door to the main part of the castle. I could have come in that way, but I might have met a member of my family.

The door was closed, but I could hear voices inside. Two voices, Vinny's and a man's voice. I could not tell whose it was, but Vinny was crooning to the baby in that sing-song voice of hers and telling him to smile at his daddy. So I was right, and he was in there, I thought, with a surge of excitement. I was half-tempted to burst inside, but something held me back.

It had to be someone I knew and perhaps loved. I hated the thought of it being Uncle Andrew, because of the implications of the inheritance. Neil had paled when I told him Luke was missing. Robert – I couldn't bear it to be Robert. As far as I knew Ian was busy with his packing, and surely, oh, surely not Grandfather.

There was a rustle of skirts behind me and Kirsty came storming along from the servants' door, her face fiery and tear-stained from the dressing-down she'd had from her mother.

'What are you doing here, Charlotte?' she snapped rudely. 'Agnes is looking for you, and I have to go and make my peace with that wretched Vinny.'

She pushed past me, tapped on the door and went inside without waiting for a reply. I hurried through the connecting door to the castle, but not before I had seen Ian and Vinny embracing, the baby held tightly between them.

18

I certainly didn't want to see Agnes just then. My head was in an absolute whirl as I hurried up the long staircase and shut myself in my own room and turned the key. I could hardly believe what I had seen. Of all people, it was Ian who was Luke's father, the least complicated of my cousins, the most artless of companions. I had never seriously thought it might be him. It didn't matter to me, and I was mightily relieved it was none of the others, and yet there was a sense of disappointment all the same, a sense of being let down by my own judgement, as if truly nobody here was quite what they seemed.

Kirsty obviously knew and didn't care. That was another peculiar fact. I'd have expected her to be deeply resentful of Ian's attachment for Vinny, not that any one of them had ever given the slightest inkling of it. I wondered if anyone else knew. Grandfather and Uncle Andrew did, I thought instantly. That was why it was thought best for Ian to be sent away. I supposed the matter was kept quiet because of family pride, and that was perfectly understandable.

But I was still conscious of a feeling of shock. Ian, *Ian!* But it wasn't Robert, was the next wild thought that raced into my mind. He hadn't after all been the one to lie with her, and my heart leaped at the knowledge. At that moment I could forgive him anything, even calling me by *her* name at the moment when his seed exploded into me. I would only remember the exquisite pleasure and none of the pain.

'Charlotte, are you there?' His voice was in the passage outside my room and I unlocked the door quickly. There was a relieved look on his face. 'Everyone's wondering if you're the next one to get lost. You've heard the bairn's been found, I take it? I knew he would be. That girl shouts before she's hurt. Hey now, my darling, what's all this?'

His voice softened as the tears brimmed up in my eyes again, and he mistook my emotion for single relief over the baby being found. But it was so many things – relief that Luke hadn't after all been snatched up in the cause of witchcraft; relief that I knew the baby's father's identity after so much uncertainty; most of all, relief that it wasn't him. Not my Robert, my magnificent Robert.

Before I could stop to think I had thrown my arms round his neck and pressed my mouth to his. There was an immediate response from his lips and his body as he kicked the door shut behind him. He held me close in his arms and somehow he was propelling me towards the bed. I wanted to protest weakly that I hadn't intended any of this, that my door was unlocked and anyone could come looking for me, that it was the middle of the morning on the Sabbath day and that being pushed back on to a bed and suddenly feeling the hard warmth of him inside me hadn't been my intention at all. But there were no words between us, only the pressure of his body on mine, his mouth covering mine, his soul touching mine, quick and urgent and glorious. I gasped with the ecstatic first moment of our uniting, marvelling again at the way our bodies moulded together, thinking with an exquisite headiness that this was so wonderful and so wanted.

It wasn't prolonged, yet just as fulfilling as if it had taken all the hours of darkness. He was a champion, a lion, and when he held me tightly to him for the final shuddering together it was my name he whispered against my mouth, and everything was vindicated in a single moment.

'I love you, Charlotte.' His voice was thick with emotion. 'For you satisfy a need in me that no other woman ever could or ever will.'

'It's the same for me,' I whispered, regardless of any modesty or reluctance to speak so freely, for what need was there for modesty between us? None at all while his body still covered mine and we were as close as any two people could ever be. But there were movements along the passage and reluctantly Robert drew away from me and covered me, a smile still lingering around his mouth.

'I knew from the beginning that your fire would be a very welcome place, Charlotte. Didn't I tell you so?'

I laughed back at him. 'You did, and I was outraged, I seem to recall. Thinking I had come to a land of savages.'

'And am I too savage for you?' he said teasingly.

Oh no, savage or tender, slow and sensual or urgent and thrusting – as long as he loved me that was all I needed to know and he could take me any way he pleased. Any time, anywhere. I caught my breath, knowing how much I loved him, but I told him provocatively I should need to consider that question after further consultations. He laughed delightedly and moved away from the bed to the window, while I went across to the dressing-table and tidied my rumpled hair. My eyes were like stars, my mouth parted, my cheeks red. I looked like the portrait of Maddie, but there was a difference. She had looked voluptuously inviting, enticing. I looked happy and satisfied, without the eternal searching that was to be found in her eyes. I had my happiness, right here at Blackmaddie, and I could barely remember the moment not very long ago when I had wished desperately I had never come here. If I had not, I would never have met Robert, and fulfilment would have been forever denied me.

The sounds in the passage came nearer, and I realised it was Agnes and Neil outside my room. I called to them to come in, and I was struck immediately by the unhappiness on Agnes' face. They looked less like an engaged couple than a pair of squabbling hens. But I made no comment, and said instead that it was a relief that Vinny's baby had been found or the whole castle would have been thrown into a frenzy searching for him.

'We might have unearthed some long-hidden treasures.' I tried to lighten the atmosphere by some teasing words, dismayed at the trembling look of Agnes' mouth after my own new-found joy. Something had clearly happened between her and Neil, and not to her enjoyment. I glanced at him, and his face was dark and scowling, and he made no attempt to hide it.

'There's no treasures about this place,' he growled, 'and no perfection anywhere under the stars.'

Robert glanced sharply at him too, clearly sensing Neil's withdrawal into his old nature.

'I gather you're composing one of those deep poems that nobody else can understand and off in another world, brother,' he grinned, as if hoping to jolly Neil out of his morass of gloom.

'Another world might be preferable to this,' Neil muttered.

'Well for the present we'll all have to be content with this one.' Robert's voice was brisk as he clapped his brother on the shoulder and led him out of my room. 'And there's something I want to talk to you about since you've expressed an interest in taking over some of the running of the estate.'

I thought I heard Neil mumbling that it all seemed farcical now, but I wasn't listening to him any more. I was anxious at the numb look on Agnes' face as she stood motionless in the middle of my room, a little as she had looked after those men had raped her. I crossed the room and closed my door firmly, then went and put my arms around her.

'What's happened?' I said softly. Her dark, expressive eyes filled with tears. I could feel her trembling and led her to the bed and made her sit down with my arms still holding her.

'He – he came to tell me the baby was all right,' she said haltingly. 'I was lying down on my bed. I'd loosened the bodice of my dress to be more comfortable. I was glad about the baby, Charlotte. Any woman would have been, and I sat up to tell him so. He – he was looking at me very intensely, and he gave a sort of gasp and reached out his hand to touch me – here – ' she motioned towards her breasts, and I felt a sense of despair, almost knowing what she was about to tell me.

'It was a tender movement, Charlotte, but as he leaned towards me everything seemed to tighten up inside and I was pushing him away, fighting in panic to get away from him. He couldn't believe what was happening, and he got angry and asked if this was how I'd behave when we were married.'

She stopped, as if unable to tell me the rest, but I made her go on.

'I was crying and shouting at him, hardly able to breathe, telling him I wasn't sure I wanted to marry him or anybody, and anyway, he probably wouldn't want to marry me now.'

'You didn't tell him about last night?' I was appalled. 'Not about Big Jake and Scouse – all of it?'

'All of it,' she said dully. 'Just how painful and humiliating and hateful it was, and how I didn't know if I could ever bear another man's touch after what they had done to me.'

'Oh, Agnes! What was his reaction, for heaven's sake?'

But I had already guessed. Robert had discovered about me and Ruskin and had been able to leave it in the past where it belonged. But Neil; Neil was a different kind of man, sensitive and creative with an artist's temperament.

'He looked as if he hated me,' she said shrilly. 'As if it were all my fault. As if I were the guilty one because of what those two had done to me. I feel as if we have gone so far apart in the last half hour it will be impossible for us ever to grow close again. And I love him so, Charlotte. I wanted his understanding – not his forgiveness, for I have done nothing wrong, have I? But he could give me nothing, and I doubt if our engagement will continue.'

She leaned against me and I could feel the sobs shaking her body. I wept for them both, but there was no comfort I could give her. I could understand each of them for I knew their characters so well, but I wished fervently that Agnes had not felt the need for confession at that moment. It was something that should have been kept a secret for ever from a man such as Neil. But it was too late now and the damage had been done, and I could only hope it was not permanent.

I did not like to think of Neil's state of mind at this precise moment. Always volatile, precarious, and he had shown his fury when he had killed Boucca with his bare hands after its attack on Agnes. Now the woman he loved had been defiled and heaven knew what revenge he might seek. He'd never find the two who had raped her, but I was more afraid of some self-inflicted hurt, though I knew better than to say so to Agnes. I could only hope Robert had prised the truth out of his brother and managed to instil some sense into him. If anyone could help him, Robert could, and I realised how often I leaned on his strength and how confident I was that he would solve every problem for me and everyone else.

I heard the distant sound of the gong and told Agnes we had better go downstairs for lunch.

'I couldn't eat anything,' she said. 'Please, Charlotte, make my excuses, will you?'

'I will not,' I told her gently. 'You must eat. You barely picked at breakfast, and you'll feel better with hot food inside you. I shan't leave you, and I shall insist that you come for the ride with Robert and me this afternoon.'

'Not to the harbour.' The association with sailors was obvious.

'All right,' I soothed her. 'He said he had to go to the village, but then I'll ask him to take us up in the mountains. It will be like being in . . . '

'Another world?' Agnes finished for me as I hesitated. She gave a twisted smile. 'I almost wish I were there too, in Neil's other world, so that I didn't have all the unhappiness of this one. But take that anxious look off your face, Charlotte. I know you're right and I should not be sitting here and brooding on something that's happened and can't be undone. I'll do whatever you say.'

I tried to cheer her up, but her face was a mask of politeness, so that even Kirsty's barbs couldn't touch her. Neil spoke little to anyone at luncheon, and when I told Robert Agnes was coming with us, Neil didn't comment.

Once outside in the cool afternoon and well wrapped in our cloaks, I asked if we might go to the mountains and not the harbour.

'Of course,' he said at once. 'We won't bother with the village anyway. My business can wait, and it's time you saw some of our natural beauty spots from close range.'

I knew at once that Neil had confided in him. The closeness of our bodies seemed to have communicated itself to our minds and given us a sixth sense as to each other's thoughts. I was touched that he dismissed his business in the village so easily and turned the gig away from Blackmaddie and towards the mountain paths that were wide and easily accessible on the lower slopes, though higher up we would have to proceed on foot if we were to appreciate the beauties of the surrounding countryside.

'Can you manage, Agnes?' I said anxiously, when we finally alighted, and the cool wind stung our faces. I did not want her getting short of breath and collapsing up here. It was suddenly reminiscent of Katrina, only there had been no one here to help her.

'I'm perfectly all right,' she murmured, 'as long as I can hold on to Robert's arm.'

He offered it immediately, and I was the one forced to pick my own careful way along the stony path and try not to think how different it might have been if Agnes had not joined us after all.

We were nearing a wider stretch of track, and Robert paused and suggested we rested for a few minutes. We had hardly looked below us until that moment, but now we had a chance to gaze around at the panorama spread out below, and it was magnificent, awesome, a kaleidoscope of colour. Blue-white mountains stretching as far as the eye could see on one side, with the glimpse of the harbour and the wild grey sea beyond it, almost lost in a hazy mist. And in between the spires and turrets of Blackmaddie, grey with a dull sheen in the occasional shafts of sunlight that appeared from behind the clouds. Around it the dark green of trees and the russet and gold of bracken, and the dark blue waters of the loch. A fairy-tale place out of a children's fantasy world, unreal and imaginary.

I could see Robert's eyes on my face, reading in it the same emotions he had seen on the day I arrived at Blackmaddie. I remembered his words then: *Welcome home, Charlotte Brodie.*

And I think we had both known, even then, that a bond had been forged between us that nothing could ever break. I shivered all the same at the inevitability of it.

'There's a hut not far from here where we can rest

properly and take a drop of brandy,' Robert said at once. 'Can you both manage to go on?'

Agnes said of course she could. She seemed determined not to be thought a nuisance, though she looked very tired to me. She had had two terrible shocks in the last twenty-four hours, I reminded myself. First the rape, and then Neil's rejection of her when she needed him most. But the last thing I wanted to do was to go to the little hut. Maybe it wasn't the one where Katrina had waited for a lover who never came, and yet surely it was the most likely, the nearest one from the castle. Maybe we were following her footsteps, and Robert's? *Was* he the lover who never came, I wondered?

I shuddered, wishing now that I hadn't suggested coming here. But the other two were already some distance away, and unless I wanted to stay here all alone and look as if I was throwing a tantrum, I had no option but to follow them.

After all, it was a relief to be inside and close the door. From the window there was still a good view, without the keenness of the wind to snatch at faces and fingers. I rubbed my cold hands together while Robert dusted off a bottle of brandy and two little cups. There was a chair and a mat on the floor and a cruisie lamp, and in the small cupboard with the brandy some hard biscuits were kept in a tin, though they didn't look very palatable to me, and Agnes and I both refused. The brandy warmed us, and after I had finished my cup, Robert drank from the same one. Agnes sank gratefully on to the chair, while Robert and I gazed out of the window at the scene below.

'You won't mind if I have a little doze, will you?' she murmured. 'I shall be quite all right to walk down again if I can just close my eyes for a few minutes.'

'That's all right, Agnes,' Robert assured her. 'Take as long as you like. We can afford a good hour up here before the light even begins to show signs of deteriorating.'

She closed her eyes thankfully, the brandy lulling her senses. But somehow it heightened mine, and all I could think of was Katrina: Katrina gazing anxiously out of this very window, full of anticipation at first, of excitement and the thrill of knowing she would spend the next hour in a lover's arms; and then the gradual realisation that he wasn't going to come. The darkening skies, the first soft flakes of snow that became a blizzard, the sudden claustrophobia, the need to get out and find her own way back down the mountain-side where she was found, frozen, dead.

My breath was coming very shallowly in my chest as the images ran through my mind as if I could see it all happening in front of me. I had to know if this was the place.

'Robert,' I began tremulously. 'Katrina . . . '

I turned to look at him. He was gazing outside, his face blank and staring. I knew he was reliving it too, but how much of it? I wondered despairingly. And just how much had he loved her?

'Yes,' he said at last, 'Katrina. We have to talk about her, don't we? She was very much involved with some secret society, Charlotte.'

I started, for this wasn't quite what I had expected to hear. I glanced at Agnes, already asleep, her head resting against the side of the chair. I drew nearer to Robert so that even if she stirred in her sleep she would not overhear us.

'You mean a – a coven?' I whispered. 'Witchcraft – was that it?'

'She was headstrong and wilful.' He neither acknowledged nor denied my question, but there was no need. He seemed to be talking to himself rather than me, trying to get things clear in his own mind. 'And secretive, too, in the last months of her life. I thought at first it was harmless, a sudden urge to do something different and exciting. They seemed to treat it as a new game . . . '

'They?' My heart gave a jump.

'But she wanted to get out of it.' Robert's voice suddenly took on an intense low note. 'I know it. She wanted to be free of it, and it wasn't time, you see.'

Seven years, the book had said. Once you gave your allegiance to the devil, you were committed for seven years. My mind was spinning with all he was telling me. I was half-mesmerised by the low drone of his voice, the only noise in the silence of the mountain save for Agnes' regular breathing. I couldn't speak, only listen.

'I'm afraid for Kirsty. She wanted so much to be like Katrina. She adored her, and she's so easily led. I was shocked when I found she'd moved into Katrina's room after she died. It was unhealthy, and I didn't know how she could bear to be surrounded by all Katrina's belongings like that, as if she wanted to assume Katrina's personality and absorb everything that she was. It was – obscene in a way.'

I shuddered, his words echoing my own feelings about it exactly, though I hadn't realised the full extent of Kirsty's obsession until now.

'And was Katrina so very lovely?' I said hesitantly, despite everything feeling a stab of jealousy at hearing him speak about her so emotionally. Robert gave a sort of strangled laugh.

'She was the loveliest girl on this earth at one time.' He spoke almost angrily. 'I even thought I was in love with her myself for a time, though it could never be, of course. And then she changed. It was as if there were a sheet of glass between her and the rest of the world. She looked the same, spoke the same, but she wasn't Katrina any more. She wasn't the same girl and we just couldn't reach her. She was – someone possessed.'

'This hut,' I whispered. 'Is this the one . . . ?'

'Oh aye.' He turned from me and stared out of the window. 'This is where she waited. I wonder how long it took before she realised her lover wasn't going to come? If she guessed that it was deliberate, that he'd expect her to wait? He couldn't have foretold a blizzard on that day. Even he couldn't have ordered it specially, could he, and he was certainly roaring drunk when he arrived at Blackmaddie, babbling about forgetting to meet her on the mountain. But by then it was too late, of course.' His voice was despairing.

I took a step backwards from him, my heart pounding. What was he intimating? That Katrina had been left here to die deliberately?

'What are you saying, Robert?' I could hardly get the words out, and my voice was hoarse with fear. Agnes and I were alone with him up here, and no one knew where we were, and Agnes was sleeping. It was just Robert and me, and he sounded so strange I hardly knew him any more. I was afraid.

He turned sharply and I couldn't see his face as he stood against the light from the window, only the dark shape of him. He moved forward and pulled me into his arms.

'Not me, darling,' he said urgently in my ear. 'Not *me!*'

'Are you two having a quarrel?' Agnes' voice penetrated my jangling senses. 'Hadn't we better be getting back down? I'd hate to be up here if the mist came down, though one could always drink oneself into a stupor until it lifted, I suppose.'

I leaned weakly against Robert's chest, thanking God for her prosaic words at that moment.

'Agnes is right, Robert. Let's leave here.' I tried not to shudder. 'I'm beginning to feel stifled in this place.'

'It's not too sweet, is it?' Agnes roused herself, completely unaware of my tumultuous emotions. But it was better so. If she was to marry Neil and live at Blackmaddie, it was best that she knew as little as possible about the dark side of my family.

If she was to marry Neil . . . I remembered that even that was less of a certainty now. I followed the two of them down the mountain until we reached the gig, my mind still interpreting all Robert had told me. Not him, he had said, not *him.* And I believed him implicitly. But if not him, then who? If what he had intimated was true, then the would-be lover who had failed to meet Katrina was very much involved with the coven as well, so who at Blackmaddie . . . ? Neil, Ian, Uncle Andrew, a servant, a stable-lad? If I mulled over it much longer I was going to drive myself over the edge of madness, imagining the whole of Blackmaddie engaged in witchcraft.

'Charlotte, are you feeling quite well?' Agnes looked at me anxiously as we rode back in the gig. 'I think the outing has done me some good, but you look very pale.' Her hand reached out for mine, exclaiming at its coldness, and I tried to smile as naturally as I could.

'I do feel chilled,' I murmured. 'I think being so high up and realising how insignificant we really are took me a little by surprise. I am sure I shall be fine once we are back at Blackmaddie and I have a hot drink inside me.'

'We had better see about that as soon as we return,' she agreed, almost as if she was the one who belonged, and I was merely the guest. But she would belong as much as I did when she was Neil's wife. Anyway, it made no difference to me that she was taking me over at that moment. It was perhaps what I needed, for I couldn't seem to think properly by myself. My own churning feelings and the sight of Robert's still, silent face put barriers between us again and I knew it. We had had to bring Katrina out into the open eventually, but now that it had happened, it was more unnerving that I had ever imagined it would be.

I forced myself to think of the one good thing I had learned. Robert had said he'd even thought he was in love with her for a time, but the very way he'd said it led me to believe he had been quickly disillusioned, and I hugged the knowledge to myself like a living thing. He might have loved her a little, even when she was – possessed – but it was a love of which he was ashamed, I was sure of it. And in a burst of illumination, I knew that the moment he had spoken her name during our act of love, he had been mourning the Katrina that was, before something evil took control of her, and not really fantasising about her in the way it seemed. No one here, I thought again, was exactly what they seemed.

There was a gig outside the castle when we arrived back at the stables. Duncan hurried out to help us down, an anxious look creasing up his gnarled old face.

'The laird's been took fair bad,' he told us without preamble. 'Some sort of heart attack by the looks. The doctor's been with him a time now and there's such a wailing going on in the kitchens you'd think he was in his grave already.'

Agnes gave a little cry. She was very fond of Grandfather, and there was genuine distress on her face at Duncan's words. Robert told him tersely not to be so morbid until there was real cause, and went striding ahead of us towards the great door. I felt a clutch of fear at my side, for Black-maddie without Grandfather was unthinkable, like a forest without trees, a sky without sun. But he was old, and the very fact that he had wanted Mother and me to come here was because he knew he was ailing. He hid it well behind the brusque mask he wore and his roaring voice, but his advancing years were against him, and we must all be aware of it.

Aunt Morag and Kirsty were in the drawing-room, and Kirsty's face was tear-stained. She did have feelings then, I reflected, and immediately bit my lip at such a mean thought at this time.

'How is he?' Robert asked at once.

Aunt Morag shook her head. 'Not good,' she admitted. 'The doctor does not give much hope for his recovery. Your brothers and Andrew are with him now. The doctor sent us out as he said Father needed air.'

Robert waited to hear no more, but was mounting the staircase two steps at a time. The four of us looked at each other uncomfortably. I knew Agnes felt embarrassed in the midst of a family crisis, but she was Neil's fiancée now as well as a guest, and had every right to be here with us. I tried to convey it with the pressure of my hand on her arm. I still felt the need of a hot drink, but somehow it seemed wrong to ask for something for my own comfort when Grandfather was dying upstairs.

My eyes blurred at the thought. That fine old man, a giant among them all, a true Brodie in the old tradition, fierce and proud – never to hear him roaring out his orders again, knowing they would be obeyed to the letter. Mother and I had agreed to leave our home and travel to the farthest part of the country at his command. Only it hadn't worked out that way for Mother, and it had been left to me to come here, bringing the likeness with me that I hadn't even known I possessed. I was even glad at this moment that the sight of me had been such a joy to Grandfather because of it. Perhaps he too had seen in me the Katrina that was, before her beauty had been tainted by the character change she had undergone.

There was a movement from upstairs and Ian came halfway down the stairs. He looked older, as if everything young in his face had been replaced by lines I hadn't noticed before. He looked haggard and grey.

'Will you all come up?' His voice was heavy. 'He's not gone yet, but he's slipped into a coma. The doctor thinks he'll not come out of it, so it makes little difference how many surround his bed.'

They must all be remembering Katrina, I thought, as I followed my aunt and cousin, with Agnes behind me. But I was remembering Mother and how I had held her in my arms while her eyes popped and her mouth opened and shut like a fish. I was afraid of death and I didn't want to see it again. But I was hardly able to turn and run, even if all my instincts told me to do so, and at last we all entered the room. I felt my nostrils pinch together at once, for it didn't need telling that Grandfather was dying. The smell of death filled the room, and he lay there under the covers, the great mound of him barely moving, already grey, the cheeks sunken, eyes closed, the faintest movement of his throat the only perceptible sign of life. A small bubble of spittle appeared at the side of his mouth, and I wanted to weep for the spirit of the man who had been so dominant until today.

The Blackmaddie men surrounded him, two on either side, while the women stood at the foot of the bed. It was like a frozen tableau as we waited for Grandfather to die. It was a ritual, the waiting, because once he was pronounced dead the waiting mourners would suddenly spring to life and move about their duties, proving to themselves, maybe, that they lived while he was dead. I could hear muffled sobbing beside me. Agnes and Kirsty. But my own eyes were dry. The mourning time had not yet begun, only inside me.

Every few minutes, it seemed, Doctor Fraser stepped forward and held Grandfather's wrist or touched the feeble pulse at his throat. It fluttered on, but no one made any attempt to move or even speak except in hushed whispers. And then, just as the daylight was beginning to fade and candles had been lit in the room, Grandfather seemed to gather up enough strength to give a loud sigh, and the next minute exhaled the final breath from his lips, and all was still. Grandfather had died with dignity.

'He's gone,' the doctor said gently, and Aunt Morag immediately burst into noisy crying and rushed from the room. We could hear her outside, trying to compose herself, for she was not given to public displays of grief, even on such an occasion as this. The tears were in my eyes now, and running down my cheeks, and I would not stop them. I watched as one by one Uncle Andrew and the Stewart boys bent and kissed the face of my grandfather, and then Aunt Morag returned and did the same, followed by Kirsty and me, and finally Agnes. I leaned towards the old face, knowing I was seeing it for the last time, for I could not endure seeing it laid in a coffin, and whispered my own good-bye to the old man who had been the means of introducing me to my love.

'I won't forget you, Grandfather.' The words were a whisper between us two, and then I followed the others outside the room, glad to breathe in air that wasn't stale and rancid. I leaned against the wall for a moment to recover, though the others were already moving downstairs to congregate in the drawing-room, needing to be together at a time of grief. I was touched to see that Neil had put his arm round Agnes' shoulders as she seemed to be overcome by a sudden rush of weeping.

'Charlotte.' Uncle Andrew suddenly stood in front of me, his voice ragged. 'Will you please come with me to Father's study before we join the others in the drawing-room? There is something I have to tell you.'

19

It seemed a strange time for Uncle Andrew to want to see me alone. The others would consider it very odd, and I couldn't think what reason he had for the request. But I felt bound to follow him, and we faced each other across the heavy leather-covered desk that had been Grandfather's. Uncle Andrew now sat in Grandfather's chair, the laird of Blackmaddie. There was a lump in my throat that I had to force down. He poured two glasses of brandy and handed one to me, bidding me drink. It was the second glass of brandy I had taken that day, and the fiery liquid burned my throat.

'You'll think it strange for me to ask you to come here.' His voice was more gentle now. 'And at such a time. But many years ago I was brought to this study with the same request, Charlotte, on the death of your grandfather's father. It is the custom of Blackmaddie.'

He drank deeply of his brandy and poured another while I sipped at mine. I could understand his emotion, but not his words.

'Won't you explain, Uncle?' I said tremulously.

'The reading of the will takes place one calendar month following the laird's death,' he informed me. 'Not at any funeral feast, but one calendar month afterwards. It has always been that way, and we abide by tradition here. But before then you and I will have been to Edinburgh to call at the solicitor's chambers to examine old documents that are meant for certain eyes and no others.'

I started in my seat. Kirsty had mentioned old documents when she had shown me the family tree. I had thought no more about them until this moment. But now I was aware of my heart beating very fast, and of my fingers gripping the stem of my glass.

'If your father had lived, I would be telling him all this,' Uncle Andrew went on solemnly. 'For it is the custom that as soon as the old laird dies, his successor takes the prospective heir to Blackmaddie into this study and tells him what the documents contain. But before you jump to the wrong conclusion, my dear, I must tell you that Blackmaddie can never pass to a woman.'

'Kirsty has already told me something of this,' I nodded slowly; so she had been telling the truth, even if her words had been said with spite at the time. So why had I been brought in here if none of it applied to me? Why was I to be taken to the solicitor in Edinburgh to examine documents that were apparently too old and fragile to be brought here to Blackmaddie?

'Then you'll know that the line could end here unless I were to marry again and produce a male heir.' He smiled faintly. 'I think that is an unlikely possibility, though not to be entirely ruled out, one supposes. But for the immediate need to adhere to the old traditions, Charlotte, you and I are to toast each other and the spirit of Malcolm Brodie in a vintage brew from the cellars of Blackmaddie which I will now ring for Duncan to bring to us. And then we will hurl the glasses against the stone fireplace so that no other will drink from them and deny us our birthright.'

'But . . . ' This was making no sense to me. 'If I can never inherit, what is the sense in all this? Why go through the ritual with me, Uncle Andrew?'

I wondered if his mind was touched since his father's death, that he still had to act out the little charade, though it meant nothing. I watched him tug at the bell-pull, and then he smiled at me.

'When you read the documents you will see that provision has been made for such an eventuality, Charlotte. When I said the line could end here unless I married again and produced a male heir, that was not strictly true. Not as long as you are capable of child-bearing, my dear, and I am sure it will not be too long before some worthy young man wants to take you for a wife. And your son will inherit Black-maddie.'

I was conscious at that instant of a sudden sensation such as I had known several times before: a holding of my breath, a moment out of time, a flooding and emptying of the senses all at one instant so that everything blurred and sharpened in front of me at once. My son, my son would inherit Black-maddie. I almost felt like placing my hand gently on my abdomen to guard him. I heard myself give a shaky laugh to relieve the tension that gripped me.

'But what if I should have only daughters?'

'If you have a dozen daughters, then the first of them to bear a son will bear the heir to Blackmaddie,' he said simply. 'There is no disputing it.'

There was a knock on the door while I was still gathering my startled thoughts together, and Duncan appeared with the bottle of vintage brew, as Uncle Andrew had called it. It was on a tray with two tall glasses. Duncan's face was set and grieving, knowing what this occasion was all about, but he gave me a brief smile, and I knew he was glad for me that I was taking my father's place in this ceremony. Uncle Andrew drew the cork from the bottle and poured the wine into the two glasses. He stood up and handed one to me, and I felt obliged to do the same. I felt weighed down by the oppressiveness of centuries of Brodie tradition, and too emotional to speak, knowing I was now so essential a part of it.

'To the laird,' Uncle Andrew intoned. 'To the one past, the one present, and the one to follow.'

He drained his glass and I did the same, though the wine was strong and bitter, and after the brandy it made my head swim. Then Uncle Andrew hurled his glass at the fireplace, where it shattered, and I did the same. Then his hand reached out and clasped mine across Grandfather's desk, and I couldn't stop the tears bubbling up inside me and pouring down my face. My shoulders shook uncontrollably, and within seconds Uncle Andrew was round the desk at my side and comforting me. All the solemnity was over, and he was the kindly uncle again, drying my tears, and consoling me in a shared grief for someone we had both loved very much.

'I'm all right now,' I gasped when my shaking had finished. 'It was all so unexpected, after Grandfather ... '

'I know, my love,' he said gently. 'And being a woman, you would feel more tenderly about him. But he would not want you to mourn too long. He had lived his life and was ready to depart to the next one, and he's probably roaring at the angels by now and getting them in order.'

'Uncle Andrew!' I was half-amused, half-shocked by such irreverence, but it helped me to recover all the same, and in a little while we were re-joining the rest of the family in the drawing-room. There was a moment when I felt everyone turned and looked at me, but then Aunt Morag was insisting I had some food and a hot drink the same as everyone else.

'I don't think any of us feels like eating dinner tonight,' she commented. 'But Cook will be bringing hot soup into the dining-room in a little while. For now, try to eat a little toast, Charlotte. Nothing seems quite so bad if you give your hands something to do to occupy them.'

I supposed she was right, and I tried to eat the toast. The hot drink was the most welcoming, and I wished she was not going to insist on our taking soup in the dining-room that night. Seeing Grandfather's empty chair – but perhaps it was best after all that we all gathered there as soon as possible. We all had to face that empty chair sooner or later. However, I was glad when Uncle Andrew made no attempt to take his place at the head of the table right away, though he had every right to do so.

Conversation seemed stilted and hushed that evening, all of us wishing we were not together, yet none of us wishing to be the first to get up and leave the others. Finally, Agnes said she was feeling very tired, and looked hopefully at me. I guessed she did not want to sleep alone, and I said quickly that I would retire as well if no one minded, and that I thought I would stay in Agnes' room for a few nights.

'As you wish, Charlotte,' Aunt Morag said distantly, clearly not caring what I did. 'Goodnight to you both.'

We said goodnight quickly. Uncle Andrew and Robert were busy in the study going through Grandfather's papers. It seemed a grisly task, but one that had to be attended to, and once again, I supposed the sooner the better. Ian and Kirsty were in a huddle at one corner of the room and hardly noticed our leaving. But Neil came to the door with us and after a moment's hesitation he put his arms round Agnes and kissed her. A gentle, platonic kiss that made me turn away my head, but at least it was a communication between them that neither seemed to reject.

I was glad to be with Agnes that night. We reassured each other just by each other's presence in the room. And naturally she was curious to know why Uncle Andrew had taken me off with him so soon after Grandfather had breathed his last.

'It seemed clear that everyone else had a good idea, but I didn't feel it was my place to ask,' Agnes said diffidently. 'Don't tell me if it's private family business.'

'There's no reason why you shouldn't know.' I told her about the little ceremony Uncle Andrew and I had performed and of the details of the inheritance, and in the darkness I heard her intake of breath. Her hand reached out across the space between our beds and squeezed my own.

'I'm so glad, Charlotte,' she said softly. 'It's so right somehow. It must give you a reassuring feeling of continuity. It's like having the future being assured for the right person, no matter what happens in the intervening years. I'm glad – and proud – to think I shall be a part of such a family – God willing.'

She took her hand away from mine, and I knew she must be very tired, for she seemed to fall asleep almost at once. But it was much longer before I slept. How could I, with so many different things milling around in my head? All the things Robert had revealed to me about Katrina; Grandfather's death; the unexpectedness of the half-hour with Uncle Andrew in the study. There were still many things unanswered, but suddenly they seemed of less importance compared with the grief that was beginning to overwhelm me again. I had known Grandfather such a little time, yet he had influenced my life. He had brought me here, knowing it was my right. I was the only one of true descent, except Kirsty.

But what of Kirsty? My eyes had been half-closed, drowsily half-asleep. Why could it not be inherited by Kirsty's son? the thought rushed into my mind. If Katrina had lived, then her son could have been the next heir at this moment. And if I died before I had a son, Kirsty's son would be the next in line. I felt at that moment as if the coldness of death was settling around me. A woman could not inherit Blackmaddie, but the son of a Brodie woman could. And my son would come before Kirsty's because the line, through my father and me, was more direct. Or so I interpreted Uncle Andrew's words. I felt sure that when it was all explained properly by the solicitor in Edinburgh I would discover I was right.

The thought that I – and any son I bore – stood between Kirsty's son and all the magnificence of Blackmaddie was enough to make me terribly uneasy and afraid. This time my hand went physically to my abdomen as if to protect a foetus that did not even exist.

It was a strange week that followed. The men were hardly in the castle at all, it seemed, for there was so much to be done: people to be informed, arrangements to be made. It was left to the women to receive callers who came to pay their respects and offer their condolences. I had not experienced the trappings of death to this extent after Mother, I realised, nor of course had her death been mourned on such a large scale. Grandfather had been the laird, and as such was to be accorded an impressive funeral and a feast to follow on a grand scale.

'It seems ghoulish to be feasting afterwards, as if there were something to celebrate,' I commented to Agnes one afternoon. We were sitting together in one of the downstairs rooms, and I was putting the final stitches to some black garments that needed to be altered. Kirsty had been sitting lethargically gazing out of the window, but her eyes sparkled at my remark.

'Well, you certainly do have, don't you, Charlotte?' she snapped.

My hands paused over my stitching, for I knew they were trembling with anger. I had almost been waiting for this moment and I stared levelly at her.

'None of us can help being what we are, Kirsty,' I said. 'I certainly did not ask for it to happen.'

'I hate it. All of it.' She twisted her hands together, and I remembered how she hated going into a sick-room. She must have been appalled standing there and watching Grandfather die. I couldn't help pitying her at that moment, for she couldn't help her feelings.

'It'll be better once the funeral's over,' I said sympathetically. 'And at least Ian's still here. He'll be there to support you.'

She gave a funny little laugh. 'Ian won't go to the funeral!'

'Not go?' I was shocked. Ian had been very odd ever since Grandfather died, refusing to go back to university and stating that he had no intention of returning at all now that Grandfather was no longer here to insist. He seemed somewhat deranged, as if the shock had affected him very deeply, but to refuse to go to the funeral was almost blasphemy, I thought.

'He's too upset,' Kirsty said in a clipped voice. 'It's no use sitting there with your mouth open, because he won't change his mind. He refuses to talk about it and I haven't seen much of him in the last few days. He takes himself off into the woods to be on his own. At least, he says he's on his own.'

She got up and walked out of the room, banging the door behind her.

'Well! What on earth was that all about?' Agnes stared at me. 'Ian's not the only one to be behaving strangely, is he?'

'They're a strange couple,' I said lightly, and began to talk of something else. But I wondered about Ian taking himself off to the woods and being on his own so much. I'd have expected him to be with Kirsty. Though he had certainly lost a lot of his boyishness these past days, and I realised he wasn't such a youth after all. He never had been in years, of course, but he had always given that impression until now. And I couldn't help wondering, too, if he was meeting Vinny in the woods and seeking consolation in her arms. Now that I knew he was the father of her child, what could be more natural?

But I put them both out of my mind and got on with my work, for the garments would be needed in a few days' time, and I dreaded the occasion myself. I had missed Mother's funeral, but I was not going to be allowed to miss this one.

I grew hourly more nervous as the time approached, though when it came, the service at the kirk passed in a kind of dream for me. I was conscious of figures dressed in black and solemn faces and weeping, of voices droning and a wooden coffin from which I couldn't seem to take my eyes. But I couldn't believe that Grandfather was inside it. It was all unreal, and perhaps better so. Only when the coffin was being lowered into the ground did it have any meaning for me, and then I couldn't bear the thought of walking round the open grave in yet another ritual, looking down as if to make sure the coffin was well and truly there. I had a sudden grotesque image in my mind of Grandfather looking up at the narrow portion of sky left available to him and seeing all the faces gazing down at him in their various masks of mourning: Uncle Andrew and Aunt Morag; the Stewart boys who had all loved him; Kirsty, Agnes and me; the Sinclairs and other friends and acquaintances who had come to mourn; Duncan and nearly all the servants who had loved him too.

But not Ian, I thought angrily. And not Vinny either. It enraged me to think these two were so conspicuously absent, but if no one else thought to comment on it I decided it was better not to stir up a hornets' nest within the family. I whispered to Kirsty to show me where Katrina was buried. She looked at me, and her voice was tight and sort of strangled when she answered.

'Not here. At Blackmaddie.'

Not here in the kirkyard. Not in consecrated ground, the realisation shrieked at me, because she had sold her soul to the devil. Though she had become restless and thought to change her mind and renounce her vows, it had been too late; the seven years still had a long time to go, and long before then she had been left to die on the mountainside.

'Come away, Charlotte,' Agnes and Neil were pulling at my arm as I went dizzy with the way my thoughts were careering on. It was all too horrible, and the sobs were filling my throat as they led me away, sobbing for poor lost Katrina, who had sought to come out of the wilderness too late, as well as for Grandfather, who must have known all about it and insisted that her body could not be buried with the blessing of the kirk.

Once back at the castle, with the next ritual of eating and drinking and talking over the dear departed with friends and relatives, however, some of the horror did lessen. Had it not, I would surely have become completely demented myself.

Ian appeared at some stage, though I did not see him enter the room. I only remember noting for the first time how like Luke's eyes his were. I had always thought Ian's were grey, innocently disarming, but today they had that almost transparent greenish look that so disturbed me about the baby. He must be more affected by Grandfather's death than I had realised, I thought, and so I generously forgave him for the strangeness of his behaviour.

Anyway, I had no time to ponder on Ian or anything else, for Uncle Andrew informed me that he and I would leave for Edinburgh in the morning.

'So soon?' I exclaimed.

'There is no point in waiting, and the sooner the business is done, the better. We shall stay one night in an hotel, Charlotte, so perhaps you will pack an overnight bag. There is no need to take very much, as this is hardly a pleasure jaunt. I have sent word to Mr McGregor that we are arriving during the afternoon and he will make arrangements for us at the hotel for that night. We shall see him first thing the next morning, and after our business is finished, we shall return to Blackmaddie in time for dinner that evening.'

'Very well, Uncle.' I was clearly not expected to argue.

Once the last of the funeral guests had gone I told Agnes I had better pack a small bag as requested, and she came to my room with me to sit on my bed and watch me with a miserable expression on her face.

'I wish you weren't going, Charlotte,' she said nervously. 'Though I couldn't expect you to sleep in my room for ever I shall miss your company.'

'There's nothing to be afraid of from the dead, Agnes, and everyone here is your friend.' Someone had said something of the same to me once, I seemed to recall. Then I shuddered, remembering Ruskin again for an instant with the usual revulsion. I wondered how Agnes was feeling now about her experience in the wood on All Hallows' Eve. So much had happened since then we had hardly mentioned it, and perhaps it was better to leave it in the past where it belonged, particularly since she and Neil seemed to have grown closer again since Grandfather's death. How close it was impossible for me to guess, but I hugged her impulsively and said perhaps Kirsty would be glad of her company, since Ian wasn't quite the old companion she'd been so happy with when I first came here.

'Perhaps,' she said. 'In fact, she did seem a bit more friendly towards me after we came back from the kirkyard. I think she was relieved it was all over. She said if I liked, she would go riding with me one afternoon. I did tell you she suggested it once before, but nothing had ever come of it.'

'Well then, perhaps you can suggest it while I'm away, and it's only two days, after all, Agnes.' I smiled encouragingly, though I was surprised at Kirsty. Surprised and pleased. Despite all her antagonism to me, there would always be a soft spot in my heart for my foolish cousin, and if she could be friends with Agnes instead of me, well, I must try to find it in my heart not to be jealous of it. Because Kirsty seemed to me to be in need of friends who were more mature than the Sinclair girls.

*　　*　　*

The next day Uncle Andrew and I departed for Edinburgh. I wanted to cling to Robert as I said good-bye, but with everyone about at that moment all I could do was smile at him and try to convey my love in my eyes. I was nervous about the journey, but my uncle was good company and apparently understood my bewilderment. He hardly referred to Blackmaddie or the intricacies of the inheritance as we jogged along mile after mile of scenic road or through busy little villages, but pointed out various landmarks and made a few witticisms and told tales about the old days, and I was grateful to him for this.

Still, we were both relieved when we came to Edinburgh. I had never seen the city before and the sight of the castle, towering over all on its high craggy mound was enough to make me gasp with awe. Blackmaddie had an awesome quality of its own, but the sight of this was beyond anything I had seen before.

'Aye, it's an impressive place,' Uncle Andrew agreed. 'The whole city is built on crags, you know, Charlotte. It's a maze of tiny alleyways and closes, dark and dingy in places, but with the great castle looking down on it all on Castle Rock. They do say it's built on the site of an Iron Age fort, and I could go on telling you stories about it all day if we had the time.'

'Oh, haven't we?' I urged, for anything that put off the moment when we would be closeted with Mr McGregor reading the mysterious documents was welcome to me just then.

Uncle Andrew laughed. 'We have not, lassie!' We jogged on in the carriage. 'Though you must know it was there in the castle that Mary gave birth to James VI in 1566, and that the Honours of Scotland are housed there – the Scottish Crown Jewels. Older than your English ones in the Tower, I'd have you know, Charlotte.'

We clattered on along the cobbled streets, and I was fascinated to hear snippets of a country's history that I was almost ashamed to admit I had known nothing at all of. I *should* know something, I told myself, and when I returned to Blackmaddie I would find some books in the library on the subject. It would be a more wholesome occupation than reading about witchcraft.

But Uncle Andrew was eager to get us settled in the hotel and have a meal, and then I supposed it would be nearing bed-time, for I did not imagine he would want to wander about in the city during the hours of darkness pointing out places of interest to a curious Sassenach. And I was beginning to feel very tired, I admitted to myself, so I was not altogether sorry when he stopped the carriage and we alighted in the courtyard of a modest hotel, and a uniformed man came out to greet us.

It was a pleasant enough hotel, and one where Uncle Andrew had clearly stayed before. I realised that we were receiving deferential treatment; everyone knew I was Miss Brodie, and offered condolences when they learned of Grandfather's death. It was all so unusual for me, and though I tried to act naturally I was not altogether at ease.

I was quite glad to leave in the morning, after a fair night's sleep, but my heart beat unsteadily when we arrived at the solicitor's chambers, walked up the narrow flight of steps and were ushered inside. Mr McGregor was a tall thin man with piercing brown eyes and a black bushy beard. He wore a black coat and trousers, and reminded me of a funeral attendant. But he was kindlier than his looks suggested, and bade me come to the desk to examine the documents which told me all that Uncle Andrew had forewarned me about. They were certainly old and yellowing, but what touched me was the accompanying document, signed and witnessed by previous heirs to Blackmaddie. Grandfather, Uncle Andrew, now myself, in proxy for my future son. It was a weird feeling to sign my name to follow those, witnessed by Uncle Andrew and Mr McGregor and his clerk.

It wasn't a terribly long ceremony, and yet one that was deeply moving to me. I was told the documents would now go back into the solicitor's vaults, and that they never left the building. It was the way things were, Uncle Andrew told me gently, and there was no arguing against it. Still, it was good to come out into the daylight again and put the solemnity behind me.

Uncle Andrew did not want to prolong our stay, and soon we were back on the road to Blackmaddie. I would be glad to be home, I thought suddenly, glad that this part of the legal proceedings was over, though there was still the formality of the will one calendar month from the date of Grandfather's death.

'We are fortunate with the clement weather this year,' my uncle remarked as we rode along the bustling Edinburgh streets and out of the city. 'It is not every year we have such a slow start to winter as this one. If all the signs are right, we will not have the snows until into the new year, and that will be a blessing.'

'You must hate the snow,' I said involuntarily, thinking of Katrina. It sometimes bothered me that he never mentioned her, for she was his daughter and he must grieve for her, but I bit my lip immediately, wishing I hadn't spoken. To my surprise his voice was steady and unemotional.

'My dear, one rotten apple in a box can soon taint all the others. Katrina had taken a road that could only lead to self-destruction eventually. She had been lost to me long before the snows claimed her, and I had said good-bye to her long before her death. It was a relief in a way that she died with so much beauty still about her, even though that beauty was rotten.'

I was too shocked to answer. Whether he knew that I followed his meaning exactly I could not tell, for he began to speak of other things at once. But it was clear to me that he knew all there was to know about Katrina's involvement with the coven, and I shuddered, imagining his anguish when it first became apparent to him that there was no hope of saving his daughter. It sounded almost as if he was glad when she died, I thought, and that was a terrible admission for a father to make. Unless – unless he was so bitterly ashamed of her and incensed by her association with evil that he himself had arranged it so that the would-be lover was too drunk to meet her at their little hut on the mountain. No, I would not let myself think such a thing. Uncle Andrew was a kindly man and surely could never be so devious. But my heart pounded and I thought again that no one was just what they seemed at Blackmaddie.

I dozed off several times in the carriage, for Uncle Andrew's conversation dwindled away after several hours, and so the journey was not too tedious.

I think we were both glad when we arrived home again, our business completed. Nothing could alter the course of history now, I thought suddenly. Blackmaddie was assured for my son, and it was a comforting feeling now that I had become used to it.

Kirsty greeted me quite cordially and Aunt Morag ordered hot drinks for us at once, saying we must both be tired and thirsty. It was pleasant to feel welcome, even though it was probably on Uncle Andrew's account, I thought, a little uncharitably. Coming back with the knowledge that Grandfather's roaring voice would no longer be heard made me feel a little thick in my throat, but there was no use grieving for things that could never be changed, and I was relieved to see that Agnes was looking less upset than when I left.

In fact, she followed me into my room when I took my small bag upstairs to unpack, and I looked at her with sudden interest. Agnes looked different. There was a bloom about her and a new awareness in her expressive brown eyes, and I knew something momentous must have happened to put it there.

'What is it?' I asked softly. 'Have you and Neil made your peace, Agnes? I know there's something.'

She ran across to me and sat down on the bed beside me, taking my hands in hers. Her voice was soft, caressing the words she spoke.

'Oh Charlotte, please don't think it wrong of me so soon after your grandfather. I cannot think it was wrong when it brought Neil and me so close. I – I was on edge after you left and he could see it, of course. Partly because I felt so alone without you. The others – they were all part of the family, but I was very much the outsider. It wasn't their fault – it was something I felt inside myself. So I went to bed early, but I couldn't sleep. I kept thinking of him – that dear old man, and I started to weep for him. Neil tapped at my door to bring me a milky drink, but I didn't hear him. He opened the door and came inside and saw the state I was in.'

She took a deep breath that was a sigh and her eyes were faraway, in a place of her own remembering. She spoke so quietly I had to lean towards her to hear the rest of her words.

'He came to me, Charlotte. Took me in his arms and held me, and I think we were both weeping for your grandfather. And then . . . oh, don't ask me how it happened for I don't really know, but it was as if all the hurt and the sadness I had ever experienced was being washed away, and there was only warmth and tenderness and love in the world. It was just as you told me. With the right person, it is the most wonderful experience under the sun.'

'Oh *Agnes*!' I hugged her, glad beyond words that she and Neil had come together at a time when they most needed comfort, and that all Neil's hurt pride should have been wiped away, and all Agnes' fear and disgust. I was thankful too that Neil had obviously proved himself a man, and therefore my fears for him were unfounded.

'You – you don't think badly of us, because it was so soon after your grandfather?' she whispered.

'I think he would have been delighted to think he was the means of bringing two people he loved back to their senses,' I said softly.

She looked as if she would tell me more, but tiredness suddenly overcame me and I could not stifle a yawn. She kissed me quickly and said she would see me in the morning.

'I'm feeling tired too – and a little bruised in places. I had my first riding lesson with Kirsty this morning. It was very enjoyable, but I did not know I had so many muscles,' Agnes smiled. 'She says I must pursue it if I am to become an expert, so we may have another ride tomorrow. You will not mind if I go with her in the morning, will you, Charlotte? Just for an hour or so? I daresay you could join us if you wished.'

'I think tomorrow morning I shall lie in bed until luncheon,' I smiled back. 'Or at least until I have recovered from so much travelling in two days. You go and enjoy yourself, Agnes, and don't worry on my account.'

I was glad to think Kirsty had fulfilled her promise of taking Agnes riding. It was good for both of them. And I was so happy for her and Neil. The world was suddenly a much brighter place, I thought sleepily, even though I had not seen Robert since my return, for he was not yet back this evening from visiting some of the outlying farms on the estate. But tomorrow I would see him again, and all the other tomorrows. Life was good, and I was not going to think of the past any longer, nor of things that could not be changed. I would not even mourn too sadly for Grandfather, for he would not have wished it. I would not forget him, ever, but I would remember him with joy and not sadness.

I did not find it hard to fall asleep that night, and I drifted off in an almost euphoric state, the way one often did without realising it was merely the calm before the storm.

20

I did not stay asleep until luncheon the next day, though it was well into the morning when I awoke. It was Vinny bustling about with washing-water who stirred me. I asked her if Agnes was awake yet.

'Everyone else is up and about, Miss,' she told me pertly. 'Miss Agnes said I was to tell ye she and Miss Kirsty are about to go riding and will see ye at luncheon.'

'Already? They must be feeling more energetic than I am then,' I said lazily.

'It's the best part of the day, Miss,' she said pointedly. I laughed, knowing she liked to have the beds made and be back downstairs fairly early.

'All right, I'll get up in a minute,' I said in an agreeable tone. I was still feeling cheerful and optimistic, and now that I was fully awake I was beginning to agree that it was a shame to waste the day lying in bed.

'Is Master Robert about?' Suddenly I couldn't wait to see him again, but Vinny's words squashed the idea at once.

'He's taken the Missus over to the Sinclairs to see old Mrs Sinclair, since she's still no so well. I think she took cold standing around at the laird's funeral, Miss.'

'Oh. Well, I'm sorry to hear that. Vinny – you weren't at the funeral, were you?' It suddenly occurred to me. 'Do they upset you greatly?'

She paused in her task of laying my clothes out on the bed.

'No more than they do most people.' She shrugged. 'Somebody had to stay behind to see to the preparing of the feast, Miss. And somebody had to be here to see folks out and show them back in. It's the custom. So I said I'd do it. That's all.'

'Oh I see.' It made sense, I supposed, but Vinny seemed such a curious sort of girl, I'd have expected her to want to view every little detail of the proceedings.

I was disappointed that Robert was to be away for the morning, and Agnes too. As if to answer my unspoken questions as to the whereabouts of the rest of my family, Vinny spoke cheerfully.

'Master Neil and his father have gone off round the estate, and the last I saw of Master Ian he was coming out of the stables, Miss. Now I'd best be getting back downstairs and I'll come back and see to yer bed later, if there's nothing else ye're wanting.'

'No thank you, Vinny.' I threw off the bedcovers. I was glad she hadn't brought Luke up this morning; just lately she had got out of the habit. I still couldn't explain my aversion to the child, but it was very real and the less I saw of him the better.

So everyone seemed to be away on their own pursuits but me, I realised. Still, it would be pleasant to take a stroll around the grounds of Blackmaddie by myself, enjoying its peace and grandeur without the need for conversation. The events of the past weeks had been tumultuous, and the last two days very tiring with the journey to and from Edinburgh. I would be glad of some time to myself, to *be* just myself.

I washed and dressed in the soft grey wool dress I had asked Vinny to put out for me. Not deep mourning for Grandfather, for I had not done so for Mother, and I hated black clothes anyway. But the cool grey was sufficiently demure to show my respect. I took a shawl, so that I didn't need to return to my room before I went out, and eventually I went to the dining-room and made my breakfast of toast and butter, which was all I required.

When I had finished, I went to the library to look for some books as I had promised myself yesterday. I wanted to learn more about the stormy history of the country of my ancestors, and of the beautiful city of Edinburgh that had so enchanted me in my short visit. It took a little while until I found just what I required, but later, with several books in my hands, I made my way back through the passage towards the main door of the castle.

As I neared it I glanced automatically at the little side table just inside, where visitors left calling cards, or any letters for the family were placed. And my heart gave a giant lurch in my chest. On the silver salver on the side table lay an open note, in hand-writing I had seen once before. The words danced and blurred in front of my eyes: *Come to the shed where the hawk is kept.*

I realised I was holding my breath. I glanced around me as if expecting to see Boucca's great wings spreading above me in a lethal swoop, as if I expected to feel the cruel talons piercing my skin. But there was no sound at all except for my own heartbeats. The castle was silent, unusually silent, as if I were the only person living within its walls. It unnerved me. Seconds before I had been cheerful, optimistic, happy; now, in an instant, all of it had vanished. I was afraid, insecure, suspicious, fearing something nameless and unknown. It was the worst kind of fear.

I tried to force myself to think logically. It was the same note Agnes and I had seen before. There was no doubt of that. And that other time, when she had assumed the note was for her and had gone to the shed with such disastrous results, when we had returned the note had gone. Someone had taken it, and I believed then it had been destroyed to get rid of the evidence. But it hadn't been destroyed, after all.

My mind cleared a little. Vinny was still here in the castle and there were other servants in their quarters. Some of them were young girls. Perhaps after all the note had been left for one of them, for an assignation with one of the stable-lads as we had guessed at the time. Perhaps it was as innocent as that, and there was nothing at all sinister in the fact that it had been placed where I was bound to see it again, and that I seemed to be the only one of my family left here this morning. Except Ian, but heaven alone knew where he had got to.

In any case, I would have to find out the truth. If there was some simpering little servant girl kissing and cuddling a stable-lad behind Boucca's shed, then nothing would make me happier or more reassured. If it was something else . . . I crunched the note tightly in the palm of my hand, unable and unwilling to consider any other possibility. I knew I had to see for myself.

I stepped outside the castle, still clutching the books from the library in my hands. In a few minutes I hoped I would be able to laugh at my foolish fears and continue my stroll around the gardens, find myself a warm secluded spot and enjoy my reading until Agnes or Robert returned.

And even if my fears were not unfounded after all, even if it was all a hideous trap and I was walking blindly towards it, it seemed as if I was impelled to go to the shed by some force outside myself. My nerves were hypersensitive as I neared the wooden building, my eyes searching and my ears straining for anything outside the normal, for the swish of a maid-servant's skirt or the deep laugh of a stable-lad.

I suddenly stopped, for there was another sound above the pounding of my heartbeats, the crunch of leaves and gravel under my feet: the sound of low, intoning voices, mumbling, chanting, the way I had so often imagined them in the castle. Were they still all in my head? I wondered for an instant. But they certainly were not. They came from the shed. And I was suddenly filled with a hot rage, because someone was determined to frighten me and I was going to let them unnerve me no longer. It was time for a confrontation. I laid the books down.

I strode towards the door of the wooden shed and wrenched it open. I was met with blackness that stopped me at once. For a second I was unable to think what it was, for it seemed that inside the door was a black curtain that impeded my entry. What nonsense was this, then? I pushed it aside, and stepped into the shed, and as I did so there was a rustling from behind me and someone pushed the door shut and stood between it and me. And as the voices penetrated into my brain the mounting terror gripped me like icy bands as I stared disbelievingly into the small room of the shed.

'Oh no!' The despairing words were torn from my lips in

a thin whisper, for my mouth was too dry with horror to emit any real sound. 'Oh God, no, no!'

The voices still droned on in that awful chant, and my eyes took in the scene in front of me. The window was draped with the same black cloth that made the curtain over the door, shutting out every bit of daylight. The stench was sweet and rancid at the same time, from the incense that was burning steadily in a crucible on the floor, the four black candles lit within the chalked circle there, the oil-lamp that Neil had always used when he tended Boucca, and the storage jars of oil normally kept in the shed. There was also a horribly misshapen wax model that I wouldn't attempt to identify.

There were other objects and implements that I couldn't take in immediately, for none of them were as horrific as the three people in that room. My breath was rattling in my throat as I gaped at them. Ian, my cousin Ian, as I had never seen him before. There was nothing young and innocent about him now. He looked totally evil, head thrown back and eyes half-closed so that they glittered in the candle-light, completely naked beneath a black cloak that was thrown back from his shoulders so that every part of his body was visible, hair-covered chest, firm belly, flaccid phallus crowned by the red hair characteristic of his family.

I glanced to the right of me where Vinny was moving slightly away from the door, but not so far as to let me escape. Vinny, also in a black cloak, thrown back to reveal those huge melon breasts, the nipples standing out like darts, the circles of the areolas so dark I wondered if they had been painted black for this occasion, the great rounded belly beneath, and a tangle of hair at her groin.

But it was the third person who really made me want to retch. The baby, Luke, an innocent participant in all of this. And yet how could such a being be innocent, when he sat propped up in his basket, draped in a black cape round his little naked body, his greenish eyes taking an avid interest in his parents, seemingly mesmerised by the flickering candles.

For the few seconds it had taken my horrified eyes to absorb all of this, I had been frozen with terror, unable to believe that outside in the daylight the everyday world went about its business, while in here the epitome of evil stood in the shape of my cousin Ian, his witch-'wife', and their hideous offspring. I had no doubt in my mind about them now. And with this realisation came the knowledge that I had to fight for my life if I was to survive, for I knew they were bent on my destruction for some devilish reason of their own.

The chanting seemed to get louder and more unintelligible as Ian inclined his head slightly and Vinny moved forward as if to pick up the wax model. Whatever her intention I seized my chance, and gave her an almighty push towards the chalk circle. Whether or not this would have interfered with their evil performance I did not know, but she gave a scream of rage and lurched away from it, losing her balance. She fell heavily against the small table at the side, knocking the oil lamp to the ground. The glass smashed immediately and a gush of oil poured out, to be instantly ignited by the candle-flames as the candles too fell to the floor, brushed by Vinny's cloak.

Everything happened within seconds after that. Vinny was screaming, her cloak spattered with oil and burning, the dry straw on the floor streaking into flames, the tinder-dry wood of the shed catching alight at once.

'The babby, the babby,' Vinny was shrieking. 'Save him, Master!'

The two of them made to snatch the child from the basket, but I waited to see no more of it. It was horrible to see them lunge towards Luke, his greenish eyes wide and petrified, the flames already licking round his face. I was coughing and choking as the smoke and flames threatened to engulf the shed in minutes, and I dragged the black curtain aside and wrenched open the door. I almost fell outside, gasping in the good, clean air, and running as fast as I could from the shed towards the direction of the stables. Even before I reached them I heard the sound of explosions behind me as the storage jars of oil burst into flames, and then I was collapsing, sobbing into Duncan's arms as he rushed out of the stables to see what was causing the great spiral of

297

smoke and flames to shoot skywards as high as the turrets of Blackmaddie.

'What in God's name . . . ?' he began. 'Are ye all right, my little lassie? No hurt, are ye? I'll call the lads to fetch some water, though by the looks of it there's no saving it.'

'No! *No!*' I screamed, my mind reeling at the possibility of saving any of the occupants of the shed. 'Let them burn. Let them *burn!*'

I shook uncontrollably as I saw Duncan's shocked face in front of me. It swam about as if it were under water as I tried frantically to hold on to my swooning senses. He held me tight, looking beyond me over my shoulder and I knew by the series of explosions that still echoed that there would be no hope of salvaging the shed or its contents. And I was glad, *glad*. Something primèval, stronger than pity, would let me feel no other emotion at that moment.

'It's beyond help anyway.' Duncan's words forced themselves into my spinning brain. 'The wood was ready to go up with the slightest spark with all this dry weather we've been having. God knows how it started.'

'God and the devil,' I stuttered through dry lips. They felt swollen for some reason, as misshapen as that horrible little wax model. That had been meant for me, and I knew it, and suddenly the tension in me relaxed and I leaned weeping against Duncan's strong shoulder, while he held me to him as if I were a child.

I could still hardly take in the fact that Ian could have been so evil. And Vinny also, a simple village girl. But so many things about them both were becoming clear to me now as the thoughts raced through my mind with breakneck speed. The way Vinny had paled when I had asked about Luke's baptism. Her refusal had been nothing to do with keeping the identity of the father a secret after all, but because she would not wish to have him entered in the Christian church. I could see too why neither Ian nor Vinny had been present at Grandfather's funeral, for neither of them would have wanted to set foot in the kirk.

I caught my breath on a sob, remembering how Vinny had screamed to Ian to save the baby when they started burning, calling him 'Master'. That time in the garden when I had seen Kirsty lean over Luke and croon at him, and Vinny had said softly that the master was well pleased with the baby, I had put a different, milder interpretation on the word. Now I saw Ian as the master of the coven. I shuddered violently as Duncan still held me tightly to his chest.

Was this the reason Kirsty had invited Agnes to go riding today? The thought exploded in my head. Knowing that everyone else was occupied, had Ian urged her to keep Agnes well out of the way while he and Vinny lured me to Boucca's shed for their own evil purpose? I was ready enough to believe anything, with the stench of burning still in my nostrils and black smoke rising like a pall into the sky above Blackmaddie.

Dimly I heard the sound of horses' hooves as Agnes and Kirsty returned to the stables, and minutes later the two of them came running across towards us.

'What's been happening here?' Kirsty gasped out.

I wrenched myself out of Duncan's arms and rounded on her, a red rage blinding me to everything but the sight of her, standing there so horrified and so innocent, so open-mouthed. I took hold of her by the shoulders and shook her until her teeth rattled in her head.

'Surprised to see me, are you?' I screamed at her. 'What were you expecting then? That I'd be stuck full of holes like that disgusting little wax doll they had? Perhaps you helped them make it, did you, Kirsty?'

'What on earth are you talking about?' she shouted back. 'Have you gone completely mad, Charlotte?'

Oh no, I wasn't mad, whatever they had tried to make me believe with their voices in the night. I was quite, quite sane and clear in my head about a lot of things.

'I'm talking about you and your precious Ian! Only he wasn't really yours when it came to the point, was he? He belonged to everybody, if what I read in that disgusting book was true – and mostly to Vinny and that loathsome little Luke, didn't he? Well, you'd better take a good look over there, my so-innocent little cousin! Because that's all that's left of them.'

I twisted her round until she stood in front of me, facing the shed that was now little more than a smouldering pile of wood and ash, with nothing recognisable among the smoke and flames that billowed from it. I dug my nails into her shoulders and forced her to look.

'Charlotte!' I heard Agnes' voice, horrified at my outburst, uncomprehending.

'What are you saying, Miss Charlotte?' Duncan's shocked face gasped at me. Then Kirsty gave a terrible cry and broke away from me, running towards the remains of the shed and screaming Ian's name.

'He won't hear you,' I called after her, hardly aware of the gloating note in my voice. 'He's past hearing anything any more, and I'm *glad*. Do you hear? *Glad!*'

There was a sudden sharp blow to the side of my cheek that rocked my senses and sent me staggering for a moment, and when I focused my eyes properly and felt the grip of the strong hands that held me, it was to see that Robert had returned with Aunt Morag, and the two of them had overheard most of what had been said. Aunt Morag's face was white and frozen, and Kirsty was now down on her knees by the burning shed, sobbing and mumbling incoherently. I felt that she was not beyond stretching out her hands and scrabbling in the red-hot ashes to find what was left of Ian. I shuddered into Robert's chest as he held me.

I heard Agnes speaking quickly, in a high, shrill voice. 'I just don't know what happened, Robert. Kirsty and I returned from our ride and we could see the smoke from some distance away. By the time we got here the shed was almost burnt out. And Charlotte was in hysterics . . . ' Her voice trailed off helplessly. She put a tentative hand on my arm, clearly thinking I was deranged and in need of medical help, but suddenly all the fury in me subsided like a spent match. I was surrounded at this moment by people who loved me – Robert, Agnes, Duncan.

'I'm sorry,' I managed to stammer. 'I've had a terrible shock. Robert – Ian and Vinny were in the shed. And Luke.'

Agnes caught her breath, her hand going to her mouth. 'Oh, how terrible. And you saw it all happen?'

I saw Aunt Morag out of the corner of my eye. She had run across to Kirsty and hauled her to her feet. Her hands were on Kirsty's shoulders and she seemed to be talking to her rapidly and sternly, though I couldn't hear the words. But at last Kirsty allowed her mother to take her into the house, still sobbing uncontrollably.

Suddenly the full horror of all that had happened really came home to me. And I had expressed elation at the deaths of three people, however wicked, and been partly responsible for those deaths when I pushed Vinny, though I couldn't think anyone would condemn me in the circumstances. But the shock of it welled up inside me again, and I felt myself tremble in Robert's arms as I lifted my head and looked into his eyes.

'Oh, Robert, it was so awful,' I babbled. 'They were in there with all their horrible paraphernalia surrounding them. Black candles and incense and a chalked circle . . . '

'Hush, my darling, calm yourself. It's over now, for ever.'

I couldn't help being aware of the sorrowing note in his voice, and a lump came to my throat. Whatever he was, Ian had been his brother. It had been easy to forget that when I had seen Ian in his black cloak with evil in his eyes and in his heart.

'Can we go inside?' I heard Agnes whisper. 'She should be away from here.'

Far away, my mind begged, away from Blackmaddie for ever. But I allowed Robert to lead me inside as if I were a child, his arms supporting me, his love surrounding me, and never had I needed him more. I dreaded the moment when Neil and Uncle Andrew would return. I couldn't begin to imagine what their reactions would be and if they knew, or how much they had guessed, about Ian. I felt loving hands pushing me into a chair, caring voices murmuring around me. A glass of fiery liquid was pushed into my hand and I was forced to drink. A feeling of unreality lifted me somewhere into a dream-world, but it soon became a nightmare-world, where I fancied I saw Ian and Vinny and Luke, three faces horribly distorted in grotesque laughter with flames leaping all around them. Laughing, even while they were being consumed by fire, because their ashes would be scattered in the wind over the land and waters of Blackmaddie in order that they may rise again.

'I think she's coming out of it now,' I heard a voice close to me say. The faces swam about beside me as I struggled to return to sensibility. I wanted to tell them about my nightmare, to shriek at them that the fire had merely been a transitionary phase for such as Ian and Vinny, but I stayed silent. They had had enough anguish without that.

I must have been unconscious for a little while, for Neil and Uncle Andrew were in the room, both pale but surprisingly controlled. I knew then that everyone here had either known or suspected something of what had been going on, but they had been powerless to stop it. *I* had stopped it, I realised. Was that why I had been sent for, commanded to come to Blackmaddie, even when everything in me had rebelled against it at first? Was this the purpose of it all, to stamp out the evil that was here? Perhaps it was all a fanciful idea, but it was the one consolation, the one comfort at that moment, and I clung to it like a lifeline.

'Are you feeling better now, darling?' I realised Robert's arms were still holding me. No wonder I felt safe, I thought mutely. Here in his arms, the best place in the world. I nodded. And then Aunt Morag came into the room, her face tight, and I could see she had been weeping. She walked straight towards me.

'Kirsty wants to see you, Charlotte,' she told me. 'She has something to say to you, and I hope very much you won't refuse to talk to her.' Her face suddenly seemed to crumple, and I could see at once how afraid she had been for her daughter. '*Please*, Charlotte. Let her talk to you.'

My first reaction had been revulsion. I never wanted to speak to Kirsty again. But there was something in this pathetic woman's face that told me I must. And if Kirsty wanted to make her peace with me I could not find it in my heart to turn my back on her. I nodded slowly. I knew I must see her alone, but I could not quite rid myself of the fear inside me. After all, might she not feel obliged to finish whatever it was Ian had started? As if Aunt Morag could read my mind, she suddenly bent and kissed my cheek. It touched me more than anything.

'She does not wish to harm you,' she whispered. 'She only wants to beg your forgiveness if you can ever give it.'

I was unsteady on my feet, and Robert insisted on coming with me to Kirsty's room. He told me he would wait in my room until Kirsty and I had finished our conversation to see that I got downstairs again, and I felt a rush of love and gratitude towards him, knowing that he understood my fears.

Robert left me at Kirsty's door and went into my room to wait. My heart was beating unevenly as I went inside, not quite knowing what to expect. The first thing that I saw was that all the obscene pictures had been stripped from the wall and piled up on the floor, and that she was pulling her clothes from the closet with frenzied hands. Her face was blotchy and red, her hands trembling. She was a different Kirsty from the arrogant girl who'd run wild with Ian. She motioned towards the pictures.

'They will burn too,' she said jerkily. 'And I shall move out of this room tonight. I thought she was so wonderful, you see. All of them. With the power to change people's wills to their own wishes. It was exciting and different. And Katrina, she was so beautiful too. I always envied her because she had the likeness. You never knew that, did you? She was so dear to Grandfather, not just because it would be her son to inherit Blackmaddie, but because of the likeness. He couldn't believe anyone who looked like Maddie could be evil. He always affirmed that Maddie had two sides to her personality, one good, one black and evil, and he could never admit that Katrina had inherited the evil side.'

I just stood there and listened while she rambled on. It seemed that was what she wanted. She wandered restlessly about the room, still gathering bits and pieces from the walls, the furniture, as she talked, as if she wanted to rid herself of everything that had been Katrina's as quickly as possible.

'I wanted so much to be like her.' Kirsty's voice rose more shrilly. 'Even when I knew what she was doing – though I didn't want to join the coven. I resisted, even though she tried to persuade me, and Ian too. Then, after she died, Ian began to put the idea into my mind that it was the most perfect way I could find to be like her – to take her place with *them*. He drove me nearly to distraction, wondering what to do. I wanted to in a way, because I loved him and it was what he wanted, but something always held me back.'

'Thank God it did.' I spoke for the first time. She looked at me with brimming eyes.

'God? Do you think He helped me decide?' She brushed that aside, her hands twisted together. 'Now they've gone – Ian and all of them – Mother said I must tell you – I *want* to tell you, but I don't know how to find the words.'

I moved across to her and caught her restless hands. At that moment she was a child again. One of the children at my school in Bristol, coming to me for comfort with pricked fingers from a sharp needle, and the panic in me went. Kirsty was lost and trying desperately to find her way back to sanity again, and it seemed I was the only one who could help her.

'Just tell me,' I said softly. 'Why did Ian want to harm me?'

'It's so shameful.' Her voice was a whisper, but I kept my grip on her hands and she took a deep breath. 'He – he began to put the idea in my head about the inheritance, you see. We all knew how it would be when Grandfather died – about your son being the future heir to Blackmaddie. And he said that if you were dead, it could be *my* son. Oh Charlotte!' She paused, biting her lip to stop it trembling. But I had already suspected as much, and so it was not the terrible shock she seemed to expect.

'That had occurred to me,' I told her evenly.

'It was the price I had to pay,' she whispered. 'If I joined the coven, virtually taking Katrina's place, which he knew I was so tempted to do anyway, he would guarantee your – your death, and he would give me the baby I wanted. It was an added incentive, you see, because he knew I loved him, while he – he wasn't capable of loving anybody.' Her voice was suddenly bitter. 'Oh, I don't mean he couldn't father a child, because he'd already done that. But it wasn't love. It was putting more of his kind on this earth. That was what he wanted, Charlotte. To own me, body and soul, and provide Blackmaddie with a child of the devil.'

It was so evil I could hardly believe it. And yet I had to believe it, because I had seen the proof of what Kirsty was saying. I had seen Ian in his other role, of the Master, the devil, the evil one. I was shocked and horrified now, and I could see by Kirsty's dilated eyes that she was reliving every moment of the time Ian had tried to persuade her. I knew I had to keep her talking before her mind gave up the struggle to remain sane.

'Was it you who chopped up my red moire dress, Kirsty? And did you take the book on witchcraft from my room? It's important for me to know these things now, for my own peace of mind. I had suspected Vinny, you see.' The words came out in a rush.

'Oh yes.' Kirsty's voice had a horrible sing-song quality about it now.

'And the time at the Sinclairs' in the game of Blind Man's Bluff? And the voices I kept hearing through the wall?' I shivered. 'Was that you and Ian in here?'

'When the closet doors are left open on both sides of the connecting wall the sound carries,' she nodded. 'It was easy for Vinny to leave yours ajar. But it wasn't me who pushed you at the Sinclairs'. That was Ian. He'd know just how far to go, you see. It was just meant to frighten you – a warning.'

'It certainly did that,' I muttered. 'And the night of All Hallows, Kirsty. Something was going on out there in the wood, wasn't it? Agnes and I saw the lights, but we were sure we had been drugged. Something in the milk.'

'That was Vinny.'

'And – today? Did you take Agnes riding on Ian's instructions, Kirsty?' Somehow I didn't want to know it was true. I didn't want to believe it of her. She nodded her head, pulled her hands away from me and covered her face with them.

'I swear to you I didn't know what he had planned,

though, Charlotte.' She gasped out the words. 'I didn't know – I didn't know – ' She suddenly burst into noisy sobbing again, and after a second's hesitation I took her in my arms. She didn't seem like an evil woman any longer, she was a pathetic child, led along a path from which there was almost no returning. Almost – I held her away from me and made her look into my eyes.

'Listen to me, Kirsty,' I said urgently. 'You nearly did me the most terrible wrong, and I've listened to you and tried to understand. But now it's your turn to listen. You're not Katrina, nor ever will be. She died on the mountain and her evil died with her. And no matter what Ian said to you, or how persuasive his arguments, he could never have forced you to join the coven against your will. You were always free to choose, and you chose right. Forget everything but that. You always resisted, always. Your will was stronger than his.' That's the most important thing of all. *Your* will was stronger than *his*.'

I could hear the sound of her heartbeats in the silence of the room as she absorbed all that I was saying.

Very slowly I saw the terrible haunted look leave her eyes. And I knew without being told that having realised what I told her was the truth, nothing and no one would ever be able to lead her into such dark paths again. If Ian, whom she loved with an unhealthy obsession, had failed to persuade her against her true nature, then no one else was ever likely to succeed. I felt an immense relief at knowing it.

'Charlotte, I don't expect you to forgive me,' she began in a whisper. 'You couldn't, after what I've done.'

'But I do,' I said simply, and almost to my own amazement I knew that it was true. I just wanted her to be a normal, happy young woman, and for that I would forgive a great deal. Especially now I knew all the danger was past. I would not let myself wonder about the coven; I hoped without its leaders, it would disband. I stopped my thoughts short, for there was still one more thing I had to know.

'Kirsty, was it Ian who should have met Katrina on the mountain?'

I held my breath, but she nodded at once.

306

'Yes it was. I wasn't sure at first, but he could always explain things so logically, you see. Telling me she had to die because she wanted to break away from him and his kind. Poor Katrina.' She shuddered, but she was able to speak more calmly about them all now, and I knew the thought of her will being stronger than Ian's was going to sustain her in the days to come and give her back her self-respect and her dignity.

So now the last piece of the puzzle had fallen into place. It had been Ian who left Katrina to die. Not Robert, or Uncle Andrew, or anyone else, but Ian. It always came back to Ian, and now he was dead and there was nothing more to fear for any of us at Blackmaddie. I hoped Kirsty would soon be able to see that, too.

'I think I'll have a little sleep if you don't mind, Charlotte,' she said. 'I'm suddenly very tired.'

'Will you be all right?' I asked anxiously. 'Would you rather use my bedroom?'

She smiled tremulously for the first time. 'The walls are stripped of her pictures, and I feel that at last she is gone for ever. Don't worry about me.' She hesitated for a moment and then she leaned forward and kissed me. It was the kiss of a friend.

I went back to my own room, where Robert was waiting for me. I had a job to fight back the tears. I truly felt as if Kirsty had come out of the wilderness and that I had helped her. It was a tremendously humbling feeling, and I felt as if the two of us had travelled a hundred miles nearer each other in the last half hour.

I closed my door behind me and leaned against it, exhausted. Robert turned from the window and held out his arms, and within seconds I was circled within them. This was not the time for explanations, for passion, for lovemaking. It was the time for being needed, loved and wanted, and comforted as only he could. Without the need for words, just by being together where we belonged. He led me to my bed, and we lay there in each other's arms, with the love we both felt surrounding us like a protective blanket, his cheek close to mine, every fibre of our beings in a communication that was beyond description.

At last I felt Robert's lips move against my cheek.

'I want you to be my wife, Charlotte. As soon as possible, for I can't live without you, and I'm impatient for your answer.'

'Is there any doubt?' I whispered back. For there was only one answer it was possible for me to give. 'It's yes, yes, *yes!* As soon as possible, my beloved.'

We sealed the bargain with a kiss that was slow and tender, a promise of the passion we knew so well. But this was not the time.

There was still so much to say. We should not stay here any longer while there were people downstairs anxious about Kirsty and myself, and explanations to be made about Ian and Vinny. And for myself, I felt the need to get right away from Blackmaddie for a time, to see things from a distance and perhaps view them differently. Perhaps to Edinburgh, that had so enchanted me, for a honeymoon. But that was something else that had to be discussed, for wherever I went, it had to be with Robert beside me.

21

One calendar month after Grandfather died, Mr McGregor faced us all at Blackmaddie for the reading of the will. He sat in Grandfather's chair, now Uncle Andrew's, in the study, with its brown-panelled walls and the smell of old books so beloved of Grandfather, and the stone fireplace where Uncle Andrew had dashed our glasses after our solemn dedication to the past and the future. But this was the present, and it was an occasion I wished to be over, though much of the horror surrounding Ian's death had begun to recede from my mind for I had my own future to think about. As yet, Robert and I had told no one of our plans.

I looked at him now, seated to the right of me, the light from the window emphasising his strong, masculine features, and as always at this sight of him, a rush of love engulfed me. Tall, broad-shouldered, bearded and aggressive, a giant of a man, a match for any woman, and I was the only woman he wanted in all the world. Nothing could change the certainty in my mind about that now.

There had already been a light, powdery fall of snow to remind us that winter was approaching rapidly, and we had been able to stand at my window one night with our arms entwined, and gaze up at the mountain with no dark doubts about Katrina to cloud my happiness, and no love for her left in Robert's heart save that of a kinsman. I knew it as surely as I breathed.

He glanced my way and the corners of his mouth lifted in a small smile as we waited for Mr McGregor to begin intoning the contents of the will. My Robert. I heard Agnes give a slight cough, almost the first time for many days. She was truly blooming now, and both she and Neil seemed to have grown in stature lately. The date for her wedding to Neil had been fixed for the first week in January, and her parents would come to stay for several weeks.

Agnes and Neil had joined Robert and me when we were browsing through some books in the library one evening, their faces alight with eagerness.

'Father and I have been discussing a matter I have been thinking of for some time,' Neil said at once, and I thought how changed he was from the rather fey, dreamy poet I had first met, always searching. He had found what he was looking for in Agnes – and something else, apparently. His attitude towards life was much more positive now.

'Tell them, Neil,' Agnes urged him. 'It sounds so exciting, Charlotte!'

He smiled at her. 'All right. Well, you know Father has had it in his mind to be rid of the wood out there? I have been speaking to some timber merchants down in the village and they showed great interest when I mentioned the number of trees that would be available. How do you fancy your brother going into the timber trading business, Robert?'

'I don't relish the idea of seeing great sheds going up within sight of Blackmaddie and the sound of saws disturbing it,' he commented.

'No, no. We would merely be suppliers – at least for the present,' Neil assured him. 'Father wants the trees gone, and so for that matter, do I.'

So did we all. Uncle Andrew had stamped into the drawing-room one night, Grandfather all over again, and it was clear he was still grieving. Not just for losing his son in that horrific manner, but for what his son had become. Knowing the wood at Blackmaddie had been used to such evil purposes, he had put it to the rest of us that it should be removed as soon as possible, leaving only a fringe of trees at the far end. There would be no whirling lights to dazzle the senses in the dead of a moonlit night in the future, no suspicion of orgies and magic practices and rituals. At least, not in Uncle Andrew's mind. But wasn't there something in the book I had read about the witches' meeting places not needing to be in woods, but in any dark or doleful place, or in a large parlour draped in black, or on the sea-shore when the moon shines bright, or on a large heath, and especially near to water, which was supposedly magical? The remains of the wood would gradually develop into such a place as a heath, I supposed, with old tree stumps and bracken to grow wild and natural, and with all the past elements of those other meetings pulsating with life beneath the surface of the ground. But in those kind of thoughts lay the road to madness, and I kept them strictly to myself.

Robert thought it a splendid idea anyway, and it was good to see Neil with some purpose in his life. He and Agnes had a good future ahead of them, and Neil and his father had grown much closer together now. I was glad of that on another score.

For Robert and I had decided to leave Blackmaddie. We would be married very quietly two weeks before Agnes and Neil; neither of us wanted a big fuss. As yet, the family had not been told. We were going to wait until after the reading of the will. But there was one thing we had no intention of telling any of them until we were well away from this place. Already, the future heir to Blackmaddie stirred with life inside me. I had suspected it for several weeks now, but it was a secret Robert and I kept to ourselves, for it was too precious, too important to risk anything happening to him. What could happen now? I reasoned. But something more basic than reason made me urge Robert to keep the knowledge to ourselves, for until our baby was born safely I would not be really at ease in my mind.

I recalled the moment when I had told him, when we lay together in my room about a week before. He had raised himself on one elbow and looked down at me, magnificent in the moonlight, his face relaxed in the aftermath of our loving, his fingers gently tracing the curve of my breasts. They paused now and went down to the soft swell of my abdomen, as yet giving no hint of the new life inside me.

'Our son,' he said huskily, and neither of us gave thought that it might be a daughter. He bent and kissed me, the weight of him covering me again, the passion rising between us anew at the knowledge of what we had created through our love, and my body was ever ready to receive him and glory in the fulfilment we brought to one another.

I wondered now if he was remembering it too, as Mr McGregor cleared his throat and referred first of all to the documents Uncle Andrew and I had signed at his chambers in Edinburgh, and asked if there was anyone present who disputed his right to succeed Grandfather or that the next of true descent was myself and then my son, to whom Blackmaddie would eventually belong. I kept my eyes lowered, not wanting to see the slightest sign of antagonism on Aunt Morag's face or discontent on Kirsty's. But when I was almost compelled to glance at them both, there was nothing there to alarm me, and I concentrated on the will which Mr McGregor was now reading.

Of course we all knew that Uncle Andrew was the chief beneficiary as to the castle and land and the tenancy of various farms and estate cottages. But Grandfather had made detailed and ample provision for everyone else in his family. Agnes was not mentioned, of course, and was only present because of her imminent marriage to Neil, but Aunt Morag was handsomely provided for, and a large sum of money – larger than I could imagine – was to be shared equally between his grandchildren. It would have been a magnanimous bequest between the six of us, but now that both Katrina and Ian were dead it was to be divided between Robert, Neil, Kirsty and me. When Robert's share and mine were added together it would make a wonderful investment for the plans we had mulled over long into the night on many occasions now.

It was a relief when the will reading was over, and everyone left the study that was becoming stuffy and a little claustrophobic. Uncle Andrew thanked the solicitor formally for all of us, and then Mr McGregor shook us all by the hand, one by one, and the two men went off to break open a bottle of good Scottish whisky together. The rest of us settled for a more homely kind of refreshment as Aunt Morag rang for afternoon tea and buttered scones to be brought to the drawing-room.

'Charlotte, Kirsty would like to come to the village with

us when we go to choose some material for my wedding-dress,' Agnes said. 'Is that all right?'

I smiled at Kirsty. She was still a little wary of my reactions, still nervous and diffident after the shock of Ian's death. 'Of course it is. I want to buy some material for myself anyway, so it had better be a full afternoon's outing if we can persuade Duncan to wait about for us.'

'There's no need to trouble Duncan, Charlotte,' Robert offered. 'I shall have some lengthy business matters to deal with in the village, so I will arrange to take you young ladies myself. It's not every day a man has the pleasure of escorting the three most beautiful girls in the Highlands and having them all to himself, so I intend to avail myself of the chance.'

I could see that Kirsty was pleased to be included in his gallant invitation. And I knew, too, about his business matters, feeling my heart give a little leap of excitement as his eyes caught mine and smiled at our shared secret.

At last Uncle Andrew returned to the drawing-room, rubbing his hands after walking outside with the solicitor to see him on his way. Aunt Morag handed him a cup of tea, which he said teasingly was poor stuff after the nectar he'd just swallowed, but he took it all the same. And then Robert came across and took my hand, pulling me to my feet so that we faced them all.

'Charlotte and I have something to tell you,' he said in the firm, rich voice I loved so well. 'Although it's so soon after Grandfather's death and the other tragedy, I'm sure we all agree that life must go on, and the past is dead and gone. Therefore, Charlotte and I intend to be married three weeks from now.'

There were cries of delight from Agnes and Neil, and a look of pleasure from everyone else, to my intense relief. But Robert hadn't finished yet, and he asked them to postpone the congratulations for a few minutes.

'I don't want Neil and Agnes to think we're stealing their thunder,' he went on smilingly, 'but partly on that account, partly out of deference to Grandfather and Ian, and mostly because it's what we both want, we wish only for a quiet, simple ceremony, and will leave the big celebrations to Neil and Agnes. I know Charlotte wants to busy herself with making dresses and all the rest of the business of preparing for a wedding, and now that it's two weddings you'll realise that I shan't see too much of my future bride in the next few weeks! However, you must all make the most of her company.' His fingers tightened round mine. 'Because I am going to book our passage to America at the end of January.'

I was prepared for astonishment, and for the dismay on Agnes' face as she stared at us, open-mouthed. But it was something Robert and I had discussed from every viewpoint, and we were very sure it was what we wanted. There were fortunes to be made across the Atlantic, and we were young and strong and not afraid of hard work. We had the enormous advantage of Grandfather's money behind us and were not going there as some emigrants did, with little money and nothing but hope to sustain them. Robert had already made enquiries as to farmlands and the price of livestock and building materials, and we planned to build a fine new home where our children could grow strong and healthy with no shadows of the past to haunt them.

Robert was relating much of this information to Uncle Andrew, and I could see he was impressed at the detail we had gone into before we made up our minds. Kirsty wished us both every happiness in our new life, and although she and I shared a kind of friendship now, there would always be a certain barrier between us, and I thought she was probably relieved that I would be leaving Blackmaddie. She and Agnes seemed to get along remarkably well after all. I looked at Agnes; leaving her was my only regret, and I could see the tears in her eyes as she walked over to me and hugged me.

'Oh, Charlotte, why didn't you give me some idea of this? And how am I going to exist without you?' she whispered.

'Of course you'll exist,' I told her. 'Because you'll have Neil. Didn't I tell you that everything would change between us once you were married, Agnes? It has to change, because you'll be a different person then, just as I will be when Robert and I are married.'

I still could not say the words without a surge of happiness running through me, and I hugged Agnes back, and told her I hoped she was going to be my attendant at my wedding, as I was to be hers. I could see Kirsty hovering in the background, and after a second's hesitation I suggested she might like to be an attendant too. She threw her arms around my neck, the old sweet Kirsty she must have been before Ian and Katrina between them tormented her so much, and I was glad I had made the gesture. Agnes said laughingly that she had better have the two of us as her attendants too, only I would be matron of honour then, of course, being already married.

It was a busy time for us all, and better so, for past events could recede into the background while there was so much preparation.

Our wedding was as simple as we both desired, in the candle-lit kirk, with only our family present, and a few friends and the family servants. We could not leave the Sinclairs out of our special day, and even though we had not planned it, there were friends from the village who made their way to the kirk to wish us well, and tenant farmers and others, and I was very touched by their attendance. But as far as I was concerned, there was only Robert and me and the minister binding the two of us together, Robert holding my hand in his, and placing the ring on my finger, and tipping my face up to his, our lips meeting in front of them all.

We had a few days' honeymoon in Edinburgh, a time of bliss and delight that neither of us would ever forget. Then it was back to Blackmaddie for the Christmas celebrations that Agnes and I insisted upon, and the wild Hogmanay activities that were so new and exciting to us. First-footing and dancing and singing, and eating and drinking until the dawn hours, and finally falling into bed almost too tired to undress, and waking up still in the circle of Robert's arms, with the nakedness of him still warming me with remembered passion and the promise of more.

'This is truly the best part of being married,' I whispered to him time and again when we awoke, 'this knowing that it wasn't all a dream. That you're still here, and it's all still happening to us, Robert.'

'The best part is having you all to myself,' he murmured back, 'and knowing that you're a part of me and nothing can ever break the bonds between us, except ourselves.'

And I would pull him close to me, knowing there was nothing within either of us that would ever want us to part, feeling him respond at once to my touch, knowing he wanted me, loved me and lusted for me the way I did for him, and being elated by the knowledge. We did not even care that our lateness for breakfast every morning could hardly be unnoticed by the rest of the family.

And then it was Agnes' turn to be married to Neil. A more pompous ceremony this time, with her parents present, and a few friends from Bristol who had wanted to make the long journey with them. But it was none the less meaningful for all the splendour, for the vows were the same, and the emotions they felt were the same, and I felt a thickening in my throat as I saw the happiness in Agnes' eyes. I was so glad for her that she had got her heart's desire.

They did not go away for a honeymoon, for they were to travel to Europe later in the year, so they were able to come to the ship with Robert and me when the day finally came for us to leave Blackmaddie. The day before, Robert and I had taken the gig and gone out by ourselves, as if to take our fill of the beauty and tranquillity of the castle and its majestic surroundings that we had chosen to leave. We stopped the gig on the high ridge where we had stopped on that first day, and Robert helped me down to gaze all around us.

You could almost hear the silence. It was like a blanket surrounding us. I let my eyes wander freely all around me as I had before. Towering mountains in their winter mantle of snow against the flat grey of the sky, trees and bracken pale now without the fiery colours of autumn to warm them, the cold grey waters of the loch, and in the middle of it all, rising majestically and solidly into the skyline, the grey sheen of turrets, the mass of stonework and glass that made up Blackmaddie. More beautiful, more at peace, I thought with sudden awareness, than she had ever been. I would not believe she could put any curse on us two for daring to leave her.

I felt Robert's arms closing around me. 'Any regrets?' His eyes looked searchingly into mine. I shook my head vehemently, for there were none. How could there be, with him beside me?

'It was never really home as I know a home should be,' I said slowly. 'It sheltered me for a while and that was all. But the moment I'm really looking forward to is when we stand and look at another home – more modest than this one – and know that it belongs only to us, Robert.'

'Us three,' he echoed, his hand moving down to guard my abdomen for a moment. 'With no ghosts of the past to haunt us. Knowing that whatever happens there will be of our own making and no one else's. It's a good feeling. Remember what I said to you that first day when we stood here?'

' "Welcome home, Charlotte Brodie," ' I said softly. I would always remember that moment. Not Charlotte Brodie now. Charlotte Stewart. There had been a prince with a name that was very similar. He had gone across the sea as well, though in a different direction, and had not returned. Would we ever return, I wondered?

I was happy at this moment. Happy and content with the man I loved, and I lifted my face to meet his kiss, feeling as if we had truly come full circle in making our own promises for the future in this particular place. This was our real farewell to Blackmaddie.

Next day everyone escorted us to the ship, and we had a tearful good-bye from Agnes, who was convinced she would never see me again. She was probably right, but I told her to smile, and that I would write to her the moment we set foot in America. Robert and I intended to tell everyone about the baby after our arrival. Until then, not even Agnes was aware of our secret.

I was relieved when all the good-byes were over, for even old Duncan had hugged me to him, disregarding the fact that it was not his place to do such a thing. But no one made any comment and I hugged him back, for he would always hold a special place in my heart.

At last we were alone. The ship set sail as darkness fell, and Robert and I could relax in our cabin for the long journey ahead. Not that it was all that comfortable, for it was small and a bit cramped and the bed was none too soft. But none of that mattered as long as we were together. That night my husband reached out his arms for me and covered my body with his; the gently rocking motion of the ship added to the sensuality of his love-making and the desire that flared between us.

He entered me slowly, exquisitely, as he had done so many times before. And yet each time was like the first time, more sweet, more pleasurable than anything I had ever known before, our movements part of the ship, complementing it and heightened by it. On and on. He was magnificent, my Robert, his hands cupping my breasts, his mouth seeking mine as the warm sweet heaviness claimed me again and again, as if neither of us wanted this night to end. For I think we both felt that this was when our marriage and our new life truly began.

'We'll have lots of babies, my darling,' Robert whispered against my mouth. 'And one day, one of them will go back to Blackmaddie and wonder how you and I could ever bear to leave it. But he'll be more than welcome to it, for this is home to me. *This!*'

I felt him twist and gasp against me, his hands gripping me more tightly, and then the warm, ecstatic sensation that filled me so explosively, and I shuddered against him as we clung together in our final completeness.

A son for Blackmaddie. Perhaps I already held him in the darkness of my womb. Or perhaps it would be a daughter first, a girl with black hair and blue eyes and full red mouth, for there was something deep within me that wanted the likeness to show itself again in my daughter, to prove to the world that Grandfather had been right, and Maddie had not been all bad. That her descendants could inherit the good side of her nature and not only the bad.

I was glad it was not possible to choose the sex of the

baby and that it was already predestined. But boy or girl, neither Robert nor I could deny that it was a part of Blackmaddie's future, whether its heir or merely a thread in a family tapestry that no miles of ocean could destroy. The thought was at once comforting and disturbing, but it was one to be locked away in the corner of my mind. For now, I had everything I wanted here in my arms, and in the warmth of Robert's embrace, Blackmaddie was already another world.